ELEPHANT WALK

* * * * * ELEPHANT WALK

A NOVEL BY ROBERT STANDISH

THE MACMILLAN COMPANY

NEW YORK: 1949

The last reason why this book should not have been written ceased to exist in the high summer of 1944. In writing it I cannot make the customary and prudent disclaimer that the story itself and all the characters are entirely fictitious, but I can say with complete truth that nothing in the following pages now has the power to hurt, embarrass, or humiliate any one of the persons portrayed, nor his or her living descendants. This seems to me the most important consideration.

In this cramped and regimented age, unable to attend to the simple details of living without the permission of a bureaucrat, it has been to me an infinite joy to write this book which is, as I see it, the epitaph of a more spacious and colourful epoch, whose tail-end I was privileged to see. Now that my task is ended, I put down my pen with a sigh of regret. In doing so I have realised that it is not only to the reader that books are a means of escape from present-day realities.

I wonder what Erasmus would have said about it all.

R. S.

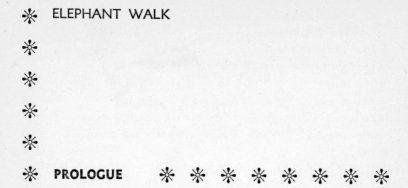

❋ PROLOGUE   ❋ ❋ ❋ ❋ ❋ ❋ ❋ ❋

A massively-built man between thirty and forty years of age stood for a few minutes looking around him with keen, appraising blue eyes, as he surveyed the wide saucer-shaped valley, the steaming low country four thousand feet below him, and the towering peak of Ratnagalla. The sheer beauty of what he saw dragged from him a deep sigh. On either side stretched miles of cultivated land. Around the upper part of the valley, the dark green shining leaves of coffee bushes glistened in the early morning sun, while the intense flaming scarlet of ripening coffee berries made it appear as though the valley were aflame.

Tom Carey surveyed the scene with the pride of achievement, as well he might, for a bare fifteen years previously the valley had been clad with virgin jungle, which had never heard the ring of the woodsman's axe. His own courage and determination had made this transformation possible. The coffee grown on Tom Carey's broad acres in the uplands of Ceylon was finding its way into every market on earth where men appreciated fine coffee, and there came back to him in return from all over the world a stream of wealth, greater by far than his wildest imaginings and greater, so it seemed, than he would ever be able to spend.

He was a big man with slow, determined movements, a strong, firm jaw, which only just missed being ruthless, and a pair of candid, fearless blue eyes. It was the face of a man very sure of himself, sure of what he wanted and of his ability to take it by force if need be. The spot on which he stood on this gay, sparkling morning of the year 1863 was where two spurs which rose out of the plains met to form a small plateau some twelve acres in extent. It faced due south, commanding a fine view of the saucer of the valley and of the plains beneath. Behind, the land rose steeply to the rim of the saucer. A hundred feet or so above him, a clear, sparkling spring bubbled out of the hillside and, spilling down a deep declivity, turned the little plateau into swampland. The feet of many creatures had churned the mud deeply.

"I shall build my home here, Appuhamy," said Tom Carey, turning to a tall, dignified Sinhalese in middle age, with sweeping moustachios, who stood patiently, his small son aged about ten beside him. "There is no better site in all Ceylon."

"Nevertheless, Master," replied the other warningly, "it lies astride the elephant trail. This is their halting place when they come up from the plains. It is not wise, Master, to make enemies of the Elephant People."

"The elephants," snapped Carey, "must for the future choose some other way." He looked at the other's dismay contemptuously. "You heard me? I shall build my house here."

"If the Master wishes to build his house here, he will build it here," replied Appuhamy gravely. "But it is a spot of ill omen. No good will come of it."

"Keep such tales for the old women, Appuhamy. I will not listen to them. They told me when I cleared the jungle that the elephants would destroy my coffee. They did not do so."

"Master did not plant his coffee across the elephant trail," retorted the other quietly.

"Nevertheless, Appuhamy, you will undertake the contract, will you not?"

"I will undertake the contract, Master, even if I do so with a heavy heart."

"First," said Tom Carey, "the land must be drained. I will have coolies here tomorrow morning."

Without further discussion, he walked to where his horse was tethered, mounted and rode away.

"The Master," said Appuhamy to his young son, "is an obstinate man."

"But," said the boy with bated breath, hero-worship shining from his eyes, "he is not frightened of the elephants."

A week later the little plateau had been drained and a spillway created to carry off the spring water. A month later a series of deep trenches had been dug for the foundations of a gigantic bungalow, while several hundred men were at work cutting a new road to the site. Six months later, from stone quarried a few hundred yards away, the massive foundations were completed. So vast were they that from many miles around the curious, seeking to confirm the fabulous stories they heard, came wonderingly to see them.

"Of what will the rest be constructed?" they asked Appuhamy.

"Teakwood," he replied, "the finest Burma teakwood, every piece seasoned and guaranteed perfect. Only the best is good enough for the Master."

"Why teakwood?" they asked. "The jungle above abounds with fine timber. It is his for the cutting."

"The Master is building for his children and his children's children. Fine teakwood endures almost as long as stone. The damp and the sun will not rot it; the ants will not eat it; in hot weather or dry it will not warp. When it is finished it will be a palace."

"Why," asked the voice of a sceptic, "does he trouble to build this fine house for his grandchildren when he has not even a son, nor yet a wife? To me it is a great folly."

"To you it may be folly," retorted Appuhamy acidly, "for you are content to live in a flimsy hut constructed of mud with a bug-ridden thatch of palm fronds, but it is beyond argument that when it is finished, this will be the finest house in all Ceylon. . . ."

"Better to say *if* it is finished," continued the other, "for I have it in my mind that the Elephant People, when next they come this way, may have other ideas. As everyone knows, only a very foolish, or a very ignorant person, would thus lightly incur their wrath."

"The Master," piped Appuhamy's son, who had heard this exchange, "does not fear the Elephant People. He does not fear anything. If the Elephant People try to stop him building his fine home, he says that he will make them help to build it. I heard him say so. He has promised me that when it is finished he will find a place for me there. . . ."

"Hush, child!" said his father reprovingly. "I am sure that if, when you are older, you go to serve the Master, he will not wish you to repeat his words to every idle loafer who has nothing better to do than to talk nonsense."

"But father," asked the child when they were alone, "you do not believe, do you, that the Elephant People can stop the Master from building his home here?"

"I do not know what I believe," was the guarded reply, "but I do know that I wish the Master had chosen another place to build. With so many fine sites from which to choose, it is strange that he could not find one which pleased him as well. The Master, as you will learn if you go to serve him, is not easily turned from his purpose."

Not long afterwards great wagons, heavily laden with teak, each drawn by six milk-white draught oxen, arrived in unending procession up the new road. Some brought great timbers to serve as corner posts, floor beams and roof beams. Others brought loads of sawn planks for flooring; fine-grained sections for interior panelling; rough-hewn pieces to be sawn and planed on the site for a variety of purposes. No sooner had one wagon discharged its load than another was ready to take its place, until more than two acres were filled with neatly stacked timber.

A few days after the last bullock cart had arrived upon the site with its load of teakwood, a seemingly unrelated event occurred in the sweltering low country far below. There had been drought across the land for many weeks. The water-courses were dried up, the grass and other herbage was parched and dry and dust-laden, while even in the depths of the jungle itself there was a dearth of fresh green leaves. A herd of elephants, looking at the desolation around them, suddenly remembered that, far up in the hills, were cool springs, sweet pastures and delicate jungle foliage such as they had not tasted for many weeks. It was the Old Bull who trumpeted the order to move. Three cows, each with a calf at her side, followed obediently. The way led across the plain to the foothills where, out of the morning mist, beckoning from afar, a light winked at the summit of Ratnagalla Peak. *Ratna* in the Sinhalese language means a gem, and *galla* a mountain, so with picturesque imagery, the peak acquired its name. At its summit a spring bubbled to the surface and then ran down a smooth rocky face which, on clear days, acted as a mirror to reflect the rays of the rising sun. Whether the Old Bull consciously set out in the direction of the gem which shone from the peak is debatable, but it was none the less a fact that the elephant trail, which led across the plain and to the foothills had, before the memory of man or elephant, always pointed directly at Ratnagalla.

By noon, a baby bull calf, sleek and round as a rubber ball, who had trotted uncomplainingly beside his mother, became acutely aware of hunger and thirst and that he was very tired. The Old Bull halted for a few moments on the bank of a dried-up river in the very centre of which there remained a small quantity of evil-smelling ooze. When the trail reached the foothills, all save the Old Bull himself were in distress, but he, knowing the dangers because of the smell of Man which lay heavy across the land, set a cracking pace upwards. The youngsters, who were hungry and thirsty and whose every muscle ached, needed an occasional thump from their mothers' trunks to help them up the steep trail.

Although he had awoken that morning with no conscious recollection of the cool delights which awaited the herd in the hills above, the decision once taken to migrate, the Old Bull now remembered clearly every yard of the way. At about three o'clock in the afternoon he remembered with gratitude that a couple of miles or so ahead there was a plateau where two spurs met. Here a cool spring ran from the hillside. Here, too, was a mud wallow where, in a few short minutes, tired and aching muscles would forget the rigours of the journey. When within two hundred yards of the spot, the Old Bull halted dead in his tracks, trumpeting softly to the others to remain hidden over the brow of a hill while he went forward to reconnoitre.

This was a spot shunned by Man and yet, there was no mistaking, the Man smell, strong and rancid, was everywhere. Myopic like all his kind, the Old Bull had to rely chiefly upon smell. As he approached closer, even his dim eyes were able to see men, dozens and scores of them, clad in brightly coloured garments, busying themselves with some strange task upon the spot which traditionally belonged to the Elephant People.

Where once there had been several feet depth of cool mud there was now a series of forbidding stone walls rising from the ground, while to the right of them, men were working amongst great piles of timber. The Old Bull trumpeted with shrill rage. It had been bad enough some years previously when the jungle had been felled and burned, only to be replaced by coffee, but at least the zone of cultivation had not encroached upon the elephant trail. From time immemorial, as clearly understood in the spirit as though it had been a written treaty, there had been a truce between Man and the elephants. Each, by tacit consent, avoided the haunts of the other, for they had nothing to give each other except enmity. Man worked his rice fields in the jungle clearings and, to avoid these, the elephants made wide detours. Man, likewise, avoided the elephant feeding grounds and the trail which led between the low country and the hills. Here, plainly, was a flagrant violation of the unwritten treaty.

Trumpeting to the others to close up and follow him, the Old Bull, screaming hate and defiance, began a mad charge in the direction of the men working among the piles of timber. The baby bull, understanding nothing of what was afoot, found from somewhere the strength to keep pace with his mother, who followed obediently in the wake of her lord and master.

On seeing the mad rush of the Old Bull, the men working quickly scattered, making for places of safety. All save one man who, clad in white, stood his ground, immovable as a rock. He waited until the Old Bull was within twenty yards of him and then there was a flash and a tremendous report and the Old Bull sank, trumpeting defiance, to his knees. Almost at that very second, it seemed to the baby bull, the earth opened. He and his mother crashed into a deep pit, cunningly concealed with little woven branches and leaves. In his mad rage, the Old Bull must have cleared the pit in his stride.

The pit was narrow: only large enough for one elephant. By good fortune, the baby bull, therefore, fell on top of his mother. From all directions men came running. The smells of them were terrifying. Wedged between the wall of the pit and his mother's back, the young bull struggled frantically to regain his feet. Somehow, he never did remember how, he reached solid ground a few seconds before the arrival of the men. With fear lending speed to his flying feet, he tore across the little plateau, cannoning into a great pile of heavy timbers, one of which, sharply pointed at one end, dislodged itself from the pile, tearing a gaping wound in his flank. Again there came the terrifying sound of the weapon which had stopped the Old Bull dead in his tracks. The baby bull felt a searing pain as a bullet glanced off the massive bone of his skull, tearing a path through the gristle of his ear. It was half an hour before he caught up with the rest of the herd, nor did they slacken the mad pace until one of the cows, who had assumed leadership, deemed that it was safe to do so. By this time, the herd was several miles deep in the cool jungle which covered the immense shoulders surrounding the peak of Ratnagalla.

The two remaining cow elephants did what they could to comfort the motherless baby bull, but it was poor comfort at best. The bullet which had torn the hole through his ear was quickly forgotten, but from the gaping wound torn in his flank by the falling timber, he had lost much blood, and it was some weeks before it healed in the cool mud of the mountains, where also there was abundant sweet food. Although the wound healed, the terror of that day was destined to live with him all through his life.

*   *   *   *   *

It was two years before the Big Bungalow, as it inevitably came to be known locally, was completed, and it was not until then that Tom Carey deemed the time opportune to return to England.

In the latter part of the year 1868 Tom Carey, longing for a son to whom he might pass on his huge heritage of coffee land, married a wife. Some three months before their child was due to be born, he returned alone to Ceylon. His son would be an Englishman, and it was right and proper for an Englishman to be born in the land of his fathers. The Big Bungalow, although Tom Carey had never lived in it, was complete in every detail. He would go to live there, he decided, when his wife and son came to join him.

For Tom Carey the year 1869 was without doubt the most eventful of his long life. In April of that year his son, George, was born to him. There was great rejoicing at Ratnagalla when the cablegram announcing the fact arrived. A vast bonfire, visible on the coast some sixty miles away, was built upon the highest point of Carey land. At a feast celebrating the event every soul working for Tom Carey received a week's pay as a gift. Eight days later another cablegram arrived, telling Tom Carey that he was a widower. Numb with grief, he moved into the huge and splendid home he had prepared for his bride, deriving what comfort he could from the knowledge that, before she died, she had given him the son for whom he longed. Even so, ten long weary years were to pass before Tom Carey first laid eyes upon that son.

The year 1869 had not yet finished with Tom Carey, nor his fellow coffee planters into whose pockets for decades a fabulous stream of wealth had been pouring, for it was in that year that the coffee blight, the dreaded scourge *Hemileia Vastatrix,* began its work of destruction, not ceasing until hundreds of thousands of acres of fertile coffee land had been put to the torch and lay in black ruin.

Tom Carey had destroyed his coffee while other planters were still hoping vainly that the scourge could be arrested; and, at a time when the smoke from the bonfires of burning coffee blackened the uplands of Ceylon, Tom Carey, whose courage had made this thing possible, looked out from the solitary splendour of his home on to more than a thousand acres of two-year-old tea which, a few years hence, was destined to restore his shattered fortunes. Tea could never produce from the soil such vast wealth as had come from coffee, but even so, Tom Carey comforted himself with the knowledge that he had created a fine heritage to pass on to the son whom he had never seen.

One evening, tired from a long day in the fields, he espied on the way home a solitary bull elephant descending the trail which led from the mountains to the jungles of the low country. It was a fine young bull, in the prime of life, one of whose ears hung at a strange angle, as though deformed, while along one flank was the deep scar of an old wound. The magnificent creature picked his way carefully through the loose rubble of the trail until he came to a spot where a detour was necessary to avoid the plateau on which now stood the Big Bungalow —so vast and portentous a structure that it seemed to challenge the very mountains themselves for domination.

The young bull halted in his tracks. The spot was fraught with hot, bitter, agonising memories. There came to him once more the hated smell as the men had swarmed around him. He remembered the flash and the hideous explosion as the bullet had pierced the gristle of his ear, and the gaping wound torn in his flank by the falling timber. He remembered, too, months after that hideous day, returning by the same trail to be greeted by the beloved and familiar smell of his own mother who, captured in the pit laid for her, had been forced into shameful servitude. With his own eyes he had seen her, harnessed like some docile bullock as, with heavy chains on either side of her, she had hauled great baulks of teakwood into position for the builders.

At the memories evoked, the young bull threw his trunk high into the air, trumpeting a challenge in which, for those with the wit to read, there was hatred, defiance and a strange, ill-understood nostalgic longing. When a bare fifty yards separated them, the young bull and the man, the latter unarmed, stood facing each other, each of them quite unafraid: it was the young bull who shrank before the steady gaze of the man who confronted him.

It occurred to Tom Carey as he continued on the way to remember the warning of Appuhamy, who had maintained until the day of his death the unwisdom of crossing the path of the Elephant People. His son, a tall, handsome young man, who bid fair to be like his father, now worked for Tom Carey in the Big Bungalow. There burned in the young man's eyes a strange light of hero-worship and devotion. Tom Carey was as sure as he was sure of anything that the young Appuhamy would, if need be, die for him. But he, too, shared his father's forebodings. Tom Carey had always thrust these aside contemptuously, as though they were old wives' tales. He was not a man easily deterred from his purpose. If he had been, he mused grimly, he might have been tempted, like so many others had been tempted, to abandon the land which was about to begin once more to produce wealth for the Careys.

The young bull elephant paused once more upon the next ridge, where his outline was silhouetted against the setting sun. Once again he threw up his trunk, shattering the still air with his mournful trumpeting. Tom Carey, although he did not quite know why, shivered and began to think of other things. . . .

When his son was ten years old, Tom Carey turned his back for a few months upon the rich tea land and returned to England. In the hold of the ship which carried him were two hundred cases of tea, each stencilled with an elephant's head and the bold legend:

ELEPHANT WALK

CEYLON TEA

It was characteristic of Tom Carey that the stencilled elephant's head was portrayed vividly in anger, its head lifted, mouth open and trunk thrown high in defiance.

Ten years after the event, Tom Carey found that the bride who had died without seeing the splendid home he had built for her, had given him the kind of son he wanted most: a tousled, fair-haired boy, with candid blue eyes like his own, sturdy-limbed and self-reliant. The image of the boy, which was never far from his consciousness, made the remaining years of their separation easier to bear.

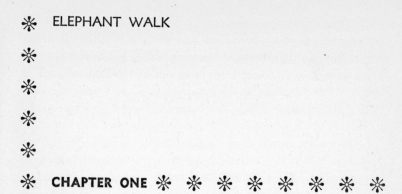

❊
❊
❊
❊
❊ **CHAPTER ONE** ❊ ❊ ❊ ❊ ❊ ❊ ❊ ❊

A tired horse picked its way carefully along the narrow trail which led around the swelling shoulders of Ratnagalla Peak. Its rider, too, was tired, although he forgot fatigue in the sheer joy of home-coming. It wanted a bare half-hour to dawn. Unless his mount stumbled, George Carey calculated that, with the first light of the new day, he should be at a spot on the upper lip of the slightly tilted saucer of the hills which, upon the maps, was marked Ratnagalla Valley. All through the long night he had been buoyed up by the prospect of watching the sun rise across the valley, which was not only his home, but the spot in which all his earthly interests and affections were centred. Esmeralda, the sweating chestnut mare who had borne George Carey through the night, seemed to share his joy at home-coming if for different reasons.

On the very rim of the valley, just as a blood-red sun was rising out of the distant sea to throw stabbing points of light across the plains below, George Carey reined in Esmeralda and sat motionless for many minutes while the glory of the panorama at his feet unfolded itself.

Many who believed they knew George Carey well were inclined to regard him as a gross, material fellow, incapable of the feelings which, as he sat there astride his tired mount, were flooding over him like a healing balm. He was a big, beefy, blond man, with tousled hair and brilliant blue eyes. If those who thought him insensitive had troubled to look a little further below the surface, they would have found instead that he was merely inarticulate. He had longed, for most of his forty-four years, to be able to put into words so many of the things which the sight of loveliness in any form evoked in his uncomplicated being. It was too late now; he knew it, but he was content, none the less, to remain drinking in the beauty of the scene spread at his feet until the sun, rising swiftly, had bathed the whole valley in golden light.

In the middle ground stood the gigantic Big Bungalow, which was his home, its bold façade standing out from the verdant hillside looking more like a Swiss mountain hotel than a private dwelling-place. Most people stood in awe of the Big Bungalow. A few laughed at it. George Carey loved it. More than the Big Bungalow he loved the well-tended acres of high-elevation tea, which swept like a gigantic green girdle around the saucer of the hills. In the twenty-four years since he had first come here, George Carey had left it as seldom as possible, and it was his most fervent wish that, for the remainder of his days, his absences would be few and brief. With a deep sigh of contentment which shook his burly frame, he guided Esmeralda down the narrow zigzag path in the direction of the familiar smells and sounds which came up to him upon the morning air.

As George Carey plunged down into the tea, a gay, laughing, chattering army of men, women and children, some seven hundred strong, extended in a long line abreast, seemed to come forward to meet him. It was the season of alternating rain and sunshine, when the miles of tea bushes, usually a dark green, not unlike the laurel, were crowned with tender lettuce-green shoots of the new season's growth for which, the world over, a hundred million teapots were waiting avidly. The army of pluckers, baskets on their shoulders, suspended from soft cords across their brows, worked with flying fingers through the flushing tea. Every one of them, from the six-year-olds at their mothers' sides, up to and including their grandparents, sometimes even their great-grandparents, worked with a cheerful intensity of purpose. Even as he came down to meet this scene which so delighted his eye, George Carey spared a prideful sideways glance at a white-painted notice-board which bore the legend: ELEPHANT WALK TEA ESTATE, and which marked the limits of Carey land.

A syce from the Big Bungalow, who had spotted George Carey in the distance, came running to meet him and to take the flagging Esmeralda back to the comfort of her loosebox. Tired as he was, there were things George Carey was in a fever to know before he, too, went to refresh himself after the long journey.

A few moments after he had dismounted, Carey plunged into the tea to work on foot past the long line of the pluckers, every one of whom he knew by name. As he passed them he exchanged here a smile, there a jest, and with another a quick, earnest enquiry regarding some sick or aged member of the family.

"Haven't you enough mouths to feed?" he asked with a smile, nodding meaningly at a pleasant-faced girl, obviously far gone in pregnancy.

"I hope your husband hasn't beaten you while I've been away?" he asked of another.

As he went down the long line, young and old, men and women, looked at him with affectionate welcome in their eyes. He was, in their estimation, a good master. For years he had shared the heat of the long day with them, listened patiently to their complaints, helped to settle their quarrels impartially, laughed at their marryings, grieved at their buryings—given them, in fact, everything to which their feudal loyalty to him entitled them. George Carey was a privileged person. He knew it. And with his privileges he assumed in full the obligations which went with them.

A tall, bearded Tamil, who had grown old in the service of the Careys, came forward to greet him.

"Everything all right, Rengesamy?"

"All is well now that the Master is back," came the grave reply from the head *kangany*.*

"Where is Wilding *Doray?*" †

"He is up at the jungle clearing, Master. He went there straight from the muster ground."

"Then send a boy," said Carey, "to fetch me a fresh horse. I will go up there to see him."

George Carey believed, and quite understandably, that nobody looked after Carey land and interests as well as a Carey. Some two

* Foreman or supervisor.
† Literally, Wilding Master, or Mr. Wilding.

years previously, with the utmost reluctance, he had employed a young Englishman named Wilding as assistant. In those two years, except for a very occasional weekend his chief spent at Badulla or Bandarawella, Wilding had never been left on his own. This time, however, Carey had been absent for two weeks, and he was in a fever to know how this untried assistant had borne the full responsibilities of Elephant Walk during that time.

At first, Carey had been very doubtful whether he could ever make a planter out of John Geoffrey Wilding. Later, he had come to revise that judgment. Wilding had taken to the work as a duck takes to water. He had one quality without which all the others were worthless: he knew how to handle labour; when to be firm and when to be lenient; when to see everything and when to turn a blind eye. In justice, Carey realised that his views about Wilding had been founded upon the fact that Wilding was so many things which he, Carey, was not.

Wilding was a man approaching thirty, dark, good-looking, with bold, reckless brown eyes. He was well-poised, graceful and precise in his movements. He had well-shaped hands, with the long tapering fingers of an artist. While other planters were content to wear khaki shirts, shorts and puttees, Wilding always appeared immaculately turned out in cream-coloured silk shirts, Savile Row riding breeches and shining boots. Wilding was a highly educated man, too, which created an impenetrable barrier between him and Carey, who had merely acquired the smattering of education which is interlarded into the curriculum of an English public school between the more important cricket and football.

"Too much education will be no help to you, my boy," Tom Carey had insisted. "Merely make you discontented."

"Wouldn't it be a good idea, dad, if I spent a couple of years or so at a school of tropical agriculture somewhere?" George had asked. "Some knowledge of scientific agriculture should be useful."

"There's only one scientific agriculturist around here," Tom Carey had replied, "and that's God Almighty. While He provides alternating rain and sunshine, the tea is going to flush, no matter what the text-books say. The coolies, bred and born here, know more about tea than you'll ever know if you live to be eighty. To be a successful planter you've got to understand how to handle labour. That's ninety per cent of it. The other ten per cent is just a matter of keeping your head in a crisis and keeping your mouth shut when you know nothing."

George Carey had had twenty-four years since to reflect upon the wisdom of his father's words, and in that time he could find no fault with them.

"Glad to see you back, Carey," called Wilding, as his chief rode into the pocket of jungle which was being felled and cleared.

"Everything all right?" asked Carey, offering a firm handshake.

"Everything right as rain," was the easy reply.

"Nothing went wrong while I was away?" asked Carey, trying vainly to keep the anxiety out of his voice.

"Nothing that I couldn't put right. You know, the little day to day upsets."

Suddenly Carey began to laugh at his own fears. "I might have known you'd have sent me a wire if anything had gone wrong. Still, you know, one can't help worrying."

"What did the doctor say to you?" asked Wilding.

A shadow came across Carey's eyes as he replied, "The doctors— I saw three of them, and for once they were in agreement—told me there's nothing wrong with me that won't be put right by a few months at home in a cold climate. It's over ten years, you see, since I've been back to England. Hell! I don't want to go back to England! I've lost touch. There's nothing there for me any more. The last time I went back, I was bored stiff. This is my home now."

"Are you going to obey the doctors' orders?"

"Probably. That depends," replied Carey.

"Depends on how I've run the place while you've been away? Is that it?" asked Wilding, a glint of amusement in his eye.

"Well—er—I suppose, if you must have it, yes. That's it."

In Carey's estimation, Wilding was too infernally quick on the uptake. It embarrassed him sometimes. As he saw things, remarks such as that, however obvious, were best left unsaid. Wilding had a quick, clever tongue and on a good many occasions Carey had been uncomfortably aware, during conversations with his assistant, that the latter's thoughts were far ahead of the conversation. George Carey's mind and body moved rather slowly. He arrived at his conclusions by easy stages, after due deliberation, and there was in him, although he suspected at times he was being unjust, a mild antagonism towards those who reached their conclusions more quickly than he did, even if the conclusions were the same as his own.

"I quite understand, Carey," continued Wilding, not in the least abashed. "This is a valuable property, and it sticks out a mile that you can't go home on leave for months with an easy mind leaving it in the hands of a man you couldn't trust, or who was likely to make a fool of himself. I think you'll find everything all right."

"You're a funny chap, Wilding," said Carey with a friendly smile.

"Perhaps," said the other slowly. "I've always had an unfortunate knack of saying things that most people only think. That's what cut my Army career short. Nobody told me at Sandhurst, don't you see, that if you want to get on in the Army you must keep your mouth shut and learn to enjoy kissing the backsides of the mighty. I was fool enough to believe that all I had to do was to learn to be a good soldier. However, planting suits me down to the ground, and I hope we don't fall out about anything, Carey, because I like it here."

When George Carey rode homewards through the tea the sun was high above the horizon, the long line of pluckers working steadily through the tea flush under a brazen sky. Sweat was showing in dark patches through gaily-coloured Manchester prints in an infinity of patterns, which must have looked grotesque except against the green background of the tea, the intense blue sky above and the brilliant golden sunshine, which seemed to set off the harsh barbaric colours.

Awaiting Carey at the top of the wide flight of stone steps which led to the Big Bungalow stood a tall, dignified Sinhalese, with sweeping iron-grey moustachios, his sparse hair tied in a bun at the back and held in place by a curved tortoise-shell comb. He wore a long white duck gown, immaculately laundered, fastened down the front with massive silver *tikals,* brought back from Siam thirty years previously as a gift from Tom Carey.

"Everything all right, Appuhamy?"

"Everything all right, Master. I am happy," said Appuhamy, the light of devotion and affection in his eyes, "that the Master has returned."

"Anybody staying here?"

"Nobody, Master. But several guests will be here tonight, I think."

A few seconds later, George Carey felt himself enfolded gratefully within the cool, sombre immensity of the home which had been built as a queenly setting for his mother, who had never seen it. Nor was there in his eyes anything incongruous in the fact that this huge establishment existed to administer to his bachelor solitude. It was home. He had never known any other home since leaving school. It satisfied him mentally and physically. He loved the lustrous sheen, the perfection of the waxed teak floors and panelling, the huge beams which supported the cavernous roof, the heavy teak doors which swung noiselessly on their brass hinges, the gigantic teak four-poster bed in which Tom Carey had died peacefully in his sleep. Every table, chair, cupboard, wardrobe and shelf in the bungalow was teak which, to George Carey, as it had to his father, symbolised stability, permanence, solidity: qualities desirable in a home and, as Careys saw things, essential in a man.

For close on fifty years, the life which had gone on in the Big Bungalow, for the greater part of the time under Appuhamy's zealous eye and control, had been smooth, easy and, seemingly, effortless. Strife and turmoil had never been allowed to mar its placid surface. For almost forty years, up to the time of its builder's death, the Big Bungalow at Elephant Walk had been a symbol all over Ceylon, and indeed far beyond, for the kind of princely, open-house hospitality which swiftly changing conditions had already put into the past tense almost everywhere else on earth. The life of the Big Bungalow ran in long, deep grooves. With the death of his father it had not occurred to George Carey to lift the wheels out of the old grooves or to establish new ones. To him, as to Appuhamy, change, however slight, would have implied a criticism, a dissatisfaction with the way of life which Tom Carey had established and found very good. A few weeks after his father's death, when the shock of his passing had become a little dulled, George had moved from his own bedroom to his father's. Except for this, nothing else in the routine of the establishment had been changed. The white coats of the servants, with the elephant's head emblazoned upon the breast, still bore, in bold letters, the initials T.C.

Shaved, bathed and clad in fresh clean clothes, the fatigue of the long night ride forgotten, George Carey addressed himself pleasurably to a pile of letters and newspapers upon a large silver salver beside his favourite long chair on the veranda. Silently, waiting until his master should look up, Appuhamy came bringing a tray. Four drops of angostura bitters, gin up to the first line cut in the glass and water up to the second. On working days, one gin and bitters at noon had been the established rule of the house for a very long time.

Even when seated at the head of the immense teakwood dining-table, at which sixty and more guests had often sat in comfort, George Carey was not aware of any incongruity. He liked the huge expanse of polished teak and the line of massive cut-glass flower vases which seemed to fade away into the distance from him. Indeed, one of the things which had irked him most when last he visited England had been the relatively cramped quarters in which he had been compelled to live in hotels and in the houses of his friends, and it was the thought of having to endure this again which wrinkled his brow and, now that he was home again, was the only small black cloud upon an otherwise perfect horizon.

* * * * *

Late on a golden afternoon in the year 1913, George Carey rode lingeringly through the tea as though reluctant—as indeed he was—to leave the familiar scene. Arriving home, he threw the reins of his horse to a syce and, mounting the steps to the Big Bungalow, turned for a moment at the top to watch as, in the last rays of the setting sun, hundreds of tired coolies, their day's work done, streamed from the fields to the bowls of steaming rice awaiting them in the lines.

Already Carey was beginning to feel the pangs of parting. It was a Saturday, and on the Monday he was due to leave for Bandarawella, take the train for Colombo, there to join his ship for England, in obedience to his doctor's orders.

"The Master is sad," said Appuhamy, interpreting Carey's mood rightly. "Everyone here is sad, too. But it is better, Master, to obey the doctors. They should know."

"They should know, Appuhamy, but I sometimes wonder if they do. I've half a mind to tell them to go to hell."

"The Old Master always said that Master should go to England every five years," observed Appuhamy reprovingly.

That somehow, seemed to close the subject. That Tom Carey had already been in his grave some nine years made not the slightest difference to Appuhamy's unswerving loyalty. Fortunately for these two, master and servant, no situation had ever arisen since Tom Carey's death in which George Carey's authority had come into the smallest conflict with his father's. George Carey had often wondered whimsically whether, in such an unlikely event, his own authority would prevail.

"Anyone here tonight, Appuhamy?" asked Carey.

"Yes, Master. Everyone coming to say goodbye to Master. Mr Gilly, Mr Wilding, Mr Norman and Mr Cullen are having their baths now. Mr Oswald has come from Badulla, Mr Martin from Passara, and there are two gentlemen I have never seen before. Their servants say they belong to the Irrigation Department."

"The two gentlemen you do not know, they have everything they want?"

"Of course, Master," replied Appuhamy, in a surprised and injured tone.

"Give them my compliments and say I shall look forward to seeing them before dinner."

"I have already done so, Master."

In the few moments during which this exchange took place, the swift curtain of tropical night fell. Carey, poised upon the dividing line between the opaque blackness outside and the warm friendliness within, stood appraisingly surveying his home. The long veranda, just over eighty yards in length and twelve yards in depth, looked very inviting in the soft light shed by the line of oil lamps hanging from the roof rafters and swinging gently in the cool evening breeze. The lamplight was reflected from the heavy cut-glass set out upon a silver tray atop a teakwood trolley, which a servant was pushing along the veranda on silent, rubber-tyred wheels. This, by long-established custom, arrived every evening of the year at sundown exactly.

While George Carey was feasting his eyes upon the familiar scene, from which he would soon be separated for some months, a raucous voice called: "Have a drink, Gilly?"

"Thanks, I will," remarked a man of roughly George Carey's age, who emerged from one of the bedrooms and helped himself. "Here's to you, Erasmus old sport!" said the newcomer, lifting his glass to an incredibly aged and disreputable parrot, who occupied a huge teak-wood perch.

"I'll have one too, Gilly," observed Carey, stepping into the lamp-light.

It was apparent that these two were close friends. Although physically alike, the resemblance ceased there. John Gilliland, whose estate, Donaghendry, adjoined Elephant Walk, was a more subtle, polished product. He was a hard-bitten, self-opinionated Ulsterman, good-humoured when his will was not crossed, with keen grey eyes and a tongue whose wit was ready enough, but often tinged with malice.

"It's amazing," said Carey, "how that dam' bird Erasmus still remembers the old guvnor's voice. 'Pon my soul, I'd feel lost without it! There are times, you know, Gilly, when I almost wonder whether, in some queer fashion or other, the old guvnor didn't manage to reincarnate a bit of himself. Appuhamy, of course, won't hear anything to the contrary, but that's because he's a Buddhist. Still, nine years is a long time—even for a parrot."

"Here's to you anyway, Erasmus old sport, whoever you are!" said Gilliland, lifting his glass. "Tell me, George," he went on more seriously, "how did young Wilding shape while you were away?"

"First-rate, thanks. He's an odd chap in many ways. A bit difficult to get next to him, if you know what I mean. But the truth is, he ran the place as well as I could. Otherwise, I couldn't face the thought of going home."

"Well, he has a soft billet here, provided he keeps his nose clean," observed Gilliland. "And, unless I misjudge him, he's smart enough to know it."

"You don't like him, do you, Gilly?" asked Carey uneasily.

"I don't know. Everything's been plain sailing since he came here, and I sometimes wonder just how far one could depend upon him in a crisis. But he's a likeable chap and, frankly, on the whole I'm inclined to like him. He's got brains, imagination and some very queer tastes—for a planter."

"Such as?"

"Ever seen any of his water-colours? I don't set myself up to be a great judge of that sort of thing, but to me they're first-class."

"You mean," asked Carey, "that those pictures round his living-room wall he did himself?" Gilliland nodded. "Good God! Next time I go there I must look at them. Anyway, Gilly, I'm going to rely on you to keep an eye on him while I'm away. It isn't the man I mistrust, you know, it's his judgment. Hang it all! He's only been here two years. He speaks Tamil and Sinhalese fluently, and the coolies like and respect him, but . . . only two years."

As George Carey turned thoughtfully in the direction of his bedroom, there came the tattoo of a rain squall on the roof, followed a few seconds later by the cascading of water, trapped from the vast expanse of roof, down the drain-pipes and into the ravine below. The sound of horses' hooves outside brought servants running with huge umbrellas to escort the guests up the steps and into the bungalow. The immense dripping umbrellas were collapsed and stood to drain in the row of elephants' feet converted to use as umbrella stands. The four largest had belonged to an old bull who had fallen many years previously to Tom Carey's gun for presuming to question the latter's right to build his home where he pleased.

From the lounge which, like every other room in the Big Bungalow, opened on to the veranda, came softly but insistently above the tattoo of the rain, the sound of a rosewood grand piano, dwarfed to tinny proportions by the immensity of the room in which it was housed. Like everything else in the Big Bungalow, the piano was a hangover from the past. It had been imported specially for George Carey's mother, whose fingers had never touched the ivory keys. Indeed, since the day when more than a dozen coolies had staggered up the steps with it, almost the only time its forty-odd-years silence had been broken had been when the Eurasian piano-tuner from Badulla came on his tri-monthly visits.

As he sat at the piano, Geoffrey Wilding was acutely conscious of an unbalance and frustration in his life. Everything he turned his hand to he did well, but not so superlatively well that any one of his talents set him out far in advance of his fellow-men. He played the piano well, but not well enough to believe himself the master of the superb instrument whose keys he thrummed with a vague discontent. His water-colours were good—they had received commendation at more than one exhibit—but no one was more acutely aware of their limitations than John Geoffrey Wilding. He was a good horseman, but would never be a great horseman. He read voluminously and was, in the strict sense of the phrase, well-read, but the pinnacles of human thought towered a little beyond his reach. In his own bungalow, when the servants had gone to bed and he was sure that he was not observed, he liked to darn his own socks. The simple, homely task satisfied something in him. A hole in a woollen sock was nothing. Darned, it became something, giving him the satisfying sense of creating something; something that would endure, as it often did, longer than the sock itself.

It had been easy to learn Tamil and Sinhalese, for Wilding had a flair for languages; their structure and forms interested him. He was too intelligent to wish to parade his many accomplishments, for he knew this, from long experience, to be the surest way of antagonising the people around him. Nor did he take any great pride in the possession of accomplishments which his fellow planters and neighbours lacked. He knew only too well that, aesthetically speaking, he was like the one-eyed man who is monarch in the kingdom of the blind.

On this evening, with the driving rain as an *obbligato,* he drew comfort from the piano as a means of self-expression or, as he liked to think of it, a kind of emotional safety-valve. Almost involuntarily his long, tapering fingers drew from the piano strange, mournful discordancies and plaintive, wailing melodies in the minor key, with the drawn-out pathos of Gaelic laments. His neighbours were too hearty for him. Even when sober, he did not find them very bright, but when drunk, as they undoubtedly would be before midnight, they were abysmally dull. Wilding held his drink well—even as recently as the year 1913 this was a *sine qua non* of social acceptance—but usually drink bored him.

Closing the piano quietly, Wilding slipped into the convivial group which had centred itself around the trolley on the veranda.

Robbie Norman, a soured, elderly, misanthropic Scot, with his hand carefully shielding his glass, was splashing out a huge tot of whisky, on to which he poured, more as a ritual than for any practical purpose, a few drops of water. Sam Cullen, John Gilliland's young assistant, was already flushed of face and a little incoherent, the re-sult of trying manfully to drink level with men who were already seasoned to alcohol when he was in his cradle. The officials of the Irrigation Department, a little bewildered by the setting in which they found themselves, were trying vainly, from the behaviour of everyone on the veranda, to determine who was their host, a task which was quite beyond their capacity, because the tradition of the Big Bungalow demanded that everyone, invited or not, behaved as though he were in his own home. By the time they had run George Carey to earth at the billiard table, Appuhamy had announced din-ner.

At the Big Bungalow hospitality was on a careless, princely scale. Guests were expected to accept the good food, drink and service they found with the irreducible minimum of fuss and thanks. In the past, men had come for a weekend and had stayed for months. Others had been known to come and go without their host being aware of either their coming or going. One did not write and ask Carey of Elephant Walk if one might come. Some wrote to say they were coming: others just came.

It was, as the Careys—father and son—had always seen things, a privilege to be able to entertain lavishly, and to do so was the only way of justifying the magnificent bungalow erected as a memorial to Carey success and tenacity.

Since George Carey was about to go home to England for some months, it was inevitable that his friends and well-wishers would gather to give him a good send-off. It was equally inevitable that, until all his guests were sitting around his table, George Carey would be unaware of either their identities or numbers.

"Half the fun of life for me," old Tom Carey had once been heard to say, "is to ride home in the evening not knowing whether I'm going to dine alone, or find the place full of friends."

It was a way of life which already belonged to an epoch which had passed, and those who enjoyed Carey hospitality were privileged per-sons, who must have sensed that, before many years passed, it would vanish. Perhaps that was why their laughter and their talk endured far into the night and why, on the Monday morning when George Carey rode off to catch his train at Bandarawella, his guests—or some of them—were still under his roof when the ship taking him to England was nearing Aden on the other side of the Indian Ocean.

* * * * *

The Ratnagalla Gun Club was an uninspiring palm-leaf thatched structure, measuring some forty feet by twenty, built roughly of wood and raised a few feet off the ground on piles. The lounge occupied most of the space. It contained a dozen or so of the ubiquitous long chairs in which sleep was more practicable than conversation. In one corner was a tiny bar, beside which were stacked cases of whisky and still more cases of bottled soda water. On a shelf behind the bar there were, it is true, a few fly-specked bottles of other drinks, but it was years since any member or guest had asked for anything in the way of refreshment except tea in the afternoon and whisky at all other times. Behind the club-house were the dingy living-quarters of the resident club steward who, for six days a week, had nothing to do, while the seventh usually left him in a state of prostration. For those members who did not live entirely upon suction while visiting the club, the steward would kill and cook an indiarubber chicken, open a can of sausages, make what he euphemistically called an omelet, or serve a curry.

The Ratnagalla Gun Club, which had long since ceased to have anything to do with guns or shooting, had been created some years previously as a more central meeting-place for the district, where members could meet upon a level footing without the burden of entertaining falling unduly upon any one of them. The chief redeeming feature of the club was its two hard tennis courts. Upon these, rather than upon the amenities of the club-house, its slender resources were lavished.

On this Sunday afternoon, six of the club's long chairs were occupied by somnolent, sweating planter members. It was a leaden day. The heat was terrific, and not even the hardiest enthusiast present contemplated playing tennis until around four p.m. when, theoretically at least, the slanting sun's rays would be less deadly in their effects. Of conversation there was none. The silence was broken variously by the snores of Robbie Norman and occasional expletives at persistent flies. From behind newspapers came the hearty belches of those who at noon had sampled the club curry.

Shortly before four o'clock, a horse's hoof-beats were heard approaching along one of the narrow trails which met and intersected at the club-house, and were the reason for its location. Streaming with sweat and, when he had removed his helmet, looking unusually grave, John Gilliland strode into the lounge. Throwing himself into a long chair, he called loudly for tea. Until this was served, he did not speak. Several of the members, awakened by his entry, staggered out into the rear premises in a vain effort to refresh themselves under a shower of tepid water.

"I'm afraid," said Gilliland, in a voice of doom, when assured of a wakeful and attentive audience, "I've got some bad news."

There was a pause while Gilliland fumbled in his pocket. "Boy!" he called, producing an oblong slip of pink paper, unmistakably a cheque. "Pin this on to the notice-board."

Attached to the cheque was a single sheet of notepaper addressed to "The Treasurer, The Ratnagalla Gun Club" and, in George Carey's handwriting, "Herewith please find cheque value Rs. 500, in accordance with Rule No. 17. Regards, G.C."

In turn the members rose gloomily from their chairs to examine the notice-board, leaving it with blank looks of incomprehension.

"I didn't know there were any rules," observed Wilding. "Nobody's ever shown me any. What's Rule 17, anyway? Do you know, Gilly?"

"Rule 17," replied Gilliland, in a voice heavy with emotion, "provides that any member of the club being such a purblind crass idiot and bloody fool as to permit himself to be bamboozled into marriage, pays the club five hundred rupees."

"Is this, do you suppose," asked Robbie Norman, "Carey's way of breaking the news that he's married?"

Gilliland nodded gloomily. "My God!" he groaned. "A woman at Elephant Walk! And poor old George of all people! If it'd been one of the young fellows," he added, "I could have understood it. When I was about twenty-five I nearly made a fool of myself during Colombo Race Week. Would have done, too, only old George Carey nipped in just in time and told the bride's mother that I had five illegitimate children and there was insanity in my family. It was a bloody lie, too.

I only had three. And drink's the only trouble in my family. However, old George saved me. I wish to God now I'd taken a spot of leave and gone home with him. If I'd been there I could have saved him from—this."

"Dammit all, Gilly," said Wilding, "you're being a bit hard on the girl, aren't you? You haven't even met her yet. For all you know to the contrary, it may be the best day's work George Carey ever did. She may be a damned nice girl, a good sort and—er—all that sort of thing."

"Yes," growled the other, "it's all that sort of thing I'm scared of. I don't doubt she'll be nice. Why else would George want to marry her? First thing you know, she'll be wanting to give pink tea parties on the lawn at Elephant Walk. She'll arrive out here with trunkloads of frippery and, just so's she'll be able to have an excuse to doll herself up, she'll expect us in boiled shirts and dinner-jackets. Well, I haven't got a boiled shirt, and the moth have eaten my dinner-jacket. What's more, I don't intend to buy another. She's probably a good-looking piece—trust George for that! She'll be inviting all her plain-looking girl friends out to stay with her—you can bet your life she won't ask the good-looking ones—and they'll come out here on the rampage for husbands, and by God!"—Gilliland surveyed the room fiercely— "Don't say I didn't warn you!"

"You know," said Wilding, breaking a gloomy silence a little later, "I'm not so sure a few women in the district wouldn't liven things up a bit. God knows there's not much social life here the way things are!"

"Aye, my lad," said Gilliland, a strong North of Ireland accent emerging, as always in moments of stress, "she'll liven things up all right! Holy God she will! Yesterday you had one boss. Next week, my lad, you'll have two—and I hope you'll like it! I don't mind admitting, you fellows," he continued in a broken voice, "this has hit me pretty hard. George and I have been pals for a long while. There's nothing I wouldn't do for George, and the same's true where he's concerned. Elephant Walk has been a second home to me. The cook there knows my likes and dislikes better than my own does. And only a few weeks before George sailed, my new girl remade all the curtains in my bedroom there. No, I don't mind admitting, this has just knocked the heart out of me . . . no, I won't play tennis this afternoon. I'll sit and watch some of you. My God! . . . a woman at Elephant Walk!"

"You fellows," said Wilding, seeing that the sentiment of the club was against him, "may be woman-haters, but I'm not. And, in case you don't know it, you behave like a pack of bloody savages."

"Woomman hater—me! I like that!" exclaimed Robbie Norman. "I've got three. How many have you got?"

"None at all, thanks!" replied Wilding.

"Then you're no' qualified to express an opeenion on the subject," was the dry retort.

"While we're on the subject," said Gilliland, a twinkle of amusement in his shrewd grey eyes, "why don't you do as Rome does, and get yourself a nice girl? You never know, it might take that discontented look off your face. Why don't you, Wilding?"

"I don't do so," retorted Wilding, keeping a check on his temper, "—not, mind you, that it's any of your damn business—because it doesn't happen to appeal to me. It's too easy. I was taught, you know, that it isn't sporting to shoot a sitting pheasant. And since we are on the subject, if ever I do take either a wife or a concubine, my preference would be to have a little romance mixed up with it. Perhaps I'm old-fashioned."

"It isna a matter o' romance, ye ken," remarked Robbie Norman, "but it's rather a concession to a climate which is conducive to an awfu' lot o' low thinkin'. Ma wee lassies come when I call them and disappear when they are told to. Romance? Phooey! It was romance that made me leave Aberdeen twenty-five years ago in a hurry, and I havena' been back since. Romance has nothing to do with it. With me it's strictly medeecinal."

"Have it your own way," said Wilding wearily. "Who's ready for a game?"

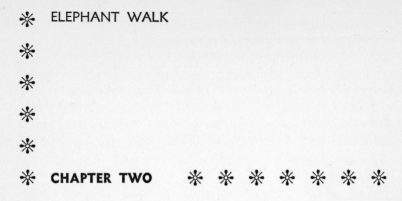

❋ CHAPTER TWO   ❋ ❋ ❋ ❋ ❋ ❋ ❋

John Hartington always proposed to Ruth Lakin on Saturday afternoons. Indeed, he seldom saw her at any other time. The bank claimed him on ordinary days until five p.m., or later, while his evenings were dedicated to his studies, by means of which he hoped, at some future time, to augment the pitifully meagre salary paid to him by the London & Home Counties Bank as cashier in their Shillingworth-on-Thames branch. On Sundays he had to be content with gazing longingly across the aisle in the direction of the Lakin pew in the parish church on the rare occasions when Ruth was present, while for the rest of the day his duties as churchwarden and teacher in the senior Sunday-school class occupied his time fully.

On the only Saturday afternoon in John Hartington's life with which this story is concerned, Ruth Lakin had listened to another in a long series of impassioned proposals.

"I like you very much indeed, John," she had replied, to soften her refusal as much as possible, "but I don't love you. Besides, you say so yourself, the rules of the bank don't permit you to marry for another year and—well, I don't think long engagements are good for people. You mustn't forget either, John, that I'm older than you are."

With what grace he could, John Hartington accepted her decision, in the phrasing of which he was still able to read a small ray of hope.

"Won't you stay to tea, John?" she asked, touched by his miserable expression.

"No, Ruth, thank you. I'll go home. I don't somehow feel I could face the rest of your family. But you wouldn't care for an hour or two on the river after tea, would you?"

"I can't, John," replied Ruth firmly. "I've got to go and play in the tennis tournament. My partner and I are in the semi-finals."

Looking the picture of dejection, John Hartington walked down the narrow pathway between the twin rows of geraniums and blue lobelias, to the gate of No. 11, Lawn Crescent, and although he did not know it, out of Ruth's life for ever.

Mrs Lakin, peeping through the lace curtains, watched him go. She was a faded, unhappy woman who for years had worn a sense of guilt at having produced three daughters when, as she had always known, her late husband, not long retired with the rank of colonel from the Indian Army, had so ardently desired a son.

Mrs Lakin did not understand Ruth, her youngest daughter, nor, it is pertinent to add, had she ever understood Eleanor and Dorothy, Ruth's two elder sisters, both of whom were unmarried and, now it seemed in all human probability, would remain so. Although neither Eleanor nor Dorothy could at any time have been called beauties [by any stretch of the imagination], they had been presentable young women who, in India in their early twenties, had not lacked suitors. Ruth, however, had good looks, charm, vivacity. "There's one that won't be left on the shelf!" Colonel Lakin had said pointedly, at Ruth's coming-out party in Poona.

"Mr Hartington's gone early," observed Mrs Lakin, with the air of one who would like to pursue the matter further.

"I asked him to stay to tea, mother, but he wouldn't."

"I don't think you're being quite fair to that young man, Ruth," observed Mrs Lakin with pursed lips. "It isn't always wise, you know, to believe that you can go on dangling a man on a string for ever. Men do not like to be made to look ridiculous, and I am very much afraid that is what you are doing to Mr Hartington. Why don't you marry him, my dear?" she added after a brief silence, seeing the ugly look of annoyance which crossed her daughter's face.

"I don't love him, mother. Surely that's enough?"

If Mrs Lakin could have brought herself to the point of being completely honest, her reply to this would have been "Fiddlesticks!" Instead, she indulged in what was known in the family circle as "one of mother's martyred sighs".

Mother and daughters were all acutely aware of the inadequacy of the widow's pension allocated to Mrs Lakin since her husband's death. She was not a heartless woman, but she realised that the marriage of one of her daughters would simplify so many things. It was true that John Hartington was not, in the matrimonial sense, a good catch, but he was an earnest, worthy young man with an assured position and, in a world whose *tempo* had already begun to accelerate, this, in Mrs Lakin's eyes, was something not to be lightly disregarded. Ruth was and always had been a puzzle and a sore trial to her mother.

"I don't want to try to influence you," said Mrs Lakin gently, "but . . ."

"But what?" asked Ruth bluntly and forbiddingly.

"Well, dear, you'll be twenty-seven next birthday and, as they say, you're not getting any younger. Your sisters may not say it, but I'm very sure they wish they'd not been quite so—hasty, that time in Peshawar. Eleanor was quite sure Major Hendriks would propose again, but he didn't. But now run along and we'll talk about it some other time."

As she pedalled her rattling and decrepit bicycle down towards the village, Ruth gave way to one of her rare moods of self-pity. She was growing to loathe the cramped, confined life which went on in the narrow confines of Shillingworth-on-Thames and the shabby, genteel atmosphere of her home, filled with ugly Benares brassware and frowzy Indian bric-à-brac which had survived from twenty years of what had once seemed glamorous service to the Empire. Ruth wanted love, romance, excitement. She was a normal, healthy young woman who had reckoned the price carefully and was determined, if she could, only to surrender her freedom for these, the things which seemed so logically to be her birthright. She was not infatuated with the idea of lavish spending on clothes, jewels, luxuries, but being honest with herself as she always tried to be, she knew that a few pretty clothes would help. She had often seen in imagination a big pigeon's-blood ruby, in a rough red Indian gold setting at her throat, and she knew how well it would suit her white skin, dark eyes and dark brown hair. The very thought was exciting. It seemed to typify, in some vague way, the kind of life to which she felt herself entitled. On the other side of the picture, she saw a little bitterly the kind of lives to which some of her contemporaries, similarly situated, were condemned, and she did not relish the thought of spending years in genteel poverty, surrounded by the odours of frying herrings and damp diapers.

Ruth arrived several minutes late at the tennis club, and her partner, a tall, cadaverous young man named Lancaster, was waiting for her somewhat impatiently. He took tennis, as he took everything else in life, very seriously, playing with a precision and a deliberation which was at times very irritating. Ruth, on the other hand, was in this respect a good many years ahead of her time. She really played tennis: played to win. The garb which was affected by women on the tennis courts in 1913 was quite adequate for the innocuous game of pat-ball which most of them played. Ruth, however, seemingly oblivious of the odd looks cast at her, wore a daringly—some said indecently—short frock, with elbow length sleeves, giving her the maximum of freedom.

The secretary of the club introduced Ruth and her partner to their opponents. "Mr Carey," he said in an undertone to Ruth, "is an immensely wealthy tea planter from Ceylon."

"What on earth's he doing here then?" asked Ruth bluntly.

"Staying with his cousins: you know—the Careys who have that lovely place by the river," the secretary replied, completely missing the import of the spontaneous question, which was perhaps just as well.

Although he did not look the part, it quickly became apparent that George Carey, despite his forty odd years, and his bulk, played a better game of tennis than Shillingworth-on-Thames was in the habit of seeing. It was apparent, too, that for all practical purposes his partner was a passenger, somewhat bewildered by the speed of the game. Ruth found herself wondering how, with such a handicap, Carey could have reached the semi-finals.

George Carey, who was not used to playing with or against women, irritated Ruth in the early stages of the game by playing, as he would have described it, "chivalrously", until a series of smashing drives from Ruth, which eluded him, caused him to change his tactics. From then on, although there were four people on the tennis court, it became obvious to the spectators that the game was in effect a singles match between George Carey and Ruth Lakin. The other two players were only in evidence when it was their turn to serve. By winning two straight sets, George Carey and his partner were declared the winners, but although on the losing side, Ruth had enjoyed every moment of the match. Her eyes dancing with pleasure, more than a little out of breath, and perspiring in a way which was not considered ladylike, she sank gratefully into a deck-chair on the veranda of the pavilion, smilingly accepting the glass of lemonade which was thrust into her hand. George Carey, who loved the kind of ferocious tennis they had been playing, lowered himself into a deck-chair alongside Ruth. The chair, a more fragile piece of furniture than the massive teak chairs which were provided at the Big Bungalow tennis courts, splintered to matchwood under his weight, to the consternation of everyone except Ruth and George Carey.

"Won't you have a lemonade, Mr Carey?" asked Ruth solicitously. "Surely you must be thirsty? Or is it so hot in Ceylon that you call this cool?"

"It's quite hot enough for me, Miss Lakin," Carey assured her, "but the truth is, lemonade doesn't agree with me. I suppose there isn't . . . ?" Ruth shook her head. Her companion's look of blank amazement and horror spoke volumes.

The court furthest from the pavilion fell vacant shortly afterwards, and it seemed the most natural thing in the world when George Carey challenged Ruth to a singles match, "without," as he put it, "our encumbrances".

They played three sets of savage tennis, such as no woman certainly had ever played upon the club courts. George Carey won the first set easily, the second set not so easily, while the third set dragged out to 10-9 before George Carey, closing up to the net, smashed home the winning stroke.

"I know we don't know each other very well, Miss Lakin, but I've got my cousin's motor-car here—couldn't we—I mean, wouldn't it be a good idea to pop over to Henley and have a quick one? I've got such a beautiful thirst, it would be a pity to ruin it with"—he shuddered—"lemonade."

Cars in 1913 were almost as rare as nicely brought up young women who rode in them alone with comparative strangers for the avowed purpose of "having a quick one". Ruth Lakin had only been in a car once before in her life. Those who observed the phenomenon were scandalised, and the fact that, in his precipitate departure, George Carey had forgotten that he was due to play in the finals, did not ease matters.

At the Red Lion in Henley Ruth did not, of course, enter the saloon bar but, more than a little aghast at her own daring, sat at a window-seat in the lounge overlooking the river, sipping what Carey assured her was a genuine Tom Carey. "My old guvnor invented the recipe forty odd years ago," he told her. "There's nothing like it. I suppose I ought to tell you though, that the true recipe calls for limes, not lemons. How do you like it?"

"It's"—Ruth paused for a word—"heavenly!"

For more than an hour Ruth listened to stories of Elephant Walk, the lovely valley that lay within the saucer of the hills in far-off Ceylon; the wonderful bungalow which had been built for George's mother, who had never seen it.

"I've got a photograph of it here, if you'd like to see it," said George, charmed by Ruth's qualities as a good listener. "To tell you the truth," he added shamefacedly, "I look at it two or three times a day. I can't get back there soon enough."

"But," said Ruth in amazement, when she saw the photograph, "it's huge! It's a—a—palace!"

"It is a bit on the big side," George agreed, "but the old guvnor liked to entertain people."

"Does your wife," Ruth asked casually, "like entertaining on a big scale?"

"My wife?" said George in a shocked voice. "Good God! I'm not married. What ever made you think that? I suppose really I'm not what you might call the marrying kind. Who'd want to marry me?"

It is hard to say whether Ruth's absence until nearly ten p.m., or the arrival of the huge shining limousine outside No. 11, Lawn Crescent, caused the more consternation.

"Don't you want any supper, my dear?" asked Mrs Lakin, when the recriminations were over.

"No thank you, mother. I'm not hungry. I think I'll go up to bed now."

Downstairs, the talk engendered by Ruth's late home-coming, the sight of the splendid limousine which had brought her home and her own radiant appearance, lasted far into the night. Her sisters, consumed with curiosity, tapped vainly upon the door of Ruth's bedroom, but she, disinclined for talk and wanting to be alone with her thoughts, feigned sleep.

But there was no sleep for Ruth Lakin until, sitting at the window, she had heard the mellow bell in the parish church clocktower strike four. Only then did she turn reluctantly away from the window. Before climbing into the narrow and not very comfortable brass-knobbed bed, Ruth turned up the gas light. During the hours of her thoughtful vigil, strange processes had been going on within her. New purposes had been born, so far-reaching that she was impelled to wonder whether they had left any outward mark upon her.

Wearing a badly-cut cotton nightgown, with a narrow wisp of machine-made lace at the throat and sleeves and the mark of a hot iron on the left shoulder, Ruth surveyed herself in the cracked mirror of the wardrobe. She looked at herself searchingly from top to toe. And then, impelled by thoughts she did not quite understand, tore off the nightgown to survey herself mother-naked, clothing herself in imagination as she believed Ruth Lakin should be and would be clothed when she became Ruth Carey.

She was not in love with George Carey. She knew that. But she warmed to him with a feeling of enormous friendliness. He was kind, direct, unsubtle and, despite being a good many years older than she was, wore an unconquerable air of youthfulness. There was something about George Carey which would always remind Ruth of a small, mischievous, untidy, inkstained, irrepressible schoolboy. In the process of growing to middle-age some little part of him— perhaps the best—had forgotten to grow up. Now, if never again, Ruth knew she must be completely honest with herself and not invest her actions with motives which were false. George Carey was a means of escape. She believed that she could make him very happy:

perhaps, indeed, ideally happy. On his part, if he could not make her ideally happy—and she faced the possibility—he would be kind, considerate and, in his awkward fashion, gentle. He could give her, furthermore, so many of the things for the lack of which life was quickly becoming intolerable. George Carey had said he was returning to Ceylon in five weeks' time. Ruth was resolved that he should not return alone.

* * * * *

Life at Meldrums, the pleasantly-situated house belonging to Mortimer Carey and his wife Isobel, was, to George Carey's way of thinking, excessively dull. His fellow guests, invited for the week-end, were a worthy couple called Bennett, who talked so far back in their throats as to be barely intelligible. They were, so they informed George Carey at lunch, deeply interested in Buddhist mysticism. Indeed, it was because George Carey lived in Ceylon that they had been invited to meet him. Ceylon being, in theory at least, a Buddhist country, they envied him his opportunities of studying at first-hand this fascinating question. George, who had not the least notion of what they were talking about, remarked that the only Buddhist priest he had ever come in contact with had seemed to prefer small boys to mysticism. The conversation thereafter flagged.

The whisky decanter at Meldrums, never more than a third full, was kept under lock and key until after dinner, to be produced at the moment when Mortimer Carey, yawning, remarked pointedly, "What about a nightcap?" George, of course, kept a bottle of whisky in his room, but it taxed his ingenuity to the utmost to devise pretexts for the many journeys upstairs during the hours in which he was accustomed to helping himself to a drink. It irked him, too, to have to drink flat water from a bedroom jug when he infinitely preferred soda.

George Carey viewed England through jaundiced eyes. It ranked with him in the same category as taking a dose of castor oil or quinine. Being so excessively unpleasant, it must, he forced himself to believe, be good for him. He had firmly resolved that this was to be his last visit to England, so his stay with his cousin was in the nature of a final farewell to his only kith and kin. The only bright spot, he realised during the Sunday afternoon following the dreary luncheon, had been the meeting with that nice girl—he couldn't remember her name—who had played such smashing tennis the previous day. Despite the coolness, which he realised he would have to face for his discourtesy in forgetting the finals on the previous day, he haunted the tennis club for the remainder of the afternoon, in the hope of catching a glimpse of Ruth. In the early evening, telling his outraged cousin he would not be in for dinner—he felt quite unable to face any more chit-chat with the Bennetts—he made for the saloon bar of a riverside pub, where he gave the local yokels a demonstration of the absorptive powers acquired during some twenty-four years in the tropics.

At closing time, tucking a bottle of whisky under his arm, he strolled back to Meldrums, firm in his resolve to find out this nice girl's name and, if possible, arrange some more tennis with her. "If she plays like that on a grass court," he mused, "what a magnificent game she would play on the faster hard courts!" Although not consciously aware of it—and there is little doubt that if he had been he would have returned to Ceylon by the first ship—the hard courts he had in mind were those at Elephant Walk. She seemed, for all her clean-limbed, good proportions, so very frail. And yet, he mused ruefully, her tremendous forehand drive nearly beat him. She would have beaten him, too, had he not discovered in the nick of time that, like most women, her backhand, probably because of a lack of wrist power, was her weakest point.

Mortimer Carey solved George's perplexity the following morning at breakfast, which at Meldrums was a chatty family affair. "I hear the Lakin girl gave you a tussle at tennis on Saturday," he observed.

"Even if she isn't very—er—ladylike," continued Isobel, "she plays a wonderful game, don't you think?"

George agreed with enthusiasm and pigeon-holed the name.

"It might be a good idea, my dear," said Mortimer, "to invite Mrs Lakin and the girls to lunch one day this week. It's a long time since they've been here." Somewhat reluctantly, George thought, Isobel Carey agreed.

"I must say, Isobel," George blustered, "I think you're being a bit unfair on this Miss—er—Lakin. Struck me as a dashed nice girl.

And you can take it from me, she didn't do anything unladylike when I was around."

"I daresay, George," cooed Isobel, "that, tucked away here in Shillingworth, we're a wee bit old-fashioned, but a good many of us have noticed that on the tennis courts she dresses in a way that is —er—well, a little revealing."

"Well, hang it all! You can't expect a girl who plays tennis like that to cramp her style with crinolines or bustles, can you?"

"And you know, George," continued Isobel inexorably, "although I hadn't intended to mention it, I do think it was a little—er—peculiar of her to allow herself to be seen drinking in a public-house."

"Good God, Isobel!" retorted George in an irritated voice, "one would think from the way you talk she'd been out on the booze. The fact is that after tennis at the club, where all they had to give a man was lemonade, I felt I needed a couple of quick ones, so I drove the girl over to Henley and, just to keep me company, she had a couple of Tom Careys. For God's sake don't make mountains out of molehills."

"I'll try not to, George," replied Isobel sweetly, "but you see it happened to be cook's afternoon off. Her sister lives in Henley and works at the Red Lion. Although perhaps I shouldn't say so, you must see that it was a little embarrassing for us, George. Wasn't it, Mortimer?"

"Well, my dear, we don't want to spoil George's holiday, so let's not, as he says, make mountains out of molehills." It was very evident, nevertheless, that Mortimer, too, oozed disapproval at every pore.

Ruth Lakin, when news of the invitation to lunch with the Careys arrived, credited George, wrongly as it happened, with having engineered it. This, as she knew, was her moment. Opportunity had knocked. It might never knock again.

"You'd like to go, would you, girls?" Mrs Lakin asked. Eleanor and Dorothy agreed eagerly. "What about you, Ruthie darling?"

"Oh yes, we might as well go," Ruth replied, concealing her elation behind a veil of indifference. It would not be wise, she knew, to allow either her mother or her sisters to gain an inkling of what she felt. Mrs Lakin, with the kindest intentions, was not distinguished for her tact. Ruth remembered hearing her mother, a few weeks previously—she flushed at the recollection—saying archly to John Hartington, who was waiting impatiently for her in the garden: "You must be patient, John. Ruth won't be long. She's upstairs putting on her prettiest frock for you." This time, Ruth was resolved, her mother's tactless tongue was not going to be allowed to play any part in the plans she was weaving.

From the wardrobe in her attic bedroom Ruth took down, with bitter thoughts at the memories it evoked, a flowery muslin frock bought, by dint of many soul-destroying economies, for Ascot two years previously. There had been a telegram at the last moment from the man in whose honour she had bought the frock and, never worn in public, it had hung in the wardrobe ever since. Many stratagems were needed to iron out the creases of long disuse from the frock, but Ruth managed to accomplish the task without the knowledge of her mother and sisters.

On the morning of the luncheon Ruth dressed herself with great care. Her dark hair, worn in a low bun on her neck, looked striking. Hats did not become her, so she resolved, on some pretext or another, to carry the floppy, frilly thing that went with the dress. George Carey, she was quite sure, would not know whether the dress were one of this year's latest Ascot models or ten years old and, as she judged him, knowing, would not care. Ruth was aware that, in this frock, sadly thrust aside for two years, she looked her best. She was tall, moved well and, when she had them, knew how to wear good clothes as they should be worn. George Carey, she guessed, liked his women frilly and fluffy. The svelte, sophisticated type would, she believed, frighten him to death.

"You look very sweet, Ruthie dear," her mother observed as the hired open Victoria arrived at the door of No. 11, Lawn Crescent. "I'm glad, after all this time, you've decided to wear that frock. I always thought it suited you so well."

Isobel Carey, more far-seeing than her husband, regretted the hastily-given invitation to the Lakins. Her two sons away at school were, although the subject had never been openly discussed, George Carey's logical heirs. During the preliminary skirmishing which took place before lunch, her quick eyes caught the quicker glint of understanding which seemed to be exchanged between Ruth Lakin and George Carey. She was aware, too, that George Carey, the confirmed bachelor, was at a very impressionable age. Tennis, it seemed, was a bond of understanding between these two. But, as Isobel Carey well knew, tennis could lead to anything. Making some excuse for her disappearance, she bustled into the dining-room to change the place-cards at the table so that George Carey and Ruth Lakin should sit on the same side of the table at opposite ends. In this stratagem, however, she had reckoned without her husband's cousin George, who was as easily deterred from his purpose as a steamroller. In his years of bachelor freedom he had acquired no social graces, but he did not suffer from any sense of embarrassment from lack of them. He liked some people, disliked very few and was quite indifferent to what the rest thought of him. With Isobel Carey dinning into his right ear the doughty achievements of her two sons on the football field, and a good lady on his left who talked a great deal about the "poor heathen", George nevertheless, sometimes leaning forward, sometimes leaning backwards, managed to carry on a spirited conversation with Ruth Lakin. Before lunch was over, with a suitable handicap agreed upon, a blood match had been arranged for the following afternoon upon the far court of the Shillingworth Lawn Tennis Club.

Isobel Carey gritted her teeth in rage. Mrs Lakin looked aghast, while Eleanor and Dorothy wondered whether Ruth should have drunk the second glass of claret cup. Mortimer Carey, a gloomy man at the best of times, took refuge in gloom. He felt himself able to bear with fortitude his cousin George's imminent return to Ceylon.

Mortimer Carey owned an electric launch in which, on rare and infrequent occasions because of the excessive cost of charging its batteries, he liked, on sunny afternoons, to ride in solemn state up and down a four-mile stretch of placid river.

"I'm sure you won't mind, Mortimer old boy," observed George Carey while the guests were saying their formal farewells at the front door, "if I borrow the launch this afternoon?"

A few seconds later, without waiting to hear Mortimer's reaction to the suggestion, George Carey and Ruth Lakin, laughing like two juvenile conspirators, were sneaking down the garden path to the boathouse where the launch was kept.

For a few seconds Ruth was sobered by the thought that in this escapade she had socially, in so far as Shillingworth was concerned, burned her boats. There was no coming back along the road she had taken, but, as George Carey bundled her into the launch, she reflected grimly, the time was not far off when Shillingworth could think and say what it pleased, for she, unless her plans miscarried, would have escaped from its smug orbit.

The non-appearance of the couple delayed the departure of Mrs Lakin and her two daughters for some minutes, during which Mortimer Carey made a perfunctory and half-hearted search. Murmuring, "Really, one doesn't know what to expect next from the young!" Mrs Lakin climbed into the hired Victoria and, with considerable embarrassment, drove homewards. By the time Mortimer Carey arrived at the boathouse, his launch was a quarter mile upstream and disappearing round a bend in the river.

By paying an enormous deposit to a riverside hotel for the complete makings of a picnic tea with all the necessary equipment, George Carey ensured the privacy he demanded for the afternoon. He was thoroughly enjoying the adventure. Ruth Lakin, he mused, was a girl in a million. She laughed at a good joke unrestrainedly as though she enjoyed it, instead of simpering. She met him on level terms in everything. He had the feeling that if the impulse came upon him—and he hoped it would not—to say something shocking, she could laugh it off with him. His clumsy gallantries were so spontaneous, naïve and lacking in self-consciousness that Ruth, despite the disparity in their ages, found herself regarding him as a big, good-natured boy.

There was nothing subtle about his enthusiasm when he talked of Ceylon. The gentle look which came into his eyes when he talked of Elephant Walk so obviously sprang from a deep, abiding affection. A less acute woman than Ruth Lakin would have seen an underlying purpose in George's enthusiasm, but Ruth had the wit to see that there was no underlying purpose. George's enthusiasms bubbled out of him spontaneously because he wished to share them. He was not, as many women might have been pardoned for believing, painting his life in Ceylon in glowing colours as a species of ground-bait preparatory to a proposal.

From a riverside pub higher upstream, George telephoned Mortimer

Carey that he would not be back for dinner, leaving Ruth to send a telephone message to her mother, via the doctor who lived next-door, that she, too, without any explanation, was unavoidably detained and would not be back until late.

There came a moment during the afternoon when George Carey, so subtly that he was unaware of the fact, crossed the bridge which divided bachelordom from that other condition in which bachelordom appeared less as freedom than as bleakness and incompleteness. In that moment he became spiritually receptive to ideas which he had always thrust resolutely from him. The changed outlook came so stealthily that there was no time to repel it. For the first time since his arrival in England, he was inwardly bemoaning the fact that in a few weeks he would be returning to Ceylon, where he would not be able to spend jolly afternoons with this charming, friendly girl. It seemed such a pity. Although he did not quite know why, it was much more fun playing tennis with her than with his good friend Gilly and his other neighbours at Elephant Walk.

The fact that this afternoon on the river had been stolen from right under the noses of his cousin Mortimer and, as he put it, "that acid bitch Isobel", made it so much more delightful. He chuckled as he recalled the look of dismay on Mrs Lakin's face when he had whisked Ruth off through the shrubbery. At Elephant Walk, of course, the shrubbery, and in fact the whole setting, was infinitely larger and in every way more delightful than the rather gloomy grounds with which the gloomy Mortimer had surrounded his home. But at Elephant Walk—and the very thought made him feel disloyal—there would not be this nice, friendly girl scuttling through the shrubbery with him. Probably for the only time in his life, George Carey was seeing Elephant Walk as anything short of sheer perfection.

George, as he looked at Ruth sitting in the launch in front of him, lips parted a little, eyes sparkling with excitement, her hair blowing in the wind, was quite sure, although the fact had only just struck him, that she was the prettiest girl he had ever seen. George was short of adjectives to describe feminine beauty, and there was in his vocabulary no higher accolade than 'pretty'.

In the dim tunnel of a leafy backwater George Carey made the launch fast to the bough of an overhanging willow and, when he had ensconced himself comfortably upon a pile of pillows, became aware that a silence had fallen between him and his companion. His own thoughts had been tinged a little with melancholy, so perhaps, he mused, some of them had communicated themselves to Ruth.

Suddenly, as most brilliant ideas are said to come, it flashed across George's mind that his return to Ceylon need not involve the parting which had given rise to his melancholy broodings. After all, he said to himself, men did marry. Why shouldn't Ruth return to Ceylon with him?

George Carey looked up apprehensively towards the sky where there was, he decided, still a little too much light. In the past, during moments of aberration, when imagination flies fancy free, he had often imagined himself proposing marriage. It had been just an idea or an ideal, for there had never been in his mind any clear picture of the woman involved. He remembered that she had always smelled very nice of lavender water and had looked very fresh and clean, but her personality had always eluded him. But—and this was important —these proposals of his imaginings had always taken place in the fading light when—he had sometimes blushed at the thought—he had been unable to see whether She were laughing at him. It had been a real fear always, that of laying his heart at a woman's feet and baring his soul to her, only to be greeted with mocking laughter. George Carey did not think he could bear that. As he looked at Ruth Lakin, almost obscured in the soft shadows of evening, somehow he did not believe that, if he could bring himself to the point, she would laugh. She might, indeed probably would, refuse him, but she would do it, he was sure, in a way that would not be humiliating.

"Miss Lakin—er—Ruth—you don't mind if I call you Ruth, do you?" he blurted out, breaking a long silence.

"I think I would prefer it—George," replied Ruth, looking up with a quick smile.

"Ruth," said George soberly, clamping a vice-like hand on to her left shoulder, "I've spent the last few minutes trying to summon up courage to ask you something and—well, it isn't very easy because I'm not very good at this sort of thing. Although we've only known one another a short time, it doesn't seem like that to me. I expect lots of fellows have said that to you. But it's true. Then, you see," he rambled on, "it sticks out a mile that we get along splendidly together . . . laugh at the same things . . . if you know what I mean. Look, Ruth," he faltered, "it's no good my beating about the bush any longer. I'd like to get down on my knees and say what I want to say to you, but if I did that I'd probably upset the damn boat. The fact is, you see, Ruth, I've been thinking . . . I've got to go back to Ceylon soon and I don't mind telling you, a few minutes ago I was feeling pretty gloomy about it, when all of a sudden—'pon my soul, it came to me like a flash!—the idea struck me, why," he gasped, "couldn't you come with me? I know, Ruth, I'm not much of a catch. . . ."

Ruth, although she did not quite know why, winced at the word.

"I know I'm a clumsy, ham-handed devil. But—I see it now—I'm desperately in love with you, Ruth and—well, what it amounts to is, will you marry me?"

With the nightingales singing above them as though they would burst their hearts, the sweet scents of the peaceful English countryside in their nostrils and the water lapping gently beside them, strange thoughts ran through Ruth Lakin's head and new emotions gave her a queer ache under the heart. She was able, during those enchanted moments, to forget that this hulking, good-natured man whose grip on her shoulder nearly made her cry with the pain of it, was a rich man, able to give her all the things she wanted. She was able, too, to forget that only a day or two previously, in the solitude of her shabby attic bedroom, she had resolved, with all the cold-blooded deliberation of a hunter stalking his prey, that come what might, she would marry this man. It flashed across her mind that here was a man offering her simple-hearted devotion and, although she had never thought of it in quite this way before, able, if the gods were kind, to make her very happy.

"I know, George," she said gently, "that all nice girls are supposed to say 'It is so sudden!' But it *is* sudden, you know. Don't you want to know more about me? Oughtn't we to know more about each other? Oughtn't we to—well, wait a little?"

"I never will know more about you until we're married," said George with more wisdom than he knew. "I don't think people ever do. I love you, Ruth. Do you love me? That's all that matters."

"I think I do, George," said Ruth softly.

At that moment Ruth Lakin was so near to being in love with George Carey that she quietened conscience by the reflection—and in that moment it was an honest one—that if he had been a poor man her answer would have been the same.

"Then what are we waiting for?" asked the impetuous and delighted George. "We're growing older every minute. I've been told that somewhere in London there's a place where they dish out special licences. Let's get one!"

In the years that lay ahead there would be time, Ruth mused, to analyse the ingredients of the tears which streamed down her cheeks. Another could only guess that in them was the salty sweetness of relief that the cold-blooded thing she had planned had, when the time came, been done in warm blood.

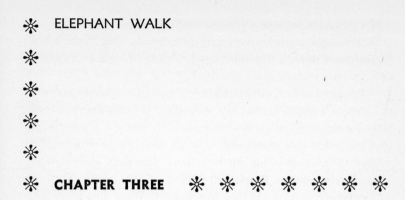

❋ **CHAPTER THREE**   ❋ ❋ ❋ ❋ ❋ ❋ ❋

The news of the impending wedding, which raced round Shillingworth with the speed of a prairie fire, roused the village from its summer calm, causing more excitement than anything which had happened since the time when Mr Phelps, the church organist, had been discovered romping in a haystack with the buxom barmaid from the Goat & Compasses.

"The man must be feeble-minded!" was Mortimer Carey's only comment when the news reached him. His wife Isobel bit her lip with vexation when she remembered that by inviting the Lakin family to lunch she had furthered the match. For ever afterwards she would regard Ruth Lakin as one who had come between her sons and their inheritance which, bearing in mind the amount of whisky George Carey drank, could not, in her jaundiced view, have been long delayed.

At No. 11, Lawn Crescent the news was received emotionally, as might have been expected. When Ruth returned home shortly after midnight, looking radiantly happy, Mrs Lakin exercised her parental privilege of demanding from her an account of her movements.

"As you so often remind me, mother dear," said Ruth, taken aback by her mother's uncompromising attitude, "I am nearly twenty-seven years old, and I don't have to explain my every movement. However, you may as well know it now as later. I've been with Mr Carey— George Carey—and"—she threw up her chin defiantly—"we're going to be married."

Her righteous indignation forgotten, Mrs Lakin began to weep.

"Are you thinking of a very long engagement, dear?" she asked. "Somehow, I think it would be a pity. Three or four months would be quite long enough, don't you think?"

"As a matter of fact, mother, George is going to London tomorrow to see about a special licence. We're thinking of being married"—she balked at the announcement—"next week. George, you see, has to go back to Ceylon very soon and I, naturally, want to go with him."

"But it's quite out of the question, dear! Next week indeed! Why, it's positively indecent. People will think . . ."

"Let people think what they like, mother. What does it matter? It's my life and I'm not going to bother my head about—people." The last word she uttered with such venom that Mrs Lakin and Ruth's older sisters looked alarmed.

"Are you in love with this Mr Carey?" asked Mrs. Lakin. "Are you sure you're doing the right thing?"

"I'm not a child any longer," was the impatient reply. "Yes, I am in love with George and I'm as sure as I ever was of anything that I'm doing the right thing."

"I suppose you know," said Mrs Lakin, going off at a tangent, "that Mortimer Carey and his wife were most upset at the way you . . ."

"They're George's relatives, mother. George is quite capable of dealing with them."

"They may be George's relatives, dear," was the mildly reproachful reply, "but don't forget that they're our friends and neighbours and we have to go on living here."

"I've already forgotten everything, mother, except that I'm terribly happy, and I don't intend to allow Shillingworth's ideas, right or wrong, to influence me. I've loathed the smug self-righteousness of the place ever since we came back from India, and now"—there was triumph in Ruth's voice—"I've escaped!"

When he called at No. 11, Lawn Crescent, to meet the rest of the family, all the advantages were with George Carey. His great bulk and beaming sunburned face seemed to dominate the tiny formal drawing-room, making Mrs Lakin appear even more frail than she was. His effect upon Eleanor and Dorothy, despite his large amiability, was to terrify them. It was a long time since they had heard a loud, hearty, masculine voice in this room. The few male visitors who came to the house tended to talk in almost confidential tones and to sit uncomfortably on the edges of chairs. Hearty masculinity by-passed No. 11, Lawn Crescent. Her sisters looked wonderingly at Ruth, unable to understand why she, too, did not share their vague terror.

George arrived with immense boxes of costly flowers for Mrs Lakin and grotesquely large boxes of chocolates for Eleanor and Dorothy. "Even if I have stolen a daughter from you, Mrs Lakin," observed George without much originality, "just try to remember that you've got a bouncing son in exchange."

The Tottenham Court Road Chippendale chair, on which George sat precariously, began to creak. Suddenly, Mrs Lakin did not quite know how it happened, her strong sense of the proprieties seemed of less importance to her than that she liked him. As she dried the tears which followed this realisation, she tried vainly to dismiss as unworthy the thought that this large, beaming man, who was so soon to take Ruth away from her, was so obviously prosperous. Even if she had not known it beforehand, she would have known that George Carey was a rich man. His clothes, which he wore badly, were good. There was about him a large carelessness, which so often comes from a deep pocket.

The most precious of all George Carey's wedding gifts to Ruth, because the most precious to him, was Esmeralda who, oblivious of her change of ownership, was nuzzling sweet hay in the stables at Elephant Walk. Ruth was an ardent horsewoman, although she had not been astride a horse, because of limited means, since the family's return from India five years previously. The impulsive gift of Esmeralda, his beloved chestnut mare, was a token of George's delight that here was one more interest which he and Ruth had in common.

The solitaire diamond engagement-ring which George brought back from London and which, by pure chance, was the right size, was so magnificent that there hovered on Mrs Lakin's lips, happily unsaid, the word "vulgar". The crocodile leather dressing-case filled with rich gold, cut-glass and ivory fittings, acquired at great cost in Bond Street, took Ruth's breath away. A necklace of fifteen beautifully matched rubies, Tom Carey's gift to his bride, which had lain for more than forty years in a bank vault in London, brought tears of pure joy to Ruth's eyes.

They were married by special licence at a registrar's office in London, exactly eleven days after they had first met. Mrs Lakin and the two girls, Mortimer and Isobel Carey were the only people present. After the wedding breakfast, in a private dining-room at the Savoy, George and Ruth took the afternoon train to Paris.

*   *   *   *   *

The few days spent in Paris served to enrich several *couturiers,* jewellers and other purveyors to feminine extravagance and to fill Ruth's trunks with a variety of pretty things of a kind which had never been seen in the Ratnagalla Valley.

It was George's first visit to Paris, and, when he had got over his amazement, delight and admiration upon finding that Ruth spoke passable French, he found the atmosphere too exotic, too highly perfumed for his simple tastes. Only Ruth's presence made the stay tolerable to him. But for a fortuitous occurrence on the last evening, he would have carried away a very poor opinion of this glittering city by the Seine.

Paris was full of Anglo-Saxon visitors and, to the disgust of those Parisians who did not directly benefit therefrom, much of the fare provided by places of amusement was confined to British and, to a lesser extent, American tastes. On the last evening, wandering fancy-free and with no fixed plan, George steered Ruth into a *boite* where they were privileged to see "the one and original can-can". Once sure that Ruth was not shocked by the spectacle, George's immoderate laughter and uninhibited pleasure were, to a large part of the spectators, fully as enjoyable as the show itself. To see the row of waving behinds clad in long white linen drawers touched some responsive chord in George Carey's unspoiled heart. His only personal purchase in Paris was two phonograph records of the can-can accompaniment, by means of which he hoped to perpetuate the memories of a memorable evening. "Old Gilly would have loved that, darling," he observed nostalgically as they left the place. "Just up his street. He's a great chap, you know. I'm certain that you and he'll get on like a house on fire."

"He sounds a dear," replied Ruth, with an enthusiasm which she did not altogether feel. George's descriptions of John Gilliland—loyalty and enthusiasm made him overstate his case—had created in Ruth a premonition that she would not always see eye to eye with her husband's closest friend and nearest neighbour.

That night, before sleep claimed them, George, his heart bubbling over with happiness and gratitude to Ruth who had made it possible, summoned up the courage—as he saw matters, it was his simple duty —to try to tell Ruth of his youthful indiscretions. A gentle but firm hand across his mouth saved him this embarrassment. Ruth did not want to hear. If George had sown his wild oats prodigally, he had done, she assumed, what ninety-nine out of every hundred normal men had done, and she did not want to be reminded of the fact that the sowing had probably taken place while she herself was in her cradle or, at best, toddling in her nursery. To have listened, she felt, would have been the height of indelicacy.

"Don't you think, George," said Ruth when the honeymoon ship was midway between Suez and Aden, and George, his glass poised, was just about to swallow his eleventh whisky-and-soda before dinner, "that you ought to drink a little less? I'm sure drink in the tropics is good—in moderation. Daddy always said so. He always believed it was the drunkards and the teetotallers who went under first."

"But, darling," protested George in unsimulated horror and amazement, "you surely aren't suggesting that I'm drunk, are you?"

"No, of course not," said Ruth. "I can see that drink doesn't affect *you*." She glanced meaningly in the direction of three fellow passengers who were trying to retain their dignity and stagger gracefully out of the lounge, having drunk level with George for the past hour or more. "All the same, dear, I'm sure it isn't good for you and I wish, for my sake"—she put a wealth of passionate pleading into this—"that you wouldn't drink quite so many."

If Ruth's last word had been "much" rather than "many", George would have been in a quandary. But it was not. His simple and effective reply was to arrange with the bar steward that whereas in the past, as was his custom, he had been drinking single whiskies, he now be served with doubles. The nett result of this was that his usual evening consumption of fifteen to twenty single whiskies between six p.m. and the time the bar closed, was changed to an average of a dozen doubles, which represented a nett increase of alcoholic intake amounting to roughly twenty-five per cent.

In all other matters, however, George's attentiveness and solicitude was impeccable. He was quite touchingly proud of Ruth's good looks and vivacity, delighted to humour her least whim. Indeed, there were times when Ruth found it in her to wish that George would treat her rather less as though she were a piece of Dresden china.

*　　*　　*　　*　　*

It was very hot in Colombo when they landed. They lingered long enough to eat the prawn curry at Mount Lavinia, catching the night train for the hills. When, shortly after daybreak, the train came to a standstill at Bandarawella, then the terminus, Ruth was swept, although not yet aware of it, into the smooth-running, efficient orbit of the Big Bungalow, which was to be her home. From now onwards her every material want had been anticipated by Tom Carey, already nine years in his grave, who, although he had never heard of her when he died, had even formulated the plans for her reception at her new home. Tom Carey had planned the food she was to eat that day, the place and the time she should eat it. He had planned the exact positions in which the staff of the Big Bungalow should stand to receive her, the flowers and the arrangement of them in her honour and a score of other details so that her homecoming should be a momentous day.

From Aden, George had sent a cablegram indicating the time of their arrival. From the moment Appuhamy had received the cable, the rest had been automatic. Some forty-four years previously the Big Bungalow had waited many months for the bride who never came. But plans for her reception had been made, down to the last detail. Appuhamy, remembering these, put them into effect forty-four years later.

Drawn up beside the platform was a heavy cart with a team of patient milk-white draught oxen, ready to haul the baggage to Elephant Walk, while beyond this, beaming syces in attendance, were Esmeralda and a big rangy Australian gelding which, for the future, would be George's mount.

As George led Ruth the short distance across the station yard, Esmeralda whinnied with delight on hearing his voice. George went forward alone and, putting his great arms around Esmeralda's head, he seemed to whisper something to her. "She's yours now, darling," he said, turning to Ruth. "Be good to her. I've told her to be good to you."

Ruth turned in amazement to look at George, whose face was grief-stricken. His eyes were held widely open, while across his face was the look of horror seen in a child deprived of some beloved toy. "George," said Ruth impulsively, "I can't take her from you."

"Don't be absurd," said George, with a break in his voice. "She's yours. Mount her. I've given her to you. She knows that and—well, you can't play shuttlecock with a horse. Not with Esmeralda anyway."

Ruth became aware suddenly that the two syces, the other passengers descending from the train, those who were there to meet them and the station staff, were all looking at her in horror and astonishment.

"Why are they staring at me, George?" she asked.

"Are they? Then perhaps, darling, it's—er—because"—he looked down at her legs—"you're wearing those."

Ruth was wearing jodhpur riding breeches. "Haven't they seen these before?" she asked.

"Probably not on women, now I come to think of it," said George. "But anyway, don't let it upset you."

The runner who was to announce their arrival along the route was already on his way and more than a mile out of Bandarawella. The runner who met him half-way and completed the thirty-mile journey was breathing heavily when he entered the kitchen quarters of the Big Bungalow.

"They have arrived?" asked Appuhamy.

"They have arrived," said the runner.

"All is well with the Master?"

"All is well but"—he paused for the effect of his words—"the woman wears trousers!"

George and Ruth had already eaten a light breakfast on the train and, within ten minutes of arrival at the station, were cantering along the greensward outside the town, through the cool sparkling air of early morning. Before long the pace had to slacken, for the route lay along a narrow trail through the jungle-clad hills.

"Oughtn't we to have seen that the baggage was all right?" asked Ruth, worried as to the fate of her newly-acquired treasures and not yet realising that decades previously—before she was born—Tom Carey had provided for the care of her baggage with the same painstaking forethought he had given to the menus *en route*. Indeed, Tom Carey had overlooked nothing except, perhaps, the passage of time. Who could blame him for that?

"Everything'll be there tomorrow morning," George reassured her, "and the case you'll need tonight will be at home before we are."

As the sun rose higher, the heat increased until, at about eleven o'clock, Ruth, who had not been astride a horse for some years, was uncomfortably hot and conscious of muscles long unused which ached agonisingly.

"Oughtn't we," Ruth asked a little tremulously, "to have brought a picnic? I'm getting terribly hungry."

"There's a picnic arranged a few minutes ahead," said George reassuringly.

"How do you know?" asked Ruth in amazement.

"Oh, Appuhamy will have seen to that."

A few minutes later, around a bend in the trail, there was the welcome sight of a trestle-table erected by a cascade which tumbled down into a cool glade of the jungle. Over the table was a temporary shelter from the sun, made from the huge fronds of tree-ferns cunningly interlaced. The table was ready set with white linen, a cut-glass bowl of jungle orchids, and shining silverware. The neck of a champagne bottle was visible above the surface of a pool of cool spring water. A silver cigarette box and matches stood upon the table. At a discreet distance from the table was a small tent. "That's for you, darling, in case you want a wash and brush-up," said George. Inside the tent Ruth found a comfortable chair, a table, a mirror and, to her amazement, a smiling Sinhalese woman, daughter of the woman who, forty-four years previously, had been chosen to wait on George Carey's mother.

"Try to look suitably impressed when you see the table," said George, when Ruth emerged from the tent.

"I don't have to try, George," said Ruth wonderingly. "It's like a fairy-tale!"

"But you haven't seen the star-turn yet. Come and look at it."

In the centre of the table, picked out in coloured rice, grain by grain, against a background of white rice, like some delicate mosaic, was the legend: *Many happy years at Elephant Walk*.

"Fancy Appuhamy remembering that!" said George. "It was the guvnor's idea. My mother was to have stopped here at this very spot and—well, it's been done to welcome you now."

If George Carey had been a more observant man, understanding a little better how the mind of a woman works, he would have seen and interpreted correctly the quick shadow of disappointment which crossed his wife's eyes.

A Sinhalese boy, smartly dressed in a white gown, hovered by the table, while a junior cook from the Elephant Walk kitchens stood at a cooking-stove, transported especially for the occasion. Ruth's eyes popped at the delicious pilaff of fresh-water crayfish; a dish of roast snipe, each ensconced upon a piece of toast; a vegetable curry served with flaky white rice, and a bowl of fruit salad in which George identified for her benefit slices of fresh mango, papaya and pineapple, chunks of banana, the pulp of mangosteen and passion-fruit, the whole besprinkled with the juice of fresh limes. This was followed by the arrival of a gigantic silver pot of coffee, containing enough for a regiment, and an astounding array of liqueur bottles.

"And to think," said Ruth with laughing dismay, "that an hour ago I was wondering whether we could snatch a ham sandwich! I suppose I shall wake up but"—her mind flashed half-way across the world to No. 11, Lawn Crescent—"I don't want to, George."

After a rest of a little more than an hour, they resumed the journey. Part of the way lay through cultivated land, where Ruth caught her first glimpse of tea.

"That's Charley Mitchell's place over there," said George, pointing to a distant bungalow. "We'll have old Charley over for the weekend soon. You'll like Charley."

Then the cultivated land gave way to open park country, with grassy valleys and wooded crests as they skirted the swelling shoulders of Ratnagalla Peak.

Sated with new impressions, Ruth yet found time to reflect, as she looked towards George's broad back ahead of her, that upon a horse and in this setting he looked more at home, more natural than wrestling with stiff collars in London, Paris and aboard ship.

At about four-thirty in the afternoon, just when Ruth was beginning to think longingly of a cup of tea, they dismounted beside a trestle-table where a smiling Sinhalese boy had produced, apparently from nowhere, a vast silver tea-tray, and was already in the act of making tea. In a few minutes, with the ease of a conjuror, he produced buttered scones and a silver muffin-dish of anchovy toast.

As soon as they had eaten, at George's insistence, Ruth climbed stiffly into the saddle again. "The longer you wait, the worse it will be," he assured her. "Besides, I want you to have your first sight of Elephant Walk at sundown. On an afternoon like this it looks"—he paused, a little embarrassed at his own eloquence—"as though the whole valley has been dipped in molten gold. It's very beautiful, dear. I can't tell you how beautiful. You'll have to find the words for yourself."

They arrived on the rim of the valley a bare five minutes before the sun dropped behind the mountains. Ruth had steeled herself for disappointment, for she had the wisdom to know that no two people see beauty quite alike. But the scene spread out before her transcended anything she had imagined. The rays of the dying sun illumined the grim, austere, weathered teak of the Big Bungalow, gilding and softening its harsh outlines.

"We've another twenty minutes before darkness," said George. "But don't worry. Esmeralda knows every stone of the way."

When they had been descending the trail for three or four minutes, the still evening air was rent with a terrifying blast of sound, which seemed to come from a clump of trees just ahead. Esmeralda shied so violently that Ruth had difficulty in keeping her seat. A second or two later there lumbered out of cover a bull elephant, one of whose ears was cocked at a queer angle and along whose flank ran an ancient scar. He stood for a few moments contemplating the horses and riders approaching him and then, silhouetted against the evening sky, threw up his trunk and once more lifted his voice in a trumpeting so filled with hate and melancholy that Ruth shivered.

"It's that damn bull come back again," George muttered. "Haven't seen him for a year or two now and I hoped we'd seen the last of him here."

"I don't think," said Ruth in a hushed voice, "I've ever heard anything which frightened me more. It sounds so terribly—mournful, as though he were sad and eaten up with some longing he can't express."

"I'm going to try again," said George angrily, "to get a licence from Government to shoot the brute. Until an elephant has been declared a rogue, nobody dares touch him."

As he spoke, the bull shambled off into the gathering darkness, turning round once more as he disappeared to trumpet the mixture of hate and longing which was consuming him. The slate of memory was wiped clean, away from this accursed spot. But whether climbing the long trail to the mountains or descending it to the plains, the memories which flooded his little brain at sight of the huge defiant bungalow, built across the elephant trail, never failed to re-awaken in him the pain, the anguish and the sorrow which had befallen him on the first long pilgrimage from the plains.

"You sound as though you hate the elephants, dear," said Ruth, wondering at the transformation which had taken place in her husband, who looked resentfully in the direction in which the bull had disappeared.

"They're a nuisance," said George savagely. "They've done a lot of damage here over the years. In the guvnor's time they uprooted coffee, in mine they've uprooted tea. This is planting country, not an elephant reserve. The guvnor built the bungalow across their trail and dammit! even after all these years, they still seem to think they've been robbed and cheated. It's almost as though they think they still have a right of way."

"Perhaps they have," said Ruth softly. "Perhaps they don't like you calling your home Elephant Walk. I don't know much about elephants, of course," she added lamely, "but somehow, I think I know how they must feel."

"You're as bad as the Sinhalese, darling," said George with a laugh.

"They call them the Elephant People, as though their minds worked like human minds."

* * * * *

From the moment he had received George Carey's cablegram announcing his arrival with Ruth, Appuhamy had been torn between joy at the overdue coming of a bride to Elephant Walk and vague fears that the presence of a woman would prove a disturbing influence.

Appuhamy had nothing against European women generally; indeed, his knowledge of them was confined to those who, over the years, had stayed at Elephant Walk as guests. From other Sinhalese servants, however, he had heard frightening stories of wives who evidently did not know the proper place of a woman in the scheme of Creation and who made life unbearable to their servants. Appuhamy was an Asiatic and in Asia the status of women is clearly defined. Bachelors could always be assured of willing, efficient domestic help, which was available, too, for married men whose wives could bring themselves to accept the inevitable gracefully. In Appuhamy's case, however, the problem was not even as simple as this. He did not resent the coming of a woman to Elephant Walk because it might involve him personally in trouble, extra work and a supervision to which he was not accustomed. It went deeper than that. The Big Bungalow was still run, as nearly as possible, as Tom Carey had ordained. It was, in Appuhamy's eyes, perfect. To change perfection must, in the very nature of things, be a retrograde step. Besides, even if loyalty to Tom Carey had not been behind his attitude, Appuhamy was too old and set in his ways for change.

"The woman wears trousers!" the runner had said. What kind of a woman was this whom George Carey was bringing home as a bride?

Appuhamy had toiled since the first light of dawn to make the Big Bungalow worthy of the occasion. The long veranda was festooned with flowers. There were banks of scarlet, pink and white hibiscus, streamers of rambler roses and sprays of heavily scented frangi-pani. Not a blemish nor a mark marred the perfection of the polished teak floors and panelling. But after the arrival of the runner, some of the joy went out of the voluntarily imposed task.

Appuhamy had long since given up hoping that George Carey would marry. He had once hoped so ardently, for it seemed wrong to him that the rich acres of Carey tea land and the fine bungalow to which he had devoted a lifetime of toil, should pass into the hands of strangers. But there had been a time when Appuhamy, believing George's marriage inevitable, had conjured up from his own imaginings a dream bride. She had been tall and graceful. She had borne her head with a queenly air. Across her lips there had always hovered a gentle smile. She had treated Appuhamy with the same lofty graciousness she accorded to everyone. And with this lovely chatelaine as an adornment, the calm, unhurried life of the Big Bungalow had pursued its splendid way unchanged.

This bride, who was already on her way over the hills, was wearing trousers. Appuhamy winced and shrank from the thought. Would she, he wondered, be smoking a pipe? Why not? A woman who wore trousers in public was capable of anything.

Even as these thoughts perplexed Appuhamy, taking away much of the pleasure of his master's imminent return, he stifled and dismissed them as far as he was able. There was fear in his heart lest events and forces outside his control were about to conspire to impair his loyalty which, as Appuhamy looked back, had been spotless and unstained. Nor, he was in justice bound to admit, was the coming of a bride to Elephant Walk—even one who wore trousers—an unalloyed misfortune. It might well be that he would live to see this unknown woman bear an heir to the Carey fortunes.

To see a Carey infant in the gigantic teakwood cradle, which had lain for more than forty-five years without an occupant, gathering dust in a lumber-room, would satisfy something in Appuhamy: something which cried out for continuity. It would ensure that the loving care he had lavished on the Big Bungalow over the years would not have been lavished in vain, and that long after he was gone to his reward, there would be another generation of Careys to take pleasure from the lustrous teak, the gleaming silver and napery, the brandies and old wines in the cellar which, with his own hands, he had put in the storage bins. If it were not to go on, it was all so futile, so foolish. The very thought gave Appuhamy a pain under his heart. It gave him, too, the strength of purpose to put from his mind the knowledge that this bride who was coming to Elephant Walk garbed herself strangely, and to remember only that she, however clad, was now a Carey and that, as such, it was his duty to serve her to the best of his ability.

There are times in life when the temptation is strong to clothe inanimate things with thoughts, hopes and fears. There is the temptation to fall into this error—if error it be—in setting down coldly the arrival of George Carey and his bride.

The Big Bungalow had been waiting a long time for the bride to come, and now that the moment was at hand, with the hoofbeats of the horses sounding louder every moment, it was as though the Big Bungalow became a sentient, expectant thing. Never, it seemed, had the lamps along the big veranda shone so brightly. Never had silver and cut-glass sparkled more invitingly. Never had the pools of light beneath the lamps in the big lounge seemed so warm and friendly, nor the vague areas of shadow more restful and tranquil. The logs in the vast inglenook fireplace seemed to burn with a clean, smokeless flame. It was as though the bungalow itself, the things in it and the mysterious unknown something which makes the difference between a shelter and a home, sensed that the long period of waiting was ended and that the days of fulfilment were at hand.

"Tell me, darling," said George dismounting, "isn't there some old superstition that says the bride should be carried over the threshold of her new home?"

Eyes dancing with excitement, Ruth nodded. "Even if there weren't, George," she said as thigh and back muscles shrieked aloud in protest, "I don't think I could climb that flight of steps alone."

At the top of the steps, Appuhamy at their centre, the entire staff of the Bungalow stood in a beaming semi-circle. As two syces led the horses away, George Carey lifted Ruth's limp and unresisting body into his arms and began the ascent of the long flight of stone steps.

When some eight or ten steps from the top, George, who was more than ordinarily tired himself, slipped. Only by allowing his forearms and right elbow to strike the stone painfully, did he save Ruth from an ugly fall. The rest happened so swiftly that neither of the principal actors in the little tragi-comedy was aware of what had happened until too late. Ruth, unhurt, rose to her feet while George, suffering pain in one ankle and his right arm, lay where he was for a moment, muttering frightful imprecations under his breath. The line of white-clad servants broke and, in a flash, four of them, disregarding his protests, had seized George and carried him to the top of the steps and on to the veranda. Ruth, with a wry smile, completed the short climb alone. It was in keeping with a day which had been filled with surprises that it proved to be the beefy bridegroom, and not his radiant bride, who was carried over the threshold.

"Are you hurt, George?" Ruth asked anxiously.

"Nothing to speak of, darling. I'm sorry I was such a clumsy idiot."

"Have a drink, George!" came a raucous voice from the parrot perch.

Erasmus broke the tension and George, having recovered himself sufficiently, beginning with Appuhamy, introduced every member of the immense staff of the Big Bungalow.

"They don't all work here, do they, George?" asked Ruth in amazement. "What do they find to do?"

"Better ask Appuhamy about that. I wouldn't know."

In the middle of the veranda, for it was just sundown, was the teakwood trolley containing the customary hospitable array of decanters, bottles and glasses. Of these last there seemed to Ruth an incredible display. Inside the big lounge, upon a round centre table, was an oval silver tray, similarly equipped.

"You didn't tell me there was going to be a party, George," said Ruth in surprise.

"Party? There's no party, dear. There's no party, is there, Appuhamy?" he asked.

"No, Master. No party."

"Then what," asked Ruth bewildered, "is all this for?"

"Oh, that. That's just in case anyone wants a drink, darling. Perhaps I ought to have told you. Ever since it was built, it has been open-house at Elephant Walk. It was the guvnor's idea. He was a great one for hospitality. People in the district come and go just as they please. Anyway, let me pour you a drink, darling." George splashed out two whiskies-and-sodas, handing one to Ruth.

"You mean, darling," said Ruth, "that guests come and go here whether they are invited or not?"

"Sure!" said George. "It was the guvnor's idea. He loved hospitality. What was the use, he said, of having a damn great barn of a place like this if your friends didn't feel they were welcome here. You see, he built this bungalow for mother and, you must understand, it was a terrible blow to him when she died without ever seeing it. I knew nothing about it, of course: only things the guvnor and sometimes Appuhamy told me. But for a long while after mother's death he was badly broken up about it and, you see, to be able to entertain his friends was the one great pleasure left in life for him."

"But didn't you tell me, darling," said Ruth, "that the bungalow was all built and equipped before your father even met your mother?"

"Yes," replied George, not quite seeing the point of the question. "It was the guvnor's idea, don't you see, to have it all ready for his bride, down to the last detail."

"I see," said Ruth. "Just—any bride! Is that it? I didn't know your father, dear, but to me it seems just a little impersonal."

"Put that way, darling, I suppose it does," said George bridling a little. "But the guvnor told me often that, as he put it, he wanted a dream house for his dream bride."

"To me," said Ruth slowly, "that seems rather like buying a picture-frame and then having a portrait painted to fit it."

"Exactly, darling! I wish I could put things as neatly as you do."

In a few moments, with the ache of tired muscles easing in a warm bath and feeling herself enveloped by the superb comfort of this great house of which she was now mistress, Ruth wished she had not allowed a word of criticism, however oblique, to escape her lips. She was, she realised, a very lucky girl and, in a queer, impersonal way, she felt a deep sense of gratitude to Tom Carey, who, equally impersonally, had built and equipped this splendid frame of which she was determined to show herself worthy.

When George and Ruth disappeared to refresh themselves after their long journey, Appuhamy, his head proudly erect, walked slowly down the flight of steps from the veranda, pausing a few yards away from the bottom beside a cairn some ten feet high, such as may be seen in the highlands of Scotland, beneath which Tom Carey lay buried.

"She came, Master," said Appuhamy, in a voice tremulous with emotion, "wearing trousers. But I will serve her, Master, as I would have served the Mistress had she come. She is tall, Master. She holds her head proudly. There is laughter in her eyes. The young Master, I could see at a glance, is very happy, happier than I have ever seen him. It may well be, Master, that you and I are growing old, and the old must always give way to new ideas. It may—who knows?—be the custom now for women to wear trousers."

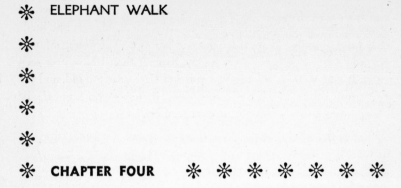

CHAPTER FOUR ❊ ❊ ❊ ❊ ❊ ❊ ❊

Usually George Carey was a gregarious soul, but at breakfast-time he liked to brood in silence and solitude. It was not until he had consumed a bowl of mixed fruits, four cups of tea and two small triangles of toast, followed by the first cigarette of the day, that his orbit widened to embrace his fellow creatures.

"Well, darling," he said to Ruth on the Saturday morning following their arrival, when these preliminaries to a new day had been completed, "you must put on your best bib and tucker tonight."

"Why?" asked Ruth excitedly. "What's going to happen? Something special?"

"Nothing exactly special, darling, but as you're going to meet the whole district, I thought probably you'd want to look your best."

"You mean you've invited all our neighbours here tonight?" asked Ruth, trying hard to keep from her voice the consternation she felt.

"Good Lord, no! They don't need inviting. They'll be here in force."

"Without being invited, George?"

"Well, you see, darling, this is the biggest bungalow for miles around. In fact, the only one fit to do any entertaining in. For as long as I can remember, everyone who could get away has rolled over here on Saturday after work. It's—well, it's a sort of local institution."

"I see," said Ruth thoughtfully. "I meet them all at once that way. I hope I shall like them, George."

"You will, darling. They're a grand crowd of fellows. And they just can't wait to meet you. I'm looking forward to watching their faces tomorrow morning when they see you play tennis."

"Oh, I see," said Ruth. "They'll come back in the morning, will they?"

"Bless your heart no! They'll sleep here. In Ceylon, you know, 'where I dines I sleeps'."

"How many do you think there will be, George?"

"Impossible to say, darling. Anything from five or six up to fifteen or so. First, there are the lads from the Ratnagalla district: they always come. Then, as I expect the news of your arrival has got round a bit, there'll be some of the lads from around Badulla and Passara and perhaps even further."

"But," said Ruth horrorstruck, "how is it possible to cater for them when you don't know if five or six or fifteen or twenty of them are coming?" She laughed a little grimly as she thought of the establishment at No. 11, Lawn Crescent, where domestic economy was balanced upon a hairline.

"Oh, that's easy enough, darling. There's always food here for a crowd."

"But are there rooms ready for all of them? I mean, oughtn't I to be making some preparations—or something?" Ruth added vaguely.

"There's tons of rooms—twenty-eight bedrooms, as far as I remember. Gilly, Wilding and a couple of the others stick to the same rooms always and keep a lot of their things here. It's more convenient. Saves them sending things back and forth. But as far as you're concerned, darling, it needn't bother you a bit. Appuhamy and the rest of the staff are used to this sort of thing. They'd be miserably unhappy if there wasn't a lot of entertaining here. Servants out East are like that: they like to feel that the house they're working for is an important one, so that they can live in a sort of reflected glory."

"I wish, George," said Ruth weakly, "it could have been possible for me to meet all of them, say, two or three at a time. It's so difficult meeting a big crowd all at once. And somehow, one never gets to know people that way. Besides, one's bound to like some people more than others and to want them to come more often."

George's look of dismay was so ludicrous that Ruth forgot her misgivings. "You know, darling," he said contritely, "I'd do any damn thing to please you, but what you suggest just isn't possible. You must see, darling, that to invite some and not others would be so"—he paused—"damned unkind. The fellows here regard this place as a second home and 'pon my soul! I just haven't the heart to invite some and tell others to stay away."

"No, of course," said Ruth. "I understand. But you'll have to stand by me, darling, because it's going to be a bit of an ordeal for me."

"Ordeal? Not a bit of it! It's going to be much more of an ordeal for some of them. Why, they're hardly house-broken! Take old Robbie Norman, for example. I don't think he's spoken to a white woman for the best part of twenty years. He had a bit of trouble with a girl in Aberdeen and he's scared stiff. Some of the young fellows are pretty near as bad. Don't you worry about any ordeal. Take my word for it: they're the ones that are facing an ordeal."

"You know, George," said Ruth thoughtfully, "it makes me feel like an outsider breaking into a bachelor paradise. From all you've told me, it seems it was easy enough for you all to get along pretty well without a woman in the district."

"Paradise my left foot!" said George, concealing a certain distress he felt at the trend of the conversation. "If they knew how happy I am, they'd all get married tomorrow. Do you know, darling, one of the things I'd always dreaded about getting married was having to have breakfast with someone. The very thought frightened the life out of me. But now, will you believe it, I rush back from the muster ground"—he laughed a little sheepishly—"just for the sheer joy of seeing you in that pretty frilly thing you're wearing, and to see you sitting there so fresh and sweet. I don't know how you do it. My mouth always tastes like the bottom of a parrot's cage in the morning."

"It could be the whisky you drink the night before, darling," laughed Ruth. "But I must say, you've been very good about cutting them down."

"By the way, darling," said Ruth, as George was about to leave the bungalow, "I think I'd like to have a room of my own—a sort of boudoir, where I can keep odds and ends and have a writing-desk of my own. There's plenty of space in our room, of course, but it's rather a—well, masculine room, if you know what I mean."

"Well, there are plenty of rooms, darling. Have a look round, take your pick and tell Appuhamy what you want."

Put like that, it seemed simple enough. For more than an hour Ruth wandered through the seemingly endless spare rooms in the Big Bungalow. But she might have saved herself the trouble, for when she had seen the first, she had seen them all. They were all of identical size; all had an identical outlook; all were identically furnished and all had the identical furniture placed in identical positions. So exact, indeed, was this placing of the furniture that the whim seized Ruth to check with a tape-measure whether the result had been achieved fortuitously or by actual measurements. In five minutes the latter view prevailed. There was no doubt in her mind that by placing beds in the exact centre of the rooms the maximum circulation of air was ensured, but at an altitude of four thousand feet the heat at night was almost never oppressive; seldom, indeed, as hot as a hot summer night in England. The aesthetic disadvantages, in Ruth's estimation, seemed to outweigh the advantages.

Hovering in the background, smiling courteously and anxious to be of assistance, was Appuhamy, who stood waiting for the superlatives of admiration to drop from Ruth's lips after her exploration of the bungalow. As there was nothing to choose between the rooms, she decided, understandably, to take as her boudoir the room nearest to the master bedroom, and accordingly informed Appuhamy of her decision.

"But, Mistress," said Appuhamy aghast, "that is Mr Gilly's room!"

"It was Mr Gilly's room, Appuhamy," replied Ruth sweetly. "It is now my room."

Ruth spent the rest of the morning in the garden and, therefore, did not see the agglomeration of clothes, books and other personal belongings, the accumulation of over twenty years, which the servants carried out of the room of which John Gilliland had had exclusive possession for so long that Appuhamy stood appalled at the probable repercussions.

"I don't think," she said when the task was done, "that I shall need the bed. Please have it taken away."

"But, Mistress," protested Appuhamy, "it can't be taken away. The bed was built here in the room. The doors are not big enough.

On closer examination, Ruth found this to be correct. The gigantic four-poster, like all the others in the house, was built in one piece. When, as a compromise, she decided to have it moved to one corner of the room, the united efforts of four men failed to budge it.

At noon Ruth told George of the difficulty. George looked blank.

"Sorry, darling. I'll get a couple of carpenters in this afternoon. They can saw the bed into sections and get it out."

"But you can't do that, George. Although it is a bit in the way, it's a beautifully made piece of furniture and it would be a crime to destroy it."

"Don't let that worry you, darling. They'll do it in such a way that it can be re-assembled—if it's ever needed. But times have changed. Do you know, darling," he said sadly, "we haven't had every bed in the bungalow occupied at one time since the guvnor's funeral. I daresay," he added, brightening as the idea struck him, "that you'd like to go and buy yourself some furniture. Something a bit more cosy and feminine. It's never occurred to me before, but I suppose the bungalow isn't very feminine."

This monumental understatement, coupled with George's obvious desire to please her, left Ruth torn between tears and laughter.

Ruth ordered her tea to be served that afternoon in the lounge. George, as almost always, was out in the fields until just before sundown. Tea arrived in stately fashion, with Appuhamy in the lead and two boys pushing the gigantic teak trolley around from the kitchen. It was superbly and luxuriously served, but on such a lavish scale that Ruth found it hard to keep a straight face. Upon the immense oval silver tea-tray was a gallon-capacity silver teapot, a large silver jug of cream, another of milk. There was white and brown bread, richly buttered and cut in wafer-like slices; sandwiches of two or three kinds; a dish of hot toast and another of teacakes, representing a quantity of food alone sufficient for a large party.

Ruth lingered over her tea reflectively. She was trying harder than she had ever tried in her life to fit herself into these strange new surroundings. The Big Bungalow sometimes frightened her, always bewildered her and, most of the time, made her want to laugh. Of one thing she was sure: unless she had seen Elephant Walk, George would always have remained in some measure an enigma. Most people's homes, she mused, were a reflection of their owners, who put upon them the subtle yet unmistakable stamp of their characters, tastes and personalities. The Benares brassware and other Indian bric-à-brac at No. 11, Lawn Crescent, were the logical outcome of her mother's nostalgic harking-back to the more spacious life the Lakins had lived in India before Colonel Lakin's retirement and death had imposed such far-reaching changes in their mode of life. Every piece of brass, every ornament, lived, not as things of beauty, but as tangible reminders of happier days that were gone for ever. On the other hand, it was plain to Ruth after a bare forty-eight hours at Elephant Walk, that so far from George having imposed his personality on the bungalow, it was the bungalow which had moulded George and his mental processes to its own unchanging ways.

There was only one personality in evidence at Elephant Walk: that of Tom Carey, who would never see it again. Vainly Ruth had searched George for signs of discontent, but there were none. The massiveness, the ordered routine and the air of wholesale prodigality which pervaded the Big Bungalow, held George in their grip. He did not consciously think of it as perfect, but rather, it never had crossed his mind to doubt it.

In all fairness, Ruth mused, she was bound to admit it would be difficult to find any imperfection in this extraordinary household. The staff was invariably courteous, willing and efficient. The food was superb and served in a manner beyond praise. Even in the spare rooms, many of which could not have been used for years, she had failed to detect a speck of dust, a floorboard or a piece of furniture which needed polishing. Magnificent quality linen sheets, clean every day, appeared on the beds; the bath towels, enormous expanses of the finest quality towelling, were luxurious beyond Ruth's wildest dreams. Why then—Ruth searched her mind for the answer—this strenuous effort to find fault in the mass with something which, taken piecemeal, she had already admitted was faultless? It would be mere petty vanity, she felt, to say that the Big Bungalow lacked a woman's touch. So did the Taj Mahal, the Tower of London and the Pyramids, which proved nothing. Ruth wondered whether the cramped and shabby gentility of the past few years had warped and shrunk her standards of comparison. Had it destroyed in her the capacity to enjoy more spacious living? She hoped not. Even if she had not been told so, it was quite obvious that no woman's hand had rested, however lightly, upon the Big Bungalow. No woman could have chosen the furniture which, again she was forced to admit, was superbly comfortable, and also handsome, in a rock-of-ages style. She found herself examining the chair in which she was sitting. Its wide teak arm-rests were covered with spotlessly clean cushioned chintz. The back could be adjusted to any angle. The woodwork itself was so cunningly dovetailed and morticed that, if such a thing had not been impossible, it seemed to have been made in one piece, as though poured from a gigantic mould. The effect achieved was utterly impersonal and yet, Ruth asked herself, was that not proof of its efficiency? Nothing which ran on such well-oiled wheels as the Big Bungalow could, in the nature of things, be so impersonal as it seemed, for behind its façade there was thought, diligence and a high understanding of domestic problems.

What manner of a man had Tom Carey been? She felt, without quite knowing why, a vague irritation against George's father who, years before she herself was born, had set in motion wheels which even now, nine years after his death, were still running in the grooves in which he had put them. He must have been a forceful, egotistical man, it seemed, or he would not have thrown this monstrous home across the elephant trail as a flamboyant challenge. He must also, beneath his domineering crust, have been a sensitive man with the same kind of simple unsophistication which he had passed on to his son. There was something touching about the story of this lonely man, Tom Carey, which found an answering chord in Ruth. Starting with nothing, he had carved wealth from what had then been a wilderness in the mountains of Ceylon. Then, later in life than the thought comes to most men, he had wanted to share the good things of his life with the wife he had fashioned from his dreams. So he had set to work to create a home for her. If he had been impelled, Ruth argued, to find a wife as a mere vehicle for his heir, he would not have given so much of himself in creating a home for her. If he had had any understanding of women, he would have known that his dream wife would have found joy and fulfilment in the creation of a home. That he had not understood this made him, in Ruth's eyes, a figure deserving of sympathy—a sad man who, in battling against adversity, had found no time to learn that there was a gentler side to life. Now she herself had fallen heir to all Tom Carey had striven so hard to provide for his wife. It seemed to place upon her the obligation to stifle the criticisms which rose to her lips and to accept gratefully the splendid way of life which old Tom Carey had made possible.

Ruth's reverie was interrupted by the sound of a horse trotting up the drive. A heavy masculine tread came up the steps and along the veranda, followed by the sound of a door being banged in anger and a voice: "What in hell's happened here, Appuhamy? Someone's pinched my bed!"

Whatever explanations were made were made in tones too low for Ruth to hear. The footsteps went down the veranda and another door was slammed angrily, while a few seconds later there came the sound of splashing water and an off-key baritone singing "Stop your tickling, Jock".

The huge wardrobe in Ruth's room was full of new and unworn dresses. After some deliberation, she chose an evening gown of blush-rose satin, its long tunic with a high waistline giving it an Empire effect, which flattered her figure. Nothing could have shown to better advantage the ruby necklace than the square neckline of this magnificent creation of the Rue de la Paix.

As she surveyed herself in the mirror Ruth wondered whether George would approve. "Of course, I want you to look your best, darling," he had said. "But, if you know what I mean, try not to stun them."

While Ruth was putting the finishing touches to her toilette, sounds from without suggested the arrival of a troop of cavalry, while a few moments later many heavily-shod feet marched in step down the veranda, but without creating the smallest quiver in the solidly constructed floors. More doors banged. The sounds of splashing water were multiplied and an unknown voice broke into an unknown song whose words were happily indistinguishable. Another voice shouted: "Shut up! You can't sing that here"—and as an afterthought—"now."

*　　*　　*　　*　　*

Nervously Ruth waited in the lounge, hoping that George would come before the others. When she had last seen him he was halfway into a white suit and was struggling with his tie.

A door opened down the veranda and the voice of Erasmus was heard: "Hallo, Gilly! Have a drink, old sport!"

"Thanks, I will," was the reply. From where she was standing, Ruth could see a man helping himself from the trolley. Glass in hand, very much at ease, he strolled into the room. "You must be the blushing bride," he remarked.

"I am the bride," retorted Ruth, "but I don't blush."

"No," said John Gilliland, with an appraisal which was very nearly insulting. "I don't believe you do. By the way, I'm Gilly. Heard of me?"

"Indeed, yes," said Ruth coolly. "But in spite of everything, I hope we shall be friends."

"I'm not so sure of that. You haven't begun too well, you know." Ruth's eyebrows rose a trifle. "First, you start by pinching my best friend and, not content with that, you commandeer a room which, after about twenty years, I've come to regard as my own personal property."

"Well, Mr Gilliland, since all the rooms are as like as peas in a pod, I don't feel somehow that the loss will be too terrible."

John Gilliland grinned appreciatively. "By the way, don't stand on ceremony with me. Call me Gilly. Yes, you know, I always have thought that this place looks as though someone put up a railway hotel, got a contractor to furnish it and then forgot to build the railway. But that, however," he added when their laughter had subsided, "is strictly between ourselves. George—bless his simple heart!—thinks it's wonderful."

"In a way," said Ruth, "I think it's wonderful." In dealing with John Gilliland, she mused [in an appraisal which had been as quick as his own], it would be no bad idea to keep him at arm's length until she had the opportunity to weigh him more accurately. Faintly, she sensed his hostility.

"You see," continued Gilliland, "dear old Tom Carey—God rest his soul!—was one in a million, but he wasn't very long on imagination, if you understand me. When he set out to furnish this place he employed carpenters who had never seen any furniture in their lives, so he sent to London for a bunch of illustrated furniture catalogues and told them to get busy making samples. Everything was a bit too small for Tom Carey's taste so, sticking to the original designs, he told them how big he wanted things."

"Considering all the difficulties," said Ruth, "I think it's wonderful that he did as well as he did. Not many men could."

"Now that you've got my room," said Gilliland, "you'll find it a nice cosy place to have your nervous breakdowns in—or doesn't it affect you that way?"

It dawned on Ruth suddenly that John Gilliland was trying to sound her out to see how far she would go in a kind of indirect disloyalty. Already she knew that to laugh at the Big Bungalow was to laugh at George. She looked at the shrewd grey eyes that watched her, believing that she read some of the thoughts they concealed. She sensed that behind the smiling, genial mask was a resentment at her intrusion into the—to John Gilliland—very satisfying life in the Ratnagalla Valley. Looking at him thus, Ruth had no doubt that John Gilliland had already, before meeting her, written her down as a designing woman who had married an unsophisticated middle-aged man for his money. This was so near the truth that it hurt. Yet the real truth was too subtle and elusive a thing to be disposed of thus simply. She gritted her teeth resentfully. Even though John Gilliland were right in his summation, she would prove to him, and to these others, that they were wrong. They were not going to be sorry for George Carey: they were going to envy him.

To Ruth's relief the tête-à-tête was brought to an end by the arrival of George himself.

"I see you two have met," he said, beaming happily and expectantly from one to the other. "Well, what do you think of each other?"

"That's a terribly embarrassing question, George," said Ruth. "It's the kind that's never answered. I'm far too shy to say what I think, while Mr Gilliland—he thinks I should call him Gilly, George—is far too polite."

"I think Ruth—may I call you that?" said Gilliland, "is marvellously like your description of her, George, and I think you're a very lucky man."

George Carey beamed. "I can't tell you," he said, helping himself to a drink, "how much I wanted you two to like each other."

At the trolley on the veranda Ruth saw a rather wizened, dried-up man with a bald head helping himself. "Have a drink, old sport!" called Erasmus.

"What d'ye think I'm doing, ye daft bird? Why someone hasna' wrung your neck years ago is past me to understand."

"Wring his blasted neck!" called Erasmus, whose quick ear missed very little that was emphatic.

Drink in hand, the new arrival came into the lounge. He was uncomfortable, shy and ill at ease.

"As a favour to me, Mrs Carey," he began, leaving no time for introductions, "would ye have yon parrot strangled? His vocabulary is a deesgrace to any decent home, and it hasna' the tact to conceal ma voice when it repeats things I've said in moments of exasperation. Welcome to Ratnagalla, Mrs Carey!" he went on in the same breath. "I hope ye'll waste no time in giving George a bonnie son. He's a good lad, is George, but easily led astray, and if I were to marry George—which heaven forbid!—I'd keep an eye on John Gilliland. He's a verra artful man is John Gilliland, Mrs Carey. The rest of us here in Ratnagalla are harmless. I don't know whether ye are a whuskey drinker, Mrs Carey—and probably by the bonnie looks o' ye ye're not—but if ye are, tak' my advice and only drink Elephant Walk whuskey. It's one o' the finest blends ever to come oot of Scotland. The others, for all their fancy labels, are no' fit to be mentioned in the same breath. Believe me, Mrs Carey, I'm speaking from pairsonal observation. Only the ither night I was calculating that

I've drunk on an average two bottles a week of it for close on twenty years. And never had a headache! That's no' a hasty judgment, ye ken, Mrs Carey, for it represents well over two thousand bottles an' entitles me to express an opeenion. I find talking is thirsty work, Mrs Carey," he said, draining his glass, "so, if you'll excuse me, I'll go and lubricate ma tonsils and, since George hasna' introduced us, the name is Norman, Robbie Norman. You're a sly dog, George, and I hope ye'll prove worthy of the lovely little leddy."

Those who heard Robbie were amazed at this taciturn man's unexpected monologue. His usual conversational fare was grunted monosyllables or—this when in his cups—a violent tirade against some unknown from the dim past. "She was an artfu' wee slut, was Jeannie," he would say, chuckling, "but no' artfu' enough for Robbie!"

Although Ruth of all those present knew him least, she was the nearest to guessing the struggle which had taken place in this shy, retiring man before he could bring himself to the point of talking so freely. Her eyes softened and, as she saw the look in his, she felt that she had found a friend.

Sam Cullen revealed himself as a big, shy, awkward young man who wore a bewildered air, as though he found life difficult to understand. As George performed the introductions Ruth heard names dimly while a procession of red-faced, hearty young men was paraded before her. Strachan . . . Newcombe . . . Wilkie . . . Somervell . . . names whose personalities hardly registered.

George Carey introduced Wilding with some éclat. Whatever misgivings he may have had regarding his assistant had vanished. During his long absence in England, the affairs of Elephant Walk had been conducted fully as well, George was ruefully forced to admit, as though he himself had never left. Nevertheless, Carey was never entirely at ease with his assistant, whom he sometimes suspected of laughing at him, as quickly dismissing the thought as unworthy.

"This is Mr Wilding, darling. Thanks to him, we shall be able to take that trip round the world soon."

Ruth noticed Wilding's easy assurance of manner, his good clothes and his carefree, reckless brown eyes, which seemed to see everything. She was aware that he was the only man in the room who realised that the gown she was wearing was a Paris model and suited her to perfection. Among these others he seemed out of place, like a canary among sparrows, standing out among the gauche, shy men as being the only one entirely at ease, except perhaps John Gilliland, in whom Ruth sensed a vague hostility.

The seventeen people who sat down at the gigantic dinner-table seemed lost at one end. The size of the room, the formality of the service and the unusual presence of a woman, conspired to dampen the party. Gilliland, Wilding and Ruth between them did their best to keep it going, but their best was not very successful.

"I was trying to remember, George," said Gilliland, "how long it is since a lady has sat at this table. 'Pon my soul, I don't think there's been one here since the Judge and his wife came up from Badulla. That must have been seven years ago, in '06 or '07."

Heads turned to George Carey to hear verification of this, but the host's chin had dropped on to his chest. He was no longer with the party. George Carey was asleep.

"George!" said Ruth in an outraged voice. "Gilly was talking to you!"

"You'll have to get used to that, Ruth," laughed Gilly. "George is like his father. I've always said that this room has an hypnotic effect on Careys."

Ruth's eyes blazed with indignation, but she was determined not to make a scene. Nor was her determination made any the easier by John Gilliland's evident amusement at her discomfiture—amusement which, it seemed, was tinged with malice.

After dinner voices grew louder and conversation, not brilliant at any time, became irritatingly vague and disjointed. Ruth made her excuses and went to bed before eleven o'clock. She made her escape thankfully. She was tired and wanted to digest her impressions.

At one o'clock she was awakened by what seemed to be an earthquake, and then again by George coming to bed. He shed his clothes, leaving them in a pool on the floor.

With George breathing heavily beside her, Ruth lay awake for more than an hour with her thoughts.

At his usual time, a little before dawn, George was awake, bright-eyed and alert as though nothing had happened.

"What on earth was that terrible noise I heard before you came to bed?" Ruth asked.

"Noise? I don't remember any noise, darling. Oh yes, that must have been when Gilly fell off the parrot perch."

"No, I heard that—and what he said, too."

"Then," said George brightening, "it must have been when I scored the winning goal. Young Wilkie and I—you know Wilkie? He's the nice-looking boy from Badulla—he and I were going like hell for the ball—he'd had a couple, you know—and just at that moment a damn fool of a boy arrived with a tray of sandwiches. Well, you can imagine what happened then! Wilkie, the boy, me and the sandwiches all went arse over kettle—but my shot won the match!"

"I don't know what you're talking about, George. And I don't think you do either. What match are you talking about? What goal? Do you mean to tell me you were playing football out there?"

"Good Lord no, darling! I ought to have warned you—in fact, you ought to have stayed up to see the game. It's a kind of polo we've invented. We clear the long veranda and instead of horses—you can see for yourself you couldn't very well have horses on the veranda, although we did try it once—we have bicycles. Four-a-side, with hockey sticks and a tennis ball. It's a grand clean, fast, sporting game, believe me, darling."

"It sounded it!" said Ruth, torn between anger and laughter. When she emerged on to the veranda for her first sight of the new day, two carpenters were at work planing the scarred surface of the floor and erasing all traces of the previous night's game. Behind them, two of the house servants were polishing the boards as though their lives depended upon it. Erasmus, happily not a talkative bird in the morning, surveyed the scene sardonically.

❋

❋

❋

❋

❋ **CHAPTER FIVE** ❋ ❋ ❋ ❋ ❋ ❋ ❋ ❋

The scores and hundreds of small and large British communities scattered all over Asia have always—perhaps because of contact with the unchanging East—been slower than the Mother Country—itself reputedly a stronghold of conservatism—to recognise the new manners and customs which have changed the face of life.

Women, far more than men, came under the baleful influence of this strange, backward-looking way of life. The white woman in Asia has, in the tradition of the American frontier, always enjoyed the privileges of a high scarcity value. Scrawny, horse-faced, spavined women with paddle teeth, a drug on the matrimonial market at home, made brilliant marriages in India and other parts of Asia, where lack of competition endowed them in the eyes of weary exiles with qualities of mind and body which were largely illusory.

By way of payment for their enhanced status and privileged position—and payment is always exacted—British women were expected to conform to certain arbitrary, and at times faintly ridiculous, conventions. As a condition of being treated like ethereal creatures from another planet, it was demanded of them that they maintain the illusion in and out of season. The first condition, this the easiest of all, was that they did not soil their hands with any menial task. They were expected to reduce personal contact with "natives" to the absolute minimum. In public at all times, and especially in the presence of men of alien race, the utmost decorum in dress was obligatory, on the theory that arms, bosoms, and legs higher than the ankle-bone, if exposed to the vulgar gaze, might arouse in lusty Asiatic hearts evil desires and passions, which in turn might, in some vague way never clearly expounded, impair that equally vague and ephemeral thing called "white prestige". Nothing illogical or inconsistent was seen in the fact that in almost every great seaport, from Port Said to Yokohama, white women of a score of races were inmates of brothels, catering with a splendid catholicity to any man— regardless of his race or colour—so long as he possessed the price.

In the rarefied air in which they lived, British women, unless very well-balanced and intelligent enough to find food for laughter in all this absurd mumbo-jumbo, tended to lose touch with reality. They were deceived into seeing themselves in the same light as that in which—they vainly hoped—they were seen by the "lesser breeds".

The British male was the culprit. Who can blame his women for falling into the deeply-cushioned and perfumed trap he laid for them? And having fallen, believing that they possessed all the qualities presupposed?

The little British community into which Ruth descended at Elephant Walk—its simplicity never having been complicated by the presence of white women—had not travelled so far along the road of self-deception. To a man, however, they were victims of that queer arrested development which characterises a womanless society. Each one of these men, although none would admit it, had ex-perienced moments in his solitary life which had given rise to vague doubts as to its worthwhile-ness, cut off entirely from the society of women. Slowly, subtly, irresistibly, each had created for himself a formless, idealistic picture of the women of his own race, so utterly at variance with the facts that it would have been laughable, had it not also been pathetic. The phantasies woven by these lonely men were, surprisingly, less sexual than social. Those to whom the urges of the flesh became intolerable had a simple remedy at hand, and one furthermore, sanctioned by custom in a land where the sun is warm, the women are willing and chastity causes the tongues of the un-charitable to wag far more than inchastity.

The arrival of Ruth in this queerly constituted community was not, as might have been expected, the signal for an outbreak of covetousness among George Carey's friends and neighbours. The peasant toiling in the field does not cast a lecherous eye upon his queen when she passes. He is content to savour the fragrance she leaves behind her and to gaze with passionless eyes at her rare and unattainable beauty.

Of the men gathered on the tennis courts at Elephant Walk on her first Sunday morning, only two were capable of seeing Ruth through eyes which did not distort her out of all recognition. These two, Geoffrey Wilding and John Gilliland, saw Ruth much as she was, if for different reasons: Wilding, because he was used to the society of women and to him, therefore, Ruth presented no great novelty; John Gilliland, because he walked through life with an armour of cheerful cynicism which protected him from the dangers of idealism. Ruth to Gilliland was merely the designing woman who had caught his best friend in a moment of aberration, subsequently having the temerity to take for her own use a room which he had long regarded as his own private property. For the rest, he considered George Carey had made a fool of himself, and hoped it would make no difference to a long friendship. Ruth herself, as a creature of warm flesh and blood, with hopes and fears, did not exist for him. If she went away, he would move back into his old room at the Big Bungalow. That was all.

The first sensation of these other men assembled on the tennis courts at Elephant Walk when Ruth made her appearance was one of shock. At a time when women tennis players wore long white skirts and long-sleeved blouses, buttoned up to the neck and at the wrists, Ruth wore a garment of her own devising, the logical forerunner of the skimpy latter-day tennis frock. It had been at least ten years ahead of its time when exhibited to the public gaze of Shillingworth. Here, in the shadow of Ratnagalla Peak, it made its bow fully a generation too soon. Prepared to ignore ankles, these men almost saw knees. In place of buttoned wrists, they observed with alarm that Ruth had elbows. The women created by their vague idealism minced delicately, required helping over negligible obstacles, shrieked with alarm at any mention of reptile life. This tall, graceful woman, with a clear skin bearing the bloom of health, eyes which danced with the joy of living, and whose ready smile embraced everyone, did none of these things. She strode down to the tennis courts and with a buoyant, elastic step, vaulted lightly over a low fence. When a snake was observed scuttling away, she asked with unconcern, "Is it a poisonous one?" She was a bitter disappointment to the chivalrous males, if only because she seemed so little in need of their thwarted chivalry. One can only guess at Sir Walter Raleigh's horror if Good Queen Bess, instead of walking upon his gallantly offered cloak, had leaped over it with disdain.

George Carey beamed happily. In his eyes Ruth could do no wrong. John Gilliland and Geoffrey Wilding seemed to notice nothing remarkable, but the rest, although they were not articulate enough to say why, were uncomfortable. Equally without knowing why, they felt a curious sense of pity for George Carey, who appeared so little in need of it.

Ruth being an unknown quantity, there was some discussion as to what her handicap should be. "Ruth gives me a hard game playing level," said George Carey, "and as I play from scratch and she hasn't got the hang of the hard courts yet, how about fifteen in alternate games?"

"That isn't enough!" protested a gallant chorus.

"I'd like to play from scratch," said Ruth, settling the matter. "I'd rather be beaten without a handicap than win with one." There were a few smiles at this, for the standard of tennis at Ratnagalla was considered high, and the idea of a woman competing on level terms seemed a little absurd.

Cullen and Wilding fought a drawn-out battle on the far court, the former playing with tremendous dash, while Wilding, who used his head, was the winner.

Ruth's first real game was against John Gilliland. "Play a back line game with Gilly," urged George Carey. "Watch his lobs and don't give him a chance to get up to the net."

Ruth, as she looked at the cheerful, sunburned faces alight with enthusiasm, found herself contrasting them with the way they had appeared an hour and a half previously, when she had observed them on the veranda, unshaven, clad in pyjamas, stretched out in long chairs, each as far as possible from his neighbour, while a procession of servants served solitary breakfasts. It was one of the many unwritten laws of Elephant Walk that breakfast was not a social occasion and must be eaten in silence.

John Gilliland, making it quite clear that he did not take his opponent seriously, began by clowning for the benefit of the gallery and to Ruth's great annoyance. At one moment it was a game whose outcome was a matter of indifference to her, while at the next she was grimly determined to win and to drive the mocking light out of the grey eyes which surveyed her so amusedly.

Gilliland was caught on the defensive and from the beginning Ruth, by clever placing, made him run three yards to her one. What disconcerted Gilliland was that this was his game, the way he used his brains to overcome the handicap of years and lessened agility. Try as he would, he could not recover the initiative. Almost before he knew it, he had lost the first set, 6–2, and was uncomfortably aware of titters from the gallery. He was breathing heavily when the second set began, and his grin did not fit so well. Somehow, the antagonism which flashed between these two communicated itself to the spectators. Even the insensitive George became aware of it. There came to Ruth the determination, she did not know why, to humiliate John Gilliland. Although she had the whip hand of him and knew it, she allowed him to win the second set, after dragging it out to 8–all. It was quite apparent to those who witnessed it that Ruth made no attempt to take the winning service. It was apparent also to John Gilliland, whose mouth was set in a thin line and whose eyes had gone cold and dead. He did not speak a word to Ruth between the second and third sets.

"The sun's getting hot, darling," said George Carey, who wanted to see the end of the situation. "Don't you think you've had enough for your first day?"

"I'm barely warm, darling. Don't worry about *me*." The emphasis on the last word was too pointed to be ignored.

In case there had been the least doubt as to whether Ruth had thrown away the second set deliberately, she proceeded to win the third, 6–0, the winning stroke being a forehand drive, in attempting to take which, John Gilliland, by the contemptuous ease of the stroke, was made to look very foolish. He walked from the court grey-faced with rage and exhaustion.

"We must have a return match some time," said Ruth lightly.

There was no applause. An icy silence had fallen on the courts two or three minutes before the end of the set. It had fallen when Ruth, leaping to take a fast volley, had exhibited for a fractional part of a second, some three inches of bare thigh between the top of a stocking and the furthest extremity of a pair of impeccably modest bloomers. The reaction to this innocent display had been a strange one. The trifle had offended against the preconceived ideal of womanhood—white British womanhood—which existed in the minds of these men. The sympathies of the spectators were strangely apportioned. To John Gilliland went sympathy for his defeat. To George Carey went sympathy because of the almost photographically quick exposure of a tiny section of thigh, and in addition because of Ruth's masculine excellence—the highest accolade—at tennis. It was not as simple as this, but essentially these were the feelings aroused by Ruth's masterly victory.

The arrival of a procession of boys with the traditional Sunday morning "King's Peg" eased the tension. This, as Ruth learned, was another Elephant Walk tradition, established by Tom Carey and carried on uninterruptedly after his death.

The "King's Peg", served at ten o'clock, consisted of a double measure of old brandy in a pint-size silver beer tankard, filled to the brim with champagne which, in wire crates specially made for the purpose, had reposed all night in deep spring water. Laughing at this slavish adherence to the tradition and, even as she did so, hoping that she would always be able to laugh, Ruth sipped her first "King's Peg". George, rather than see it wasted, finished it for her.

During the interlude created by the arrival of the "King's Peg", Ruth found herself alone, as though for a little while shut off from the community of these others who, their muzzles deep in their tankards, seemed not to be aware of her existence. Seeing her standing thus alone and a little bewildered, Geoffrey Wilding, being socially conscious and tactful, moved across to her with his tankard in his hand.

"That was a mistake, Mrs Carey," he said to her softly.

"What was?" asked Ruth sharply.

"Humiliating John Gilliland like that publicly. He'll never forgive you for it. Men—his kind—don't, you know. All cats aren't women."

"Your solicitude on my behalf is very touching, Mr Wilding," said Ruth coldly. "But aren't you taking rather a lot on yourself?"

"I'm trying to be friendly, that's all. You may need friends here." Wilding's tone and manner were light, but it was evident that he meant what he said. Even in her own estimation Ruth went down by remarking: "You aren't frightened that I shall humiliate you, as you put it, when we meet in the finals? It couldn't be that, could it?"

"No, believe me, it wouldn't bother me in the least if you beat the hide off me as you did off Gilly. I don't care whether I win or lose. Ball games aren't a religion with me: just an amusement. But of course, having said what you have said, you leave me no choice."

"Choice? I don't understand," said Ruth in a manner which she believed to be haughty. She was very conscious that in this exchange she was not showing to advantage.

"Not only am I going to beat you in the final, Mrs Carey," said Wilding with amusement, "but I'm going to win two straight sets."

"Really?"

"Yes, and the score will be 6–0, 6–0. What you won't understand, although you will later, is that in giving you a thorough beating I shall be proving myself a friend."

"I suppose you know, Mr Wilding, you talk an awful lot of nonsense. Why not explain yourself?"

"It isn't nonsense, and you know it, Mrs Carey," said Wilding, keeping his voice low. "It was a blunder not to have accepted a handicap. It was a worse blunder afterwards to have beaten Gilly and made a fool of him. You know what Talleyrand said: *'C'est plus qu'un crime, c'est une bêtise.'* Meanwhile, I, being your well-wisher, am going to make you look as foolish as you made Gilly. Then, although you don't believe me, that curious thing called public sympathy will turn against me. Because it turns against me, it will automatically restore you to some measure of favour. 'What a cad that fellow Wilding is!' they're going to say. 'Poor little woman! How dare he behave so unchivalrously?' Then, as you come off the courts, look pale and wan; plead a headache, or something like that. These musclebound Galahads expect it of you. Take my advice, and don't disappoint them."

"I think," said Ruth venomously, "you're the most odious and impertinent man I've ever met!"

"Wouldn't you rather play off the final this afternoon, darling?" asked George, bringing to an end a conversation which Ruth was finding not at all to her taste. "You've played an awful lot for your first day."

"No," replied Ruth. "If Mr Wilding is willing, I'd like to play it off now."

Very much conscious that things were afoot which he did not understand, George Carey mumblingly agreed.

The atmosphere was tense. The bewildered and distressed spectators wondered whether Ruth was going to repeat her performance. In their eyes, John Gilliland and Sam Cullen ranked as the two leading players in the district. It had been a surprise when the latter had been beaten by Wilding. The truth did not occur to them: that Wilding had never before troubled to extend himself on the tennis courts. It seemed likely, therefore, assuming his victory over Cullen to have been a fluke, that he was destined to be treated by Ruth in the same way as John Gilliland had been treated. They did not relish the spectacle. They were prepared to treat George Carey's wife with chivalry, as they understood the word, but in order to qualify for chivalry, they demanded that she be weak and helpless.

By beating John Gilliland, Ruth had lifted herself out of one category, without seeming to fit at all easily into another. People who defy classification, whether men or women, cause too much perplexity.

Ruth walked down to the courts determined to give to the coming game everything she had, but from the very first moment she knew she had met her master. Wilding, revealing a form he had never shown before on the courts, was quite merciless.

"Sure you're not feeling the heat?" called George Carey at the end of the first set, which had gone to Wilding, 6–0.

"Not a bit, thank you, darling," she called gaily and, with set lips, resumed the game.

Two or three times there came audible sounds of disapproval from the spectators as Wilding, seemingly oblivious of his duty towards the gentler sex, carried out his threat literally. Ruth did not win a single game. Curiously, those who watched him noted his absence of chivalry, but forgot to note the fact that he was outstandingly the best player among them. They had no time to wonder, therefore, why he had never before revealed this form. As he came up from the courts at the end of the match, disapproving backs were turned upon him. Thanking Ruth gaily for the game, he seemed quite oblivious of the black looks cast upon him. A voice from among the spectators crystallised the general opinion of them all. "I always thought," it said, "that Wilding had a hairy heel."

Some of the tense atmosphere engendered by the episodes of the tennis court was eased for everyone by the traditional Sunday morning "Tom Carey", which took place with full ceremony on the big veranda at noon precisely.

Since the day when it was first evolved by its inventor, the Tom Carey has spread far and wide over a large part of the earth's surface, to be drunk and enjoyed by men wherever hot suns create thirsts. The exact recipe, in Tom Carey's own words, is as follows:

To the juice of 24 limes add 6 lumps of sugar and 24 drops of Angostura Bitters. To this add one ½-pint of good cherry brandy and 2 bottles of dry gin. Stir the mixture well in a large punch bowl and when well mixed add 12 bottles of soda water as cold as possible. Stir until the sugar is melted.

The drink would have been exactly the same if mixed in smaller quantities in the same proportions, but Elephant Walk tradition demanded that the inventor's recipe be followed exactly, regardless of the number of persons to be served. In Tom Carey's day hospitality had been on such a scale that on Sundays the bowl was often filled two or three times.

"It's a lovely drink," said Ruth, sipping hers reflectively, "but hasn't it occurred to anyone to halve or quarter the ingredients? There's far too much in that bowl. . . ."

"I've often noticed," said John Gilliland, breaking a shocked silence, "that women have no feeling for tradition. How do you account for that?"

"It could be," said Ruth with irritation, conscious that all eyes were upon her, "that women prefer to do their own thinking. I was wondering," she went on as though talking to herself, "whether anyone here has had a new idea since Tom Carey died."

"Ruth!" ejaculated George, putting into the word some of the horror he felt.

"You know, Mrs Carey," observed Wilding as they went into the dining-room for tiffin, "if you aren't very careful you'll be getting into trouble. Jokes about sacred things aren't appreciated here. The Medes and the Persians were red-hot revolutionaries . . ."

"You are impossible and impertinent, Mr Wilding."

"Of course I am!" was the amused reply. "Hasn't anyone told you that before now?"

✳

✳

✳

✳

✳ **CHAPTER SIX** ✳ ✳ ✳ ✳ ✳ ✳ ✳ ✳

With the rain coming down in sheets and work outside at a standstill, George Carey was moodily practising trick shots at the billiard table. He hated these days of forced inactivity. He had never learned to take pleasure from reading. If he were not working, he liked to be engaged in some form of violent exercise, or to be surrounded by his friends. Therefore, in wet weather the men of the Ratnagalla district would congregate at one or the other bungalow, more often than not at Elephant Walk. Since Ruth's descent into this bachelor paradise, the other men in the district were a little reluctant to face her upraised eyebrows when they arrived *en masse* uninvited and unannounced.

"At last I've caught you with some spare time on your hands," said Ruth, finding George in the billiard room. "Can you give me a little of it?"

"As much as you like, darling," said George eagerly.

"Tell me something," said Ruth with an amused expression on her face. "How long is it since you've consulted *Crockford's Clerical Directory?*"

"Never heard of it," said George blankly. "Why?"

"And how often do you look at *Who's Who, Whitaker's Almanac, Ruff's Guide to the Turf* . . . ?"

"What's all this about?" asked George, bewildered. "Sometimes, to settle a bet, I look up something in Whitaker, and Ruff keeps me in touch with racing at home. Why?"

"Come with me," said Ruth with mock sternness, leading George to the rear of the bungalow, to a small room whose walls were lined with shelves, all filled with books, with the overflow piled upon the floor.

"Funny!" said George looking round him curiously, "I don't think I've ever been in here."

"Just look at these books, George! They go back donkeys' years, and not one of them looks as if it had been opened. What on earth do you waste money on them for?"

"I didn't buy them, darling," said George. "I expect you'll find it was a standing order placed by the guvnor, and it's just been allowed to run on. That's all. Don't worry yourself, darling. I'll see that they're got rid of."

"I haven't finished with you yet, George," said Ruth, leading him into the next room, whose shelves were filled with fine china, still wrapped in paper as packed by the makers, and each piece bearing the famous elephant-head design. On the floor were two huge crates of china which, from the dates on the labels, it seemed, had lain unopened for years.

"It does seem a lot, doesn't it?" observed George.

"If we have twelve children, darling," said Ruth, "and each of them has, shall we say, six children, there will be enough china for all of them for the rest of their lives. And yet you turned over to me the other day an invoice which says there's more on the way. Why, George?"

"You mustn't blame Appuhamy, darling," said George, who was uncomfortably aware that Ruth was critical of this loyal servant's seemingly wide powers.

"But I don't blame Appuhamy, George. I blame you."

"Well, you see," explained George, "years ago Appuhamy had orders to make a list of the breakages every year and to order replacements. It was the guvnor's idea. Some pottery firm in England made the design for him and keeps it in stock."

"But, George, what on earth is the use of having more sent out when we can't possibly use a quarter of what's in the bungalow already? And how long is it since you've been down into the wine cellars, George?"

"Must be two or three years," was the unhappy reply. "Why?"

"Last week you passed over to me an invoice for some wines which are on their way from England. Among them there are six cases of Madeira. Nobody here drinks Madeira, George. You said yourself you hate it. 'Sickly muck' was what you called it. Down there I found a huge cabinet of cigars that have gone mouldy. You don't smoke cigars, George, nor, as far as I can see, do any of the men in the district. Keep a box, by all means, for the odd guest who wants one, but to let them go mouldy by the thousand seems to me just wicked waste and extravagance. Everything's like that here, George. There are whole hams thrown away after only a few slices have been cut."

"Be reasonable, darling!" said George. "We can't be expected to eat bad ham. When a ham's cut and we don't eat it, the servants won't. They don't like ham."

"Then order half hams or smaller pieces."

"Who ever heard of ordering half a ham?" said George in amazement.

"There are great tins of biscuits that have gone soft and uneatable," continued Ruth inexorably. "We're only a small household now. Corea doesn't like me in the kitchen. I've only been in twice, but on those two occasions I saw enough to appal me. Meat comes in quantities big enough for an hotel sometimes when we have nobody here at all."

"The trouble is, you see, darling," said George, "we're so far from anything, and we never know who's going to pop in. It's always been like that."

"I know it's always been like that, George, and I'm trying to do something about it. Don't think, darling, by my saying this that I don't like the luxury and all the comfort here, because to me it's wonderful. Since the day Daddy died I've got sick and tired of pinching and scraping and trying to keep up some sort of a show at home on too little. It was terrible, George darling, believe me. But it's because I've been through that and, perhaps, if you like, don't ever want to go through it again, that I have a kind of superstitious fear of waste. I do want you to understand me, George, and not read into all this just a desire to criticise and pick holes in this wonderful way of living that you've made possible for me. I'm not like that, George. Truly I'm not. But every time I suggest any kind of economy, you seem to think it doesn't matter. You say you've more money than you know how to spend, but I don't think that justifies you in allowing waste. There are hungry people in the world, George: lots of them."

"I suppose you're right, darling," was the slow reply. "We ought to do something about it. I've never thought of it before. Yes, darling. You are right. We should. What do you want me to do?"

"I simply want authority from you to stop waste. That's all."

"But, darling," said George, his face clearing, "you've got authority, absolute authority, already."

"You may think so," said Ruth, "but take it from me, I've not. You have authority. You can give me authority by making it absolutely clear to the staff that they must obey my orders."

"If anyone here," said George, raising his voice angrily, "disobeyed an order from you, darling, I'd sack him on the spot; no matter who he was. Yes, even Appuhamy."

"Nobody has disobeyed an order, George. That isn't their way of doing things. Before I start giving orders, I've got to understand first what's happening, how things are run. I never seem able to get to the bottom of anything. When I asked Corea why so much meat was ordered, he referred me to Appuhamy. When I asked Appuhamy, he said that you'd said something about some guests coming."

"Well, if you remember, darling," said George, "last week, if it hadn't rained, we were talking of organising a big picnic."

"But we didn't organise it and it did rain and enough meat for a regiment arrived. I'm not saying all this with the idea of being difficult, George," continued Ruth gently, seeing the other's distress. "I'm trying to help. I want to be some use here, but"—she became very nearly tearful—"it's like fighting a featherbed. I don't seem able to get anywhere. Sometimes this bungalow frightens me, George. Everything goes along unchanged. It's as though"—a note of fear crept into her voice—"your father were still here. Don't you sometimes feel that George?"

"Of course I do, darling. I like to feel he's still here. This place— how shall I put it?—was his whole life. He was very proud of it and, if you know what I mean, to have the place run in the way he liked it is a sort of tribute to him."

"I never knew your father, George," went on Ruth. "But I'm perfectly sure he never rescued Elephant Walk from ruin after the coffee blight by sheer wanton waste and extravagance. When he was alive things were different. I can see that. You and other people have told me of whole weeks on end when every room here was full. But now, eight or ten people arrive for the weekend and, as far as I can see, the scale of buying things goes on just the same. I understand better than you know, George, how you feel. I love your loyalty to your father, but George"—she gripped his arm fiercely—"you're a man, too. You're not just a sort of echo of your father. You've got tastes, likes, dislikes, ideas of your own. You depart from your father's tastes and ideas in some things. For example, your father smoked cigars and drank Madeira: you don't. You're not living the same kind of life as he did because times have changed. People will no longer ride long distances to come here, stay for a few days, shoot, play tennis and amuse themselves. You've got to recognise these changed conditions, and change with them a little."

"Darling," said George unhappily, "if you feel like this, let's do something about it. Let's cut down in some way. I don't know how, but I'll read the Riot Act to the staff and tell them that things must be as you wish them."

"I think the first thing we should do, George, is to cut down the staff a bit. I wonder if you've any idea how many people you're feeding? I don't know exactly, but I wouldn't be surprised if it was a hundred. In the kitchen alone there's Corea with two assistant cooks, whose names I don't know, four kitchen helpers and dish-washers. Appuhamy has six houseboys under him in the bungalow. There are three men in the stables and, although I've never counted them, there seem to be eight or ten men working in the gardens. On top of these, there's a full time carpenter and two polishers, the *vasi-cooties** and two *dhobies*,† and that doesn't account for the men cutting wood for the bungalow up in the jungle. There's a small village at the back, darling, with all the wives and families and dependents."

"When you say it like that, darling, I know it sounds a lot," explained George, "but this is the East. Each man does his own job. A

* Low caste sweepers and sanitary men.
† Laundry-men.

high caste man won't do a low caste man's work, and so on. Besides, most of the servants here were here in the guvnor's time, and the others are children of people he employed. I'll give way to you in most things, darling, but I won't have old servants turned away. Even if I were to sack some of them, I'd have to go on paying their wages. I promised the guvnor I'd do that."

"Yes, I understand that, George," said Ruth with an air of numb hopelessness, "but at least make a rule that when an old servant dies or leaves for some reason or another, he is not immediately replaced. This is not Buckingham Palace, and we're not royalty."

"No," replied George sharply, "but this is Elephant Walk, and that means something, here in Ceylon. I'm a Carey, and by God! that means something, too. We, the guvnor and I, have been well and loyally served by the staff here and by the estate coolies, because they know that we look after them. I agree with you about waste: it's wrong, and I'll help you to stop it, but I don't intend to allow any penny-pinching economies here that are going to lower the prestige of the bungalow. I've been a bit slack over lots of things. I suppose it's been the easiest way. But you must remember that, away from here, I spend nothing, and what I spend here I can afford. I can quite understand that perhaps you find this place a bit extravagant . . ."

"Just a bit, George," said Ruth smiling.

"Anything you want, you know you can have," continued George with vehemence, "don't even bother to ask me. Go down to Colombo and buy it or send to England for it if it can't be found in Colombo. But you mustn't expect me to discover suddenly that I don't like a way of living that I've got used to. In a lot of ways, darling," George went on more gently, "you're such a hell of a lot smarter than I am, but although you lived in India for a bit when you were a kid, you don't understand the East. I do. Lots of people have tried to change the ways of the East, and they've failed. It's broken their hearts, darling, and I don't want to see yours broken. Changes of any kind must come slowly, or one finds oneself up against a brick wall."

In those moments Ruth realised how strong simple sincerity could be, and how much stronger than subtlety. If George had been possessed of Machiavellian subtlety, she knew he could not have turned the tables upon her more neatly, nor could he have made her feel, despite the unassailable logic and rightness of her own attitude, that she had somehow done him less than justice. She found herself looking at George Carey in a new light.

"Having said as much as I have, George, I may as well say more. I'm glad we've had this talk, because somehow I think we understand each other better for it. You see, George, I wasn't cut out to be quite useless and, since I want to do something, it should be something useful; and whether you know it or not there's a lot of useful work could be done here."

"Such as?"

"To begin with, the medical arrangements here. They're terrible. The Sinhalese dispenser does his best, but he isn't really qualified. He's all right, of course, for cuts and burns and bruises and black eyes, but there are nearly two thousand people here, George, men, women and children, and the nearest doctor is close on thirty miles away, over a rough trail."

"Well, what do you want to do, darling?" asked George patiently.

"I'd like to make a bargain with you . . ."

"We don't have to make bargains," said George with a quiet dignity. "Tell me what you want and, if I can do it, you shall have it."

"Sorry, darling," said Ruth. "Bargain wasn't a nice word. But what I want is your permission to cut down the expenses of this bungalow without making it any less comfortable either for us or for our guests, and without getting rid of old servants. In other words, all I want to do is to cut out waste. It'll soon show itself in the monthly bills, and with the saving I'd like to start a hospital for the coolies. There's a great barracks of a place behind the bungalow that's empty now. Appuhamy tells me it was used for the servants of guests in the old days. And the old days, you know, George, aren't coming back—ever."

"Do you mean you want to be a sort of Florence Nightingale among the coolies?" asked George. "Because if so, I can't permit that. They wouldn't understand it and, even if they understood it, they wouldn't like it. You're a woman and you're in Asia and, well, it just wouldn't work."

"No, I don't want that, George. I knew you would feel that way about it. . . ."

"It isn't the way *I* feel. Get that idea out of your head. It's the way the coolies would feel. But tell me," he went on in a less emphatic tone, "what makes you think a hospital is necessary?"

"Never a week passes without children being born here on your land. The babies live or die and it seems to me largely a matter of luck. I've watched the pen in the coolie lines where they put the babies while their mothers are away at work. In the northern lines two days ago all the babies had some skin disease. I don't know what it was, but I'm quite sure that only one of them had it to begin with and the others all caught it. That's wrong, George."

"Of course it's wrong, darling! Do you suppose I haven't known that for the last twenty years? We started a hospital here once, just because of the very things you're talking about. When the people got hurt, their wounds were dressed with clean surgical dressings, but as soon as the doctor's back was turned, they whipped off the dressings and packed the wounds with filthy *vederali** remedies. What makes you think you could succeed when the guvnor, who spent his whole life here, failed; and I, who have spent more than half my life here, couldn't make a go of it either? Don't you see, darling, even if I didn't believe, as I do, that these people are my moral responsibility —and they are that—it's to my interest to see that they're healthy and happy. Healthy and happy people work better."

"But, George," Ruth went on, realising that, if she were the crying kind, she would have taken refuge in tears, "the Dark Ages ended because someone was not satisfied with things as they were. And if that hadn't happened, we would still be living in the Dark Ages. I don't think it will be easy, but I still think, whatever the difficulties, you should try again. The experiment, if it fails, won't be a very expensive one."

"Won't you understand, dear," said George, "that I'm not thinking of it in terms of its cost in money. As you say, it's a small matter." He thought for a moment and suddenly his face cleared. "But go ahead. Cut out the waste here. It's right that it should be cut out. Collect your ideas about the hospital and we'll go into it together and we'll try to make a success of it. But"—the troubled look came back to his eyes—"don't hope for too much, or you're going to be terribly, bitterly disappointed. I'm not very bright, I know that. But I've got

* The name given to indigenous medical practice.

an idea that reformers don't do as much good in the world as people think they do. You can go on saying that cleanliness is next to godliness, until you're blue in the face. But it doesn't really mean anything. It's just words. Before it means anything, people have got to learn to like being clean for its own sake. Even I know that if I cut myself with a dirty knife I'm more likely to get an infected wound than if the knife's clean. But the coolies don't know that. All their knives are dirty, but their cuts aren't always infected. I don't understand the principles of antiseptic surgery. I'm told they exist, and I'm quite prepared to take someone's word for it. But if I, with all the advantages I've had, don't understand it, how do you expect these poor damn coolies to? But go ahead, darling. Go ahead. Don't ever say or think that I stood in your way, and don't think it's going to be easy, because it's not."

To Ruth it was a victory of a kind, but it did not taste quite so sweetly as she had believed in anticipation. The George revealed by this conversation was strangely unlike the George who, at one o'clock in the morning, could derive seemingly endless pleasure from playing polo on bicycles. It did not tally with the George who, tears of pure mirth streaming down his cheeks, had roared his approval at the *cancan* in Paris and who, even now, chuckled with delight when the gramophone records recalled the evening to him.

"By the way, darling," said George a little later, "I've a bone to pick with you. They tell me in the stables that Esmeralda isn't getting enough exercise. Why don't you get out and about more? Come round the estate with me, or I shall regret giving the mare to you."

A dozen times Ruth had been about to make the same suggestion, but had not done so because it seemed to her that where Elephant Walk was concerned, George reserved a completely private, sealed-off compartment of his being. She had been present on several occasions when, with a few quick phrases in Tamil or Sinhalese, George had settled various problems with the men under him. But never once had he volunteered to translate these discussions into English for her benefit. It seemed as though he were jealous of anything which touched upon the conduct of the estate he had inherited.

"I'd love to, George!" said Ruth, delighted. "There's nothing I'd like better."

"It's been on the tip of my tongue to suggest it a dozen times," said George. "But, I don't know why, I didn't think you'd be interested."

*   *   *   *   *

Appuhamy and Corea the cook viewed the newly instituted economies through jaundiced eyes. They were not, like the majority of servants in the East, in the habit of taking commissions upon their employer's purchases. The economies, therefore, did not touch their pockets. They touched, rather, something much more sensitive— their pride. Their wages were only slightly higher than those prevailing, despite long service and, in both cases, very superior qualifications for their work. Much of the compensation which was theirs for working at Elephant Walk was the reflected glory of being a part of a lavishly-run establishment of a kind which no longer existed in Ceylon. They themselves and the Big Bungalow were a hangover from another era. It was their pride, therefore, which was touched, and pride everywhere is very sensitive. Change at Elephant Walk implied criticism, even if none were actually voiced, and, like their master, they did not want changes.

The final humiliation of all, in Appuhamy's estimation, had been when Ruth had suggested to George that, as at the weekends guests arrived in varying numbers, it might be more sensible to ask those intending to come to send a chit over before beef day, which was Friday, when the beef coolie went to market with the orders. That way there was plenty for every guest that came, but no needless waste. On Thursday afternoons, therefore, his distaste barely concealed, Appuhamy would hand the chits which had come in from all round the district, to Ruth who, upon reading them, issued the necessary orders.

At sundown one day, after this little ceremony, Ruth had seen Appuhamy walk slowly down the main steps of the bungalow to the cairn which stood a few yards from the bottom. There, his lips moving, he had remained lost in contemplation for a great many minutes. ". . . and now, Master," Appuhamy was saying, "the woman counts every slice of meat which the guests eat! Had I not promised I would be faithful to the end, Master, I would not remain here another hour."

"What's Appuhamy doing down there?" asked Ruth curiously.

"Oh, didn't I tell you, darling?" said George. "The guvnor's buried there, under that cairn. It was a nice idea, I think. It was the coolies who thought of it. In their own time they brought stones from every boundary of the land and built it with their own hands. It was their way of taking leave of the old guvnor. Appuhamy pops down there to have a chat with him once in a while. You know, he likes to tell him all that's happening, like he always did. He always tells the guvnor, for example, whenever any of the best glass or china is broken."

Ruth wondered if she could believe her ears, and yet George was talking in the matter-of-fact tones he might use to order a drink.

"What on earth are you talking about, George?" she asked aghast. "Is Appuhamy mad? Are you? Your father is dead—nine years in his grave, you told me, and you talk as though it were an every-day thing to chat to him about breakages in the bungalow. . . ."

"Appuhamy was devoted to the guvnor, you must understand, darling. . . ."

"I was devoted to my father, George, but it didn't occur to me to go round to the cemetery to tell him when I smashed a cup or a glass. Normal, sane people don't do things like that. . . . George, I'm frightened. Can't you realise that? This is my home and there are things going on that I don't understand. . . ."

"What things, darling?"

"Whose voice is that ghastly parrot imitating when it calls 'Boy!'?"

"That's the guvnor's voice, darling," said George reassuringly. "Don't let that worry you."

"But it does worry me. I thought that was it, because when Appuhamy hears it—provided he doesn't know I'm here—he replies, 'Coming, Master!' and runs along the veranda faster than when you call him."

"Force of habit, darling, that's all. With Appuhamy it's a kind of reflex action—like when you cut a chicken's head off and it runs around. He hears the guvnor calling and he comes a-running. . . . It's funny you taking it like this, because I rather like it."

"You may like it, George, but I don't. I'm scared—deadly scared. I'm among things I don't understand, and your saying that you like it doesn't make it any easier for me. Feel my hand, George." The slim hand which rested in his was icy cold.

"Put it down to nerves, darling," said George, "and try to forget it."

"That's easier said than done, George. I can't shake off the thought that the bungalow has a personality. It likes some people and dislikes others, and you see"—Ruth's voice dropped to a whisper—"I'm not sure that it likes me."

Ruth was very much overwrought. George could see that. He did his clumsy best to comfort her and set her fears at rest. In large measure his solid, kindly, unruffled presence did lull her fears, even if it only put them behind her into one of the strange *oubliettes* of the mind.

"Supposing, George," she went on, in an eager, wistful voice, "just supposing a time came when I couldn't go on living here any longer. Which would be the more important to you: me or this bungalow?"

"Really, darling!" said George. "That's a damn silly thing to ask. It's like one of those 'Have you stopped beating your wife?' questions."

There flashed across George's eyes a shadow of fear. Ruth, who was watching him narrowly, knew that even George did not know the answer. Her eyes instinctively went up to the high vaulted roof of the bungalow, where the shadows lost themselves in formless obscurity. She felt as she sometimes felt during a thunderstorm: the plaything of forces which were too big for her.

*   *   *   *   *

There began for Ruth weeks of pure delight. Rising at dawn, she allowed George to go alone to the muster ground and, after their light breakfast together on his return, she set out with him on horseback around the estate.

During these long days in the saddle, Ruth was continually finding something new in George, new sides to his character, as well as new aspects to the life of a planter. Viewed through superficial eyes, tea-growing appears to be an effortless process: God makes the tea flush and man strips it as it grows.

There was so much to be done, so much to be supervised, so many things happening at the same time. It fell to Wilding, because the tea flush was at its height, to spend most of his time with the pluckers, but George Carey, because he knew it encouraged the coolies to have the Big Master taking an interest in what they were doing, made a point of spending a couple of hours daily with the plucking gang. To Ruth it was a never-failing delight to watch the deft fingers of the brightly-clad pluckers against the background of the tea.

George seemed to have a sixth sense, born of long experience, where the weeding contractors were concerned. He would walk unerringly to a small part of a big field, difficult of access, there to discover skimped work on the part of the contractors. He displayed infinite patience when training young men in the delicate art of pruning tea, so that each bush was spread and flattened to the maximum, giving the largest surface for new growth.

In mid-afternoon, despite the intense heat down below, it was a joy to go down to the factory, to smell the sweet apple-loft smell from the fermenting tables, and all the other delicate aromas given off by tea, stage by stage, from the moment it arrives at the factory as green leaf, until it emerges black and fired from the driers. George, although his palate must have been rasped by whisky and hot curries, was able, even better than De Wet, the taciturn Eurasian teamaker, to taste samples of new shipments before they went to market, and to predict with uncanny accuracy the price they would fetch at auction, price being based upon flavour.

The old women who sat on their haunches all day, picking the slightly reddened stalk from the tea, always grinned appreciatively as George entered the factory. All of them had known him for twenty-five years, ever since he first came to Ceylon. It gratified them, old, tired and almost useless as they were, that the Master remembered their names, was able to recall their little family tragedies and comedies and was never too busy to exchange with them salty, earthy jokes of a kind which appealed to them. A chuckle went down the line as George stopped before an old woman, who for years had suffered from an enormous and presumably benign tumour in the stomach, to ask her when the baby was likely to be born. The toothless old crone was crippled and had to be carried to work every morning. Two grandsons performed this task at her insistence, because she knew that when she ceased to work, she would die, and she was not ready to die. Neither her age nor her sufferings, however, prevented her from rocking with laughter at this not too delicate sally, and the old woman's dark eyes, bright with affection, followed George lingeringly as he moved on. Elsewhere in the factory Ruth saw George pause for several minutes, a rapt expression on his face, watching an old man stencilling the defiant elephant head on the outgoing tea chests. Pride was writ large upon his face. "That mark means something!" he said, when he saw Ruth had observed his absorption.

De Wet emerged from his office on one of these visits, greeted Ruth with grave courtesy and waited, a little puzzled, while George fumbled in his pocket for a small package.

"I've been keeping this for you, De Wet, for years," said George Carey, handing the package to the teamaker.

With fingers which trembled a little, De Wet unwrapped many sheets of tissue paper, until at last a massive gold half-hunter watch rested in the palm of his hand.

"Why do you give me this, Mr Carey?"

"I am not giving it to you, De Wet. It's a present from my father. He gave it to me ten years ago and said, 'Give that to De Wet when Elephant Walk tops the market.' Well, Elephant Walk topped the market at last week's Colombo sales. That's for you, and an extra day's pay for everyone in the factory."

"To see Elephant Walk at the top of the list is enough for me, Mr Carey. This"—he pointed to the watch—"is too much. What can a man like me do with such a watch?"

In De Wet was personified the tragedy of all the people who live in a void suspended between the two races from which they sprang, and acknowledged by neither.

"What does topping the market mean, darling?" asked Ruth, a silent witness of the formal presentation.

"It means," said George proudly, "that at last week's tea auctions in Colombo, Elephant Walk tea fetched the highest price of any high-elevation tea in Ceylon. I wish," he added sadly, "the guvnor were here today. It would have been a very proud day for him."

It was so like George, Ruth mused, to emphasise that this handsome gift came from his father. It would never have occurred to him to give it as from himself. It was not only through Erasmus that the personality of Tom Carey was still abroad at Elephant Walk.

Esmeralda no longer suffered from lack of exercise, for on many of these days in the open air she covered, with Ruth on her back, as much as twenty to twenty-five miles.

Ruth's stamina was a never-failing source of wonder to George Carey, and he, too, was learning things about this clean-limbed, bright-eyed wife who never complained, no matter how hot or tired, never took shelter behind her sex, and seemed to find unending interest in the things which, in his estimation, were first things.

These happy days came all too swiftly to an end. One Saturday night, not having attempted the feat for a good many years, George Carey, urged on by Gilliland and the others, tried to make a standing jump on to the parrot perch—a feat which for years had been regarded as a great achievement—but in doing so, he fell and broke an ankle. It was a bad fracture, set badly by the fumbling hands of the Sinhalese dispenser, and when the doctor arrived from Badulla some twenty-four hours later, it was so badly swollen that little could be done. When at length the swelling subsided, George Carey was told that it might be months before he could walk again.

During the first weeks of this forced inaction, George Carey was utterly miserable. On working days, in accordance with the excellent habit of a lifetime, with the exception of a gin and bitters at noon, he did not touch alcohol until sundown. Now, however, as the shadows lengthened in the afternoons, he began to look longingly towards the end of the veranda where, on the stroke of six he knew, the trolley would appear and he could try to find in the whisky decanter some of the ease and contentment of mind which he could no longer derive from violent exercise.

"No, George, not another, please!" Ruth said one evening in pleading tones, as George was pouring out a large drink when he was already looking a little glassy-eyed.

"No, George, not another, please!" echoed Erasmus mockingly, awakening the echoes with a peal of raucous laughter.

Because George Carey wanted to keep the work of the estate at his finger-tips, Geoffrey Wilding was perforce a frequent visitor at the Big Bungalow. When she saw him arrive, Ruth always tried to efface herself. She had not forgotten the airy insolence of his manner on that first Sunday on the tennis courts, and she did not like the amused indifference she read in his face on their rare meetings.

"You seem to hate the sight of Wilding, darling," said George after one of these visits. "Why?"

"I don't dislike him," said Ruth wearily, "but he's a conceited young man who wants putting in his place."

"As you know, darling," said George, "he's not my type and I don't mind admitting I find him a bit difficult to understand. But he's a good chap, really he is, and I don't know what I'd have done without him. He's doing two men's work now and there's never a peep of complaint out of him. You see, darling," he added with apparent inconsequence, "we Careys didn't come out of the top drawer, if you know what I mean. I'm not apologising for us, but the fact is that the guvnor was no one before he came out here. From what he told me, he didn't have two coppers to rattle together. He lived on curry and rice for years, saved about ninety rupees out of every hundred he earned, and as a result of that, we came up in the world. I dropped into a pretty soft billet when the guvnor died. Where young Wilding is concerned, I think it was the other way round. I rather gather he started off with a silver spoon in his mouth and then, without ever believing he'd have to, had to go to work for a living. It can't have been easy, and I think, darling, he's done it damn well. He's an odd kind of chap in many ways—reads books and that sort of thing. He's had advantages I've not had, but I expect he's damn lonely all the same. Of course, I don't want to force the chap down your throat, but be as nice as you can to him, darling."

George was lying in a long chair with his leg in splints. Ruth leaned over him and kissed him. "George," she said very gently, "in case I've forgotten to tell you, I think you're the most generous-minded man I've ever met, or am ever likely to meet."

"Don't talk damn silly nonsense, darling, but give me a drink," said George, but the look in his eyes belied his tone.

❋

❋

❋

❋

❋ **CHAPTER SEVEN** ❋ ❋ ❋ ❋ ❋ ❋ ❋

John Geoffrey Wilding sat alone with his thoughts beside a crackling wood fire. As he gazed into the flickering flames, he was thinking of a quite fortuitous meeting that day with Ruth Carey who, for the first time in some months, had been more than frigidly polite. He had come face to face with her while riding along a narrow path in the farthest corner of the estate. Pulling his horse off the path with some difficulty, he had made room for Ruth to pass. Instead of passing with her customary cool nod, she showed a disposition to linger.

"How's George's ankle?" he asked amiably.

"It's still giving him a lot of pain, I'm afraid," she replied. "Incidentally, he was wondering only last night why you didn't come more often to the Big Bungalow," she added.

"Yes, I daresay he has wondered. But then George doesn't know what you and I know, does he?"

"I don't think I understand you, Mr Wilding," said Ruth, as haughtily as she could. "I'm not aware of any secrets I share with you that I don't share with my husband." She wished now she had not been so pleasant.

"Forgive me," said Wilding with a mock gravity. "I didn't mean to suggest any such thing. I gather then that you repeated to him the little homily I read you on the tennis courts when you first came here? As far as I remember, you didn't seem to appreciate it. I'd so like to know what George said. Do tell me."

Ruth had not mentioned the incident to George, and she was perfectly sure that Wilding knew this.

"Since then, you know," continued Wilding, sparing her the necessity of a reply, "I've had some months to reflect about my outrageous conduct on that day, but I'm afraid, if the occasion arose again, I wouldn't change a syllable of what I said. What's more, Mrs Carey, forgetting your natural annoyance, tell me frankly now, in the light of what's happened since, don't you think I was right? Wasn't it a bad idea to make John Gilliland look a fool?"

"I'm not going to fence with you, Mr Wilding," said Ruth, trying to keep her temper. "You're too good at it. So good, that I can't help wondering why you became a planter."

"That is why I became a planter. You see, I had the knack of choosing the wrong people to fence with. By the way, Mrs Carey," he continued mockingly, "isn't it singling me out for too much honour to call me Mr Wilding? Frankly, I don't dislike it. If anything, I prefer it. I never have liked this modern tendency to call comparative strangers by their Christian names. But it's occurred to me that, as you call everyone else in the district by his Christian name, to go on calling me Mr Wilding seems, if you understand me, a little conspicuous."

"George asked me the same question only yesterday," said Ruth, amused by the other's impertinence.

"And what did you tell him, if I may be so indiscreet?"

"I told him that you were presumptuous and conceited and that the best way to treat you was to ignore you."

"Your character analysis is almost perfect," said Wilding, "but I really cannot say the same for your logic. It wouldn't flatter my conceit a bit, you know, to be treated as you treat the herd of overgrown boy scouts who come to the Big Bungalow to offer you their homage. Why, even where your pet abomination, Gilliland, is concerned, you call him Gilly. No, believe me, to be singled out for a mister is much more likely to add to my conceit than to take away from it."

"Gilly," said Ruth coldly, "is George's best friend."

"I know," said Wilding sympathetically. "How you must loathe him! Funny, isn't it, that as soon as a husband identifies his best friend, his wife sharpens her claws. I suppose it is that wives suspect best friends of being privy to all sorts of dark, premarital secrets. Not, mind you, that I think George had any."

"For a bachelor, you seem to know a great deal about women," said Ruth sharply.

"Now really, Ruth—or do we go on with the Mr and Mrs business? It's for you to say—aren't you putting the cart before the horse? Men who understand women remain bachelors. The others marry in order to learn."

Despite a severe struggle, Ruth's good humour prevailed. "I'm not going to argue with you any more—Geoff. I suggest that we bury the hatchet. Come and dine with us tomorrow evening. It'll cheer George up."

"Implying that it won't cheer you. Is that it? Yes, I'd love to come. Thanks. Somehow or other, I can't get used to these wholesale general invitations to the entire district to come for the weekend, lush all the drink in sight and get sentimental about the good old days. I know it's heresy to say so here, but I strongly suspect that the old days weren't so good. Besides, I don't like brandy and champagne at ten o'clock in the morning, even if it is Sunday, and even if it has been the custom at Elephant Walk since somewhere around the time of the Indian Mutiny. A custom isn't good just because it's old. Much the same is true of champagne, incidentally. Even at proper cellar temperature, an 1891 wine would be a long way past its prime in 1914. Somebody ought to tell George about it. If you won't, I will, even if he never speaks to me again. I intend to ask for a bottle of beer, which I much prefer and, while wiping the froth off it, I shall wait for the walls of Jericho to fall down. Even if poor old Appuhamy does have a fit, I refuse to drink any more champagne and brandy on an empty stomach. And, since we've buried the hatchet, I'm going to look to you for moral support."

Wilding's ideas were so amazingly like her own that Ruth was startled. It made her feel uncomfortable and, by implication, disloyal. Although choosing his words carefully, Wilding was laughing at George, while she was very much tempted to do likewise.

"You don't fit very well into the social life of the district, do you?" asked Ruth.

"No, I suppose not. I'm grown up, you see, which makes it hard.

You're grown up, too, and you feel like a fish out of water most of the time, don't you? Although I've never had occasion to tell you, I like your—George, very much indeed. He's a good chap to work for, straight as a gun barrel and a very kind host, so I ought not to say things like this. Being a woman, I think you'll understand me: I'm scared of getting caught up too much in the life of the Big Bungalow. I don't want to get like Gilly and old Robbie Norman or, for that matter, some of the younger fellows. I like a drink as well as the next man, but I don't like swimming in it, any more than I like sponging on George's generosity—because that's what it amounts to. Even the young fellows who spend the weekends there are being hypnotised by that damn great bungalow into believing that everything worth while in life has roots of tradition a mile long. I've often had the feeling there that, under that enormous teak roof, time has stood still and that anyone with a new idea is liable to have something heavy drop on him. It's got you, too. I can see that by the look in your eyes. Don't let it. Fight against it.

"I lived there, you know, for two months while George was in England. He asked me to because, as he put it, he didn't like the thought of the old place being empty. I stuck it as long as I could, but it was too much for me, so I went back to live in my own bungalow where, incidentally, I didn't live a quarter as well. But that's beside the point. I love old Appuhamy, you know; he's a grand fellow and there aren't many left in the world like him. But there were times when I had the feeling that it wasn't Appuhamy talking to me. Yes, I see," continued Wilding, flashing a quick glance at Ruth, "you've noticed it, too. I know it sounds a bit far-fetched, but 'pon my soul! there were times when I thought that the old man never did kick the bucket. I never met him, but in those two months I grew to know him better almost than I know any living person in the district. I didn't dislike him, either. I think he must have been a fine old boy, but I'd have liked him a lot better if he'd stayed in his nice comfortable grave without trying to run the lives of other people.

"Do you know, Ruth," continued Wilding, dropping his bantering tone, "one Sunday morning I was there alone and, with Appuhamy in the lead, there arrived on the veranda at ten o'clock that damn great trolley. I was alone, mark you. There was that huge Sunday morning decanter of brandy, twelve bottles of champagne—although I'll admit only one of them had been chilled—and beside them were twenty-four silver tankards! 'No thanks, Appuhamy,' I said. 'I'll have a cup of coffee.' Well, the old boy stood there with as much expression on his face as on a wooden image, as though he hadn't heard me. He poured a damn great nobbler of brandy into the tankard, filled it up with champagne and handed it to me on a silver platter. 'No thanks, Appuhamy . . .' I started to say. I was going to insist on the coffee but" —Wilding laughed grimly at the recollection—"I just hadn't the nerve! Appuhamy stood there until I started to drink. I've often wondered what would have happened if I'd chucked it over the veranda. I think he'd have poured out another and, if necessary, called for help and made me drink it. But as I was taking my first sip, he glanced over the veranda rail at that pile of stones where the old boy was planted. He'd been looking pretty grim, but then his face lit with a smile which I can only call beautiful. His lips moved and I fancied that he was saying: 'You see, Master, I made the impudent young upstart drink his King's Peg?' Then Appuhamy bowed politely and left me alone, but take my word for it, Ruth, I knew I had to drink the damn stuff. It was very odd."

"I ought not to be talking to you like this," said Ruth, with a friendly smile, "but you've done me a lot of good, Mr—Geoff. It's curious that two people so very much—well, out of sympathy with each other, should have such strangely similar feelings."

"I was on my way back to my bungalow," Wilding had said. "I usually have a cup of coffee about this time, if I'm anywhere near. Will you join me?"

"Yes, I'd love to. It's a funny thing, but although I've been here more than six months, I haven't seen inside another bungalow in the district."

They had sat for a few minutes while drinking their coffee and then Ruth had ridden home towards the Big Bungalow.

Now, in the flickering firelight, Wilding remembered how very attractive Ruth had looked. For choice, he did not like to see a woman wearing jodhpurs, but she had worn them very well. She sat a horse well, too. She was too young and gay and beautiful to be imprisoned in that great mausoleum where she had made her home. Good fellow that he was, George Carey must, he mused, be pretty poor company for a girl like that.

"It's a great pity and . . ." he paused thoughtfully, "I wish George Carey wasn't such a decent chap."

*　　*　　*　　*　　*

From the door of his own small house at the rear of the Big Bungalow, Appuhamy sat gazing out across the valley, bathed in the golden afternoon sunshine. He was lost in thought. His brow was deeply furrowed by his perplexities. Occasionally, there flashed across his face a look of anger.

As major-domo of this great establishment, his was a position of considerable dignity. In the old days, during the lifetime of Tom Carey, when visits were exchanged frequently between the Big Bungalow and Government House in Badulla, the official residence of the Government Agent, in whom was vested the chief civil authority for the Province of Uva, Appuhamy had, by general consent, ranked equally with the Government House butler. Leaving all questions of rank aside, however, he was proud of the trust which had been reposed in him for so many years, and even more proud of the fact that he had never, by word or deed, betrayed it.

Bearing all these things in mind, therefore, it was manifestly beneath Appuhamy's dignity to listen to gossip. This he refused to do. But since he was not deaf, it was quite impossible not to hear the things which were on every tongue. They were shameful things, affecting the honour of the family to whose service he had devoted his life. For days now he had burned to do something but, search his mind as he would, he could think of no course of action open to him without overstepping the ill-defined but well-understood line of demarcation which divided master and servant, even though, over the years, the relationship had become a friendship.

Appuhamy's musings were complicated further by what he had heard from George Carey's lips at the dinner-table some two or three weeks previously. If he had not heard it with his own ears, he would not have believed it. "You know," George Carey had said, turning to Wilding, "Ruth ought to get out and about more. There's no need, just because I've got a busted ankle, for her to spend all her time in the bungalow. I wish," he added, "you'd let Ruth make the rounds with you. I don't like her riding alone."

Appuhamy, whose surprise at this suggestion was only equalled by that of Wilding himself, heard it with amazement. Wilding had agreed, not, Appuhamy thought, with any pleasure. There and then, in Carey's presence, a rendezvous had been made for the following morning. Since that day Appuhamy had found it impossible to close his ears to the tales which had come down with the woodcutters and charcoal-burners working high up on the shoulders of Ratnagalla Peak; tales which, in going the rounds, had lost nothing in the telling. Without being aware of the significance of the news they brought, these simple men, coming down from the high mountains with loads of firewood and charcoal, told of seeing, miles from Elephant Walk, the woman known to be the wife of the master at Elephant Walk, riding along little-frequented jungle trails with the man Wilding, known to be George Carey's assistant. They had been seen together eating picnic meals far—or so they must have believed—from any watching eye. Their laughter had been heard echoing among the high peaks. It was true that none of the tales specifically mentioned anything further, but that was hardly to be expected. Even a child must realise that, for every minute spent under observation in the remote jungle and parkland up beyond the line of cultivation, fully an hour was spent without any observation. From one of these expeditions they did not return until two hours after darkness had fallen. The reason, which Appuhamy had taken pains to verify and which, astonishingly, had been accepted by George Carey unquestioningly, had been the casting of a shoe by Esmeralda. Naturally enough, George Carey had been worried but, as soon as Ruth and Wilding had returned, the expected explosion had not occurred. Indeed, in the friendliest possible fashion, George Carey had insisted that Wilding stay for dinner.

Now Asiatics—and the Ratnagalla district, with the exception of a tiny handful of Europeans, was peopled by Asiatics—are not less charitable in their interpretations of events than the rest of the world, even if they incline to be more realistic. Here, in their view, was a very simple equation, in essence as old as time itself. To an attractive young wife, married to a husband many years older than herself, there had come a handsome, dashing young man with bold eyes and, as every-one who came in contact with him knew, a quick tongue and ready wit. Inclination, in the general view, could be taken for granted. There remained, therefore, only opportunity to provide a solution of the equation.

In essence, Appuhamy's attitude of mind towards the situation was the general one, complicated in his case by the affection and esteem in which he held his employer. That his employer's wife could be un-deserving of the slurs on her character did not occur to him. Equally, he did not moralise about it. He was actuated only by a single-minded desire to save the son of his old master from hurt and dishonour and to put an end to the gossip and speculation which flew from lip to lip. The wish to do this was one thing: to do it another. To go directly to George Carey and to tell him what was being said and what was happening during his forced inaction was unthinkable. It would be an unpardonable breach of good manners, bitterly resented by George Carey and, because of this, would achieve nothing. But what to do?

Appuhamy's eyes turned from the golden mists which obscured the plains and to the Big Bungalow, which existed for him as the symbol and repository of Carey prestige. From the day he had seen its vast bulk reared on this remote plateau, which had happened during his impressionable boyhood, he had woven around it many queer phan-tasies, until it meant to him almost as much as the Ark of the Covenant had meant to the peoples of Israel.

Appuhamy rose from the floor where he had been squatting, combed his moustachios in front of a mirror, adjusted the tortoiseshell comb in his thinning hair and, taking from a shelf an immaculately laundered white gown, went across the garden and into the Big Bungalow. Walking softly so as not to disturb his master, who might be sleeping, Appuhamy went the length of the big veranda, straightening a pile of illustrated magazines with mathematical exactitude, frowned as he ob-served an ashtray which had not been emptied, making a note to call the culprit to book. Entering the dining-room, he surveyed the pol-ished surface of the gigantic dining-table, rubbing gently with a cloth where a finger-mark marred its glossy perfection and then, soothed by contact with the cool, sombre magnificence of what he saw, col-lected his thoughts again to wrestle with the perplexities which beset him. As it had never failed him in the past, the Big Bungalow did not fail him now. There was something about the dull sheen of teak floors and panelling conducive to ordered and unhurried thinking. The strong, durable timber, too heavy to float, so hard that it turned the edges of the finest tools, so durable that it mocked the very processes of time itself, was to Appuhamy, as it had been to Tom Carey, a symbol of permanence and stability in a world of shifting values and shallow appraisals. Surrounded by teak, the mind was not prone to jump to hasty conclusions, nor to think in terms of a day, a week or a year. Teak was like the eternal truths: slow, sure, solid and unchanging.

When he had been inside the bungalow for a few minutes, Appuhamy's brow cleared. He believed he had found a way.

"If the Master will allow it," he said when he removed George Carey's tea-tray, "I would like a few days leave. There are important matters which require attention."

"Of course," said Carey at once. "Take as long as you like. Dammit man! I don't believe you've had a holiday since my father died."

"For me, Master," said Appuhamy gravely, "it is not a holiday to be away from Elephant Walk. I will arrange matters so that everything goes on as usual during my absence and, if the Master permits, I will leave tomorrow night on a bullock cart which goes to Bandarawella with tea. From there I will catch the morning train for Kandy."

* * * * *

Sitting bolt upright in a hackery drawn by a fast-trotting bullock, Appuhamy surveyed the luxuriant vegetation of the low rolling hills, which spread out from Kandy in the direction of Matale. He was tired and hot after his long journey, very conscious of the fact that what he was about to do was unworthy and only pardonable because of the great need. The driver of the cart, to revive the flagging energies of the tired beast, twisted its tail mercilessly and, after another half-hour of uncomfortable jogging, halted on the outskirts of a pretty village set amongst incredibly green rice fields.

"You must continue the journey on foot," the driver said in surly manner. "If you are not too particular to enter the village, I am. I will wait for you here."

From a man working upon the narrow *bund* of a rice field Appuhamy enquired the whereabouts of the house he sought. With a surprised look, the man pointed out a small house, thatched with palm fronds, nestling beneath the shade of a fine mango tree, alongside which were half a dozen coconut palms and a few tall, slender and mathematically vertical areca nut palms. Appuhamy thanked him, walking across the rice field by the narrow way indicated.

The village, too small to have a name, was inhabited by tall, graceful people, light of skin, holding themselves splendidly and proudly erect. They were people of the Rodiya caste, once the proudest in Ceylon, humbled centuries previously as a punishment for their misdeeds. For Appuhamy thus to enter the village was an act of self-degradation, almost as degrading in his eyes as the mission which brought him there.

Surprised to see a Sinhalese of relatively high caste coming in their direction, a middle-aged couple sitting in the shade by the door of their house, both of them naked from the waist up, rose to their feet curiously. They were about to eat their midday meal. Hospitality demanded that they offer to share the meal with this stranger, but iron-bound caste laws told them that to do so would be to offer an unpardonable affront.

In brief, concise terms Appuhamy stated the purpose of his mission.

"I am told," he said, "that you have a daughter whose beauty passes all belief. It is to arrange a price that I am come here."

Nodding their understanding, his hosts invited Appuhamy to be seated, and for two hours the talk flowed back and forth, like waves beating upon a rock.

"As to her beauty, that you must judge for yourself," said the man at length. "At the school in Kandy they taught her to bake cakes, to sew. Indeed, her stitches are so fine that the eye can hardly see them. She is a girl of rare accomplishment for she speaks English well. She even reads and writes the language."

"The price you ask is high," said Appuhamy, "but I think the time has now come for me to see the girl."

In answer to her mother's call, there came from the rear of the little house, where she had been playing with a litter of newborn puppies, the loveliest young girl whom Appuhamy in a long life

had ever seen. She, like her mother, was naked from the waist upwards, in accordance with a harsh law, centuries old, which condemned Rodiyas to appear thus as a mark which distinguished them
from the rest of the people. Her unblemished skin, of so light a
brown that it could scarcely be called brown, had the translucence
of youth and bounding health. She held herself with immense pride,
walking as gracefully as a young deer. Firm young breasts, perfectly rounded, seemed to accentuate the pride of her bearing. Quite
unafraid, she smiled a greeting to Appuhamy, looking enquiringly
from him to her parents. She had known for more than a year that,
when a high enough bidder came along, she must go away from her
home, to spend a few years as the mistress of a man of some alien
race. Being a Rodiya, no Sinhalese would want her. The villages round
about contained scores of women who had left the district while
the bloom of youth was upon them, returning a few years later with
a handsome dowry, to marry men of their own kind. Most had
gone to live in the bungalows of planters in lonely districts. These
were the most fortunate. Others had sold their charms to fat *chettys*
in the bazaars, rich Tamils in Kandy, Colombo and other cities.
Even these were seldom heard to complain of their treatment.

The girl—Rayna was her name—looked sad when Appuhamy's
mission was explained to her. "He is too old," she protested, the
light of revolt shining from eyes which, a few moments previously,
had been alive with the sparkle of insouciant youth.

"It is not to my house you will come, child," said Appuhamy
gravely, "but to the house of a fine, handsome young Englishman,
who carries himself with a pride that matches yours. He is handsome
and bold, never without a jest on his lips. Have no fear, for you will
be the envy of many."

"Have no fear, child," echoed the father. "This man is the agent
of another. He comes introduced by a trusty friend. Well," he continued, turning to Appuhamy, "is she to go with you or to stay?"

"The price is high," said Appuhamy in a heavy voice, "but I will
pay it. Tell her to pack her belongings. I have a bullock hackery waiting on the road."

"It is not worth the trouble to bring my poor rags," said the girl
sadly. "When I have taken leave of my parents, I am ready."

"But, child," protested Appuhamy, "you cannot travel thus, naked above the waist. You must be clothed, for we have a long journey ahead of us among people who seldom see those of the Rodiya caste and would not understand. Run to the village shop," he added, thrusting a few rupees into her hand, "and find something to cover you. When we reach Kandy, I will see that you do not lack fine clothes."

While Rayna ran off happily enough on her errand, Appuhamy concluded the sordid bargain with her parents.

At the hour of sunset the girl, excited by all the new sights she was seeing, looked upon the lake at Kandy, the busy streets and the famed *Dalada Maligawa,* which houses Buddha's tooth. The pain of leaving home was lessened by an hour of brisk bargaining for finely worked blouses and lengths of rich shimmering silks of whose possession she had often dreamed, without ever really believing that the dreams would materialise.

On the train from Kandy to Bandarawella Rayna plied Appuhamy with questions regarding the new life which lay just over the horizon. "Will he meet me at the station?" she asked eagerly.

"No, child, he will not, for as yet he does not know that you are coming. When we get to the end of our journey, for a little while you will come to keep house for me. I have a small house in the garden of my master's bungalow. This Englishman is a strange young man who lives quite alone. It may even be that he will be a little shy, but when he sees your beauty, you can be sure that he will forget his shyness—forget too, the madness which is bringing dishonour to an honourable house," he added under his breath. "To the curious, child, you will give no answer save that you are my grand-niece, the grand-daughter of my sister."

"He is brave and handsome, the young man?" asked Rayna. Appuhamy nodded. "He has a fine house?"

"Yes, he has a fine house with many books and fine pictures."

"Then," said Rayna, closing her eyes, for she was tired from the journey and the excitement, "I think I shall be very happy."

"I hope so, child. I hope so. God forgive me!" groaned Appuhamy.

*   *   *   *   *

On the western slope of Ratnagalla Peak, the slope furthest away from Elephant Walk, the dense jungle thinned, opening out into parkland with wide vistas of grassy valleys and low, rolling hills, to whose crests clung strips of virgin jungle, like some dark fringe to the pale green shawl of grassland. Here, because the soil was too poor, the virgin solitude had never been broken by cultivation. It was a land of pure enchantment, where clean breezes, exhilarating as champagne, swept across the roof of Ceylon, and where the sweltering low country on either side was unimaginable. It was a land, too, where horses, exultingly free of the narrow precipitous paths of a tea estate, on which a wrong footfall could spell disaster, were able to stretch their legs, open their lungs and thrill to the rhythm of a wild gallop as the greensward rolled away beneath their flying hooves.

Wilding saw the distant elephant herd first, almost as soon as his frightened horse smelled it. "We're down wind from them," he said. "Would you like to make a detour behind that pocket of jungle and watch them at close quarters?"

To this Ruth eagerly acquiesced. Some twenty minutes later, their horses tethered out of sight and sound, they crept softly through a clump of flowering rhododendrons to a point which overhung a muddy morass several acres in extent. Here a herd of elephants, escaped from the foetid gloom of the low country sweltering far below them, took their ease. There were five cows and as many calves, while aloof, vigilant, austere, as might be the captain of some great ship, an ageing bull mounted guard, sniffing the wind suspiciously. The others, content to leave their safety to his judgment, continued their games under the eyes of their old enemy, Man.

The fringes of the morass were bright green, like the bogs of Ireland, while in the centre a few inches of water covered deep mud. The calves, only recently arrived from the low country, where the springs and waterholes had dried up, soon evolved a magnificent game of their own devising. When any one of their number forgot to be watchful, he was rewarded with a terrific butt in the ribs, which sent him sprawling into the deep ooze. One little fellow, who stood the height of a man's shoulder, seemed to bounce like a rubber ball under the impact, landing in the ooze with a great splash, his forelegs waving in the air. Ecstatically, he remained there, rolling from side to side, while the rich mud trickled over his sleek pot-belly.

The old bull, who had been immobile, suddenly became tense and alert. His big ears flapped and the silence was rent by his short staccato command, sounding like a short blast on a ship's siren. In a flash the games ceased. The calves ran, each to his mother's side, and waited.

"They've smelled us," whispered Wilding. "Watch what happens now." Rising to his feet, he showed himself in silhouette against the skyline and, cupping his hands, emitted a loud shout.

With a trumpeted command, the bull started the rest of the herd on their flight, while he himself turned round, displaying a deeply scarred flank. Before he too turned in the direction taken by the herd, he trumpeted his defiance at the intruders who had broken in upon his solitude. Ruth who, on the night of her arrival at Elephant Walk, had heard that sound, shivered as she had shivered the first time, less from fear than from a half-understood sympathy. To her the anguish was more apparent than menace.

"Look at those great feet!" said Wilding. "How he'd love to trample us to pulp!"

"I wonder why it was," said Ruth after a long silence, "that George's father wanted to build his home right across the elephant trail. If it had been the only beautiful site, I could understand it. But it isn't. There are at least a dozen sites every bit as beautiful and as convenient. In fact, most of them are more convenient."

"It's funny you should say that," said Wilding, "for much the same thought was running through my mind. Tom Carey, although I never met him, has passed many an idle hour for me. I find him a fascinating character study. He should have been born an American. He'd have been happy in America, where everything's big. His was the kind of soul that would've thriven on vast stretches of prairie, huge mountain ranges. He'd have wanted to build huge bridges across impossible rivers. Instead, he was born an Englishman, and a poor Englishman at that. I don't know, but I expect he had a cramped childhood, full of frustrations. This part of the country must have appealed to him. There was in it, you see, enough of the challenge he demanded. He wasn't content merely with doing a thing well—and he did that—it had to be difficult, too, or there was no taste to it.

I'm certain that if the local wiseacres hadn't warned him that to build his bungalow across the elephant trail would incur the wrath of the elephants, he wouldn't have built it there. He only needed the hint of opposition: that was enough for him. For most of the planters, the blight that destroyed all the coffee here was a catastrophe, the end. It broke them, financially and morally. But to Tom Carey it was a beginning. He couldn't control the forces that destroyed the coffee, but that wasn't going to stop him growing tea. And it didn't. Did you ever see his signature? I mean the kind written with pen and ink, for his signature is written all over Elephant Walk. It was the kind of signature you'd expect from such a man: bold, sprawling, but each letter perfectly formed, the up strokes fine and the down strokes so firm and wide that he often splayed the pen.

"So you see, you can't blame Tom Carey for building that immense barracks of a place. It was written in his destiny. It was as important a part of him as his heart and his lungs."

"You know," said Ruth, who had been listening intently to every word, "you see human nature and character much too clearly, Geoff. Much too clearly for your own happiness, I mean. Do you analyse me as though I were a specimen under a glass? Take me piece from piece, look at both sides and put the pieces back together again? I don't think I'd like that."

"No," said Wilding soberly. "I'm tempted to, but I don't think it would be wise. Sometimes it's better not to know too much. What goes on inside you is something I don't particularly want to know. The surface is beautiful enough for me, and I'll be content with that. I sometimes suspect, you know, that the scientific botanist is so concerned with mere mechanism that the beauty escapes him. Look at those rhododendrons. They're so perfect and beautiful that they almost bring a lump into your throat. That's enough for me. I don't want to know anything about how they're made, what makes them go on living, why they chose this place to grow and not a thousand other places that to me look just the same. I don't know whether they're propagated from seeds or bulbs or cuttings, or whether they just happen. Their beauty is the only thing that matters: that and the fact that it's a lovely day and we've a long ride ahead of us."

On the homeward journey they encountered a party of charcoal-burners, encamped by a spring a few hundred yards from the jungle. The men looked up at them curiously, grinned impudently and began to laugh among themselves at some earthy jest.

"You know," said Wilding soberly, when they were left behind, "everybody in the world isn't as charitable as George Carey. It hadn't occurred to me until this minute, but I think we may as well face the fact that these little jaunts of ours have made uncharitable tongues wag."

"But surely they can't . . ." Ruth flushed a deep crimson and left the sentence unfinished.

For the remainder of the ride home, Ruth made a half-hearted effort to be honest with herself. The vista of life at Elephant Walk without these excursions with Geoffrey Wilding looked very bleak to her as she surveyed it. Of course, when George's ankle was better, she would persuade him to take her up into the beautiful country on which she had just turned her back. But, she asked herself, would it be the same? Of course it would, she insisted stoutly, knowing as she did so that she lied.

CHAPTER EIGHT ✻ ✻ ✻ ✻ ✻ ✻ ✻

John Gilliland was genuinely fond of George Carey, perhaps, because the latter was so many things that he himself was not, but his affection for his friend was coloured by a possessiveness which was a part of his nature.

During these last twenty or more years, John Gilliland was sure, George Carey had not taken any major step without either consulting him or at least confiding in him, excepting always his recent marriage. This omission on George Carey's part had been a great blow to his friend's self-esteem and, in some curious fashion which Gilliland would have found hard to justify, he regarded it in the light of a major affront. He was—and to do him justice, he would have admitted it frankly—a selfish man. Passing rich, he could well have afforded marriage, but to have married would have been, as he saw things, to have disrupted a way of life which he found very pleasant. His bachelor establishment, although not on the scale of Elephant Walk, was very comfortable. Over the years, while playing with marriage as an abstract idea, he had come to the logical conclusion that the presence of a woman of his own race would detract from, rather than add to, his own comfort and convenience, to say nothing of restricting a perfect freedom which he found very precious. So, cold-bloodedly, as he did most things, he decided in favour of a celibacy which was not, nevertheless, as he expressed it, bigoted.

At the rear of the bungalow at Donaghendry was a small house in which there had dwelled for the last many years, one at a time, a long succession of comely young Sinhalese girls on whom John Gilliland had centred his transitory affections. They had always been Sinhalese for a reason which had seemed adequate to John Gilliland: he did not speak a word of the Sinhalese language. If they were happy and contented, the fact was obvious without the medium of speech. If they were unhappy or discontented, the fact was equally evident. In either case, John Gilliland was not concerned with the details. The arrangement had always worked admirably. The girls, until he tired of them, or they became possessive—a tendency common but not exclusive to the female sex—gave him what he required of them and, in return for what he gave them, went quietly and contentedly on their several ways. In John Gilliland's eyes the fact that during the weeks, months and (in one case) as much as three years, they had stayed with him, he had not been able to exchange one word with them, had made the arrangement wholly admirable. With each in turn he had kept to the letter and spirit of his bargain and, in fairness to him, it should be added that such was his treatment of them that, without exception, they left his bed and board regretfully.

Where sex was concerned, John Gilliland was a man of simple elemental tastes. He demanded of women self-effacement, obedience, temporary fidelity and the irreducible minimum of interference with his convenience. Lastly, because he had a distaste for being the father of bastards, a certain circumspection. Posterity was one of the abstract things which interested him not at all. The world had managed well enough before his arrival and would doubtless continue to do so when he was gone. It may not have been an admirable philosophy, but it had served John Gilliland's needs well enough, causing him to wonder pityingly why it had not sufficed George Carey. Quite apart from, as he saw it, driving a wedge between him and his best friend, Ruth's arrival at Elephant Walk had caused other inconveniences. John Gilliland disliked sleeping alone. He was not used to it. The presence of a chatelaine at Elephant Walk imposed this inconvenience upon him at the weekends.

All things considered, Ruth Carey was by way of being a major nuisance. She had been inconvenient enough when, metaphorically speaking, the confetti was still in her hair, but as a married woman who (John Gilliland was now convinced) was breaking the rules, she had become an intolerable burden and one not to be borne. Besides, he had not forgotten his trouncing on the tennis courts, which still rankled. Petty? Of course it was petty, but so was what passed for society at Elephant Walk. Over the years the horizon, bounded for the most part by the rim of the hills, had shrunk. The vision of those who dwelled within the charmed circle had shrunk proportionately.

More irritating than all to John Gilliland was the unarguable fact that his friend George Carey was sublimely contented with his lot, showing every sign of happiness. Never at any time had he spoken of Ruth except in terms of unbounded affection and admiration. To have been the recipient of confidences of another kind would have been balm to John Gilliland. Now, he asked himself, what was to be done? Nothing, would have been the verdict of most men, but to do nothing, as John Gilliland saw things, would have been a negation of friendship. Further, the possessiveness which consumed him, at times to the exclusion of reason, demanded that he take a part, a vital part, in whatever was afoot.

"You know, Wilding," he said amiably, when ensconced comfortably in a long chair on Wilding's veranda, a whisky-and-soda in his hand, "we ought to see more of each other." Knowing that no flattery in the world is more subtle than to meet another humbly on his own ground, he added: "And while I'm here, I want to borrow a few decent books. Be a good chap and lend me something I can get my teeth into."

"I shot a few snipe this afternoon," said Wilding. "Would you care to stay to dinner?"

"Glad to, if you can give me a bed. You don't mind, I suppose, if I send the syce back to fetch my girl? Aside from the fact that I don't like sleeping alone, she's a saucy little slut and there's a young chap in the village below my place who's making eyes at her. I'm old-fashioned, I suppose, but while my tenure lasts, I like it to be exclusive."

"By all means send for her," said Wilding genially. "This is liberty hall. Robbie Norman came up here the other day and brought all of his women with him. Nice chap, Robbie, but he's a bit whole-sale."

"Yes," agreed Gilliland, "one at a time ought to be enough for any man. In fact, it seems to be more than enough for you," he added. "That is, if you've not changed your ideas."

To this Wilding offered no comment.

"There was a fellow called Maitland who lived in the district until about five years ago," continued Gilliland. "He had much the same ideas as you have. But after a year or two, chiefly to stop tongues from wagging, he installed a girl. If she was as pure as a vestal virgin when she came to live with him, she left him the same way. But I always thought Maitland did the sensible thing. Made him less conspicuous, if you know what I mean."

It disconcerted John Gilliland, when he looked up from his monologue to help himself to another drink, to see that Wilding was laughing.

"Now, come off it, Gilly!" said the latter good-humouredly. "What's on your mind? You didn't come here to tell me Maitland's life story, or to borrow books. What is it?"

"My dear chap . . ."

"Out with it, Gilly. Don't try to blarney me."

"All right," said Gilliland, who hated being manœuvred thus. "I'll admit that I had it in my mind to mention one or two things which may have escaped your notice."

With a look of resignation on his face, Wilding poured himself a drink.

"Thinking of Maitland made me think of you, Wilding," continued Gilliland, making his tone as casual as possible. "Because, you see, tongues are wagging about you."

"They wag about everyone. What of it?"

"It wouldn't be any business of mine if you were the only person concerned. But you're not, Wilding. Some very ugly things are being said about you and Ruth Carey."

"By whom?" snapped Wilding.

"By everyone in the district. In a place like this, my dear chap, you can't expect to go off on jolly little picnics up into the jungle with your boss's wife and not have people chatter about it."

"Granted that you're right, Gilly, just how do you fit into the picture?"

"I'm George Carey's oldest friend, Wilding. Don't forget that."

"Then, if that's the case, as Carey's oldest friend, the obvious thing for you to do is to talk to Carey."

"Look, Wilding. I'm not suggesting that your association with Ruth Carey is anything it shouldn't be. Understand that. But you must see how utterly impossible it is for me to go to George with a tale like that."

"You've come to me with it. Why not to Carey? It wouldn't by any chance be that you want to keep up the pretence to George's face of liking Ruth, would it? You haven't by any chance worked it all out that, if and when the crash you hope for comes along, you'll be able to go to Carey with clean hands and say: 'George, old pal, I'm terribly sorry for your sake that all this has happened, but I'm very glad, for the sake of our old friendship, that you found out the truth without any help from me'? That wouldn't be it, would it? You're wasting your time, Gilly, because I'm as artful as you are. You're not talking to one of the muscle-bound boy scouts who haunt the Big Bungalow at the weekends and look up at you adoringly when you reminisce about the good old days. If you want to talk to me, talk sense."

" 'Pon my soul, Wilding!" said Gilliland, who found this thrust far too near the truth to be comfortable. "Living alone here has given you some dashed funny ideas."

"It's a funny thing, Gilliland," said Wilding, surveying the other with huge amusement, "but on the day Ruth Carey gave you such a hiding on the tennis courts I told her, although I hardly knew her, that she was doing a foolish thing. I told her, you see, that she was making an enemy of you, which wasn't altogether wise. Although I knew I was giving her good advice, I didn't, until now, know how good it was. I couldn't, you see, because until now I didn't realise quite how small you are. You damned Ruth publicly three weeks before you ever saw her or even knew her name. It hasn't touched you that she's made Carey a happier and more normal fellow than he's ever been. All that concerned you was that her coming on the scene didn't quite suit John Gilliland."

"I must say," remarked Gilliland, cloaking his feelings with a heavy and not very convincing sarcasm, "Ruth has found a very loyal champion in you. But"—his voice became threatening—"don't ride the high horse with me, my lad, or you'll come such a bloody thud that you won't like it."

"Until the proper person takes over the job, I rather think Ruth needs a champion," replied Wilding. "Also, since we're now being frank, let me tell you I don't like being threatened at any time, but I won't take it under my own roof. I'm afraid," he added, getting to his feet, "I'll have to cancel the dinner invitation. That is, of course, unless you'd care to eat here alone."

"Where are you going, Wilding?" asked Gilliland, his alarm showing itself very plainly.

"To the Big Bungalow, of course. If, as you say—and you should know—that dirty tales are going the rounds about Ruth and me, the proper person to know about it is Carey himself. Marriage, you know, makes a man, so to speak, the custodian of his wife's reputation, and I don't think somehow George Carey will altogether appreciate your touching devotion to his interests."

"So that's your game, is it?" said Gilliland in a voice which would have done credit to the snarl of the villain in a melodrama. "Want to make trouble between George and me. Like hell you will!"

"Why not come along with me, Gilliland? That is, if you've got the guts to face it."

"Look, Wilding," said the other in milder tones. "Don't do anything hasty—anything you might regret. Think of poor old George laid up with a gammy ankle!"

Wilding's only reply was a laugh as he called to a boy to have his horse saddled and sent round.

In the unenviable position of having started something he did not quite know how to finish, John Gilliland rode off in the direction of his own bungalow. He was sorely tempted to accompany Wilding, but thought it the more prudent course not to be present at the heated interview which, he suspected, would shortly take place. This, at least, would give him a loophole later for presenting his own version of the facts at a time and place of his own choosing.

Darkness had fallen by the time Wilding arrived at the Big

Bungalow, but it was not so dark that he missed the look of burning resentment in Appuhamy's dark eyes as the latter came forward with his customary courtesy to show him into the lounge.

Appuhamy harboured strange feelings where Wilding was concerned. Like all well-trained servants, he loved that undefinable thing called "class". It had always given him great satisfaction to give willing, courteous service to a man who understood and appreciated good service and one who, in addition to knowing how servants should behave, knew how to behave towards servants. But in such an issue as this, however regretfully, Appuhamy was compelled to align his sympathies with his master.

"Come on in and have a drink, Wilding," said Carey heartily. "Glad to see you. Nothing wrong, is there?" he added, noting the other's unusually grave face.

"Nothing that can't be put right, Carey."

"I'll leave you alone, as I expect you want to talk shop," said Ruth, rising to her feet.

"If you don't mind, Ruth," said Wilding, "I'd rather you stayed. What I have to say concerns you, you see. I had a visit a little while ago from Gilly," he went on, addressing himself to Carey, "and we—er—had a chat that wasn't altogether too friendly. I told him, among other things, that what he said to me should have been said to you. For his own good reasons he didn't take that view and—well, here I am."

"What is it, man?" said Carey uneasily. "Let's have it, whatever it is."

"Without mincing words, Gilly came over this evening to see me. He sparred about a bit at first and finally came to the point. In brief, he said that there was a lot of ugly gossip which concerned Ruth and myself, and that, as your best friend, Carey, he came to me to see if something couldn't be done to stop it. We both said plenty and, although he did his best to dissuade me, I told him I was coming over here to tell you exactly what happened. I also told him that if, as he says, he is your best friend, you were the proper person to come to in the first place. There it is. Mind you, Carey, it doesn't surprise me a bit to learn that there's been gossip and I'm not altogether sure that we can blame people for talking. Since you've had that busted ankle, I've been seeing a lot of Ruth, as you know. But what we in this room know that the others don't is that it has been with your full knowledge and consent; in fact, at your request. I'm not going to pretend to you that it has been a painful duty, however." Wilding grinned amiably in Ruth's direction. "I've enjoyed it thoroughly."

"This is a hell of a situation—for all of us," said Carey gloomily. "What in hell's to be done?"

"If you're really asking me," said Wilding, "I'll tell you. For Ruth abruptly to stop coming round with me is going to make tongues wag harder than ever. I suggest that, until your ankle is right, Ruth continues to ride round with me, though perhaps not quite so often as before. Then, when she finally stops coming with me at all, it will be logically because your ankle's better and you can take her with you. If you know what I mean, I don't think we can ignore malicious gossip, but I really don't see that we should make concessions to it. Suppose we ask how Ruth feels about it."

"I think Geoffrey's right, George," said Ruth after a moment's hesitation.

"Yes, I think so, too," said Carey. "I suppose it was the coolies talking. Poor devils! I suppose they've nothing better to do in their spare time. But it makes me sore as a boil to think that Gilly could be such a fool as to take a thing like that seriously."

"I'm not going to insult Ruth by denying any of the things Gilliland hinted at, rather than said, Carey," said Wilding, choosing his words with care, "but equally, I don't think you can dismiss the matter quite as lightly as that. You see, Gilliland, while not specifically making any accusations, made it very clear by his manner and attitude to me that he believed what gossiping tongues were saying. I think you're entitled to know that, Carey, because if Gilliland, your best friend, is prepared to believe things like that, how much less generous are other people going to be? I'm sorry to put it all as bluntly as this. It must be very distressing for you, Carey, and even more for Ruth. But somebody has to talk plainly."

"But, Wilding!" said Carey aghast. "You must be mistaken. Gilly couldn't think a thing like that of Ruth!"

"That's something you'll have to have out with Gilliland yourself, Carey," said Wilding with a shrug. "I've been very careful not to overstate anything, and it's now up to you to decide what's best for everyone's sake."

"Thanks, Wilding," said Carey with a deep sigh. "It can't have been easy to come here like this. . . . And now suppose we drop the subject. As you're here, you may as well eat a bite of dinner with us."

"Thanks all the same, but I'll go home. I've rather a fancy tonight to wrestle with a few snipe at my own place."

"Shall I be seeing you in the morning, Geoff?" asked Ruth.

"That," replied Wilding, as he made his exit, "is something you two will have to decide. But in case you think it better to come, I shall be going the long way to the factory, getting there about nine o'clock in the morning. Good-night!"

A long silence fell between Ruth and George Carey when they were alone. George's thoughts were written plainly upon his lugubrious face, but Ruth's not so plainly. One part of her was intensely grateful to George Carey for his instant and automatic dismissal of the implications raised by Wilding's visit. That same part of her applauded Wilding for the courageous and straight-forward way he had handled what might have been a very embarrassing situation. Ruth did not find this surprising, because Geoffrey Wilding was a well-poised man. There was something about him almost catlike, she mused. He would be hard to catch off-balance.

That was one part of Ruth's meditation as she sat watching her husband whose chin, as always when deep in thought, had dropped on to his chest.

They had been very gallant, very correct, these two men. Their conduct had been impeccable, above criticism. But each of them, in his own frank, lordly way, had overlooked one very important thing: that she, Ruth Carey, was a woman, and a beautiful, desirable woman into the bargain. At least, she had hoped so, but in the last fifteen minutes had begun to nurture doubts. It was right that a husband should cherish his wife's reputation but, Ruth mused bitterly, was it so right to sit there unruffled and to take that virtue so completely for granted? Would it have been so very extraordinary if a handsome, witty, well-mannered man of about her own age, such as Wilding was, were to succumb in a moment of weakness to her charms? Even allowing for the fact that Gilliland was maliciously inclined, in Ruth's eyes the things at which he had hinted did not seem quite so laughable and absurd as these two men seemed to assume they were.

Before she was able to pursue this line of thought with any clarity, it had been necessary to lift the little curtain which divides conscious, controllable thoughts and emotions from those which bubble unchecked below the surface. Why, she asked herself, had she felt a faint annoyance at the attitude of George Carey? What right had he to dismiss as an absurdity the thought that another man had fallen a victim to her? What was so absurd about it? Geoffrey Wilding had not been very flattering, either. It would have made her feel more like a normal human being and less like a piece of negotiable merchandise if, instead of rushing over to the Big Bungalow to unburden himself of his story, he had waited until the morning to talk to her first about it. It was, after all, her virtue, or supposed lack of it, which had given rise to all this hubbub. One thought, Ruth was discovering, suggests another and another, in an endless and uncontrollable chain. An hour previously the situation envisaged by John Gilliland would have seemed utterly absurd. Now, curiously, with fancy running free, it was not quite so absurd.

In musing thus, Ruth had left out of account a very ancient law: that nothing stands still. Things, people, situations go forward, go backward, but they never stand still.

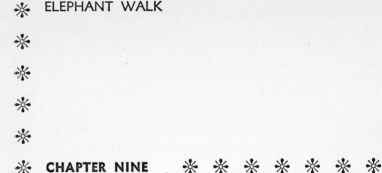

CHAPTER NINE

Fonseka, who served Wilding in the joint capacity of cook and butler, was flattered, if not astonished, upon receiving an invitation, couched in formal terms, to drink a glass of arrack with Appuhamy at the Big Bungalow.

Donning a skirt patterned after the Campbell tartan and a short white jacket, buttoned to the neck, Fonseka left the service of dinner to an underling. Urged on by a boundless curiosity, he hurried to the Big Bungalow.

"When a young man casts eyes filled with desire upon a beautiful woman," began Appuhamy, when the courtesies had been satisfied and his guest's glass was filled, "it is, I have often noticed, an almost impossible task to turn him from his purpose until the fever has run its course and his pulses begin to beat more slowly. There is alas! no quinine for such a fever."

"It is indeed sad," agreed Fonseka, "and no man can predict the ultimate consequences of such folly."

"Such a man"—Appuhamy's voice was infinitely sad—"could be dragged to his own ruin, to say nothing," he added pointedly, "of the hardship which would fall upon innocent and worthy persons who might be dependent upon him, or even"—he paused—"in his employ."

"It is too tragic to be contemplated," observed Fonseka piously. The drift of the conversation was now becoming apparent to him, but courtesy demanded that he allow Appuhamy to come to the point in his own time and in his own fashion.

"In a long life I have discovered," continued Appuhamy, in tones which suggested that the discussion was purely academic, "that the only quick and certain cure for a young man obsessed by a beautiful woman, is the appearance of one even more beautiful and desirable."

"True, how true!" observed Fonseka unctuously.

"Forgive me, my friend," said Appuhamy, with the anxious manner of a good host, "I see that your glass is empty." He clapped his hands. The bead curtains parted lightly. "Rayna, my child, bring my guest some arrack. His glass is empty."

Fonseka, who, if he had thought about the matter at all, would have expected to see the ordinary type of kitchen drab, gasped with frank amazement at the vision which came with a bottle of arrack upon a tray in answer to the summons.

Rayna was wearing a skirt of royal blue brocaded silk, which clung with superb grace to her lithe young figure. Over the top of the skirt there peeped a two-inch strip of warm golden skin, atop which was a short-sleeved blouse of rich silk, a vivid cerise in colour, on which, embroidered by Rayna's own hands, was a palm frond whose butt rested at the waist on the right-hand side, sweeping up diagonally so that the feathered tip crossed her left breast and disappeared over her left shoulder. In startling contrast against shining blue-black hair was a pair of carved bone ear-rings, dead white. The effect, as Appuhamy had intended it to be, was stunning.

"She is beautiful beyond words!" said Fonseka in a hushed voice as Rayna, moving superbly, left the room.

Even had there been any doubt in Fonseka's mind as to the identity of the young man, or the nature of the folly from which Appuhamy sought to save him, all doubt was now set at rest by the latter's manner.

"There is a little moment at the end of the day and the beginning of the evening," said Appuhamy suggestively, "when men, tired from a day spent in the hot sun, bathed and feeling at peace with the world, are relaxed, mind and body. The little moment does not last long, but while it lasts, men shed for a while the armour which protects their souls. Strange fancies cross their minds at such a time. The strong become weak. Men of ironbound habit shed habit, for the doors of the mind and the soul are open. If, my friend, at such a time the young man of whom we speak were to see the loveliness that you and I have just seen, I have a fancy that he would forget his madness. If that were to happen, I would feel myself greatly your debtor. So many people can suffer from one man's madness, is it not so? If, therefore, such a calamity can be avoided, we should be doing less than our duty if we failed at this time."

*   *   *   *   *

"If you go on improving at this rate," said Wilding, putting down his tennis racquet and pouring himself a drink, "you'll soon beat me. You are beginning to understand hard-court play."

"Pour me a drink too, please," said Ruth, falling limply into a deep cane chair. "I'm hot, exhausted and thirsty. I am improving though: I know it. But I don't think I want to beat you, Geoff. For the future, I'd rather be known as a frail little woman. Besides, what guarantee have I that if I beat you, you won't behave like Gilly?"

Wilding's reply to this was a laugh.

"You know, Geoff," continued Ruth, "although he doesn't say very much, George is very upset by it all. There's a hurt look in his eyes whenever the subject is mentioned. Gilly hasn't been over to see him, and I think it rankles."

"But when he does come to see George, mark my words," said Wilding, "he'll arrive with a long face and an I-did-it-all-for-good-old-George attitude. If Gilliland were a woman, Ruth, he'd be known as a spiteful cat, but just because he's a big hearty-looking bloke who drinks like a fish and curses like a bargee, he gets away with it."

"Geoff," said Ruth anxiously, "what are we to do?"

"We must face facts," said Wilding soberly. "There's only one thing to do, as I told you and George the other evening. You and I have got to see less of each other."

"But, Geoff!" said Ruth quickly, dismay in her voice. "That's like running away and almost admitting that the things that beast Gilly hinted at were true."

"Just as many reputations are ruined by lies as by truth. Perhaps more. Let me ask you something, Ruth. I don't care whether you answer me or not. Just tell yourself the answer. How long do you think it would be, if we go on the way we've been behaving, before we—shall I say, make fools of ourselves? Don't interrupt me for a few moments, please. Say what you like when I've finished. . . . I said we must face facts, and if you look at the thing straightly, there are only two important facts: I am a perfectly normal man and you are a dangerously attractive woman. You may be one of these strong characters, able indefinitely to resist temptations. Alternatively, you may find me very unattractive—just in case you accuse me of being conceited. Either may be true where you're concerned, or both. I don't know. But I do know, you see, that I'm not a strong character. I think of you far too much. Think of you, furthermore, in a way I ought not to. If at this moment I were not drinking George's whisky as his guest, nothing, nothing at all, let me tell you, would stop me from kissing you."

"With only a whisky-and-soda standing between me and shame, what ought I to do, Geoff? Tremble? Blush? Or run away?"

"Be sensible, Ruth, and listen to me while I'm willing to go on being sensible, and just remember that you can't count on my continuing to be sensible indefinitely. I'm not the type, Ruth, that goes on for very long struggling against temptation. That's about all I have to say, but I'll say it again, so there won't be any misunderstanding. I don't think we ought to meet and go about together alone. If we do, I don't think either of us has the right to complain if dirty tongues wag. So," Wilding added, resuming his bantering tone, "if we're going to continue to ride off into the hills together and carry on as though nothing has happened, the suggestion must come from you. But don't forget, my bonnie wench, that you do so at your peril!"

"I'm not your bonnie wench," snapped Ruth, "and in case you don't know it, you take too much upon yourself."

"I've almost finished, Ruth," continued Wilding mockingly, "and then you have the floor. I was about to say, when you interrupted me so rudely, that if the suggestion comes from you that we continue these—to me—delightful jaunts together, I offer no guarantees of good behaviour. I shall feel free to interpret your suggestion in precisely the way I please. Can I say fairer than that?"

"I always knew that the age of chivalry was dead, Geoffrey Wilding," said Ruth viciously, "but I shall always remember you as the man who drove the last nail into its coffin."

"I am at your service, gracious lady."

"Geoff," said Ruth, in a pleading tone, "you just can't slide out like that . . ."

"Slide out of what?"

"Well, you can't leave all the responsibility for—everything on me. It just isn't fair."

"So far, Ruth," Wilding reminded her gently, "you don't have to be responsible for very much, if you think of the matter. The only crime for which we are jointly responsible—so far—is indiscretion and overlooking the fact that, however well-behaved we have been— and we have, haven't we?—we could hardly expect the rest of the world to see us in that pure light. The future? Well, the future is in your hands entirely. I am leaving that in your—very beautiful and competent—hands."

"But Geoff," said Ruth, rising dismay in her voice, "you just can't mean that! I never heard anything so outrageous in my life. It's the same as saying that we can't see any more of each other unless I'm prepared to . . . No, Geoff! It isn't fair."

"My dear Ruth," said Wilding in a hard voice, "you're losing your sense of proportion. You say I'm not being fair. It's the seducer who comes softly, wearing crêpe-soled shoes, who isn't being fair. Think of me, if you like, as the would-be seducer who comes wearing iron-shod shoes, announcing his intentions with a megaphone, so that the innocent maid knows of his intentions well in advance. If, after that, she doesn't run away and hide, surely the bold bad seducer— that's me—is entitled to jump to his own conclusions? And that, my dear, is exactly and precisely what I intend to do."

"But, Geoff, we arranged to ride to the top clearing tomorrow morning."

"We did. I start at exactly seven a.m. I should be at the spot where the road forks at seven-twenty a.m. I shall wait there for exactly five minutes. If you are not there, I shall understand that you have listened to all my good advice. But if you are there, my bonnie wench, come prepared to do battle for your honour! I must be off now, Ruth," he added lightly. "Good-night, and my regards to George."

As he rode homewards through the lengthening shadows, Wilding amused himself in trying to assess, strictly for his own information, just how much of what he had said to Ruth Carey he had meant. She was, as he had told her, dangerously attractive. They had started off on the wrong foot, but once their early misunderstandings had been cleared up, he and she had become dangerously sympathetic. They saw beauty through the same eyes, laughed at the same things, and doubtless, if the occasion ever arose, would mingle their tears in pity. He hoped, as the light of his own bungalow came into view, that he had been successful in frightening Ruth, in opening her eyes, if they were not opened already, to the inevitable consequences of their continued association on this footing. Although he would miss her company, in which he had spent by far the happiest days since coming to Elephant Walk, he hoped very sincerely that, on the following morning, Ruth would not put in an appearance. If, in the face of everything he had said, she did come, the next move would be his, and he was not quite sure what it would be. In all the circumstances, she would have to be pretty hard-faced to keep the carelessly suggested rendezvous.

Geoffrey Wilding was no novice where women were concerned. Women had always been attracted to him. To many of them he himself had been attracted, but almost always to those who had been successful in hiding from him just how much they were attracted. He did not like, as he had said on another occasion, shooting sitting pheasants. Ruth, if she kept tomorrow's rendezvous, would be just that. He was too tactful a man to tell Ruth that much of his attitude to her was coloured by the fact that George Carey, whom he liked and, within limits, respected, was a good fellow who had always treated him fairly and generously. Women, as he knew, were too egotistical to appreciate such an attitude: perhaps because they understood it too well. A woman such as Ruth, he sensed rather than knew, wanted to be treated as a woman, not merely as George Carey's wife. This, he mused, was natural and logical enough, for no woman contemplating active disloyalty to her husband, wanted to be reminded of him. More prosaically still, Wilding foresaw the probability that if he and Ruth entered into an illicit relationship, it would be for him the end of his days at Elephant Walk. He was not prepared, as Ruth's lover, to go on meeting George Carey on the old terms. This would be a pity, for he liked Elephant Walk. Even the fact that he had no real friends there did not destroy the liking. Vaguely at the back of his mind was the intention, when his leave fell due in eighteen months, to return to Elephant Walk with a wife. He had not met her yet, but he was a man slow to relinquish his dreams, reluctant to destroy wantonly the plans he had made painstakingly for the future. Women, he reflected, as he threw the reins to a waiting syce, were charming creatures, but they had the unhappy knack of complicating simple lives and situations. Up till now it had been the simplicity of life under the shadow of Ratnagalla Peak which had appealed to him most.

*   *   *   *   *

To set off on the beginning of a new career, to embark upon the adventure of life for which the brief and fleeting years of childhood have been a preparation: that surely is a thrilling and unique moment in human experience? At such a moment a boy on the threshold of manhood, or a girl on the threshold of womanhood, does not pause to calculate the chances, weigh the ultimate costs or exercise the sober wisdom of maturity, which seldom comes until it is too late to be of much practical value.

Just such a moment had arrived in the life of Rayna. Events had moved swiftly for her in these last days, which had seen her translated from rags and poverty in the obscure village in which she had been born, to a wonderland which, although its promise had been dangled before her for years, seemed too fantastic to be believed. Rich silks had killed the memory of rags; a soft bed, that of the hard beaten earth floor, which she had always known. Appuhamy had been very kind, almost tender, to her, as though she were his own daughter. Already she had more affection for him than for her own father.

Rayna had never been taught to think of her body in moral terms. That she was still what the world calls a virgin was a mere technicality, having no moral significance. That this was so, had been a matter of expediency on the part of her parents, who had taken pains to ensure that no little moment of frailty should be allowed to depreciate her value. They had been kind enough to her, but they had never forgotten, nor allowed her to forget, that she was the family's greatest single asset. She had been taught, since she was old enough to understand what was meant, perhaps even before that, that her body was an instrument of pleasure to be cherished like any other thing or commodity with a high market value. To give away wantonly, or for pleasure, that which would enable her parents to enjoy a comfortable old age, would have been, as Rayna had been forced to see things, a crime commensurate almost with wasting rice.

To say, therefore, in the cant phrase commonly used, that Rayna was a good girl, is meaningless. To say that she was a bad girl, would be unjust. She was neither of these. If one must give her a label to be tied around her neck for the purpose of identification and classification, she was an obedient girl, who conformed cheerfully to the pattern of her destiny.

From the shelter of a clump of bushes Appuhamy had pointed out to Rayna a handsome, smiling man with fearless, mocking eyes, who had been hitting a ball over a net to a tall, clear-skinned young woman who, Rayna thought during the brief moment she was in view, looked at him possessively. Rayna's heart had danced within her when Appuhamy had said softly: "That is the young man. With him you will find happiness."

"What will the woman say?" Rayna had asked.

"The woman does not belong to him!" Appuhamy had replied, and for the first time, wonderingly, she heard anger in his voice.

It was good to know that the woman did not belong to the young man for, even as her first glance rested on him, she knew that he was the handsome prince of her dreams, who one day would come and fetch her, carry her over high mountains, across swift rivers and through many dangers to an enchanted land so beautiful that, on awakening, Rayna had cried for sheer disappointment that it had been only a dream. Now, walking through the tea with Appuhamy in the gathering dusk, in the direction of Wilding's bungalow, it would have been more in accordance with her dreams, Rayna mused, and much more exciting if, instead of being led to him, he had come to fetch her.

"Is he expecting me tonight?" asked Rayna.

"No, child," Appuhamy replied with difficulty.

"Then," said Rayna, her eyes dancing, "my coming will surprise him? I am so very happy," she continued, when she had digested this thought, turning to Appuhamy with a sweet smile. "Tell me, please, why are you so kind to me?"

The only reply which Appuhamy could give her was a hand which rested caressingly on her shoulder. He was doing something of which he was deeply and bitterly ashamed, and he did not like the taste of it. He was wondering as he walked whether his old master, knowing everything, would approve. How much infamy—he longed to know the answer—was permissible in the name of loyalty? Wiser men than Appuhamy had pondered the same question, but none had yet arrived at an answer. The answer is one that does not come by soul-searching. It comes voluntarily, unsought in the stillness of the night, when truth is above all things paramount; when conscience refuses to be satisfied by any compromise, however plausible, with truth.

With a haste that indicated his anxiety to get this thing done as speedily as possible, Appuhamy bid Rayna a wordless farewell at the rear of Wilding's bungalow. When, on his return, he came to the cairn where Tom Carey lay buried, Appuhamy paused as was his custom. It had always seemed to him so very right and proper to tell his master all the little events of the day. Only the night before he had come shamefacedly to report the breakage of a handsome cut-glass flower bowl, which had slipped through his fingers. Appuhamy turned away hurriedly from the cairn. For the first time he had nothing to tell his old master.

*   *   *   *   *

Men who live alone tend to become creatures of habit, sensitive to any changes in a routine which has become familiar. Wilding became aware that the bead curtain across the passage which led from the kitchen quarters of the bungalow into the dining-room, was rustling. It only rustled when the rear door was open. At this hour, when the servants were supposed to be in their quarters, the rear door ought to have been shut. Why, therefore, was the bead curtain moving?

There was in the bungalow that night a very large sum of money in small notes and silver, destined for the payment of contractors. Wilding's first impulse, therefore, was to walk swiftly to the rack where he kept a rifle and a shotgun, take down the latter and slip two cartridges into the breech.

"Come out here into the light!" he called. "When I've counted ten I am going to shoot." To give the threat emphasis, he uttered it in Tamil and Sinhalese.

"I am not a thief," said a small treble voice in English.

"Come into the light where I can see you."

With small, timid footsteps, holding herself proudly erect, Rayna stepped forward into the light shed by a hanging lamp. She was clad as Fonseka had first seen her. In the lamplight the royal blue of her brocaded silk skirt seemed black, serving to accentuate the contrast of the cerise blouse.

"You are not pleased to see me?" said Rayna in a voice harsh with dismay.

"What are you doing here?" asked Wilding curtly in Sinhalese, ignoring the question.

"Do you not think me beautiful?" was the disconcerting reply, as Rayna pirouetted in the lamplight like a mannequin.

Wilding had seen the beauty of women in the sophisticated centres where, because these are the best markets, beauty is often encountered. In London, Paris and Vienna, in that order, he had seen beauty which, at the time, each in turn, he had believed peerless only to revise his judgments. Now in the hills of Ceylon, there stood before him the loveliest creature of them all. Here was innocence, of that there was no least doubt, but it was not the clumsy, bucolic innocence of the village, for the girl who stood so proudly before him, so conscious of her finery, had, despite an artless simplicity, the poise and bearing of a princess. There was hesitancy in the smiling eyes, but there was no fear. Wilding was disconcerted to observe that in them was a questing appraisal which mirrored his own.

"Do you not think I am beautiful?" the girl repeated, now in English.

"You are so beautiful," replied Wilding in an awe-struck voice, for it was he who had lost his poise in this encounter, "that I wonder if you are real. Won't you sit down?" he added, to cover his confusion.

"I do not think it would be wise for me to sit," she replied gravely.

"My skirt is too tight. It is very pretty, I think, but I have brought other clothes with me. They are almost as pretty, but more comfortable."

With a quick smile the girl disappeared into the darkness. Once again the bead curtain rustled at her passing. In a very few moments she returned, having exchanged the tightly clinging skirt for a length of palest blue crêpe-de-chine, wound round her with artless skill.

"I can see," said Wilding, who, after the brief interlude, was more master of himself, "that you are a most thoughtful girl. It is always wise, is it not, when going on a visit, to bring a change of clothes?"

"I have never been on a visit before," was the thoughtful reply. "But I have brought all my clothes. Some of them are very pretty. You shall see them, and if there are some you do not like, you shall buy me others. The shop in Kandy was filled with fine silks. There were so many that it was hard to choose."

"So you have brought all your clothes? Tell me, is it your idea to stay here?"

"Of course. At first I did not want to come, because I was frightened. But when they pointed you out to me while you were beating a ball with a woman behind the Big Bungalow, I was not frightened any longer. I knew that you were kind and that I would be happy here."

"Will you have a cigarette?" asked Wilding, stalling for time in which to collect his thoughts.

"No, thank you," was the easy reply. "But I will take one of these." She helped herself to a cheroot from a box on the table and, with the ease of long experience, lit it expertly, drawing a deep draught of smoke down into her lungs, exhaling it through her nostrils with every sign of satisfaction.

Someone, Wilding reflected, was trying to force his hand. His first thought was that it might be Gilliland, but he dismissed it as absurd. There was in this the imprint of a more delicate hand. Besides, nothing would have pleased Gilliland more than for his relationship with Ruth to reach a crisis which would end her days at Elephant Walk. No, Gilliland could be ruled out. Was it possible, he asked himself, that this was George Carey's doing? If so, he must be a consummate actor, for if he had entertained any doubts whatever about Ruth's conduct he had concealed them wonderfully. No, this was a more subtle hand than George Carey's. The bludgeon was his weapon, not the rapier, and here—he looked across at the lovely girl sitting upon the edge of her chair—here was the rapier wielded by a cunning and subtle hand.

Two small devils sat on Geoffrey Wilding's shoulders. One, which whispered into his left ear, said: "Take what the gods have given you, man! What does it matter who sent her or how she came? All that will emerge afterwards." The other little devil whispered into his right ear: "Softly, softly!" it said. "This is no ordinary lure. Its brilliance and beauty are dazzling, but remember that somewhere, cunningly concealed, is a sharp hook. There is always a hook, just as there is always a price to be paid for everything, and for beauty such as this the price is sure to be a high one. Make sure, before you accept the gifts the gods have given you, that the price is one you are willing to pay."

For a little while the argument between the two small devils rocked back and forth without either scoring any notable advantage.

"How old are you?" asked Wilding, ignoring both his counsellors.

"I am very old," was the sad reply. "I am almost sixteen years of age."

"Yes, indeed," Wilding agreed, "you are very old. How comes it that you are not married?"

"I am a Rodiya, you see," the girl replied, as though that explained everything.

"What," asked Wilding, who did not know, "is a Rodiya?"

"I thought everyone knew that," Rayna replied in wide-eyed wonderment. "I will tell you the story, if you would like to hear it. A long time ago, maybe it was more than fifty, perhaps a thousand years ago, the Rodiya people were the proudest people in all Ceylon. The women were all beautiful like me, and the most beautiful among them were chosen to be the wives of the King of Kandy. He was a bad man, I think. He found one day that his wives were unfaithful to him, and he did not like it, so he punished all the Rodiya people. Now, instead of being very high-caste people, we are the lowest. Other Sinhalese people will have nothing to do with us. There is a law which says that we must wear no clothes above the waist. Of course, there are no Rodiya people here, so it does not matter, but"—she laughed engagingly—"although this"—she touched the cerise blouse —"is very pretty, it is not very comfortable. I only wore it, you see, because I had to look very beautiful the first time you saw me. I think now I shall take it off."

With the greatest unconcern, Rayna removed her blouse. "That is better," she said, more at ease, stroking her breasts luxuriously.

"Yes," said Wilding, "that is better. Sit exactly as you are sitting now and do not move." Picking up a sketch block and a piece of charcoal, Wilding, with a few deft strokes, caught the pose perfectly. "That is enough," he said when the outline was finished. "There will be time for the colours in the morning."

The two small devils, tired of their fruitless persuasion, in which neither had seemed to make any headway, were gone away, leaving Wilding to reach his conclusions without their help.

A little reflection had persuaded Wilding that the author of the evening's events could only be Appuhamy, who alone had both the subtlety and the interest. Appuhamy went up a great deal in his estimation. It had been Wilding's guess from the beginning that Appuhamy's resentment at the coming of a woman to Elephant Walk would make him anxious above all things to see her go. In thinking this, he had done less than justice to the old man, whose loyalty to the Careys permitted him to over-ride self-interest. Wilding, on the last two or three occasions he had seen Appuhamy, had noted the look of resentment in the latter's eyes. It was now possible to interpret that correctly. He resented Ruth's presence, but he reckoned that a trifle beside the shame which would come upon George Carey—and the Big Bungalow—if Ruth should prove a faithless wife. Although he resented Appuhamy's interference, Wilding found it in his heart to respect the old man. Maybe, he mused, Appuhamy was right, and this was the best way for all.

At the end of half an hour spent in tumultuous thought, punctuated by uneasy conversation, the counsel of neither of the small devils prevailed. Rayna, with a wondering look upon her face, was given possession of the bungalow's only spare room. Having keyed herself for an eventuality which she regarded as inevitable, it was a bitter disappointment to realise that she must pass yet another night upon a virginal couch. There was, however, compensation: in the spare room was a full-length mirror, something she had never seen before. For a long while, surveying her slender body closely, she looked in vain for the imperfections which had caused this strange young man to turn away.

Agonising sobs shook Rayna before sleep claimed her. She was already old. If the flower of her youth were not plucked soon, it would fade and die.

*   *   *   *   *

George Carey, still chained to the bungalow by his injured ankle, listened eagerly to Wilding's brief, concise account of the week's happenings.

"I think," said Wilding, glancing out at the lengthening shadows, "I'll be getting on my way."

"But you're going to stay for the night, aren't you?" There was distress in George Carey's voice.

"Thanks, no. I've made plans to be home this afternoon."

"But it's Saturday!" said George Carey aghast.

"Do stay, Geoff," urged Ruth. "We never seem to see you these days."

"Thanks all the same, I'd like to, but," Wilding explained, "I've promised myself to paint a picture tomorrow. It's in oils. The first ambitious one I've ever attempted. The canvas and the colours came yesterday. I'm going to be up at dawn so as to get all the light possible."

"I wish," said George Carey earnestly, "you'd be a pal and paint a picture of the Big Bungalow one day. It looks wonderful from the ridge over there with Ratnagalla Peak in the background."

"I thought, George," laughed Ruth, "that you were going to ask Geoff to paint one of me."

"I would have, darling," said George contritely, "but I didn't think he went in for that sort of thing. The only ones of his I've seen were odd-looking flowers, large chunks of scenery, and palms waving against dashed funny looking sunsets. They were all a bit above my head, but the colours were nice and bright. Be a good chap and paint one of Ruth one day. It'd be grand to have a portrait of Ruth. It might make you famous, you never know. She's beautiful enough."

"Be quiet, George, or you'll make me vain. Well," Ruth added, turning to Wilding, "if you're determined not to stop, I'll see you off the premises and count the spoons."

"Make him promise to paint you!" called Carey, wondering why the idea had not occurred to him in the first place.

"Geoff," said Ruth in a hard voice when they were out of earshot, "you weren't there at the fork at seven o'clock the other morning as you promised. Why?"

"Because," Wilding replied, "I knew you wouldn't be there. I knew you wouldn't be so foolish as to come. Anyway, how do you know I wasn't there?"

"If you must know, I looked through George's field-glasses from the hill behind the bungalow. You reached the fork a full fifteen minutes before you said you would, and then you didn't even look in this direction to see if I were coming, but rode straight on down towards the factory."

"Well, since you didn't come, don't you think it was just as well I didn't wait?"

To this Ruth offered no answer.

"Geoff, I'm serious. I must see you sometimes. It does me good to talk to you, and this place is getting on my nerves."

"You haven't forgotten the conditions, have you?" asked Wilding.

"No, I haven't forgotten the conditions, Geoff, and although they might have frightened me a few days ago, they don't—now."

"Be careful, Ruth!" said Wilding mockingly, "or I shall jump to conclusions and have you calling me conceited again."

"I'm not frightened by what you call your conditions now, Geoff. Not a little bit! You may have meant what you said the other day on the tennis courts, but I know you don't now. Something's happened. You're changed. Why, at this very minute you're itching to mount your horse and be on your way. What is it?"

Wilding was saved the embarrassment of replying by the arrival of Appuhamy with a clean handkerchief on a silver salver. "The master dropped this," he said gravely.

"Thanks, Appuhamy," said Wilding, who remembered quite clearly that the only handkerchief which had been in his possession on entering the bungalow had been a soiled one, and that still reposed in his shirt pocket. The one brought by Appuhamy must, therefore, have been left behind on some prior occasion. Why had Appuhamy chosen this moment to return it? Was he actuated by a desire to break up this tête-à-tête? Looking at Appuhamy standing pointedly waiting for him to take his departure, Wilding had no doubts upon the subject, just as no doubts remained that Appuhamy had been guilty of other interference in his private life.

With Wilding's shrewd eyes upon him, Appuhamy did not flinch, returning the other's level gaze with eyes which were no longer troubled and which no longer burned with resentment.

"Well, what are you waiting for?" snapped Ruth in a tone she had never before used to Appuhamy. The latter bowed gravely, but before he turned to enter the bungalow, his face, without losing its marks of grave courtesy, seemed somehow to radiate triumph.

"Old Appuhamy seems very pleased with himself, doesn't he?" remarked Wilding.

"To me," said Ruth irritably, for her nerves were on edge, "he looks like the cat who has found where the cream is kept." Why, she asked herself, as Wilding rode off homewards, had Appuhamy worn that triumphant air? The incident of Wilding's handkerchief had not deceived her. That could not have made Appuhamy seem so triumphant: it was too petty. Had it, Ruth wondered, anything, however remotely connected, to do with Geoffrey Wilding's anxiety to ride home? She dismissed the thought. Doubtless, her nerves were playing her tricks.

"Anything wrong with Wilding?" asked George, when she returned to the bungalow.

"His manners might be improved. Why?"

"I wasn't thinking about manners," replied George. "It struck me that he wasn't looking too well. A bit drawn and worried, I thought. I hope nothing's wrong. Wilding's a nice chap, even if he does paint the damnedest-looking things I ever saw."

*   *   *   *   *

"Keep still just a little longer," said Wilding. "Another five minutes and you may rest. If you move now, I know that you will never look quite the same ever again, and I want this to look just as you look now."

"I am very tired," said Rayna, "and the *chatti* is very heavy. Please, please be quick."

Rayna, wearing only the pale blue silk skirt she had donned on the first evening for comfort's sake, maintained her pose with difficulty. Balanced upon her head was a huge terra-cotta water *chatti*. She was standing on the flight of steps leading from the garden to the veranda of Wilding's bungalow, raised on the balls of two bare feet, one of which rested upon the bottom step, and the other on the one above. The lithe young body was a mathematically vertical line from the back of the head to the heel of the foot which rested on the bottom step. She had held the pose for long minutes and was beginning to sag with fatigue.

As he worked, Wilding was an artist rather than a man. He felt inspired as, with quick strokes of the brush, he captured and imprisoned upon canvas the beauty which was Rayna's sole equipment for the battle of life. When that faded, there would come oblivion.

"Well, well, well!" said an amused voice with a chuckle. "I seem to have interrupted a verra pretty domestic scene."

Wilding looked up at the broad smile of Robbie Norman. So engrossed had he been in his task that he had not even heard the approach of the other's horse.

"Go on in and help yourself to a drink, Robbie," said Wilding, concealing the annoyance he felt. "I'll join you in a minute, but I want to finish this."

"I apologise for the intrusion, Wilding, but I thought this was the one bungalow in the entire district where a man could call unannounced without embarrassing his host. It seems, however, that ma information is a wee bit out of date. Man, man! but she's a bonnie wee lass! Ye're a lucky chap, Wilding. Ye've been a long time coming to the conclusion that old Mother Nature knows best, but ma' certes, ye picked a bonnie partner to share your fall from grace. She's a credit to you, Wilding, and let me tell you that, in a life that hasna been entirely without its tender and romantic moments, it's never been ma good fortune to find an armfu' like yon lassie. Man, but she's lovely!"

"You think I am beautiful?" asked Rayna, smiling with pleasure and maintaining her pose with difficulty.

"Beautiful? That's no' the word for it. If ye knew some of the thochts which are runnin' aroond inside ma heid, lassie, you'd give me the slap across the face that I desairve. An' if at any time you find that ma' old friend Wilding is unappreciative of his good fortune, come and discuss the matter with Robbie Norman. As a matter o' prudence, try to let me have ten minutes warning of your coming, and by the time you arrive I'll arrange to send your predecessors aboot their business. An' I must say," he continued, turning to Wilding, "for a man supposed to be in the throes of some obscure but alarming malady, my lad, ye look the picture of health."

"I don't follow, Robbie," said Wilding, putting down his brushes and palette and telling Rayna to drop her pose. "What's all this about me being ill?"

"I was compelled, much as I like to spend ma Sundays at the Big Bungalow, to leave immediately after tiffin, to attend to a small matter of domestic trouble at home. As I was leaving, Mrs Carey, knowing that I had to pass your bungalow, intimated that it would be a kindly act on my part if I called in to see all was well with you. It seems that you left yesterday afternoon before the customary weekend festivities began, and Mrs Carey exhibited, I consider, a verra proper consairn for your health."

"I can't imagine," said Wilding, "what could possibly have made her think I was ill."

"Ah well, it's the matairnal instinct. All women, you know Wilding, are mothers at heart. Perhaps I should return to the Big Bungalow to save the poor lady any further alarm. She would be relieved, I know, to learn that it was a proper anxiety for the bonnie wee lass ye've installed here, rather than ill-health."

"Don't jump to hasty conclusions, Robbie," said Wilding. "I haven't taken to cradle-snatching yet. Good God! the poor kid's only fifteen!"

"Fifteen, to ma way o' thinking," said Robbie judiciously, "is bordering on senility. Now, for ma taste . . ."

"Shut up, Robbie! I don't want to hear anything about your tastes."

"Ye know, Wilding," continued the other, quite unabashed, "there's a look in yer een that I don't like. Ye have the air of a man who is aboot to make a fool o' himself. The air of a man who is building himself little romantic castles in the air. Ye're mixing sentiment with something that's strictly a matter of business, and it's a mistake, Wilding. Ye'll have noticed, I make no doubt, that a bee taking honey from a flower doesna' linger aboot the business. It takes the honey wi'oot sentimentalising aboot the beauty of the flower."

"Don't talk damn nonsense, Robbie!" said Wilding. "But thanks for coming anyway."

"Aye. I'll be going. Robbie Norman kens well enough when he isna' wanted. It's as well, I'm thinking," he added, "that Mrs Carey didna' take it into her head to ride across here with me."

"He thought I was beautiful," said Rayna, when Robbie Norman had ridden away. "But you do not think so?"

"If I did not think you were beautiful, Rayna," said Wilding, "why do you think I should trouble to paint this picture? It does not look much now, but in a few days you will be able to see on this canvas how my eyes see you. Then it will be for you to ask yourself if you are beautiful."

"Picture!" said Rayna scornfully, looking unutterable things. "What is a picture?"

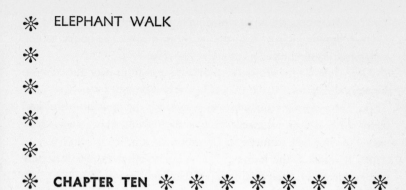

✳ CHAPTER TEN ✳ ✳ ✳ ✳ ✳ ✳ ✳ ✳

The day had been hot, heavy, full of menace. A leaden sky had pressed down upon the world, fraying tempers, magnifying petty annoyances. It was with no great pleasure that Ruth looked forward to entertaining The District—the dreary circle of the same faces which re-appeared around the huge dining-table at Elephant Walk.

They were all coming to dine and, of course, to sleep. For dinner there was corned hump of beef, the protuberance above the shoulders of the draught oxen, provided by nature, seemingly, to thrust against the heavy wooden yokes. Corned hump was a great local delicacy. Indeed, the only delicacy which the most skilful butcher could cut from the tough and tasteless beasts which furnished the raw material of beef.

From a huge wardrobe full of pretty clothes, Ruth was trying to choose something to wear for the evening. It was not a satisfying task. George Carey, whom she could hear splashing in his bath—why did he have to bath so exuberantly?—was no help. He either had no tastes or could not express them. Asked once to choose a gown for evening wear from the huge array before him, he had seized unerringly upon a yellow and pale blue negligée, which Ruth sometimes wore at breakfast. It was one of the very few garments George Carey had ever admired. Even this admiration was tempered by his somewhat lame confession that: "I didn't know it was possible for anyone to look nice at breakfast."

To wear lovely clothes in the company of people who did not see them, Ruth mused, was like cooking for people who had no appetites, or singing to the deaf.

After several whole minutes of indecision, Ruth's hand rested upon a dress which, horrified at the price, she had bought in the Rue de la Paix. It was not only the most expensive, but the most beautiful garment she had ever possessed. On its only previous appearance, Geoffrey Wilding had admired it. "It expresses you, Ruth," he had said when he entered the lounge. The words themselves, she was fully aware, meant precisely nothing, but they had been as balm alongside George Carey's blank inarticulacy when asked what he thought. Geoffrey Wilding noticed clothes, sometimes expressing his opinion about hers with a freedom that was irritating. Nevertheless, it showed an intelligent interest.

Ruth was angry and puzzled by Wilding's recent conduct. It would have been very easy for vanity to have allowed her to believe that his avoidance of her sprang from a worthy and chivalrous desire to avoid causing her embarrassment and worse. It would have been easier to believe that, but Ruth knew, with unerring certainty, that this was not so. Nevertheless, it was with Geoffrey Wilding's approval in mind that she took down from its hanger a dress which would have been sensational in Paris or London but which, to every pair of eyes except one, would this evening rank a long way after corned hump as a feature of interest. It was a lovely thing of white slipper satin with gold embroidery in a wide Greek key pattern at the waist, hem and boat-shaped neckline. The long skirt, which hung straight from the waist with very little fullness at the hem, gave an almost clinging impression. Gold kid Louis-heeled shoes completed the ensemble. Ruth hesitated about wearing the ruby necklace which had belonged to George's mother, deciding against it.

While she was putting the final touches to her appearance, the seal was put upon an unpleasant day by the shrill and familiar trumpeting of a bull elephant who, like the rest of creation, must have been feeling the oppressive heat. The sound was close; closer, indeed, than Ruth had ever heard it. She was to remember afterwards, giving the fact a significance to which perhaps it was not entitled, that the note of rage and anguish and melancholy was absent. There was something about it, it seemed to her distorted imagination of the moment, malignant, gloating, triumphant. Even to George's insensitive ear something of the kind seemed to have been communicated for, from the next room, he called out: "That damn bull seems very pleased with himself about something. I'm getting tired of him. It's been going on too long."

"It gets on my nerves," said Ruth, going into the next room. "It must be three or four months, perhaps more, since we heard them and yet, for over a month now, I've been waiting, waiting, thinking that every day they must be coming up from the plains."

"Say the word and I'll shoot them, darling, and let the government do what it likes. I'd have done it before now, if you hadn't begged me not to. I can't understand why, when you hate them so much."

"I don't quite know why myself, George. But sometimes, when I see umbrellas standing dripping in those pathetic feet out there on the veranda, I can't help feeling a queer kind of sympathy for the elephants. They were here first, George. It's we who are the interlopers. If we feel like that about them, how do you think they feel about us? I try to keep that before me."

"I think," observed George, with a false gaiety, "we'll both feel better for a little drink."

At the precise moment when George Carey, having carved for everyone else, was in the act of cutting for himself a thick, juicy slice of hump, well down towards the base, Appuhamy, shedding for a moment his slow-moving dignity, entered the dining-room with a silver salver upon which reposed an envelope. "A special messenger has just come with this, Master," he said softly.

"Take it away!" said Carey, with good-humoured irritation. "You know perfectly well I don't read letters at night. I want to enjoy my hump."

"But, Master," insisted Appuhamy, "the letter has come from the Government Agent in Badulla by special messenger, and it is marked 'urgent'."

"Put it on my desk, give the messenger a meal and a bed and I'll look at it in the morning."

Reluctantly, feeling unable to say more, Appuhamy left the room, and it was in this fashion that, for twelve more hours, the Ratnagalla

Valley, in the world but never of it, was, true to form, spared the agonising knowledge that the long-simmering cauldron of international jealousies had come to the boil, and that the murder of an Austrian Archduke by a young Serb patriot had been used as a pretext to shed a river of innocent blood.

That night, although still limping, George Carey led his team to victory in the last game of bicycle-polo that was ever going to be played upon the huge veranda of the Big Bungalow.

A strange fancy came to Ruth, lying alone in bed, vainly trying to sleep against the uproar outside her door. Although it had always irritated her in the past, she found it in her heart, without knowing why, to look with more tolerance upon the boisterous rowdiness of these overgrown boys and to wish that she were able to share their fun with them.

At seven o'clock the following morning George Carey opened the fateful envelope, which informed him, in his dual capacity of Justice of the Peace and senior officer of the Ceylon Volunteer Forces in the district, that a state of war existed between Great Britain and Germany, advising him that his presence was urgently required in Badulla, when further instructions would be forthcoming "as the exigencies of the situation may demand."

*   *   *   *   *

Geoffrey Wilding was packing. It was a melancholy task, complicated by not knowing whether he would ever see his well-loved possessions again. The books, prints, saddlery, guns, tropical clothes, private papers and his own water-colours, which littered the bungalow, were a part of him, perhaps the most telling part, for the things with which a man chooses to surround himself reveal him as he really is. Some things had to be taken away, others left. Without being morbid, he had to decide what was to be done with things if he should not return.

It is small wonder that there are and always have been so many men in the world to glorify war, for war is above all things the great simplifier, the great leveller. War provides, and always has provided, a way out of seemingly insoluble difficulties and perplexities. Nobody ever questions the motives of the man who, dropping everything, goes off to the wars. During these last weeks, Geoffrey Wilding had felt himself being sucked ever closer to the vortex of affairs over which he seemed to have no control. He and Ruth had been drifting towards —anything. He found her very sympathetic, enormously attractive, but he was not in love with her. Being brutally frank—as he always was with himself where possible, and so frequently with others that he was doomed never to be a very popular man—to have broken up the Carey ménage would have left him certainly with the moral and probably with the actual responsibility for Ruth, which was one he was not prepared to assume. It may not have been a very heroic attitude, but it was at least realistic.

Twice before in his life Geoffrey Wilding had philandered with married women, and in each instance the women concerned had been ready and willing to face the divorce court and the scandal involved. But he had not been willing. Though young and inexperienced, there was a cold logical streak in him which told him that, if they were prepared to deceive their husbands, the time would come when they would treat him similarly. Where Ruth Carey was concerned, to say that this alone was his attitude of mind is to do him less than justice. There were other arguments at work upon him. The presence of Rayna in the bungalow during these last weeks had reminded him— brutally again—that if his attraction to Ruth were mere sensuality, there was nothing which Ruth could give him which Rayna could not.

Wilding hated drifting. He preferred to do what he did of good and evil with his eyes open, aware of all the possibilities and implications. But during these last weeks he had been drifting, and war presented to him an end to drifting. He had no enthusiasm for war, for he was sceptical of the moral issues involved, but he was going because, as a soldier, it did not occur to him to do otherwise. He knew, none the less, a sense of relief that war was taking out of his hands decisions which might have been hard to make.

Within an hour of hearing the news of the outbreak of war, Wilding had told George Carey of his intention to go. Thereafter, the decision made, he had felt strangely at peace with himself. There came to him the thought that he might never come back to this enchanted valley; might never again see the gem shining in the brow of Ratnagalla Peak at dawn; might never again see the tea in all the glory of its flush, nor feel the thrill of a long gallop through the park country above, nor smell the fragrance of the tea factory below.

They had been happy enough years which he had spent in this splendid setting. If he left now, there would be nothing ugly to soil memory.

There were few things to be done. His life at Elephant Walk had been a tidy one, with no loose ends lying about. Rayna, he was now thankful, was no responsibility of his. When admitting to him that it was Appuhamy who had fetched her from her native village, she was astounded that Wilding did not already know this. Her future, therefore, was in Appuhamy's hands and, although he would miss the sunny presence about the bungalow, the artless chattering and the engagingly amoral outlook on life, Wilding laughed grimly as he thought of Appuhamy wrestling with the problem.

Last of all to be packed and put away into temporary oblivion was the completed portrait of Rayna herself, which still stood upon its easel. He parted with it reluctantly, for he had put so much into it. He had the feeling that if he went on painting in oils for the rest of his life, he would never achieve anything half as good. Although he had never attempted the task before, he had captured to perfection the colour and translucent quality of Rayna's skin, and the queer mixture of youth and ageless wisdom in the smile of this child, brought up to believe that youth and beauty were marketable commodities. If they could be sold to someone sympathetic and not too old, life could be very pleasant. Wilding did not think that he would ever forget the mixture of youth and maturity in the smile of this girl who had been cheated of her youth.

Salt tears fell into open cases while Rayna, with deft precision, packed strange thick clothes such as she had never before seen, for the journey to Europe. There were so many tears shed that year that it is small wonder Rayna's passed unnoticed. Wilding had been kind. He had talked to her on level terms. He was handsome. He had a quick smile. She liked the way his hair was brushed off his forehead. She liked the way he walked, and the friendly, polite way he lit her cheroots for her. She had come expecting to be his mistress. That she was not had been no insuperable disappointment. Nor had she perplexed herself much on the subject. Now, however, it was different. He was going away, and already she could feel the void of his going. Life had begun. Now it was coming to an end and new plans would have to be made for an uncharted future. So Rayna wept.

Trunks were being locked and strapped, packing-cases nailed down. Drawers were being emptied of their accumulation of debris. Everything pointed to such utter blank finality. Robbie Norman had offered to give a home to the cats and the dogs, and a coolie stood at the bottom of the veranda steps of the bungalow waiting to take them away.

Wilding was due to dine at the Big Bungalow that night. Not relishing arriving there in daylight with Rayna perched behind him on his horse, he waited until dark. Instead of riding to the front steps of the Big Bungalow, he rode round to the stables. Appuhamy, whose small house adjoined the stables, was coming out of the door as Wilding arrived.

"She is your problem, not mine, Appuhamy," said Wilding, helping Rayna to dismount. "You seem to think of everything, don't you?"

The old Sinhalese and the young Englishman stood face-to-face in silence for some moments. There was it seemed, a clear understanding between them.

"I try," said Appuhamy, slowly and with great dignity, "to serve my Master."

"Goodbye, Rayna," said Wilding lightly. "Take good care of—your great-uncle."

"Come, child," said Appuhamy sadly as Wilding turned to enter the bungalow. "It is well that he goes from here," he muttered to himself, "and it will be well if he never comes back. Yet," he went on in a softer voice, "he is a fine young man who goes to war bravely and with a smile on his face. How he can turn his back on such beauty is beyond me to understand. A strange, strange young man!"

"I love him very much," said Rayna, who was sobbing pitifully, "and yet he does not seem to see that I am beautiful."

Appuhamy, an arm round the girl's shoulders, led her into his house.

George and Ruth Carey were playing billiards when Wilding arrived in the bungalow. While George was playing a trick shot, Ruth pressed a small piece of paper into Wilding's hand. This he quickly slipped into his pocket.

"I must talk to you alone before you leave. Come to look for me when I go out into the garden. I will wait at the summer-house. R."

Wilding debated with himself whether to ignore the note or to keep the proposed rendezvous, deciding at length upon the latter. Let her say what she wanted to say. It would make her feel better and could do him no harm. Besides, it would save any bitter feelings.

"All ready to go, Wilding?" asked Carey. "What are you going to do about all your stuff?"

"That's one of the things I wanted to talk to you about. Sorry to be morbid and all that, but these things have to be thought of. If anything happens to me, there's a box marked 'Private Papers'. I'd be grateful if you'd have it destroyed unopened. For the rest, I don't care what happens."

Hearing Wilding talk thus calmly of the possibility of not returning, Ruth felt a sudden stab of pain. Up to this moment, the excitement attendant upon the departure of Wilding and the other young men had precluded any personal sense of loss. Like most people then, Ruth had believed that the war would in all probability be over before Wilding and the others reached Europe. She knew now that she dreaded life at Elephant Walk without him and, although she could not guess what lay over the horizon, she was frightened when she surveyed the future.

The District, of course, turned up in full force for dinner: those who were going away, who were the majority, and those who were staying behind. Dinner was one of those hollow feasts, for it is an Anglo-Saxon convention that farewells must be noisy and hearty. "Tipperary" and its contemporary anaesthetics were bawled loudly into the still night air. The drink flowed in a volume which, even for Elephant Walk, was startling. Good fellowship and forgiveness were in the air. Even John Gilliland, perhaps under the influence of whisky, made clumsy peace-overtures to Ruth, although there had never been any open declaration of war.

"By the way, Wilding," said Carey, "before I get too tight to remember it, there's half-pay for you until you come back."

Wilding, who had just seen Ruth disappear into the garden, wished that Carey had not chosen that moment to make the announcement.

Geoffrey Wilding did not hurry to follow Ruth into the garden, partly because it would have been conspicuous and partly—this perhaps was the greater part—because he was not ready to go.

When going to keep an appointment of any kind, whether tryst or business, Wilding liked to have definite intentions and some idea of what he would say and how he would behave in given circumstances. To do otherwise was, as he saw it, to put himself at a needless disadvantage. In going to meet Ruth he did not know whether it was to be a sentimental leave-taking or whether he would have to defend himself against impassioned charges of neglect. It might even be that Ruth had learned of Rayna's presence at his bungalow. In this latter event, there were bound to be recriminations to which, Wilding resolved, he would not even listen.

Meanwhile, the party was at its height, growing rowdier every minute. The heartiness and some of the laughter were tinged with hysteria, as though those about to embark on what they were pleased to call "the picnic", had some inkling of the grim, bloody years which lay ahead. Because he had been a soldier, keen on his profession, Wilding, better than anyone present, knew that the war was going to be long and hard and that its outcome was far from sure. He had too much respect for Prussian military skill to believe, as these others seemingly believed, that the war would be over with an easy victory in a few months. Although he had little enough in common with them, he looked tonight with understanding and pitying eyes at these others who were going off to the war with him. He knew, despite George Carey's promises of the tremendous party he would give them all when they returned, that the chances of any of them, himself included, seeing Elephant Walk again were very small. The knowledge made him feel sad and strangely old. He laughed bitterly when he heard bets made and recorded that the war would be over by Christmas—Christmas of 1914!

George Carey was another reason why he did not hurry to the summer-house where Ruth was waiting. Carey, Wilding mused, although he was such an unimaginative ox of a man, was also such a damned good fellow. It was a pity he could not see that Elephant

Walk, which satisfied him so completely, was not enough for Ruth.

As he watched his good-natured employer, who was rapidly getting very drunk, Wilding longed to take him aside and tell him how to keep on a level keel a marriage which, unless a miracle occurred, was bound to end upon the rocks of Ruth's boredom. But Wilding knew, even as the fancy crossed his mind, how absurd it was. Even if he were to say the things which hovered on his lips, Carey would not thank him. There were some things about life which men, no matter how painful the process, had to find out for themselves. Knowledge of that kind at second-hand was not worth having. Perhaps, Wilding mused, what he needed was a drink. He was quite sober and, because of this, the antics of his fellow guests jarred upon him.

The drink persuaded him that his concern for another man's problems was foolish. Tomorrow he would be gone and his own problems would prove a heavy enough burden. If Carey were too blind or too supine to hold his marriage together, then nothing an outsider could do would help.

Meanwhile, Ruth was waiting in the summer-house. The party had become so riotous that nobody had remarked her absence.

"Your very good health, Erasmus!" said Wilding, lifting his glass to the parrot and scratching its head. "As the only other sober person in the room, what would you advise?"

"Have a drink, old sport!" replied Erasmus sagely.

"Thanks, Erasmus. Why didn't you say so before? Tonight let us eat, drink and be merry, for nobody knows what's going to happen tomorrow."

"Go to hell!" was the chatty reply.

"Hell's bells!" said Carey indignantly. "You're not teaching that bloody parrot anything more, are you? Ruth threatens to wring its neck as it is. By the way, where is Ruth?"

"I expect," replied Wilding, "that she's gone to bed. The party is getting a little rowdy, don't you think?"

"I didn't think it had—yet," said Carey. "But perhaps it's just as well Ruth has gone to bed because at a farewell party like this, anything can happen."

"Yes, anything," said Wilding, with a far-away look in his eyes. "Anything at all!"

"You know, Wilding," Carey maundered, "all of us here, me included, are a bit too tough and rough for Ruth. We haven't got enough spit and polish, if you know what I mean. I'm damned sorry you're going off to the war, Wilding, because you're the one chap here who can give Ruth—bless her heart!—what she wants. You're educated, Wilding, and you've mixed with the kind of people she knows and understands. Ruth's going to miss you, Wilding. So shall I. At first, I don't mind admitting it, I thought you were a bit too high-toned for Elephant Walk, but I was wrong. Well, go off to your war if you must, but come back soon. I'm an older man than you are, Wilding, and there's a damn good billet for you to step into when the war's over. You're a good chap, Wilding, but don't teach that bloody parrot any more bad language. It knows enough already. Where are you going? Anything wrong?"

"I'm just going out into the garden to be sick."

"That's just like you: always such a bloody gentleman! Look at Cullen there! He doesn't care where he's sick. But hell's bells! a man who's going off to fight for his king and country can be sick where he damn well pleases. That's what I say."

"I call that a very right and proper attitude, Carey, but if you don't mind, I prefer the garden. I'm a little old-fashioned about things like that."

Outside, in the soft, cool night air, he lingered for a few moments before making his way along to the summer-house which lay some two hundred yards from the Big Bungalow. Wilding groped his way there with difficulty, for the night was intensely dark. He sighed with relief at his escape from the maudlin sentimentality which he left behind him.

"I thought you were never coming," said Ruth. "There's nothing wrong, is there?"

"Nothing, but it wasn't easy to escape without being conspicuous. That's all."

A silence fell between them.

"Geoff, I'm going to miss you terribly!" And then, in a strange, cool little voice, Ruth added: "I think George is going to miss you, too."

"Yes," said Wilding, "and I daresay Appuhamy and, for that matter, Erasmus will miss me, too. But just now I'm not terribly interested in

George's reactions. Suppose we leave him out of the discussion?"

"You sound cold and aloof, Geoff. Come and sit beside me," said Ruth, moving to one end of the cane settee to make room for him.

Twice Ruth started to speak, but Wilding's hand, softly across her mouth, silenced her. "Talking is only going to spoil the evening," he said gently. "If you and I, sitting here together on a perfect night like this, can't tell, each of us, what the other is thinking, without the help of words, then, don't you see, we ought not to be sitting here. It was Voltaire, wasn't it, who said that the art of speech was given to man to enable him to conceal his thoughts?"

In coming to the summer-house, their feet had crushed hundreds of sweet-smelling frangi-pani blossoms with which the ground was littered. The evening air was heavy with their perfume. Bull frogs and crickets, which had been silent for a little time—for there was the threat of rain in the air—resumed their song. High on the slopes above them came the plaintive bleating of a goat, while from the valley beneath came the fitful barking of a dog. From time to time sheet lightning flickered across the distant horizon. By its light these two were able to catch brief fleeting glimpses of each other's faces.

It was a night of pure enchantment, marred only by gusts of harsh drunken laughter from the Big Bungalow which, looming out of the darkness, looked like some giant liner. It was the kind of night when reason, good resolutions and the copy-book maxims seemed very unimportant beside the oldest urgency of all.

A man, a woman and a scented garden under the immense violet dome of a tropical sky, with the thought hanging implicit between them: We two may never meet again.

"Geoff . . . ," whispered Ruth.

"Be careful, or you'll break the spell," whispered Wilding, putting his hand gently across her mouth.

George Carey's bellows of laughter came clearly across from the bungalow. The sound now was harsh and very ugly. Wilding, in whose arms Ruth lay limply, felt a shiver of disgust stir her. He understood that disgust. It had touched him also, and it helped to destroy the few scruples which had not already been destroyed by the enchantment of the night and the limp surrender of Ruth.

Tomorrow, Wilding mused, it would be too late. Tomorrow there might be oblivion. Worse, there might even come sanity tomorrow. Only tonight mattered.

Treason! Treachery! Betrayal! What were these but words? What was night for but to wrap such thoughts in the mantle of darkness where they could lie hidden from the questing, uneasy eye of conscience.

In Ruth, the battle between conscience and desire had ended. It had ended when she pressed the note into Wilding's hand. Conscience, by then, had gone down to ignominious defeat. Now she lay limply, unresistingly, with desire her only master.

When the false dawn flushed the eastern sky briefly, a cock crew in the valley below, awakening them. "Come back to me safely, darling!" whispered Ruth.

The true dawn was just beginning to break when she saw him ride off towards his own bungalow.

As Wilding entered his bedroom, dimly lit by the early light which filtered through the chinks in the shutters, he sniffed with disgust, for the room was heavy with cigar smoke. The stub of a cheroot still smouldered in an ash-tray on the bedside table. It was not until then that he saw Rayna.

The finely embroidered cerise blouse and the royal blue skirt, which she had worn when she first came, lay where they had been dropped on the floor. The cheroot still alight in a tray full of ashes told the story of an all-night vigil. She could only have been asleep a few minutes. Now Rayna lay deep in the sleep of exhaustion, her slender golden body curled up like that of a tired child.

Moving very softly, Wilding changed for the journey. The cart which was to take his baggage was already creaking slowly up the hill.

Rayna's lips moved and a smile hovered across them, as though an angel had kissed her in her dreams. Wilding was very glad, as he turned away, that he had not returned home that night.

❋

❋

❋

❋

❋ **CHAPTER ELEVEN** ❋ ❋ ❋ ❋ ❋ ❋ ❋

To George Carey the war being waged on the other side of the world ranked as something in the nature of a personal affront. Nothing short of such a catastrophe could so have changed the changeless life of Elephant Walk. At an age when he felt himself entitled to relax a little—and it was with this in mind that he had engaged Geoffrey Wilding as his assistant—he was once more doing two men's work. In point of fact, there were few if any tea estates in Ceylon of the size of Elephant Walk which did not employ two, three or even four assistants. It was so monstrously unfair that the war had come along just when, it had seemed to Carey, Wilding had demonstrated so very clearly his aptitude for planting.

During the three months which had elapsed since Wilding's departure to the war in September, the grind had been as much as Carey could stand. At a little after five o'clock in the morning, with blood-curdling imprecations on his lips, he now had to crawl reluctantly from his comfortable bed to make his way to the muster-ground some three miles distant. Here, trying to collect his muddled and resentful early morning thoughts, conscious of little else but his own martyrdom and the dank chill of the dawn hour, he had to grit his teeth, plan the day intelligently and allot the labour force, approaching two thousand in all, their daily tasks. He had never thought that sun could be so hot nor rain so chilling as they seemed to be these days. Long hours in the saddle irked him as never before. He might have skimped his work, so lessening his own burden, but he could not bring himself to do so. He knew that, unless constantly watched, the pluckers, who were paid by weight, would rip coarse leaf and stalk off the bushes to gain more weight; that the weeding contractors, if he relaxed his vigilance by one iota, would skimp their work. He could not bear the thought of allowing the pruners to grow careless, just as he knew that if he did not make constant trips to the factory, show himself, take an intelligent and active interest in what was being done, in a few weeks or months the factory staff, from De Wet, the teamaker, downwards would be gripped by the sloth and indolence natural to a people who, however well they may do their work when organised and supervised, take little joy or pride in work for its own sake.

Prior to Wilding's departure, Carey had been putting on weight, but now it was stripping off him alarmingly—too fast, indeed, for health or comfort. At the end of a long day he was so tired that it was only by a tremendous effort of will he was able to apply himself to the desk work which, with the war, seemed to have multiplied. Sometimes, by three or four o'clock in the afternoon, the rivulets of sweat he had been shedding since early morning dried up and ceased. When the most marvellous of thermostats, the sweat glands, ceased to function, it seemed as though, like a stoked boiler, the temperature was building up inside him. When this happened, he experienced spells of dizziness. To hide these from the coolies, he would dismount in casual fashion, try to find something of engrossing interest under a shady tree, so that none should suspect the punishment he was enduring, nor know the fears he was experiencing. Careys were strong, oxlike men, immune from the weaknesses which afflicted lesser men. This was the legend built up over the years at Elephant Walk, and this was the legend which must be perpetuated.

The impact of this changed way of life hit Ruth as hard, although in a different way, for she and Carey saw almost nothing of each other these days. At their hasty breakfast George inclined to be silent and thoughtful. At their midday meal they saw more of each other than at any other time. But immediately it was eaten, George fell asleep in a long chair on the veranda. Much as the practice irritated her, Ruth's heart went out to him because she suspected, by his instant dropping off into deep sleep, that he was wearing himself out and, at times, not very far from collapse. It was the evenings which were the worst for Ruth. Carey would arrive home a little before sundown. She contrived on these occasions not to see him arrive, but she could not help hearing the dragging, lethargic footsteps as he climbed the front steps, nor fail to note that, when he eased his tired body into the bath, he no longer did so with a song on his lips.

If Ruth had wanted to have Erasmus destroyed before, now she longed to wring the bird's neck. Although it had only once heard her say, reproachfully and persuasively: "No, George, not another, please!" now, choosing it seemed the most pertinent moments, as though it understood the significance of what it said, Erasmus, in lifelike imitation of her own tones, would call mockingly down the veranda: "No, George, not another, please!"

George these days was in the grip of the famous vicious circle. It was only with the help of whisky that he could' summon energy enough to deal with the desk work accumulating for his attention. The whisky, while giving him temporary new reserves of strength on which he could call, also took its toll, making the task of early rising the following morning an even harder one and, as time went on, the quantity of whisky required to give him the stimulus he needed became progressively greater. It meant, so far as Ruth was concerned, that when dinner was announced at eight o'clock, George would leave his office, amiable but muzzy. He had now given up all attempts to battle against the inclination to sleep between the courses at dinner, so that, except while actually carving or eating, the meal passed in silence, accentuated by the cavern-like immensity of the dining-room.

The social life of the Ratnagalla district had creaked almost to a standstill, for only John Gilliland and Robbie Norman remained. These two, like Carey, were feeling the weight of the years and the added burden of work thrown upon their shoulders. Weeds grew on the tennis courts at Elephant Walk, while without any formal closing, the Ratnagalla Gun Club just ceased functioning and died.

When Lord Kitchener made it clear that, in his opinion, the war would be a long one, Ruth began to wonder how long she would be able to endure the drab monotony of her life. Kitchener to her, as to many millions of others, ranked almost as an infallible being.

On Christmas Eve, while Ruth was engaged in decorating a pretty shrub, which was to do duty for a Christmas Tree, the *tappal* coolie * arrived with a large batch of mail, amongst which there was a brief, impersonal note from Wilding, addressed to "Mr and Mrs George Carey". In it he said that he had rejoined his old regiment, while his address, which was % the British Expeditionary Force, indicated that he was already on active service.

"This is a messy, untidy war," he said. "I don't like it at all. Although so far mud is much more in evidence than blood, I daresay there will be enough of both before long. Personally, I prefer Elephant Walk, and I'm beginning to wonder what persuaded me to leave."

The rest of the letter recorded various meetings with men from Ceylon. To Ruth it was hideously insufficient.

That evening John Gilliland and Robbie Norman came to dine and sleep. They, like George, were beginning to show signs of the strain. Their faces were drawn, their smiles less spontaneous. There was no horseplay now and, with an eagerness that was pathetic, they slumped into long chairs.

Despite her own isolation, Ruth found it in her heart to be sorry for these three men, who seemed to huddle together for comfort. Their lives had been a mixture of hard work, hard play and hearty gregariousness. Now, only the first was left to them. They showed the bewilderment of men who did not know where they were being led.

After dinner, Ruth left them to their gloomy talk and the unconvincing heartiness which the sight of the Christmas Tree evoked in them from time to time. Locking herself in her own room, she sat at the writing-desk. A few sheets of blank paper, she felt, would make a better confidant than none at all. She wrote intently for more than an hour and then, on reading what she had written, destroyed it. She burned to confide in someone the knowledge which was consuming her, like the proverbial penny burning a hole in a spendthrift's pocket. The obvious someone was Geoffrey Wilding, but she could not bring herself to tell him, as she longed to, that the baby

* Mail courier.

she was going to have was his. Aside from a dozen other considerations, there was the ghastly, hideous uncertainty whether he would welcome the news.

The impulse to make a clean breast of everything to George had, during these last days, been almost irresistible, even though the true motive for doing so was obscure. Indeed, it was only because of the lack of an appropriate opportunity that she had not done so. It had seemed unfair, somehow, to make her confession when he was so tired that he could hardly drag one foot after another, and it was impossible to tell him when he was drunk or asleep. There were, these days, it seemed, no other occasions, and the burden of knowledge which she could not share was becoming increasingly heavy.

That civilisation was in flames and a tortured world groaning under the tyranny of war, made no difference to the unshakable traditions of Elephant Walk, for at ten o'clock precisely on Christmas morning Appuhamy, with two boys pushing the teak drink trolley, arrived with the "King's Peg". Although there were only three weary middle-aged men and an unhappy woman to drink it, the customary twenty-four silver tankards and dozen bottles of champagne arrived, just as though coffee were still king and scores of guests thronged the dismally echoing bungalow.

From the Christmas Tree Ruth pulled down a gigantic cardboard box bearing her name. In the centre of it, after unwrapping innumerable sheets of paper, she found a huge unset cabochon emerald. There was a lump in her throat as she saw the anxiety in George's eyes that the gift should please her. If John Gilliland and Robbie Norman had not been present, Ruth would have chosen that moment to tell him everything. But they were present, and the little moment passed.

"You're not looking at all well, darling," George said later in the day.

"I'm not feeling well," said Ruth. "I think I'd like to go away for a week or so. Perhaps I need a change and a few new faces. I'm not complaining, George, but sometimes"—she marvelled at her own understatement—"life here is a little dull, you know."

"Why not go down to Colombo?" suggested George. "It isn't too hot there now, and while you're there you could get the emerald set in the way you like it."

Although she knew very few people in Colombo, installed in a comfortable suite at the Galle Face Hotel, overlooking the sea, she began to feel better. It was a joy to see so many new faces. Ships came and went; their passengers stayed one, two or three nights in the hotel and were on their way. There was life and movement. The busy intentness of people conveyed to Ruth the sense, which she had almost lost in the year she had been at Elephant Walk, that life had a purpose. She did not know what that purpose was, but it was written in the faces of strangers, and from it she drew a new strength.

Although she was no nearer a solution of her own problems, this contact with another world helped her to face them. Finally, it was events rather than her own muddled thinking which came brutally to Ruth's rescue.

One morning at breakfast she skimmed the dreary and uninformative war communiqués and was about to put down the newspaper in disgust, when the type began to blur as a paragraph caught her eye:

"We announce with regret that news has reached Ceylon that Captain John Geoffrey Wilding, formerly of Elephant Walk Estate, Ratnagalla, has been reported missing, believed killed."

For two days Ruth remained in her hotel suite in a state bordering upon collapse. Her little world narrowed and she realised, through her numb, dry-eyed grief, that she was now more than ever alone and that she must find from within the strength to continue. It was not until the blow fell that she realised with any real clarity what her feelings towards Geoffrey Wilding really were. Now she knew that she loved him very deeply. She did not know—never would know now—how much she herself had meant to Geoffrey Wilding. It might have been—and she faced the fact—very little. Even if this were so, she could find now no resentment. Life had ended for Geoffrey Wilding: it was beginning for his child.

During the long hours spent alone in the hotel, Ruth found herself coming under the influence of new thoughts and a new attitude to life. The sense of guilt and betrayal of George Carey began to recede into the background of conscience. She had owed a duty to him. She had failed in that duty. These were the stark facts. The lover whom she would have been ready to acknowledge as father of her child, was now beyond recall, for even thus early in the war the words "missing, believed killed" left very little room for hope.

She had failed George Carey, and nothing could alter that. Now there was another life to consider. Would it help to undo one betrayal by perpetrating another? Because she had been a bad wife, did it necessarily follow that she had to be a bad mother too? Whereas a week ago it would have eased her soul of much of its burden to have confessed everything to George Carey—and that she had not done so had been more for his sake than for her own—now she was not so sure. There had been three persons to consider before, and although one of them, Geoffrey Wilding, no longer need be considered, there were still three, only one of them completely innocent. Her own offence and Geoffrey Wilding's were too obvious. George Carey's had been a crime of ignorance, in supposing that the life he had offered her at Elephant Walk had been a complete life and one which should have satisfied her. His other crime, also one of ignorance, perhaps of false pride, too, had been in thrusting her, as he had, into the society of a man who had infinitely more to offer a young and attractive wife than he had himself. They were not grave crimes, those committed by George Carey, but they were crimes. As such, he had to pay for them. But the infant whose coming could not now be concealed much longer, had committed no crime, and Ruth was determined, even if she had proved a bad wife, she would try to be a good mother.

Some of her thinking was straight. Some of it perhaps was sheer sophistry, founded on expedience. But most of it sprang from the biological processes going on within her, processes which were changing a fearful and guilt-oppressed woman into a mother, whose horizon was beginning to be bounded by the needs of the new life conceived by her own fault and folly, but guilty of nothing itself. Whom would it benefit, Ruth asked herself, if she blazoned to the world the true story? *Cui bono?* Her own disgrace she could bear, just as she had been able to bear the knowledge of her own guilt but, as she now began to see things, she had no right to saddle the unborn son—and she knew it would be a son—with the burden of her own guilt.

Several long days and sleepless nights were to pass before Ruth reached her decision, but when she finally sat down to write to George, telling him the news that he was about to become a father, she marvelled—such is the resilience of the human conscience—that she could ever have been in doubt as to the proper course to adopt. She wrote to George Carey gladly, conscious as she did so that she was his benefactress, giving him the news which above all else, she knew, he would be happiest to receive.

There remained only, before she returned to Elephant Walk, to assuage her own sense of grief and loss that her son would never look up from his cradle into the eyes of his own father. That grief was peculiarly hers and must remain hers as part of the price she had to pay. She faced that, knowing that it would not be a small price. In a queer fashion, she was not able fully to understand, she did not doubt her ability to create, in order to house that grief and loss, a separate water-tight compartment of her being. She could never forget, nor indeed did she want to forget, for in the very act of forgetting there were the seeds of more betrayal. She must bear this son gladly, just as she had given herself gladly to the man who was his father. But to forget the night of passion they had spent together under the stars would, as Ruth saw things, be a betrayal. The adjustment of the balance between the conflicting memories and loyalties was just another part of the price she must pay, and that it was worth while she now no longer doubted.

In the letter which she wrote to George Carey, Ruth told him that she would return in another week, but if she stopped to think, she might have known that George Carey would be unable to wait so long. They met by accident in the lobby of the Galle Face Hotel. Ruth was just leaving for an early morning stroll before the heat of the day, while George had just arrived on the night train.

George's joy was too incoherent for repetition. To the amazement of staff and guests alike, George seized both Ruth's hands, dancing a mad fandango around the lobby with her, deaf to her laughing protests and blind to the possibility that such violent treatment might not be that prescribed for expectant mothers. There were tears in their eyes when they entered the lift which carried them up to the privacy of Ruth's suite.

Looking mistily at George's ruddy, beefy face and red-rimmed eyes, seeing the pride and joy he radiated, Ruth knew that, come what may, she had burned her boats and that the guilty knowledge in her heart must be smothered below the surface of conscience.

"Did you tell anyone, George?"

"Of course I did! What do you suppose? I told everyone. Do you think I could keep the news to myself? There wasn't time to see people, of course, so I just sent a chit to Gilly and Robbie before I dashed off to catch the night train. You should have seen old Appuhamy's face!"

"What did he say?" asked Ruth.

"He didn't say much, but the first thing he did, as you can imagine, was to pop out into the garden and tell the guvnor."

"Yes, he would," said Ruth thoughtfully, trying to check a deep sigh which would not be denied.

On their return to Elephant Walk, Appuhamy was at the top of the steps to greet them. His face smiled a welcome, but his eyes, as they met Ruth's, were cold, hard and suspicious, for Appuhamy remembered a bed which had not been slept in and a horseman cantering off into the first light of dawn.

Somehow, Ruth was able to forget Appuhamy's eyes in the anti-climax of homecoming, for out in the centre of the long veranda stood, shining in all the glory of new polish after some forty-five years of gathering dust in a lumber room, the most gigantic cradle Ruth had ever seen or imagined. Like everything else in the Big Bungalow, it was built massively of teak. No slender woman's arm could have rocked it, nor chance wind overturned it.

"But it's big enough for a baby elephant, George!" protested Ruth when her laughter had subsided.

"Well, you see, the guvnor was on the heavy side himself and, well, I suppose he thought I'd be, too. I can't wait, darling," said George in a hushed voice, "to see him in it."

"Nevertheless, George, I'm afraid you'll have to wait for a few months. Even at Elephant Walk, you know, these things take time."

In a spare bedroom, brought out from some obscure hiding-place, were vast piles of baby clothing. These, too, had been intended for George. While from another hiding-place a dozen baby's feeding bottles had emerged.

"You don't mean to tell me, George," asked Ruth in astonishment, "that you went and bought all these things?"

"Good Lord, no! I knew they were here somewhere. The guvnor showed me the trunks when I first came out to Ceylon, so I told Appuhamy to dig them out. It's rather a nice idea, I think, for him to wear the things that were intended for me. Unless"—he saw Ruth's face fall—"you'd rather get a new outfit?"

"I haven't examined them, George, but I expect, you know, that babies don't wear just the same things that they used to forty-five years ago."

"Yes, probably you're right, darling. We'll give this lot away and you must order whatever you think he ought to have—and don't forget that the best isn't too good for him."

*   *   *   *   *

"I think," said George, in the early part of the evening, his face puckered with distaste for his task, "I ought to tell you some bad news, darling."

"Bad news? What is it, George?" asked Ruth.

"I didn't want to spoil things by telling you before," said George, "but Geoffrey Wilding's missing. The paper says 'missing, believed killed', whatever that means."

"I'm very, very sorry, George," said Ruth. "It seems only a week or two since he was here."

✳

✳

✳

✳

✳ **CHAPTER TWELVE** ✳ ✳ ✳ ✳ ✳ ✳ ✳

Appuhamy returned to his little house at the rear of the Big Bungalow with slow, dragging footsteps. He had no taste for the task to which he was committed. He found Rayna prinking herself before a mirror, trying on the assorted finery he had bought for her in Kandy and, seemingly, deriving immense satisfaction from the task.

"There is bad news I must tell you," said Appuhamy. "The young man Wilding is reported by the newspapers to be dead: killed in the war."

The smile left Rayna's face. Appuhamy waited a little for the tears which did not come. After two or three minutes of silence Rayna went out into the garden, returning with four or five vivid scarlet hibiscus blooms. These, with the utmost deliberation, she arranged in her hair. Appuhamy sighed a sigh of relief. He had feared that the news would strike this gay, careless child a terrible blow, but it seemed the impact of it had scarcely touched her. It shook him, nevertheless, to observe such callous acceptance of the news.

"Child!" said Appuhamy reprovingly, watching while Rayna arranged the blooms with great care. "It is not seemly to go on strutting before a mirror when you have received such news. The young man Wilding was kind to you, was he not?" Rayna nodded. "Then, surely you can cease your games for a little while, if only as a mark of respect?"

"I am doing this for him," said Rayna, drawing herself erect and speaking in a tight voice. "He always said that I was most beautiful with the red flowers in my hair. I do this to please him."

It was not until then that the tears came, and then they came in a flood which would not be checked.

Life was not sitting so well on Appuhamy's conscience during the days which followed, when he remembered that it was his willingness to sacrifice this child upon the altar of Carey pride which was responsible for the heart-rending sobs which shook the girl's slender body.

The price he had paid for Carey honour was too high. What made it more bitter was the suspicion, if not the knowledge, that it had been paid in vain. Would the infant for whom the giant cradle had been made ready have a drop of Carey blood in its veins? Appuhamy doubted it. Nor was there any comfort to be gained by confiding his suspicions to his old master. He dared not do so.

The sobs of Rayna, who was paying the first part of the price, were *obbligato* to his solitary musings.

* * * * *

These days Ruth spent most of her time in the little summer-house at the end of the garden, which had been furnished comfortably. A canvas screen had been arranged in such a fashion that she could see the glorious panorama of the valley spread out beneath her, without being able to see the immense bulk of the Big Bungalow which, as the weeks passed, she liked less and less. It was a peaceful, beautiful spot, redolent with sweet smells. There was always the song of birds, the humming of bees and the multifarious sounds which came up from the valley below. These helped to destroy any feeling of loneliness.

Looking up from her book one hot breathless afternoon, Ruth found herself under the scrutiny of the loveliest young girl she had ever seen, who stood motionless, a very sweet but sad smile playing across her lips.

"Who are you?" asked Ruth, using English instinctively.

"I am Rayna," came the reply, surprisingly in the same language. "Appuhamy is my great-uncle."

"Do you live here?"

"I have lived here for some months."

"Then why is it I have never seen you before?"

"That is because Appuhamy told me I must not speak to you. If I did so, he thought you would be angry. But I have seen you many times, and to me it always seemed that you are lonely, so," she added with a shrug, "I have disobeyed Appuhamy and have come to talk with you."

"Was there something special you wished to say to me?" asked Ruth.

"No," was the surprised reply, "but I am lonely too, and I came to talk with you. That is all."

Rayna sat chatting for more than an hour. She came again the next day and for several days thereafter. Ruth found herself looking forward to these visits, which served to break the monotony of her life.

Appuhamy, when word of Rayna's meetings with Ruth came to his knowledge, did his best to prevent them. It was not until George Carey, at Ruth's insistence, pressed the matter, that he withdrew his opposition. His attitude towards Ruth was still one of watchful suspicion.

Everything in Appuhamy's life stemmed from Tom Carey. He loved and respected George Carey as an individual, but first and foremost he regarded George Carey as a trust reposed in him by Tom Carey. The respect he accorded to Ruth, which was unfailing, he gave to her because she was the wife of Tom Carey's son, and as such was entitled to respect. He had never dared to voice his suspicions during his frequent visits to Tom Carey's grave, because he did not like to contemplate his old master's wrath if he should know that a grandson who would be only a grandson in name was to inherit Elephant Walk. Upon such a matter, Appuhamy realised, he must be certain or remain silent. Now, whatever his suspicions, there could never be certainty.

Appuhamy, however, did not hate Ruth. If hate were the proper word, he hated the situation which might so easily have brought shame to the Careys. Indeed, from close observation of George Carey since the latter had learned of Ruth's pregnancy, Appuhamy noted with satisfaction many changes in his employer. George Carey was no longer morose and sullen. He was drinking less. The prospect of a child had opened new vistas to him, and Appuhamy was philosopher enough to realise that whether the child Ruth was bearing were his own or not, George Carey could only be hurt now by the knowledge that he was not the father. If such were the case, the knowledge must at all costs be kept from him. So, stifling his early antagonism, Appuhamy watched wonderingly while Ruth and Rayna fell into an easy relationship which, in so far as their different races, stations of life and outlook would permit, was intimate.

"I have watched you with the Mistress," Appuhamy said to Rayna one evening. "It seems to me that you are too familiar. You do not treat her with enough respect. She is, do not forget it, the wife of my master."

"She is a woman," replied Rayna, with an indifferent shrug. "I am a woman. Women do not think so much of respect."

Appuhamy realised with a shock that any control of Rayna's actions and thoughts which might have been his had passed from his hands.

It was strange that these two widely-differing women, thrown so much into each other's company, never mentioned the one human being who, during these long weeks, was uppermost in the mind of each.

Until Rayna's contact with Ruth, she had always, like most of her people, regarded the business of childbirth lightly and was, accordingly, appalled by the many evidences of Ruth's discomfort and suffering.

"I," said Rayna airily and without self-consciousness, "have never shared my bed with a man. Tell me, is it worth all you are suffering?"

"That," said Ruth, embarrassed by the frankness of the question, "I do not know yet. Tell me, Rayna. Why don't you marry? You are so beautiful, you could take your pick of all the young men."

"I am a Rodiya," replied Rayna, "and I can only marry a Rodiya."

Ruth listened with interest while Rayna told the sad story of her people.

"There is something I do not understand," she said at length. "If you are Appuhamy's great-niece, then Appuhamy, too, is a Rodiya, whereas I have always been told that he is of high caste."

Rayna hung her head in shame and did not reply. Ruth found herself wondering why Appuhamy should have embarked upon the deception of calling Rayna his great-niece, but since this seemed to be none of her affair, she did not press the matter. "Surely," she went on, "you will want to marry sooner or later?"

"I will not marry a low-caste man and live like a pig in a village," replied Rayna fiercely. "I do not think I shall ever marry. Sometimes I think that my heart is broken."

Ruth smiled at this. "It's too early to say that, Rayna," she said gently. "Hearts don't break easily. You will find that to be true."

"Of that I am not sure," said Rayna. "Once, a long time ago, I loved a man very much."

"It cannot have been so very long ago, Rayna, if you are not yet sixteen."

"Perhaps. But it seems a long time ago. I lay awake all one night in his bed, waiting for him and he did not come. Then, when I was so tired that I could not keep awake any longer, I fell asleep, and while I slept, he came, saw me and went away. I was very ashamed."

"Ashamed? Why?"

"Because he knew then that I wanted to give myself to him and he did not want me."

"You should think yourself very fortunate, Rayna, that he did not take what you offered him before he went away. What was he like, this man?"

"He was tall and strong, like a prince. He had eyes which laughed. He did not mean to be cruel, but he was cruel. Sometimes I hated him because he behaved as though I were a child. But most of the time I loved him, and I was very unhappy when he went away."

Life and fiction are full of the strange fancies which come to pregnant women. Ruth had her share of these, but more than all she began to see things through clear, unclouded eyes. It came to her in one of these moments of clarity that she must not, like Rayna, be ashamed. The thought which preyed upon the mind of this lovely girl, whom Ruth was beginning to love, was not shame that she had offered herself to this man, but shame that the offer had been rejected. Ruth now saw that in trying to assuage her own grief at Wilding's presumed death, she had been wrong in being so willing to accept as a possibility that to Wilding their relationship had been nothing more than a light episode. This was wrong thinking, and to go on allowing herself to believe this was to soil the memory of the child's father and, therefore, to allow her own sense of shame to communicate itself to the child already stirring within her.

To admit, as so many did, that an innocent baby was conceived in sin and born into shame was to damn a young life. Her son, Ruth was determined, should be a happy child, conceived of a great love and, cost what it might in suffering, she would go on thinking of Geoffrey Wilding as a very gallant man who had loved her dearly and who, if he had not laid down his life for what he believed to be his duty, would have come gladly to claim his own.

How, Ruth asked herself more soberly, would this new attitude reconcile itself to her life with George? How was she going to fill her baby with the sense of this heroic love and still, while doing so, endure George Carey's pride and joy in the embryo Carey whom he had not, in fact, sired? That, Ruth recognised, was not going to be easy. Geoffrey Wilding and George Carey must, for the future, occupy separate compartments of her being, and the task of keeping them thus apart was going to be her own private hell: the hell she had created for herself. For a little while, she knew, George Carey must not exist for her. She must at all costs keep him at bay, thrust him out of her consciousness until her son should be born. Until then her love for Geoffrey Wilding and his for her must remain a beautiful thing, unsullied by any sordid thought or admission. Geoffrey, her beloved, must remain the knight in shining armour who had loved her only less than the honour which had sent him off to the war.

The great stumbling-block in the way of this new concept was somehow the Big Bungalow itself. Ruth knew now that at all costs her baby must not be born there and that, during the weeks she remained at Elephant Walk, she must see as little as possible of it.

"George," she said gaily on the day this thought came to her, "I want a place here that belongs to me and to my son, and to us alone. Somewhere where nobody can come—nobody, not even you—without express invitation. Will you give orders that nobody, unless I call, may come to the summer-house? Please humour me in this George. I and my son both want it."

"Our son, darling," said George reproachfully.

"He is mine now, George. Later he will be ours. Humour me, please George. Pregnant women must be humoured. Please give instructions at once that nobody, nobody, must come to the summer-house unless I ask them."

"Can't I come there sometimes?"

"No, George; not even you. My son will share it with me."

"But he's my son too, darling," said George obtusely, in a way that made a black rage enter into Ruth's heart.

"Not yet, George," said Ruth, controlling herself with difficulty. "He will be, but just now he is mine, and he and I want the summer-house to ourselves."

"Leave it to me, darling," said George with a sigh, "but while you're up there with him alone, don't let him forget his father."

"I won't, George. I promise."

The Big Bungalow began more than ever to grate upon Ruth's nerves. She was beginning to hate it. A strange fear came to her that her baby would be born marked with the elephant's head which was stencilled on the tea-chests at the factory, embroidered on the servants' coats, engraved upon every piece of silver in the bungalow, and was the central design of every piece of crockery. The thought so preyed upon her mind that, at her urgent request, a coolie was sent to Badulla to buy plain white china, knives, forks and spoons, and pieces of linen which bore no mark at all. Appuhamy was horror-struck when, upon George's stringent orders, he and the other servants had to wear completely plain jackets.

"Even a pregnant woman," Appuhamy muttered angrily, "should be proud of the mark of her husband's family. It is a fine mark, known with honour all over the world where men drink tea, and the woman wants to hide it. . . ."

In late May, during the eighth month of Ruth's pregnancy, when the south-west monsoon was at its height, confined by torrential rain to the gloom of the bungalow, she knew that she could not remain any longer. For the sake of peace, she had seemed to give way to George's urgent insistence that the baby be born in the Big Bungalow, but in her heart she had never intended to allow this. Arrangements had already been made, at very great cost, for a doctor and two nurses to make the journey, when Ruth announced to the horror-struck George that, in defiance of the monsoon and his own wishes, she wanted her baby to be born in a Colombo hospital.

"But you don't know what you're asking, darling," George protested. "During the monsoon the road between here and Bandarawella is impossible. Great chunks of the trail get washed away every year. I just can't allow you to do it."

"Whether you allow me to or not, George, I am going. Either you will make arrangements for me to be carried there in a chair or—it's no good looking horrified—I shall ride to Bandarawella. Esmeralda knows the way and she will take me there."

The battle lasted several days, but at length George, fearing that continued opposition would do more harm than acquiescence, agreed to the mad proposal.

The night before Ruth left, even above the roar of the rain, was heard the shrill trumpeting of the bull elephant, leading his herd down from the dank chill of the rain-soaked jungle in the mountains to the warmth of the plains below. This time Ruth could again detect mockery, derision and triumph in the hideous sound, and to her fevered imagination, it seemed that the knowledge denied to any other human being—the imminent birth of a Carey heir who was not of Carey blood—was known to the malicious brute who lurked out there in the darkness, trumpeting his mockery of everything belonging to the Careys. For the first time in more than thirty years the herd penetrated the stout fence which surrounded the Big Bungalow, smashing it to matchwood. They uprooted a score or more of young peach and orange trees, trampling and destroying most of the kitchen garden and, as they continued on their way downhill, smashing through a poultry house which barred their way.

Ruth restrained George from going out with his gun in what would probably have been a vain attempt to locate and shoot the beasts. Although she lay in stark terror listening to the din without, there came to her once again a sense of sympathy. She felt that she understood the hatred and the anguish which tortured the elephant herd when they saw the gleaming lights from the huge bungalow which had been thrown astride their ancient trail and upon their time-honoured resting place.

In the first morning light Ruth saw the havoc wrought the night before, and a great sense of oppression lifted from her as the four stalwart chair-coolies, the rain streaming from their bare backs, carried her up the hill and out of sight of the bungalow she had learned to loathe and fear.

It was easier, somehow, lying in the small white-washed room in the Colombo nursing-home, from which the rest of the world was excluded by shutters against which the sun beat vainly, giving place to torrential rain the day after Ruth's arrival.

Although doctor and nurses wondered why this healthy young woman had come to the nursing-home several whole weeks before she need, Ruth was thankful that she had done so. The characterless impersonality of the room was restful. It evoked no memories. There was nothing about it anyone could like or, equally, dislike.

She experienced a strange languor: the kind which comes from complete surrender. In the dim light and cathedral hush which surrounded her all day, were no problems, no responsibilities. She felt herself borne upon a gentle rhythmic tide against which, even had she the inclination, it were futile to struggle. Only one thing worried her now, and this worry was put behind her within a very short time of her arrival in the nursing-home.

"Doctor," she said, "I expect my husband asked you to telegraph him so that he could be here, if possible, when the baby is born. Did he?"

"Why, yes, Mrs Carey. He did."

"And, of course, you agreed?"

"Yes, Mrs Carey. It was a very normal request, and I saw no reason to refuse."

"Then, doctor, I want you to break that promise."

"You place me in a very difficult position, Mrs Carey."

"Would it place you in a less difficult position if I had another doctor? I am prepared, you know, if necessary, to go to a hospital or another nursing-home, but I can't and won't have my husband here when the baby is born."

The doctor was used to strange requests and stranger fancies on the part of his patients so, reluctantly, he agreed to her request. At these times, he knew from experience, women took strange and unreasoning dislikes to their husbands and to other people. His first duty, as he saw it, was to his patient.

With this promise to reassure her, Ruth fell gratefully back on to her pillow, content to wait until the tide, which was carrying her along in its soft arms, should reach the flood.

Thomas Lakin Carey was born with the minimum of fuss on a sultry day in June 1915. Almost up to the hour of his birth torrential rain had been falling, but it ceased abruptly and the sun came out to welcome him. It was not until he was four days old that George Carey first saw him. The telegram despatched two or three hours after his birth took two days to reach Elephant Walk, for the rain had washed out the roads and travel was dangerous, almost to the point of impossibility.

"I don't as a rule think babies look like anything except suet puddings," said George Carey, as he surveyed the infant held out for his approval, "but 'pon my soul! he looks every inch a Carey. Even I can see the likeness, darling, can't you?"

Ruth chose that moment to close her eyes, and a moment later George Carey was whisked out of the room. "Let her sleep, Mr Carey," said the nurse. "It's sleep that she needs more than anything."

In the six weeks which elapsed before Ruth brought her son to Elephant Walk, there was time to begin the discipline which she knew she must impose upon herself if the months and years ahead were to be borne. She had to grow accustomed to the idea that Geoffrey Wilding's son was going to be fathered by another man, and must be brought up to love and respect that other man. Otherwise, the whole sorry business would be too impossibly unfair, and it had already been unfair enough. It now seemed to Ruth that if George Carey were to derive great joy and a new interest in life from the son he believed to be his, some of the wrong at least would have been righted. Selfishly, she knew too that the more happiness she was thus able to give George Carey, the lighter would be her own burden.

✳

✳

✳

✳

✳ **CHAPTER THIRTEEN**   ✳ ✳ ✳ ✳ ✳ ✳

The rain clouds were coming in from the south-west, piling up above the parched land like some stupendous staircase, tier upon tier, until it seemed that on the horizon there had been created a vast and incredible snow-covered mountain range. But still the rain did not fall.

Everywhere there were cracks in the rich earth. Tea bushes lay dying where the earth had broken away to expose their roots. No longer was the tea flush lettuce-green. The bushes were covered instead with harsh dark green leaves, dust-covered and brittle to the touch. The monsoon, nearly always as punctual as the rising and falling of the tide, had chosen this year to be late. The dry weather had not only been longer but hotter than usual. The whole valley was gasping for breath. Human tempers were already frayed. The nights, for some time past, had been hideous with the quarrels which arose in the coolie lines. Dry-weather boils and ugly sores added to the general misery. Caked with dust and pus, flies settled on them in clusters. The morning sick-parades had swelled to outrageous numbers.

Thomas Lakin Carey, almost lost in the immensity of his teak cradle, which also served as a play-pen round which he crawled on long voyages of discovery, was in tune with the rest of the world: hot, flushed and fretful. He, too, turned his eyes from time to time in mute appeal in the direction of the rain clouds. In his almost eleven months of life, he had never been quite so uncomfortable.

Nevertheless, Tommy, despite the heat and the flies and the dust, was the picture of health. The same could not be said of his mother. Ruth was pale and drawn. She wore now, like a familiar garment, an air of hopeless impassivity. Much of it was due to the weather, but much was due also to the circumstances of her life. It had been a hard year for her.

George Carey, for the first two months after Ruth's return with Tommy, had turned his back upon the tempting array of whisky decanters. But after that, their allure had been too much for him, and he was drinking steadily, sullenly, as though to anaesthetise himself from a world which was changing faster than he could adapt himself to it.

The heat throbbed and pulsated as though it were a living, sentient thing which made the landscape dance dizzily before the eyes. Life waited tensely, as though hung in a void, until the healing rain should fall.

George Carey, despite all the difficulties, was making more money than he had ever made before. Prices had risen as a thirsty world cried out for more tea. Already, from the Ratnagalla district alone, more than a million pounds weight of tea had gone to the bottom of the sea. Ruth found herself trying to think of a million pounds of tea in terms of the flying fingers of the pluckers, the sacks of green leaf sent down the wire chutes to the factory. So much human sweat, thought, care and intelligence wasted.

Ruth and Tommy were almost strangers to George Carey these days. In the early morning George visited Tommy briefly before going out into the fields. At noon when he returned, Tommy was having his midday sleep. When George returned in the evening, his first thought now was the whisky decanter and, after he had taken two or three stiff drinks, Ruth refused to allow him to approach Tommy too closely.

"You surely don't want the child to grow up thinking of you as the man who reeks of whisky, George? Children's noses are very sensitive, you know. I've watched Tommy wrinkle his nose with disgust, as I want to sometimes, when you breathe whisky over his cradle."

"Good God, Ruth! Be reasonable!" George replied. "With the work I'm doing, surely I'm entitled to a drink?"

"Yes, of course you are, George," said Ruth, "but all I'm asking you to do is to come and say good-night to Tommy before you start drinking, and not afterwards."

For reply, George Carey turned away angrily and a few seconds later came the shattering sound of a door being banged violently. Somehow, although Ruth hated admitting it even to herself, the rare occasions when George Carey allowed his usually good temper to be ruffled, made things easier. It lessened, in some queer fashion, her sense of guilt. When, as was usually the case, he gave way to her, tried to turn away her irritability with a soft answer, treating her as though she could do no wrong, she became filled with a mixture of shame, gratitude and wonderment that this awkward, unobservant man could be so considerate. His humility and devotion added to, rather than subtracted from, the agonies of remorse she was forced to endure in her own private hell.

Strange and ill-understood processes had gone on in Ruth during the months of her pregnancy and the weary weeks in the nursing-home and afterwards. In order to heighten the illusion in her mind that Tommy was born of a great and heroic love, she had woven stirring little romantic tales through the fabric of her daydreams until they had assumed the guise of reality. So vividly had these fancies imprinted themselves upon her imagination, that it was Geoffrey Wilding who was, not only Tommy's father, but her husband and lover, and this gross man who beamed so amiably over Tommy's cradle was an interloper who had to be suffered, if not gladly, then in silence. The mere touch of George Carey's hand upon her shoulder was now so repulsive that it made her shudder, and much of the time she spent with him was devoted to little artifices designed so as to make actual contact unnecessary, as well as hiding the aversion she felt.

Only Tommy, Ruth mused, now made life tolerable, and there were moments when even he accentuated its difficulties.

Still the rains did not come. The cracks in the parched earth grew wider. A deathly stillness brooded over everything, broken only by the dry, rasping cacophony of the cicadas which, alone of all creation, seemed to enjoy the heat and oppression, as though these had been created for their express benefit. The cicadas had always been present as an *obbligato* against the pattern of all the other noises, but now these last were still, and only the cicadas raised their voices in their hideous, tuneless, rhythmless chorus. It seemed to Ruth's jangled nerves so much in keeping with a futile world when she read in some natural-history book that the grating, rasping song of the male cicada was his mating song and that—irony of ironies!—the female of the species was deaf!

One morning when the rain clouds had approached so close that it seemed the hoped-for rain could not be long delayed, George Carey returned early to the bungalow, wearing a worried, harassed expression.

"From now onwards, and until I give you the word," he told Ruth, "you mustn't go outside the garden. The coolies are in an ugly mood," he went on to explain. "I've never seen them like this before. There's nothing to be done now except wait for the rain. Work has come to a standstill, and idleness isn't good for them, but in this heat I just can't invent useless tasks to keep them occupied. There's no flush to pluck, and even the blasted weeds have stopped growing. I've shut down the factory this morning. Good God!" he said, holding his hands to his temples, "I feel as though I'm going to burst!"

"Have a bath and a change, dear," said Ruth gently, "and then let's drink a jug of cold limejuice and water. I can't think of anything nicer."

"I can!" said George in a voice which was very near a snarl. Breaking the habit of years, he rang for whisky, pouring himself out several big ones.

What a strange thing it was, Ruth mused wistfully, looking at George, who was lying slumped and miserable in a long chair, that although she could not bear to have George touch her, she still harboured none but the kindest feelings for him. Indeed, now she came to reflect upon the matter, her inner feelings towards him as a human being had never changed.

"I have a terrible feeling," said Ruth that evening, "that we're wasting our lives. It's not only the weather and the war news, but we seem to be living our lives as though each day means nothing: living for some future that may never come. Can't we learn somehow to live for today, so that just sometimes we can go to bed in the evening with the satisfying feeling that we've extracted something, something that can never be taken away from us, out of the day?"

This and the talk which followed made George more thoughtful than usual. He drank less that evening although, by the way he eyed the whisky decanter, Ruth knew he was longing to drink a lot. They chatted pleasantly of light, cheerful things, in a way they had not done for months. And as they chatted, Ruth's mood of irritation and vague fear passed. When it was gone, she found herself contemplating George, despite the difference in their ages, in a maternal way. The illusion lingered that he was a clumsy small boy and that she must look after him. But the more she thought of him indulgently in this manner, and the more she warmed to him with the old friendliness, the less acceptable he became to her as a husband. This last, she knew, was something out of her control and no mere matter of mood.

"In this heat, George," she said as they were going to bed, "I think I'd prefer to sleep alone."

"I know, dear," said George with quick sympathy in his voice, "I toss and turn all the time and I expect I snore like hell."

"You do snore sometimes, George, and it can be very trying, you know. So I'll sleep in my own room until the weather changes."

"I'm sorry," said George contritely. "Try and get a good night's sleep, dear. That's half the battle."

Ruth, however, believed as she entered her own room and closed the door that, no matter how the weather changed, she could never again share that hideous, gigantic four-poster bed with George.

When dawn broke, the clouds were still banked high and a parched world still gasped for breath. In the middle of the morning Ruth looked up from her bandage rolling as she heard the clatter of a cantering horse's hooves. "I think something is the matter, Rayna," she said, sensing that George would rather talk to her alone if anything serious had happened.

Flinging the reins to a servant, George strode quickly up the steps to the veranda. "Come into the lounge here, Ruth," he said in a tense voice. "I don't want anyone to hear what I have to say."

"What is it, George?" asked Ruth anxiously.

"Get together a few things for yourself and Tommy as quickly as you can—now, at once—and ride to Bandarawella. There's not a moment to be lost."

"But why, George?"

"There's no time to argue," was the fierce reply. "You've got to be on the road within an hour. I've already arranged for a stretcher for Tommy."

"But what's the matter, George? You've got to tell me."

"Cholera's the matter," he said, in a subdued voice. "So far, I'm the only person who knows it. It must have been brought here by one of the coolies back from the coast, and I've got to report it. Don't you see that once I've reported it, the whole district'll be quarantined and we'll be cut off from the rest of the world for weeks? Aside from that, there's the danger to Tommy and yourself. Cholera isn't pretty. Now, there's no time to be lost. Get packed."

"Will you come with us, George?"

"Don't talk like a fool!" he snapped in reply. "I've got to stay here, whether I like it or not. If I'm not here to give orders and see that they're obeyed, the coolies would go to pieces. As soon as you're out of sight over the brow of the hill I'm going to segregate the sick man and everyone who's been in contact with him. I'd be shot at dawn for letting even you go, but it's a risk that I'm prepared to take. There'll be stark panic here before many hours are out. You've never seen a crowd of scared Tamil coolies. I have. You wouldn't recognise them for the docile, tractable people you know. . . . When you get to Bandarawella, behave normally. Appear surprised when you hear that there has been a cholera outbreak here."

"Tommy and I aren't going, George," said Ruth firmly.

"Don't talk like a damn fool! I'm ordering you to go—now!"

"It's you who are the damn fool, George," said Ruth quietly. "It isn't any good shouting at me because I'm not going. Nor is Tommy. Our place is here, with you. I daresay I'm not much of a success as a wife, George, but at least I'm not the kind that leaves when—who knows?—she may be most wanted . . ."

"There's no time to go into all that sort of thing now," blustered George.

ELEPHANT WALK   185

". . . and even if our marriage hasn't been anything very wonderful," continued Ruth, as though she had not heard him, "we're friends, and one doesn't leave friends in the lurch. It isn't the smallest bit of good arguing with me. My mind is made up. Besides, it's much too hot to argue."

George Carey looked searchingly and wonderingly at Ruth, realising that she meant what she said. Since he had no means of enforcing his orders, he accepted the decision with the best grace he could find.

"I'm frightened, Tommy, terribly frightened," said Ruth, looking down into the fretful child's eyes. "I'm frightened for you, and even frightened for me. But it wouldn't be right to go now. He is staying, because it's his duty to. Our place is with him, Tommy, don't you see? We can't take everything and give nothing. We have a duty, too. Your daddy was killed doing his duty, and we'll do ours."

Ruth did not see George again until the late afternoon. "There's no doubt about it," he then said gloomily. "There are only eight cases so far, but by the look of them, not one of them will last the night. The coolies know what it is now, and they're almost frantic with fear. I've sent a man for police help, and I'm hoping that by tomorrow, every road and path out of the valley will be guarded. Only the threat of being shot will keep the contacts where I've put them. At the moment, I've got two armed watchmen keeping an eye on them, but if I don't go back, I expect the watchmen'll bolt."

"Isn't there anything I can do?" asked Ruth.

"Yes. Look after Tommy. Cholera's a fly-borne disease. See to it that no flies get near his food or anything he handles. For that matter, the same applies to everyone in the bungalow. Have every fly-trap and every fly-paper put into service. Swat any fly you see and, I don't care how much it upsets the staff, give orders and see that they're obeyed. In the meanwhile, I'll see to it that the bungalow and outbuilding are flooded with antiseptics."

"But, George," Ruth reminded him, "the servants don't take kindly to orders from me."

"If one of them shows any signs of being awkward," said Carey, "I'll kick him from hell to breakfast time. Meanwhile, don't stray beyond the garden and, when I'm not here, every minute of every hour have your shotgun and a few cartridges handy. Maybe I'm scaring you unnecessarily, but better that way than the other."

"But why, George, should I need a gun?"

"Because," replied George, "people in a panic are unpredictable, and from now onwards nobody—nobody bar me and the people I authorise—may come near the place."

Ruth herself in these moments felt a fear bordering on panic.

"It's not a damn bit of good getting scared now," said George roughly. "You're here at your own wish. You could have gone when I told you to. And you should have gone. Now it's too late and," he added with a ferocity Ruth had never seen in him before, "by the Holy God! if anything happens to Tommy, I'll never forgive you— never. Do you hear me?"

Cholera!

Only one block of coolie lines was affected so far. All the eight cases lived within a few yards of each other and had shared the same sanitary arrangements. Fortunately, in the estate storerooms were huge quantities of disinfectants. These were scattered around with a prodigal hand, while George Carey, a revolver strapped to his belt and a double-barrelled shotgun in the crook of his arm, enforced his orders and compelled the terrified people who had been in contact with the eight cases to remain where they were.

"We shall die of the sickness if we stay here," they wailed.

"You'll die with bullet holes in you if you try to get away," replied George. "Everything is being done that can be done to keep you safe from the sickness. Your pay will go on as usual. All you have to do is to stay here and obey orders."

Two young men, wide-eyed with terror, bored their way through the back of one of the houses in the lines and began to crawl through the tea to freedom. George Carey allowed them to get to a distance where a charge of shot would not injure them severely, and then fired in their direction. Screaming with pain, the men were brought back ignominiously and for an hour were tied to posts so that everyone could see their peppered backs and be warned by the example.

On the second day after the outbreak the dispenser vanished at the time when he was most needed.

On the third day there were fourteen new cases. The first eight were all dead and, under supervision, had been buried hastily in a pit filled with quick-lime.

On the fourth day there were only three fresh cases. By now some of the burden had been taken off Carey's shoulders by the arrival of armed police, who patrolled every road and pathway out of the Ratnagalla Valley. A hundred times a day eyes were turned upwards to the skies in supplication for the rain which would not come.

George Garey, meanwhile, was going about like a sleepwalker. In ninety-six hours he had only had some four hours sleep, snatched at odd intervals.

"Isn't there something I can do, George?" Ruth kept asking.

"Nothing," was the terse reply, "except see that no harm comes to Tommy. Any trouble with the staff?"

"No, George. They obey me in everything. I think they're badly scared, too. Any new cases? How's everything going—outside, George?"

"Forty odd cases so far, and every one of them fatal. But only two new cases this morning. God! If only the rain would come, the cholera would go as quickly as it came."

The rain clouds came tantalisingly near and then receded to the horizon, where they piled up in mockery of the suffering world beneath.

To Ruth's eyes, George Carey seemed to be shrinking. The flesh left his cheeks and jowl. Twice she saw him pierce new holes in a leather belt. She realised for the first time, seeing his bone formation as it was intended to be seen, that, as a young man, he must have been very handsome. Now he looked so drawn and ill that Ruth was frightened for him.

"Surely you've done enough?" she said when, on the sixth day, he seemed on the point of collapse.

"There's nothing much I can do now," he said, slurring his words with fatigue. "Provided the dead are buried at once, all I have to do is to let the others see that I'm not scared. If they really knew how scared I am, it would communicate itself to them in a flash and they'd die like flies from sheer fright."

"But surely, now the police are here, you can relax?"

"Listen, Ruth," said George wearily. "I don't think you quite understand. We Careys have done pretty well out of Elephant Walk. The old man created a sort of legend of Carey superiority. It's all my eye and Aunt Fanny, of course, but I've managed to live off it pretty comfortably. They can't look after themselves, poor devils, so somebody's got to do it for them. That someone's me. They nearly panicked this morning. A fellow I had been talking to ten minutes before, suddenly pitched over and fell on his face. I took his temperature—not that that did him any bloody good—and it was 105. He was dead an hour later. Don't you see, they've got something to be scared about, and if they really took it into their heads to stampede, nothing I or the police could do would stop them. They'd just be shot down like rabbits. Some would be bound to get away and then, before you knew it, there might be cholera loose all over the island. At the moment, they're more scared of my shotgun than they are of cholera, but God help us if it goes the other way!" He slumped into a chair. "Just going to take half an hour's shut-eye," he said thickly. "Half an hour, not a minute more. I rely on you to wake me."

At about noon on the eighth day the silence which brooded over the valley became intensified. With an abruptness that was startling, as though in obedience to a word of command, even the cicadas ceased their hideous, futile cacophony. The dense cloud banks which had come up from the south-western horizon seemed to press down upon the earth. The silence which brooded over everything, instead of being negative, the mere absence of sound, had become positive, highly charged with menace.

Ruth was startled out of her daydreams by the sudden silence, in the manner of a ship's engineer who wakes from the deepest sleep when the rhythmic beat of his engines suddenly stops. There came to her the strange fancy, as she stepped out on to the veranda, that an army of trumpeters, their trumpets at their lips, were drawing in deep breaths preparatory to sounding a tremendous blast when the signal should be given. It was as though pent-up forces, incalculably great, were about to be released. Instinctively, Ruth held her breath, bracing herself for the shock which, it seemed, could not be long delayed.

Something heavy fell with a plop on to a dusty flower-bed. Ruth looked at it puzzled. It moved, gathering dust as it rolled into a little hollow, and then stayed still. It was some seconds before she realised that it had been a rain drop. A full half minute passed before another fell. Instead of leaving a wet splash upon the parched soil, it had the qualities of quicksilver, for it divided into two parts upon a tiny hillock of earth, each part running, covered with a skin of dry dust, leaving no trail of moisture. A third. A fourth. A dozen together. Then once more a brief lull.

Then, as though the prayers of a suffering world had been heard, a chill breeze stirred the lifeless air like a ghostly whisper, and the blessed rain began to fall. There were no raindrops now. The rain fell like rods of polished glass which, when gusts of wind broke their rigidity, became solid sheets of water.

Even now relief had not come to the earth, for the water ran off its surface, leaving it dry, gathering in crevices and in every hollow. Every tiny channel became a rivulet, every steep gulley a cascade and every ravine a mighty roaring torrent. The tattoo which beat upon the roof of the Big Bungalow was like the chorus of ten thousand kettledrums. Then, when the earth was ready, it opened its arms to the blessed rain. The water no longer ran like quicksilver over dry dust. The earth took on again its rich, warm, natural brown as it sucked up the healing rain, dragging the life-giving moisture down to parched taproots, making it possible for life to go on.

The rain brought the end of the cholera. The healing water washed the lines clean while, for the first time, even the sick showed signs of wanting to recover.

When George Carey, stumbling like a drunken man, staggered wearily on to the veranda of the Big Bungalow that evening, there was triumph in his bearing.

"It's all right now," he said thickly, barely able to keep his feet. "They'll stay put now without me. Thanks for staying, darling. Only half of me wanted you to go, and I'm glad you didn't. I expect," he said, pouring out the first drink he had tasted for more than a week, "that this will make me as drunk as a lord! 'Fraid I've been a bit rough with you lately. If I have, I'm sorry, darling, I . . ." George Carey was asleep.

Ruth looked down upon him with friendly, understanding eyes, wondering at his unsubtle ability to play upon her heartstrings. If he had tried to do so, she knew he would have failed grotesquely. These last days had given him something he had never had before. Ruth realised now what it was: the look of maturity. Just in these few days his face had become hardened and lean. He had seen his duty and had done it simply, without fuss, and effectively. He had no subtlety. None at all. In time of crisis, Ruth mused, there was not much use for subtlety. Subtle people were so often all polish and no ballast, whereas George—she laughed a little grimly—was just the reverse. Looking at him through narrowed eyes, she wondered in a curiously detached fashion, whether it would be possible, upon the foundation of this new-found respect for him, to rebuild their moth-eaten, tattered marriage into something worth having. Gently, so as not to wake him, Ruth planted kisses on the eyes of the sleeping man. When she stood erect again, she found herself looking at Appuhamy, in whose eyes there was now no resentment. The look he gave her was gentle, tender and approving. He bowed more profoundly than usual and, when he stood erect, there was a smile of infinite sweetness upon his face.

*   *   *   *   *

Tired from his long ride from Bandarawella, John Gilliland threw the reins to a syce who came out to meet him, and fell gratefully into a long chair upon the veranda of the Big Bungalow. Appuhamy, with long experience to guide him, produced a whisky-and-soda.

"I've got some good news, Appuhamy," said Gilliland wondering shrewdly whether Appuhamy would find the news so good. "I learned last night in Colombo that Mr Wilding is not dead. He was badly wounded and taken prisoner and, somehow or other, managed to escape into Holland, and from there got safely back to England."

"That is indeed good news," said Appuhamy with an expressionless face.

"I thought you'd be pleased," said Gilliland. "Now I'd like a bath."

Appuhamy returned thoughtfully to his own quarters, where he found Rayna happily knitting a pair of tiny slippers in the fading light. It was upon the tip of his tongue to tell her the news which he knew would set her pulses dancing, but he decided to delay the announcement. A few minutes could make no difference to the girl, who had already abandoned all hope, whereas—who knew?—to make the announcement in his own fashion and in his own time might help him to turn suspicion into certainty.

Ruth was bending over Tommy's cot in the room that had become the night-nursery, when Appuhamy tapped on the door.

"Come in," called Ruth, without looking up.

"I came to tell the mistress that Mr Gilly has arrived. He will dine and sleep here."

"Thank you, Appuhamy," said Ruth in tones of dismissal, wondering, with a certain irritation, why he did not go.

"Mr Gilly brought news, Mistress," said Appuhamy softly, standing erect so that their eyes met on either side of the cot.

"News? What news?" asked Ruth.

"Good news, Mistress. Very good news."

Their eyes met again and seemed to lock.

"Well?"

"Mr Gilly brought news from Colombo that Mr Wilding was not killed," said Appuhamy, his old eyes watching Ruth intently. "Mr Wilding was taken prisoner and escaped. The master will be glad to hear the good news . . ."

The softly uttered words struck Ruth like a blow. She struggled to retain her hold on consciousness while a pair of keen old eyes, blazing with triumph, were fixed upon her. Appuhamy did not shift his gaze until Ruth toppled over in a dead faint. Because he was a well-trained servant, it was almost instinctive for him to go to her aid, but just as he was about to help her to her feet, he paused. For three or four whole minutes he stood, with arms folded and eyes blazing, waiting for her to recover consciousness.

When at last Ruth's eyes opened, she saw him standing there. Coldly Appuhamy looked down at the sleeping Tommy and then at his mother, who still lay where she had fallen, her eyes rounded with fear and horror. Slowly, contemptuously, Appuhamy turned on his heel and walked out of the room. His doubts were doubts no longer.

"Mr Gilly is here, Master," said Appuhamy to George Carey when the latter arrived some fifteen minutes later.

George Carey took the proffered whisky decanter and glass greedily. "Does the mistress know?" he asked wearily.

"I have told the mistress," replied Appuhamy gravely. "The master's bath is ready."

"Hallo, George," called John Gilliland, emerging from his room. "What do you think of the news?"

"Hallo, Gilly! Have a drink, old sport! What news?" asked George Carey.

"The news of young Wilding's escape, of course. Didn't Appuhamy tell you?"

"Good God!" ejaculated Carey. "That's wonderful! Why didn't you tell me, Appuhamy? Good news isn't so plentiful these days that I want to have any kept from me. Why on earth didn't you tell me, man?"

"I am sorry, Master," replied Appuhamy, "but I forgot."

"Forgot!" said Carey when Appuhamy was out of earshot. "There you are, Gilly. There's the difference between an Asiatic and a European. Forgot! How the hell could he forget? I must tell Ruth the good news. She'll be tickled pink. Wounded badly, eh? Taken prisoner and escaped through Holland. By God! that's wonderful. Go on, Gilly, you tell Ruth," added George as Ruth herself appeared on the scene. "Gilly's got some good news for us, darling."

"That *is* wonderful!" said Ruth, when John Gilliland had repeated his story. "Simply wonderful! I think, George, I'll have a drink. Make it a good big one, just to celebrate."

"I'm proud that he worked here at Elephant Walk," said Carey when the glasses were filled. "Here's good health and long life to John Geoffrey Wilding, and a speedy return to Elephant Walk. After a toast like that," he added, "we ought to smash the glasses."

Three empty glasses were hurled down on to the teak floor of the veranda. Two of them splintered into tinkling fragments, but one, that thrown by Ruth, rolled unbroken to the edge of the veranda.

"Dashed funny that!" said Carey, picking it up. "We must keep it and give it to Wilding when he returns. Now let's get tight!"

"Yes, let's," said Gilliland. "Just for a change!" Ruth's calm reception of the news was somewhat of an anticlimax to him. Indeed, looking narrowly at her, he thought she seemed quite untouched by it. Perhaps, after all, his suspicions had been unfounded.

George Carey, meanwhile, was writing a cablegram. "How does

this sound?" he asked when he had finished: "'Congratulations. Have just heard wonderful news. Best wishes from George, Ruth and Gilly.'"

"We mustn't forget Tommy!" said Ruth.

"Good Lord, no!" said George, inserting Tommy's name. "I'll send a coolie off with this at once."

❋

❋

❋

❋

❋ **CHAPTER FOURTEEN** ❋ ❋ ❋ ❋ ❋ ❋

In the early part of the year 1917 a gaunt, emaciated man, limping badly and gazing round him from deeply sunken eyes, stepped off the night train into the cool early morning air at Bandarawella. Not far from the train he espied his old syce waiting with a horse, scrutinising the passengers as they stepped on to the platform. It was not until he met the look of blank non-recognition in the syce's eyes that Geoffrey Wilding realised how the last two and a half years must have changed him.

The syce only recognised Wilding when addressed by name in a familiar voice. He looked shocked and horrified by his employer's appearance.

"I was to give you this," he said, fumbling in his waistcloth for a letter.

Stuffing the letter into his pocket, Wilding limped painfully across to the hotel. Here, also, he was not recognised until he had signed the register. Relaxed in a long chair, he opened the letter, which was in George Carey's handwriting:

Dear Wilding: Welcome back. I know you'll understand my not being there to meet you, but with the tea flush and everything else, I just can't get away. Tiffin has been arranged for you at the usual half-way point. Ruth and I will ride out to meet you and will wait tea for you at the trigonometrical survey mark. . . .

"Then," observed Wilding, with a mirthless laugh, "you'll have a bloody long wait!"

"Dear Carey," he wrote in reply. "If I could ride a horse, I'd still be in the Army. I'll wait here for a chair and coolies. Regards, J.G.W."

When the medical board had recommended Wilding for discharge, he had pulled every string in order to get out of England and back to Ceylon. In vain they had warned him that for a great many months he should be under proper medical care. In addition to his wounds, caused by a shell splinter which had penetrated the thigh to the bone, Wilding was suffering from what was then called shell-shock. Outside the scope of medical diagnosis, he was suffering from disillusionment. He had seen more than half his battalion wiped out because of the blundering incompetence of a man holding high rank, who had subsequently been rewarded by promotion. All he wanted now—and in this he was wiser than the doctors—was peace and quiet. Left to himself, he believed now that he could fight his way back to health and a normal outlook. During the weary months in hospital, his own bungalow, the thought of Ratnagalla Peak at dawn, the smiling vista of the uplands and the hum of contentment which rose from the valley, had been for him symbols of sanity in a world gone mad. He had clung to them, believing that if he could come once again under their influence, all would be well. Curiously, he had not given a thought to any of the people who lived in this peaceful spot. It was the place itself, not the people, which fired him with the determination to return.

On the second morning after his arrival at Bandarawella, a carrying-chair was waiting outside the hotel for him at dawn. Four strong coolies, bare-backed and clad in the scantiest loincloths, smiled him a welcome.

They reached the rim of the valley about half an hour before sundown. Wilding was soothed by the panorama spread out at his feet, remembering thoughtfully and with gratitude his own jumbled feelings when, before setting off for the war, he had paused at this same spot to take a lingering look, which might well have been the last, at the peaceful valley in which he had spent happy, if uneventful, years.

Below was the Big Bungalow and some three miles beyond it, just visible in the lengthening shadows of the night, his own bungalow. Thankful to have arrived, enfolded once again in the peace and beauty of it all, Wilding's head dropped forward and he fell asleep.

Half-way down the hill the four sweating coolies were halted peremptorily by Rayna, who had come to meet them. Clad in a scarlet silk skirt and a white blouse, she stood across the narrow trail barring their way. Her eyes were eager and misty, and her lips trembled. Wilding awoke with a start when the coolies halted, thinking he had arrived.

"I am very happy," said Rayna, coming alongside the chair, putting a hand shyly into his. She had planned to say more, but a blank look in Wilding's eyes forbade her.

Wilding, although Rayna did not know it, was tired to the point of utter exhaustion. To bodily fatigue was added the emotional strain of the day and his own nervous condition.

"Hallo," he said weakly. "Who are you? Wait, I remember. You're the girl whose portrait I painted. It wasn't bad, either," he added with a grin of amusement.

Wilding did not see the tragic look of disappointment on Rayna's face, nor hear the bitter sobs which shook her as he urged the chair coolies on. He was only sustained now by visions of cool sheets awaiting him at the end of the journey. Nothing else mattered. Imagination would not focus on anything else.

When the chair coolies stopped at the steps of the Big Bungalow, Wilding was sleeping like a drugged man. Willing hands helped him to his own room without awakening him. He did not hear the ribald greeting given him by Erasmus, nor George Carey's mumbled welcome. He did not feel Ruth's cool hand on his forehead, nor the tears of pity which rained down on him when she saw his changed condition. Least of all did he know that while he slept, the sturdy boy, now almost two years old, whom Ruth held cradled in her arms as she stood beside his bed, was his own son.

"Give the poor chap a chance," said George Carey, slurring his words, when he saw Ruth with Tommy in her arms, emerge from the room. "He doesn't want to be bothered with Tommy now. What he probably wants is a drink. He didn't look too good to me. 'Pon my soul! I hardly recognised him."

Ruth did not trouble to tell her husband, who had been drinking steadily since noon, that Geoffrey Wilding was not even conscious. She was deeply shocked. "I suppose," she said, in the voice of one talking to herself, "that they call him one of the lucky ones."

For more than a week Geoffrey Wilding lay in bed as though chained by some deadly inertia. He awoke to eat small meals with apparent enjoyment. Otherwise, his continued lethargy would have given rise to alarm. He seemed to have no interest in anything or anybody. "All right," he said wearily to Ruth in a dull monotone, "take my temperature if it amuses you, but I haven't got a temperature. I'm feeling well—better than I've felt for months. I'm just very tired and, if you'll excuse me, I'd rather be alone. You are very kind, but if I am to get well, I have got to do it in my own way. . . . No, thanks, there's nothing I want. . . . Yes, if you like, leave a few books."

For a full ten hours at night and for several hours each day, Wilding slept. At other times he lay propped up on pillows, so immobile that sometimes it was hard to see whether he were asleep or awake.

As the days passed he became a little less impersonal, and from time to time a trace of warmth crept into his voice. It was as though, by rest and sleep, he were leaching the bitterness out of his soul.

Ruth came into his room brightly one morning.

"There's been a tremendous allied offensive, Geoff," she said, with excitement in her voice. "The papers say that the Hun is really on the run this time."

"When the war is over," said Wilding in a lack-lustre voice, "I expect I shall be told. Until then, I don't want to hear anything about it."

Then, quite suddenly it seemed, Wilding began to gather strength. He spent a few hours in a long chair on the veranda each day, looking out across the valley. As though the disreputable bird did not know enough already, he taught Erasmus a few more choice utterances. Later, he limped around the garden, his limp growing noticeably less. The deep lines and creases left his face as flesh returned, but the face remained impassive, expressionless as a mask.

"Sorry if I'm not very good company," he said to George and Ruth on the first day he joined them at their midday meal, "but if you'll turn the desk-work over to me now, Carey, I'd be glad to tackle it."

Blithely, with almost indecent haste, George Carey turned over to Wilding a desk deep in letters and accounts requiring attention. Wilding tackled the work with zest, as though he loved it, and in little more than a week every letter had been answered, all accounts were up to date and the affairs of Elephant Walk, as far as paper-work was concerned, were in better order than they had been for years.

For more than three weeks Ruth waited for Wilding to show some interest in Tommy, who was a noisy, lusty infant, not easily over-looked. But Wilding seemed not to see him. "Having a kid about the place must be company for you, Ruth," was the first indication he gave that he had seen Tommy.

These days, before he did or said anything, it seemed to Ruth that Wilding brooded, thought and planned and then, having reached a decision, was in a fever to put it into effect. It was with an abrupt suddenness, therefore, that he announced one day: "Thanks very much for putting me up. It's been very kind of you, but tomorrow I'll go back to my own bungalow." He said this, as he said everything, in a manner which left no room for argument or discussion. Neither Ruth nor George, therefore, felt able to demur.

The process of taking over the work of the estate was a gradual, almost imperceptible one. At first, he was only strong enough to attend to field work in the immediate vicinity of his own bungalow. Then, in the distance one day he was seen riding his horse for the first time. On the following day, a curt note arrived at the Big Bungalow:

"Dear Carey: I think I'm fit enough to relieve you of the factory work. Unless I hear from you to the contrary, I'll be ready to start next Monday. Regards, J.G.W."

In a subtle, not easily defined fashion Wilding managed to erect between himself and ordinary human sympathy an impenetrable barrier. He no longer came over to the Big Bungalow for the weekends: an omission which shocked George Carey and perplexed Ruth.

By the latter part of 1917 almost every detail of the management of Elephant Walk estate had passed imperceptibly from George Carey's into Wilding's hands and, furthermore, everything was done with an efficiency and precision which left the former no possible grounds for complaint, although Carey did complain very bitterly to Ruth: "Dammit! the fellow's hardly human! Making every allowance for the fact that he had a pretty rough time during the war, even so, he ought to be half-way polite to me when we meet."

"I understand what you mean, George," said Ruth, "but I think we should remember that as we don't know what he has been through we can't expect to understand how he feels."

What was rankling in George Carey's mind was an episode two or three days previously. Wilding had arrived at the Big Bungalow just before sunset, to secure his employer's authority in respect of certain changes in the factory routine. He had stated his case clearly, but Carey, who was far gone in drink, had given mumbling, incoherent replies. "I'm evidently wasting my time," Wilding had said curtly. "I'll come another day when you're sober." And with that, he had left the bungalow, mounted and ridden off.

"I may have had a couple," George admitted to Ruth when recounting the episode, "but dash it all, I am the fellow's boss and entitled to a certain amount of respect. God knows, I've never stood on ceremony with Wilding."

"There is the thought, George," said Ruth judicially, "that if you want respect, you've got to earn it."

Carey winced but ignored the remark. "It's not right for a chap like Wilding to be so much alone," he went on. "I wish," he added, "that you'd try and get him out of himself a bit."

"I don't think," replied Ruth, "that he likes my company any more than he likes yours, and I don't fancy being snubbed for my pains. Nevertheless, if I have an opportunity, I'll do what I can."

*   *   *   *   *

It was late afternoon. Appuhamy, making his customary tour of inspection of the Big Bungalow, saw, with sorrow in his eyes, his master sprawled in a long chair helping himself from a decanter whose level had been some four inches higher not long previously. Rayna was playing with Tommy on a shady patch of lawn below the veranda. From the near distance came the sound of horses' hooves, and round a bend in the drive Appuhamy saw Ruth Carey and Geoffrey Wilding approaching, chatting amiably and laughing as they rode. He saw George Carey's face light with pleasure on seeing them, and he saw, too, Rayna's face darken at the same spectacle, as she took Tommy to another part of the garden to avoid a meeting.

Life at Elephant Walk, Appuhamy mused, had become very sad. With so many of its ingredients at hand, happiness seemed to have eluded the grasp of the little group of people he was surveying.

George Carey who, of them all, meant most to him, was drinking sullenly and continually. He had not shaved that morning. The white suit he wore was not clean. His was the bearing of an unhappy man who did not know why he was unhappy. But Appuhamy knew.

Ruth was bored by the enforced isolation and inaction of her life, unable, like George Carey, to take refuge in drink. She was haunted at times by a sense of guilt and oppressed at others by vague fears. Not even Tommy gave her life the completeness she needed. Appuhamy saw these things clearly. He knew, too, that she knew he saw them. There were other things he knew which Ruth did not know he knew: that underneath her cool, impersonal mask, her feelings for Geoffrey Wilding were far from cool and impersonal. He knew something else which was hidden from Ruth Carey: that Rayna, now her constant companion, was eating her heart out for Geoffrey Wilding.

Only Appuhamy, standing at the end of the veranda surveying them, could take a god's-eye view of these five people, knowing how much each knew and did not know. Only Appuhamy was able to see something of what was in the hearts of these others; only he had the power to manipulate the strings, keep one in ignorance, open the eyes of another.

Appuhamy, in these moments, was very conscious of the power which rested in his hands, bitterly conscious also of his inability to use it in the best interests of George Carey. He could, he knew, open his master's eyes to everything which had happened. But what would that achieve? Such knowledge coming from a servant would only serve to humiliate George Carey more than the facts humiliated him. Besides, Appuhamy was philosopher enough to know that sometimes a fool's paradise is better than no paradise at all. If Carey were to learn now that Tommy was not his son, every hour remaining to him on earth would be poisoned by the knowledge.

Appuhamy was prepared, if George Carey's interests could thereby be served, to sacrifice any one or all of these other four. Ruth and Wilding had already, as he saw things, forfeited all claim to consideration. Rayna and little Tommy were innocent of any wrongdoing. But, Appuhamy sighed regretfully, it would not be the first time the innocent had suffered, and not one of these four must be allowed to weigh in the scales against his loyalty to the son of Tom Carey.

While he was preparing tea for the newcomers, there came to Appuhamy a little ray of light: Rayna was the key to the tangled problem. Rayna wanted Geoffrey Wilding more than she had ever wanted anything in her short life. It was beyond the power of any man, other than Wilding himself, to grant her wish, but somehow, Appuhamy was resolved, Rayna must be made to realise, if she had not already done so, that Ruth was the chief obstacle standing between her and the man who seemed not to notice the adoration she was ready to lay at his feet.

No one knew better than Appuhamy how unstable, volatile and unpredictable a woman's jealousy could be. He would, therefore, use Rayna's. She need not know—thus restricting her capacity for harm—how far the intimacy between these two, Ruth Carey and Geoffrey Wilding, had already gone. Perhaps—Appuhamy hoped so devoutly—his interference primarily in the interests of his master, might be the means of bringing back the light of happiness to Rayna's eyes.

"The mistress," said Appuhamy that evening to Rayna, who still occupied a room in his small house, "seems to me happier these days. Do you not think so, child?"

"I had not noticed it," replied Rayna sullenly, making it obvious from her demeanour that the contrary was true. "But why," she countered, with a swiftness that disconcerted the old man, "do you trouble yourself whether she is happy or not? You hate her. You always have hated her. I have known that ever since I came here."

"Child! Child!" protested Appuhamy feebly, feeling himself at a disadvantage. "How can you say such a terrible thing?"

"Because," replied Rayna, looking him straight in the eye, "it is true. So," she continued, "the mistress is looking happier these days. What of it?"

"I was, I suppose, wondering, child, whether it could be because the young man Wilding is restored to health. The mistress—although I will admit to you frankly that I do not bear for her the affection I have for my master—has nevertheless a kind heart."

"I know nothing about her heart," said Rayna bitterly. "But one man should be enough for her. I have seen them alone more than once," Rayna went on fiercely. "They talk in whispers and they laugh. What," she asked, "do you suppose they talk about?"

"Ah!" said Appuhamy wagging his head. "Who can guess what such a handsome young man would say to such a beautiful woman as the mistress? I have lived long, child, but I have never before seen such rare beauty as hers. The young man would not be human if he were blind to it."

"I am tired," said Rayna irritably. "I will go to bed."

A few minutes later, as he passed the door of her room, Appuhamy heard Rayna sobbing, and he knew then that he had not cast his seed upon barren ground.

*   *   *   *   *

The pale moon rode high over the Ratnagalla Valley. It filtered into Ruth Carey's bedroom where, despite the massive teak panelling, she could hear the rhythmic snoring of George Carey who, seemingly, of all living things in the valley, was not touched by the silver reflection of the sun's splendour. He occupied, nevertheless, an important place in the thoughts of those who could not sleep that night.

Ruth pressed her hands to her ears to shut out the hideous rhythmic snoring. Tommy, whose cot was now in Ruth's room, stirred in his sleep, uttering a plaintive cry, as though he shared some of the perplexities which were keeping his mother awake. Tommy was always restless on the nights of the full moon. Imagination wandered fancy free, flitting from thought to thought like some haphazard butterfly. Why, Ruth asked herself, when Tommy's regular breathing had told her that all was well, had Rayna begun to behave so strangely? She had grown to love Rayna and the fresh spontaneity which characterised her utterances. There had been no disagreement. Nothing had been said. But unmistakably, the girl's manner was changed. Instead of warm friendliness, she seemed to radiate hostility and—the thought was inescapable—a watchful suspicion. Suspicion of what? Had Appuhamy in some way poisoned Rayna's mind? Even as the thought came to her, she dismissed it as foolish. Appuhamy could have no purpose in estranging her and Rayna.

Then there came to Ruth another thought: why had there been this elaborate pretence that Rayna was Appuhamy's grand-niece, when it was quite evident that this was not the case? Why and how was it that this penniless village girl was always dressed in costly silks? Who paid for them? Was it possible—Ruth's mind gagged on the thought—that George was in some way involved? Could it be that, when the household was asleep, Rayna came from Appuhamy's quarters to visit George? No, the full moon was playing tricks. Ruth had no vast experience of men, but it was impossible to believe that this was the kind of thing George would do, least of all under his own roof. Yet, how otherwise to account for the absurd fiction that Rayna was Appuhamy's grand-niece? Appuhamy, as Ruth well knew, would do anything—anything at all—for George. Furthermore, Ruth mused bitterly, if it were something that would humiliate her, he would do it with pleasure.

Then a little moment of cold justice and sanity came to Ruth. It made her shudder. If, in fact, George were doing this thing under her nose, was there such a great difference between this and what she had done to him? Had George, perhaps, known everything from the beginning? Was this a part of some subtle, diabolic revenge? It was not in George's character as she knew it, but perhaps she knew less than she believed. Bitterest of all, Ruth realised that, even if her vague suspicions were well founded, it was a situation which she must endure because of her own guilt. That was justice. Somehow she thrust George and Rayna out of her mind, together with her suspicions. She must not harbour such thoughts or they would poison her.

The moon seemed to emphasise Ruth's aloneness. She was conscious of being frighteningly alone. Thought turned to Geoffrey Wilding, and for a little while she tried to see him uncoloured by her own vanity and the other factors which cloud human vision. She wanted desperately to see him as he really was. So much might depend upon it. Health and strength had come back to him, but very little of the gay wit she had known and loved. He remained cold, aloof and impersonal. There was no warmth even in his laughter. She had once read that all humour was founded upon somebody else's misfortunes. This was now very apparent in Geoffrey Wilding. Where she herself was concerned, was he being gallant? Acting in what he believed to be her best interests, behaving as though they were no more than light acquaintances? That could be the explanation, because never for one instant since his return from the war had he let down the barrier between them. The alternative was—and she shrank from the thought—that he was completely indifferent, and that the night they had spent together had been no more than a light amusing episode, taken in his stride on the way to the war.

A part of Ruth wanted to tell Geoffrey Wilding that Tommy was his son, although she knew that to do so would be another betrayal of George Carey. Another part of her feared to face the chilling indifference with which Wilding might greet the announcement. Why, she asked herself, had nature decreed that to be a mother meant so much, and to be a father so little? The man who was Tommy's father did not know it, and if he knew, might not care; while the other man who thought he was Tommy's father and was not, lacked any intuitive sense. No woman, Ruth believed, could fail to know her own child.

Ruth gritted her teeth as George's snores rose to a crescendo. Was this, she asked herself, part of her punishment? Was George, she wondered, thrusting her into Geoffrey Wilding's company for some deep, horrible purpose? Appuhamy had shown quite clearly that he knew everything. It might be that he had told George. Even as this last thought crossed her mind, Ruth knew it to be absurd. George Carey could never have feigned ignorance of such knowledge. He, because it was in his nature, would have ended everything in a tremendous explosion of rage. His love for Elephant Walk was such —and Ruth clung to this as to a rock—that he could never have endured the thought of Tommy, without a drop of Carey blood in his veins, inheriting Elephant Walk, the Big Bungalow and the wealth which Carey drive, stubbornness and enterprise had carved from the jungle. Appuhamy perhaps—Ruth shivered at the thought—had whispered what he knew at the graveside of old Tom Carey whose voice, re-incarnated in Erasmus, still echoed through the bungalow. The macabre thought came to her that perhaps old Tom Carey would never be able to rest until his voice, with the grotesque mimicry of Erasmus, was stilled for ever. Ruth had never liked the bird. Now she hated him, even going so far as to play with the thought of ending his obscene chatter for ever.

Rising from her bed, Ruth pulled the curtain, shutting out the moon which gave rise to such thoughts. Presently she fell into a fitful sleep, dreaming that someone was sawing wood in the next room, fashioning it in the form of a cross.

The moonlight seeped into Appuhamy's little house. Sleep eluded him, too. Conscience and moonlight between them kept him awake. He was bitterly aware that Rayna, into whose life he had presumed to obtrude his loyalty to the Careys, could not sleep for the pain which was in her heart. In bringing Rayna to Elephant Walk he had unchained a tiger—a tiger which roamed free, its capacity for harm unchecked.

Upon Rayna, too, the pale moon was playing strange tricks. Her love for Ruth had turned to something near hatred. The seed had been sown in her mind by Appuhamy, but it had made no difference to her until the moment she had seen the exchange of a quick, understanding look between Ruth and Geoffrey Wilding. It had endured only for the fraction of a second, but Rayna thought she understood that look. There came back to her a fragment of gossip she had heard in the stables. Young as she was, Rayna had the wisdom to know that a man and a woman did not exchange such a look unless there were something behind it, some point of understanding, some knowledge shared to the exclusion of the rest of the world.

The moonlight, which was playing in the forgotten nooks and crannies of so many human souls, did not neglect to stand between

Geoffrey Wilding and his sleep. He was feeling too wakeful even to go to bed. He read fitfully and then, putting his book aside, plucked idly at the strings of a guitar-like instrument that he had fashioned himself from pieces of a hard, resonant wood he had found growing in the jungle high above the tea. It was a melancholy instrument, whose throbbing notes lingered like those of the Hawaiian guitar. All he achieved from this was the curses of his servants whom he awakened.

The fight to regain something approaching a normal outlook on life had been a long and hard one. Wilding was aware, furthermore, that it was not yet completely won. Indeed, as he strolled in the garden, he wondered if there were such a thing as a completely normal outlook, for to be normal, a man would have to be balanced with infinite exactitude upon the hairline which divides what is called sanity from insanity.

Wilding looked out across the valley bathed in moonlight, with a great gratitude, for he was aware that to its peace and serenity he owed the banishment of so many of the ugly thoughts which, at times, had made life seem an intolerable burden. Now he was aware, as he stood upon the threshold of normal health of body and mind, that not for long would he find contentment here.

Ruth Carey was in his thoughts too often these days. She had become a disturbing factor. When he had first returned, he had shunned everyone's society, passionately desiring solitude in which to climb back up the ladder at whose foot the war had left him, broken and shaken, a pitiful, trembling thing which even he had despised. There had been no conscious avoidance of Ruth on his part, but it had seemed to him better, having once cut himself off from his fellow countrymen who lived in this remote spot, without feeling the loss of their company at all acutely, to leave matters as they were. Ruth, however, had thought otherwise, and it had been quite obvious for some weeks that she had deliberately sought him out. It had seemed to him the fairer, more decent way to allow the emotional night of their parting, when he went off to the war, to be forgotten as though it had never occurred, and he had assumed, without going very deeply into the matter, that Ruth would have been glad not to be reminded of her own weakness. The fact, however, that she had not been willing to leave the past buried in obscurity could, he decided, have only one meaning.

Always a little hard, the war had made him harder. Always inclined to be selfish, he was become more selfish. If, as seemed evident, Ruth Carey wanted to play with fire—well, she was over twenty-one and fully aware of what she was doing. The consequences, inevitably, would fall more hardly upon her than upon him. Where George Carey was concerned, the other episode had always left a dirty taste in Wilding's mouth, and many times he had wished that, instead of spending that mad, reckless night in the summer-house of the Big Bungalow, he had returned to his own home. Rayna would have caused much fewer complications than Ruth. But, he thought harshly, it was not worth while wasting regrets on George Carey. He was a decent enough fellow, but if he was such a fool as to believe that he could maintain a happy marriage with a woman of Ruth's type by surveying it through the bottom of a whisky glass, then he forfeited the right to all consideration. No, Wilding determined, however he might behave for the future where Ruth was concerned, he would leave George Carey out of his reckonings altogether.

Gossip? Yes, there would be bound to be gossip. Nothing would ever still the clacking of the coolies' tongues. Well, there had been gossip before and the roof of the world had not fallen in. Let them talk! Let them say what they damn well pleased!

✳

✳

✳

✳

✳ **CHAPTER FIFTEEN** ✳ ✳ ✳ ✳ ✳ ✳ ✳

To Ruth it seemed as though the old Geoffrey Wilding had been able to remake himself from the fragments left over by the war. He was once again gay and amusing, even though his humour was at times tinged with bitterness. After the gloom and monotony of life in the Big Bungalow it was, she found, a joy to be with him.

Ruth remarked on this change as the trail widened, enabling them to ride side by side.

"It's good to see you like this again, Geoff," she said. "I was beginning to believe that you—well, hated everything and everyone. You never talk about what you have been through, but I expect it was pretty hellish."

"If it was," said Wilding brusquely, his face darkening, "I've forgotten it. Nature, you know," he went on, in a more gentle voice, "is very cruel at times, but she can be wonderfully kind. Some poet— I don't know who he was, although I've searched all the dictionaries of quotations for him—put it perfectly. I wonder, do you know the lines?

"Ships of pleasure and ships of pain,
Ships of losses and ships of gain.
Only the ships of pleasure remain
In the haven of memory.

"Try for example," Wilding went on, "to remember the pain you yourself suffered when young Tommy was born. You can't, can you? Old Mother Nature didn't intend you to. Every year somewhere around fifty millions of women the world over go through the ordeal of child-birth, and a year later the huge majority of them are willing to repeat it. Why? One can only suppose they remember the ships of pleasure and forget the ships of pain. . . . Yes, as you say, I went through a bad time, but I've put it behind me. And now let's talk about something else. Would you like to see my weekend cottage?"

"Your what?"

"I've been spending Saturday nights and Sundays up here for a long while. I've found a spot that I don't think has been visited for fifty years or more. It looks down upon the world and, amazingly, it makes even the Big Bungalow look small."

"Yes, Geoff, I would."

"Very well, I'll take you there. But on one condition, that you tell nobody—not one living soul—where it is. Are the terms acceptable?"

Ruth nodded, and for a while they rode on in silence.

Wilding led the way up a steep and narrow path, almost dark because of the dense vegetation on either side and the interlacing branches and creepers overhead. All along the way were the marks where the undergrowth had been chopped and hacked to make the passage possible. From occasional clearings it was apparent to Ruth that their destination was the flat top of Ratnagalla Peak. Sometimes it was necessary to crouch low over Esmeralda's neck, while at others the elbows of the khaki blouse she wore were torn by thorns which had strayed across the trail since the last time it had been traversed.

The gloom ended abruptly. They emerged into brilliant sunlight on the flattened mountain top, where the air was sparkling and clear after the shut-in atmosphere of the green tunnel on the way up. The horses whinnied with delight at the sight and smell of sweet pasture.

They dismounted and, after hobbling the horses, Wilding led the way to a small stone building, crumbling in ruins, set on the edge of the plateau which formed the mountain-top. To cover the gaping holes in the roof a tarpaulin had been stretched. At the entrance was a small painted board bearing the legend: *Gem Cottage.*

Within was gloom, contrasting with the brilliant light outside, but Ruth was able to distinguish a folding chair, a table, a camp bed, an oil stove and a vast bronze urn. As they entered, spiders and other creatures scuttled for cover.

"Why Gem Cottage?" asked Ruth.

For reply, Wilding took her outside to a spring which bubbled out of the earth some twenty yards away. Its clear water ran down a steep rock-face to lose itself in the dense undergrowth below. "It's from this spot," Wilding explained, "that the peak derives its name of Gem Mountain. When it gets too hot and dry down on the plains, perhaps the elephants look up here, see the gem shining in the early dawn light, and then remember that up here on the high slopes there are cool springs and tender herbage. Don't you see, with the gem to beckon them on their way, they come up the valley, and the only thing which spoils the journey for them is that damn great bungalow sitting right in their path."

"Let me forget the Big Bungalow today, Geoff—please. Show me more of Gem Cottage."

Upon the oil stove they fried some canned sausages and eggs, brewing the inevitable tea. They were the ordinary canned sausages of commerce and very ordinary eggs, but the enchantment of the place and the day gave them qualities which flattered them. For dessert, they scooped out a dozen or so ripe passion fruit, which Wilding gathered from a vine close by.

When the meal was finished, they sat smoking cigarettes in silence, watching while the morning mist lifted from the valley and plains below them.

"A strange feeling has come over me, Geoff," said Ruth very softly. "It comes at moments like this. I want to drink in all this beauty and peace—saturate myself in it, so that, no matter what happens tomorrow or the other tomorrows, I can keep today always. Nothing can ever take it away from me. Look!" she said, pointing to where curlicues of smoke rose from a pile of burning weeds into the still air. "Even that's beautiful."

"I have only eyes for you, Ruth," said Wilding. "The rest—the valley and the low country down there—they're lovely enough, but I've seen them so often when I've been alone and not particularly happy. Now they're only a background for you."

"You must have been very lonely and unhappy, Geoff, to have come up here alone."

"Was I? I don't remember."

The next thing Ruth knew was that she was in Wilding's arms, being carried across the greensward into the little house. "Geoff!" she protested vainly. "You're being terribly rough. It—it makes me feel like the Sabine women—all of them—the ones in the picture, being carried off by the brutal soldiers."

"It shouldn't," said Wilding tersely. "They had to be dragged away from home. You came willingly!" Saying which, he dumped her unceremoniously on to a pile of dry bracken.

Suddenly Ruth was a little frightened by the look she saw in Wilding's eyes. "Geoff, really!" she protested, more to cover up her own embarrassment than for any effect.

"Your voice then," said Wilding with a laugh, "sounded as though you were having tea on the vicarage lawn and reproving a small boy for taking a second piece of cake. We're miles from that now, my bonnie wench, so forget it. We're on a mountain top, looking down on the world. It's my mountain top," he said exultingly, "and I make all the rules here. We've a lot of lost time to make up and there's none to spare for modesty."

Hours later, gorged and surfeited with sensation, feeling bruised bodily and mentally, Ruth knew that she had surrendered because she wanted to surrender, but she knew from the hard set of Wilding's jaw and the glint in his eyes that further protests, if she had uttered them, would have availed her nothing. The knowledge thrilled and frightened her at the same time, for during these hours together, Geoffrey Wilding had stripped off the mask of civilisation. He had been a brute, even if, Ruth reflected, a wonderful and an adorable brute. With him she had run the gamut of all the emotions, but there had been moments when of them all, fear had predominated; moments when she would not have dared to cross his will. The fear was heightened by the knowledge that she was bound to Geoffrey

Wilding by chains of steel, chains which he could throw off or break, but which she could not.

"Gem Cottage," said Wilding when, becoming a civilised being, he set about brewing tea, "was once a Buddhist temple. A wise hermit lived here. That bronze urn in the corner was where the pilgrims who came to consult him threw their offerings in return for his advice. Although he was not here today to give it, you must have heard some echo of the advice he used to give to the unhappy people who came to see him."

"What was his advice, Geoff?"

"He used to tell them that there was greater joy in giving than in receiving, and that the greatest joy of all was in giving oneself. Now, tell me before we leave, what are you going to put into the urn as an offering?"

For reply, Ruth crossed to the urn and clambered into it.

"On those terms, my bonnie wench, and upon no others, you may visit Gem Cottage again."

"I doubt very much, Geoff," said Ruth timidly, "whether your hermit meant quite what you seem to think he meant."

"I doubt it, too," laughed Wilding, "but I am the hermit now. I don't give advice. I make terms, and you've heard them."

Darkness had fallen some twenty minutes before they reached the Big Bungalow.

"I think, Geoff," said Ruth, "it would look better if you came in."

"I don't care how it looks," was the indifferent reply, "but if you would like me to, I'll come. There was a time," he continued with grim mirth, "when in like circumstances, I wouldn't have much cared for the taste of George's whisky, but the last years have cured me of old-fashioned ideas like that."

"You sound terribly, terribly hard, Geoff."

"I am hard. I've seen things which make me hard and I've lost all sympathy for weaklings like George."

"He's never done you any harm, Geoff."

"You imply that I have done him harm. But you're wrong. He lives in a fool's paradise because he likes it. I've taken from him —borrowed, if you like the word better—something he didn't know how to hold anyway: that's you. For God's sake don't let's get sentimental about poor old George. He's perfectly happy with Erasmus and a decanter of whisky."

"Geoff, don't, don't be so hard!" Ruth begged him. "I can't bear to hear you talk that way of George. After all, I am his wife."

Geoffrey Wilding's bellows of mocking laughter seemed to fill the night.

"You'll be the death of me, Ruth," he said when it subsided. "What have I done to poor old George that you've not done? If you feel like that about it, go back to him and don't allow your dainty little feet to stray from the straight and narrow path again, and for heaven's sake don't talk in hushed cathedral whispers about it. You're an unfaithful wife and I"—his tone was cold and mocking —"am your devoted and adoring lover! If either of us felt the respect for George that you imply by your manner, you know perfectly well that we wouldn't have wantoned away the day as we have. At least, that's how our grandmothers would probably have expressed it. You want the best of both worlds, Ruth, and you ought to be old enough to know that you can't have it."

The brutality in Wilding's voice shocked Ruth, even though she could find no fault with his logic.

There was silence in the Big Bungalow as they entered it. It was Sunday evening when, ordinarily, John Gilliland and Robbie Norman would have been there, but now George Carey was alone. At the top of the steps Appuhamy barred the way, his eyes blazing with indignation.

"Is something wrong, Appuhamy?" asked Ruth.

"I think," said Appuhamy with dignity, realising the enormity of his behaviour, "that the master does not wish guests tonight."

"And I think, Appuhamy," said Ruth, recognising the moment as the crisis in her relationship with him, "that you are impertinent. You may go to your own quarters now. Now, I said!" Ruth added, noting his hesitation. "Unless"—their eyes met darkly—"you wish to be dismissed."

"The mistress," said Appuhamy, reeling from the shock, "would do well to go to the nursery. Master Tommy is very ill."

With his head high, Appuhamy went along the veranda to his own quarters. He wished, with all his heart, that he could save

George Carey from the humiliation of being seen in his present condition. As he passed he glanced at his master, who lay sprawled in a long chair in a drunken sleep. But he knew that if he disobeyed the curtly-given order, he would, as threatened, be dismissed. Life would end if he were banned from the Big Bungalow and from the service of George Carey, to whose interests the rest of his life was bound. He knew that, in uttering the threat, Ruth was fully aware of the consequences to him if it should be implemented.

Panic-stricken, Ruth ran to the nursery where Rayna was sitting beside the child's cot, worried and helpless. One glance at Tommy sufficed to show that he was in a high fever. Rayna looked up with anger and reproach in her eyes as Ruth entered the room.

Tommy's temperature, Ruth ascertained, was over 104 degrees. Half an hour later it had risen a trifle. There was no rash, nor any other indication of what was wrong. There was despair in Ruth's heart at her own helplessness. From time to time forcing a tea-spoonful of limejuice and water between Tommy's parched lips, she sat beside the cot watching anxiously as the fever mounted in the restless child, seeming to burn up his little body. Wordlessly, Rayna had left the room within a minute or so of Ruth's arrival, and her voice now came clearly from the veranda along with bursts of drunken laughter from George and the mocking tones of Geoffrey Wilding, who was evidently deriving great amusement from George's condition. With rage in her heart, Ruth went out on to the veranda. "Shut up! Shut up!" she cried hysterically. "Tommy's desperately ill and you, all of you, behave like a lot of drunken hooligans!"

Abashed, the other three followed Ruth back into the night nursery. The gravity of Tommy's condition penetrated even George Carey's consciousness, shocking him back to something resembling sobriety.

"What's his temperature, Ruth?" asked Wilding.

They took it again, noting with alarm that it was just over 105 degrees.

"I don't pretend to know what's wrong with him," said Wilding, "but we must get the temperature down."

With strong, competent hands and a gentleness which surprised Ruth, Wilding sponged Tommy's body with tepid water, repeating this every fifteen or twenty minutes, from time to time forcing limejuice and water between his lips.

For more than two hours hardly a word was uttered. All eyes were upon Wilding and Tommy. At about ten p.m. the temperature ceased to climb. An hour later it was dropping, and by midnight was a little over 100 degrees.

"Oughtn't we to send for a doctor?" mumbled George.

"Send for one if you want to," replied Wilding. "He'd take twenty-four hours to get here, and by that time, either way, it would be too late. The chances are that Tommy will awake in the morning with a normal temperature."

Although of them all Wilding had been the one to keep his head in the crisis and to deal with the situation with practical common sense, Ruth found herself resenting bitterly that Wilding was not apparently touched spiritually. Here was a sick child—any sick child. He had done his best, and that best, it seemed, had allayed the fever which was destroying Tommy. If Tommy had died, as might well have been the case if the fever had mounted, Wilding would have been sorry, as any ordinarily constituted person is sorry, at the death of a child. Knowing that she ought to be grateful, Ruth found herself instead resenting bitterly the fact that Wilding, despite his brisk competence, was not sharing with her any of the agony of the long night. It was illogical, unjust, but however hard she tried, she could not escape the thought.

Towards morning all four of them, feeling the need for food, sat down to a light meal. George, who had been drinking steadily since midnight, sat at the table swaying, but did not eat. Rayna, after leaving the sickroom on Ruth's arrival, had changed into her latest finery and was looking devastatingly lovely. As they rose from the table, Ruth caught a quick look exchanged between Wilding and Rayna. The look might have meant nothing more than the fleeting admiration of a man for a beautiful young girl, and the latter's acknowledgment of the tribute, but to Ruth it was like a dagger stabbed to her heart. She felt, as she returned to the night-nursery to resume her vigil, that she could stand no more. She realised, as she stood by Tommy's cot, that she hated and loved Geoffrey Wilding and that the two emotions were inextricably mixed, with hate predominating because of the knowledge that she could not escape him. She knew, with a sense of shame, that his physical attraction had enslaved her. She knew that he had only to beckon and she would go off to Gem Cottage with him again, or anywhere else, because she could not help herself. She knew, too—and of all knowledge this was the most bitter—that he was no more enslaved by her, nor touched spiritually, than he was by the cigarette-end he tossed carelessly over the veranda as he said good-night.

Rayna had disappeared in the direction of Appuhamy's house. George Carey was staggering off drunkenly to bed, and Wilding was on the way to his own room at the far end of the veranda when, as if there had not been enough drama for one night, there came from the darkness without the shrill, menacing trumpeting of a bull elephant, so close that it seemed to be in the garden of the Big Bungalow. A few seconds later there came the sound of smashing timbers and the snapping of a tree which broke with a report like a rifle.

George Carey made a great effort to pull himself together and, before anyone could stop him, he had gone out into the black darkness with a rifle he had snatched from a rack in his office. The cool air for a moment made him reel but, after a little while, his head cleared and a savage anger took possession of him. There was in him, although he did not recognise it as such, a great fear of the monstrous beasts which, from the sounds all round him, were engaged upon an orgy of destruction. It was not the physical fear, as well it might have been, of what they might do to him, but a fear which sprang from the fifty-year-old vendetta which had been waged between the Careys and the elephants, and the tenacity of purpose which would never, it seemed, allow the latter to forget that here, where a Carey had built this monstrous bungalow, was, by immemorial right, the resting-place of the elephants on their unpredictable pilgrimages between the plains and the mountains. The urge to kill obsessed the drunken man who, despite his rage, knew with a sense of guilt which would not be stilled, that he himself was the intruder.

For a few seconds George Carey saw the form of a big bull silhouetted briefly against the false dawn at a distance of some thirty yards.

He fired twice. There was, faintly audible to him and to the others huddled upon the veranda, a thud as the heavy bullets struck the mountain of flesh in their path. The bull elephant trumpeted with pain and, in a few seconds, had disappeared from sight.

"I didn't kill him," said George, when he returned to the Big Bungalow, "but," he added exultingly, "that'll give him something to remember me by!"

Despite the bold words, there was fear in his heart, fear of a tenacity of purpose greater than his own.

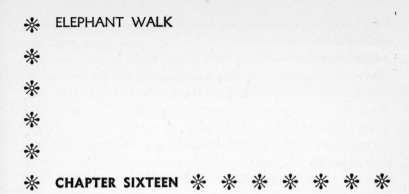

CHAPTER SIXTEEN ✳ ✳ ✳ ✳ ✳ ✳ ✳

Appuhamy surveyed through troubled eyes the havoc wrought in the grounds of the Big Bungalow. There seemed to him some significance to be read from the trail of the giant footprints leading across flower-beds to the cairn which covered the grave of his old master, Tom Carey. There had been four or five elephants abroad the previous night, as was evidenced by the varying sizes of footprints. The biggest of all, however, inevitably those of the bull, led straight to Tom Carey's grave. Appuhamy's mind went back over the years to the time when, as a small boy, he had heard his own father warn Tom Carey against incurring the wrath of the Elephant People by building upon this spot. Now, the memory of his father's warning was pregnant with ill-omen.

George Carey, sobered by the events of the night, had just come from Tommy's nursery. He was feeling bitterly ashamed of himself. He had been too drunk the night before fully to realise how sick Tommy had been. It hurt him now to remember that he had failed in his duties as a father. He stood beside Appuhamy surveying the scattered rocks of the cairn. They stood thus in silence, these two, because there was nothing to say.

Ruth and Rayna stood watching from the veranda, as did a little knot of awe-struck servants and a group of coolies come to repair the damage wrought in the night.

Fear was king at Elephant Walk. Fear of the unknown. He stalked abroad exultingly, knowing that he held so many lives imprisoned in his grip.

Appuhamy was oppressed by fear that events would bring his relationship with Ruth to a crisis which—he did not deceive himself —would mean his dismissal from the post he had held long and honourably.

George Carey was full of fear. Drunk, he was able to stifle his fears but even when drunk, he could read only too clearly the disgust on Ruth's face. He was not properly able, even to himself, to express quite what Ruth meant to him. Still less could he do so to Ruth, but the fear of losing her haunted his every waking hour. It was only by resorting to drink, which drove her further from him, that he was able to quieten his fears. There was another fear haunting George Carey: his hand was only nominally in control of affairs at Elephant Walk. Little by little he had allowed first the details and then the more important matters to rest upon Wilding's authority. So far, there had been no cause to regret this, for Wilding had done everything, Carey admitted ruefully, as well and as conscientiously as he himself could have done it. If he, Carey, were ever to become the real master of Elephant Walk again, he must, he knew, assert his authority now or it would be too late. In a little while the coolies, who had not yet realised it, would know who was their real master. A great lethargy seemed to hold George Carey in its grip. Some of it was advancing years, some of it was drink, but most was the torment of mind as he saw Ruth slipping further away from him.

Ruth, surveying the scene from the veranda, was untouched by some of the fears which oppressed the others. She had always felt a deep sympathy for the elephants, although their comings and goings frightened her. There came to her the curious sensation that the elephants were, in some vague way she could not understand, her friends. This perhaps, she argued, was because they shared her dislike for the vast, gloomy bungalow and the life within it. Another fear had been lifted from her: Tommy, as Wilding had sagely predicted, was now perfectly well, if a little weak. He was sleeping peacefully; his temperature was a point below normal.

The private fear which haunted Ruth was the shameful and humiliating knowledge that she was held in the firm grip of her obsession for Geoffrey Wilding, made even more shameful and humiliating by the realisation that to him she was little more than a plaything. Illogically, for it had been Wilding who had risen to the crisis in the night-nursery, it had been the knowledge the night before that none of her agony of mind had been shared by him which had enabled her to see him thus clearly. She had once believed that she loved him as much as it was in her to love any man. Now, even though she knew that the use of the word love in regard to her feelings for Wilding was a misuse of language and that what she felt was no more than a base physical passion, the chains still bound her. In her innermost heart Ruth knew that she was not the kind of woman that she appeared to be, or that anyone, knowing her behaviour, would be justified in believing her. The disgust she felt with herself did not help; indeed it made the grip on self-respect harder to retain. To continue her relationship with Geoffrey Wilding was to feel soiled and cheap. To end it was to create a vacuum from which she shrank.

Above all, colouring every thought, was the feeling which had obsessed Ruth almost from the time of her first arrival, that the Big Bungalow itself was not a home, designed to serve those who dwelled in it, but a monstrous thing which demanded service and obedience from those who dwelled in it. Appuhamy was its willing slave, George its slave by long habit, but she, although she could not argue the fanciful thought logically, knew that if life were to hold any more for her, she must fight against becoming its slave. It was not she who did not like the Big Bungalow, but the Big Bungalow which did not like her, and there was a world of difference. It was the Big Bungalow —and Ruth clung to the thought fiercely—which was trying to destroy her, first by allowing her to believe that a sensual fascination for Geoffrey Wilding was love, and then, when she knew it was not love, but a very base counterfeit, fanning the flames of her desire for him until they were beyond control.

That evening George Carey, shocked into sobriety by the events of the previous evening and night, turned his back on the whisky decanters, becoming the shy, adoring man Ruth had first known, sheepishly ashamed of himself, but too inarticulate to express what he felt.

"George," said Ruth gently, in the voice of one talking to a child,

"I'm sure one or two drinks would be better for you than eyeing the decanter as though you could eat it."

"I'm afraid, darling, I've been knocking it back a bit lately, and I thought perhaps I'd better lay off it for a while."

"You should try, George. It isn't good for you and it's very, very bad—for us!"

George Carey helped himself to whisky-and-soda. After a deep gulp, he began to feel better.

There came to Ruth the thought that even now, if she were able to retrieve her own self-respect and her respect for George Carey, there could still exist the foundations upon which their tottering marriage might be rebuilt. She longed in this moment, when she and George were, spiritually speaking, more in accord than they had been for months, to tell him everything and throw herself upon his mercy. It would be such a wonderful relief to slip some of the burden of guilt off her own shoulders. She had no fear of the consequences of such a confession, none whatever. But even as she played with the idea she knew, with a frightening finality, that to tell George everything would be the final injustice. George Carey would forgive her. She knew that. In his queer, groping, inarticulate way, he loved her devotedly. No other woman ever would occupy her place in his life. It was not vanity which prompted Ruth to this realisation, but insight into George's character. He would forgive her. He would accept Tommy as his own son. For the rest of his life he would never mention the ugly shadow which lay between them. Yes, confession was very tempting, for Ruth's shoulders ached with their burden. But the forgiveness which she knew was there for the asking was only to be bought at a price she was not willing to ask George Carey to pay. In unburdening herself thus, she would be exposing George Carey's consciousness to the ridicule which always attaches itself to the wronged husband. George would be clumsily chivalrous, but his soul would wince and shrink from the blow, and it would destroy his self-respect. No, she had created her own private hell and she must go on living in it. She had not the right to ask George Carey to share it with her.

"That was a deep sigh, darling," said George. "What were you thinking about?"

"I was thinking, George, that I'd not made a very great success as a wife."

"That," said he contritely, "is just your nice way of saying that I'm not much of a husband."

"The war can't last for ever, George," said Ruth, trying not to show how much she was touched. "When it's over, let's escape from here for a few months. You and I and Tommy. Let's go somewhere, meet a lot of people, laugh, play the fool and get away from this gloomy old bungalow."

"It is gloomy, darling," said George with a wry smile. "Even I am beginning to realise it now."

"In some ways, George, it's magnificent. There must be millions of women who, if they could see it, would envy me, and it makes me feel an ungrateful hussy to talk like this, but sometimes, George, I'm very frightened of it. The world is changing at a tremendous speed, and this great bungalow isn't changing. All over the world the clocks are turning round, but here they stand still. This isn't January 1918 where we're sitting now, because the clocks were stopped here in the eighteen-sixties."

"I know, dear," said George sympathetically. "It was wrong of me to believe that you would see it as I see it. Suppose we try to brighten the place up a bit?"

"Listen, George," said Ruth intensely, realising how much would hang upon his reception of what she had to say. "Don't condemn this idea until you've thought it over. Don't say anything at all now, do you understand? Nothing. But play with the idea when you're alone."

"What idea?" asked George uncomprehendingly.

"You've made lots and lots of money during the war, haven't you, George?"

"Good Lord, yes! As far as I can see, more than we could spend. Do you want some?"

"No, I don't want any, but I'd like you to spend some of it on something for me. Something vitally important to us both."

"Any damn thing you like, darling," said George eagerly.

"Don't agree, George, before you've heard my suggestion and thought it over. What I want is for you to build us a new bungalow.

I want to be consulted a little about it—not much. I don't want any-thing a tenth as magnificent as this. I'd like it built of stone, with a roof of red Mangalore tiles. I'd like Dutch tiles in pastel shades for the floors. There should be a wide veranda like this, airy rooms, but not such high ceilings. At most there should be four or perhaps five bedrooms. It should be modern in design, too, George, so that it wouldn't be necessary to have the great army of servants who work here now. No, George, don't say anything at all now. Think it over, and when you've thought it over, let's talk about it again. There's only one more thing I want to say, George. It's this: I know how much this bungalow means to you. Knowing that, don't you see, I wouldn't ask this thing lightly. It seems a lot—far more than you can ever know—to me and to us. Think it over, George."

Ruth knew, as she looked at George that, just as she was unable accurately to analyse it, she would never, so long as she might live, forget the look in his eyes, as the impact of her words struck him. There she read horror, stark amazement, fear and other things. With a great effort he flinched from the thoughts which surged through his mind.

At last he said: "As you say, darling, the war can't last for ever. Things must be pretty deadly for you. I've always known that. But they needn't be always. We'll get away, travel. I'd like to see a lot of places. I'd like to go back to Paris, wouldn't you? Then there's the Riviera. I don't somehow think I'd like America, but there's lots to be done and, unless something happens that I can't foresee, we'll have plenty of money. There's another thing, too. Wilding being here makes all the difference. I shall be able to go away with an easy mind, knowing that he's here. He's an odd chap in many ways, but it was a lucky day for me when I ran across him."

Somehow, Ruth knew, she must strive to keep back the tears which welled into her eyes. Even if she had not yet shaken off her physical dependence upon Geoffrey Wilding, she did not belong to him spiritually. There had been treachery enough. Now, no matter what the consequences, she must warn George not to place too much reliance upon a man who was not reliable. The fact that she herself had aided and abetted Geoffrey Wilding in his disloyalty to George seemed not to touch the matter. Elephant Walk and George Carey were indivisible, part of each other. To allow Geoffrey Wilding to manœuvre himself into a position where he was indispensable at Elephant Walk was to destroy George Carey.

"I'm going to give Wilding a share of the profits for the future," continued George, unaware of the tumultuous thoughts which were racing through Ruth's brain. "He's earned it and, apart from that, it'll be an incentive to do better."

"George," said Ruth, summoning to her aid every ounce of persuasion that was in her, "have you ever heard of a thing called woman's intuition?"

"Of course I have. Why?"

"Mine isn't overworked, George. I have never once, have I, interfered or tried to interfere in the smallest single detail where Elephant Walk is concerned?"

"No, darling," said George wonderingly.

"Well, at the risk of your telling me to mind my own business, I'm going to interfere now. My woman's intuition—call it what you will—tells me, George, that you'd be doing a very, very foolish thing in allowing Geoffrey Wilding any more power than he has now. I'm not blind, you know. While you've been drinking heavily, I've seen the reins slipping out of your hands and being eased gently into his. Trust me in this one thing, George, and I promise you you'll never regret it. Don't place too much reliance on Geoffrey Wilding. He's not the loyal man that you think he is."

"Now, see here, Ruth," said George, genuinely alarmed, "you've either said too much or too little. You always had your knife into Wilding, almost from the day you first met him. What've you got against him?"

"Just believe me, George, that when you've been, shall we say, in a not very observant condition, I have been very observant. Please George, don't press me to say more. If I wasn't completely sure of what I was saying, I wouldn't have gone as far as this. *Don't trust Geoffrey Wilding.*"

Ruth felt herelf flinching under the gaze of George's blue eyes which, a moment or two previously, had seemed to her bleary and a little bloodshot. Now they seemed crystal clear.

"If you are right, darling," he said slowly, "I don't mind admitting that it's a bitter blow. One day soon, maybe, it'll be easier for you to tell me more. I won't press you, but I'd like you to know that, not even for you, am I prepared to condemn a man unheard on the strength of what you've said. I don't know much about women, darling," he went on, "but if all I'm told is true, you're creatures of mood. As far as I know, Wilding has always been straight with me and, until I have proof—proof, mark you—that he's not been, I'll do nothing."

Ruth found herself withdrawing slowly and miserably into her own little hell. George Carey's simplicity and sheer decency made her feel more ashamed than she had ever felt in her life.

"I'm glad we've had this talk, dear," she said, before she went into her own room to shed the tears which would not now brook any more delay. Even so, she was able to smile through her tears a few minutes later as the bungalow echoed to the music of the *can-can* played on an atrociously cracked and almost worn-out record.

The important thing which helped Ruth to hold her head high during the days which followed was that George Carey had not refused to consider leaving the Big Bungalow. Equally he had not agreed to do so. His churning thoughts were almost visible as he mulled the idea over in his head for days. On Ruth's part, the suggestion had been a gambler's chance, for she had expected a blank refusal even to consider the proposal. That he was willing to consider it was, as she saw things, a victory in itself. It meant that George and the Big Bungalow were at least two separate entities and not, as Ruth had sometimes been tempted to think, built in one piece.

During these days Ruth was able to gain another victory, small in itself, but meaning a great deal to her. One evening, spent in a pleasant, friendly intimacy with George, Ruth knew that the atmosphere of the immense, gloomy dining-room, and the Lilliputian feeling it gave her to sit at the great table, would take all the joy out of the day. It would mean, inevitably, that within a few minutes of taking his seat at the head of the table, George would fall asleep. Even on the rare occasions when he did not do so, his struggles to remain awake were pathetic.

"Shall we have something light served on a tray here by the fire, George?" she suggested.

The revolutionary idea at first hit George like a blow, but when he had absorbed it, he said, with the air of one being amazed at his own elasticity of mind: "Yes. After all, why shouldn't we? Dashed good idea I call it."

Ruth rang the bell. In a few moments Appuhamy arrived with a grave bow to learn what was wanted.

"We'll have dinner here by the fire on a tray or a small table, Appuhamy," said Ruth amiably. "Something quite light, please."

Appuhamy looked as though he could not believe his ears. His eyes, as they met Ruth's, blazed with indignation. According to the unwritten laws of the Big Bungalow, the dining-room was the proper place for dinner, or, in extreme cases of illness, bed. People in possession of their health and senses did not eat in the lounge in front of the fire. Indeed, as he turned the matter over in his mind, Appuhamy was sure that not once in fifty years had a meal been eaten in the lounge. His whole body stiffened as his mind repudiated the idea. Ruth's eyes were firm and unwavering as they met his. So, after a few moments of challenge, his dropped. He turned instinctively to George Carey to appeal against this outrageous decision. The gesture was more instinctive than reasoned, but it gave Ruth the cue she wanted. Even George Carey recognised it as a questioning of her authority.

"Well, what are you waiting for, Appuhamy?" Carey asked sharply.

"I think, George," said Ruth, pressing home the advantage, "that this is a good time to tell Appuhamy once again that I am mistress here. He was told once before, I know, but he seems to have forgotten."

"You hear what the mistress says?" asked Carey. Appuhamy nodded humbly. "I should be very sorry to see you go, Appuhamy. Very sorry," said Carey slowly. "I think you know that. But I am telling you—and for the last time—that you must not question any order the mistress gives you. If the mistress gives you an order, it is my order. If the mistress wants dinner served in the stables, serve dinner in the stables, and without argument. Do you understand me, Appuhamy?"

"Yes, Master," was the reply, given in a small, tired, beaten voice. "I understand."

"I hope you do, Appuhamy," said Carey dismally. He could not bring himself to make the direct and obvious threat. "I hope you do, Appuhamy," he repeated, "because it would be a pity, a great pity . . ."

"Thank you, George," said Ruth, when Appuhamy had left the room. "There have been times lately when I began to feel that there wasn't room for Appuhamy and me under the same roof. What's so tragic about it," she continued in absolute sincerity, "is that I can see his point of view just as well as I can see my own. He would die for you cheerfully. I know that. I suppose I ought to love him for it and, in a queer, twisted kind of way, I do. But has it ever occurred to you, George, that his loyalty takes a curious form? He serves you wonderfully. I don't expect the world is going to see servants like Appuhamy again ever. But do you know something, George? You're just as much his servant as he is yours—sometimes even more. Even his loyalty to you is not the direct, simple thing it appears to be. He sees his loyalty to you through your father's eyes. I have a fancy, you know, that your father would never have had a meal served in here. It means really that the price you've had to pay all these years for Appuhamy's loyalty has been submission to Appuhamy's interpretation of your father's wishes. That's why, don't you see, Appuhamy rebels against any new ideas. If you were to buy an aeroplane—and I daresay before very long people will be owning aeroplanes— Appuhamy would be against it, because in your father's time there were no set rules as to what to do with an aeroplane, or with people who arrived in one. It would be all wrong because it was new.

"I understand Appuhamy being like that, but he's making you old before your time, George. If I'd let him, he'd make me old, too. I won't let him. I'll fight him, just as I have to fight this great bunga-low, every hour of every day. I'm anxious to get Tommy away from it before—it's too late. I don't want him to be moulded in mind and habit by a bungalow which lives in the past and refuses to admit that the world is changing. George!" Ruth's voice broke as she tried to express the strange fear which gripped her. "Don't you feel it—all around you? This great bungalow isn't here to serve us. There is only one way to be happy here, and that is to submit to the demands of this—this"—Ruth looked around her—"this immense, cruel house that your father built. It demands obedience and"—her voice rose to a pitch of hysteria—"I won't obey, George, I won't! It has you firmly in its grip, but it hasn't got me—or Tommy. It won't get us —ever!"

❋

❋

❋

❋

❋ **CHAPTER SEVENTEEN** ❋ ❋ ❋ ❋ ❋ ❋

Two pairs of keen eyes, the one old and sad, the other young and alert, had noted that Ruth and Geoffrey Wilding had not seen one another alone for more than two weeks. Twice during that time Wilding had been to the Big Bungalow, summoned by George Carey to discuss matters connected with the management of Elephant Walk. George Carey was gathering back into his own hands some of the reins of power which he had allowed to slip into the hands of Wilding, who was realising that his employer was not just a figurehead. In the course of these visits Ruth and Wilding had met in the most casual possible fashion, exchanged a few words lightly and Wilding had returned to his own bungalow.

Appuhamy and Rayna, whose eyes had observed these things, interpreted them each in his own way. Appuhamy was glad. He was big enough to forget his dislike of Ruth, which was resentment more than active dislike, because he knew that when relations between her and George Carey were pleasant and harmonious, it was very good for his master, who looked after his work more intelligently, ate sensibly, drank less, walked with a more brisk, alert step and smiled more readily. If Ruth could do these things for George Carey and would go on doing them, Appuhamy was content. The morality of her past conduct did not touch him. If she were able to make George Carey happy, that surely was her mission in life. More he did not seek; less he could not condone. It was a simple enough philosophy, but as Appuhamy saw things, the problem **was** simple.

Rayna, who had observed these things also, saw in them a good omen. Some few days after asking Appuhamy for money, several mysterious parcels arrived addressed to Rayna, bearing labels of a Colombo department store which did a large mail-order business. Rayna had spent not a little time lately looking at herself in a mirror, indulging in a kind of self-analysis with the object of trying to learn wherein lay any significant difference between herself and Ruth Carey. Ruth had white skin which, considered quite judicially and impartially, Rayna did not consider as beautiful as her own. Ruth was not, she thought, a very clever or amusing woman, nor was she herself. Ruth could play tennis and ride a horse, but somehow Rayna did not believe that these accomplishments made a great difference. Privately, Rayna thought most of Ruth's clothes were ugly, nothing like so graceful, probably not as comfortable either, as her own simple, Sinhalese attire. Rayna having on more than one occasion seen Ruth without clothes, had no envy. She arrived, therefore, in due course at the conclusion that any superior power of attraction which Ruth had—and it seemed that she had—was due to externals. Probably Geoffrey Wilding did not like Sinhalese clothes. If, therefore, she herself adopted European clothes, she would be quite irresistible.

With Rayna, to reach a conclusion was to act upon it. Standing in front of a mirror, wearing a low-cut evening gown of gold *lamé,* surmounted by a floppy hat, a four-year-old left-over from 1914's Ascot, and twirling a pink silk parasol, Rayna decided that she looked the part of a fashionable European beauty. Stockings, she decided, were unnecessary, particularly as they would not keep up. Shoes were another difficulty. Rayna had beautiful feet but, like those of all people who go bare-footed, they had splayed. In order to find a pair broad enough, the assistant who made up the order in Colombo had sent a pair some three sizes too long. By dint of stuffing the toes with newspaper, Rayna had made them possible to wear. They were, however, incredibly uncomfortable and she knew she was incapable of walking a hundred yards in them, let alone the three miles to Geoffrey Wilding's bungalow.

Clad thus, Rayna was sure that Wilding would be impelled to treat her with the same smiling courtesy he accorded Ruth Carey, whereas as she knew to her cost, in her own national costume, he had merely treated her indulgently as one treats a child.

"I do not think," said Rayna, as she left Appuhamy's house a little before sunset, wearing her ordinary clothes but carrying a large cardboard box under her arm, "that I shall be back tonight."

Appuhamy had grown to love Rayna. Except when in one of her black moods, she had been more comfort to him than any one of his own children or grandchildren. It pleased him to see her quick smile, to watch her lithe, splendid movements and to hear the bell-like tinkle of her laughter about the house. For the rest, there was little enough of gaiety in Appuhamy's life these days. A happy marriage was quite out of the question for Rayna. No Sinhalese of the type she would have considered as a husband would have married her, and it was very sure that she would never be content to be the wife and drudge of a low-caste Rodiya back in her native village. She had progressed too far now to return. She had tasted comfort, lived on the fringe of luxury, known the joy of fine clothes and, because she was not recognised in the Ratnagalla district as a Rodiya, had learned to meet her fellows on terms of equality. Appuhamy, therefore, hoped that, despite the long delay, his original plan for her would materialise. Now, because he loved Rayna, he added to the hope another one: that Wilding would be kind to her.

Rayna decided against using the rear entrance to Wilding's bungalow, which she now considered beneath her dignity. She arrived while Wilding, not long returned from the fields, was splashing in his bath. Going to the spare bedroom in which she had spent many lonely and tearful nights, she lit the lamp with trembling fingers, closing the door softly against any possible intrusion. Her eyes danced with excitement as she undid the cardboard box and spread her newly-acquired finery upon the bed, exulting at the thought of the mocking light so soon to be extinguished in Wilding's eyes and to be exchanged for the softer light of admiration and adoration. She felt now that she would be happy always if just once she could see in Wilding's eyes the look she had seen more than once directed at Ruth Carey.

In Kandy Rayna had observed European women twirling their

parasols. She admired the gesture enormously. It seemed so sophisticated. Those who did it seemed so sure of themselves and of their surroundings. During these last days, she felt she had perfected the art in front of a mirror.

Rayna waited for her entrance until Wilding was on the veranda, drinking a meditative whisky-and-soda before dinner. As "Wallflower" had not been a signal success years previously on her first unannounced entrance, Rayna had saturated herself with "Jockey Club". It was a full-bodied perfume, smiting the olfactory sense with a vigour not far short of pure ammonia.

Wilding began to cough as the spare bedroom door opened. Without any other evidence, he knew within seconds the identity of his visitor. He had been expecting a visit from Rayna, pleasurably so. To him, therefore, there was as yet little element of surprise. Without being very definite on the point, he had come to the conclusion that his affair with Ruth, amusing though it might be, was not altogether wise. As a long term investment, he mused, George Carey was likely to be better than Ruth. It would suit him admirably to have the Careys, as promised, gallivanting about the world after the war, leaving him in sole control of Elephant Walk. George Carey had already nearly doubled his salary in recognition of services rendered and the rising cost of living, going so far as to hold out prospects of a share in the profits of the estate. Sooner or later, if the affair with Ruth continued, even George Carey would not be able to blind himself to it. In fact, Wilding marvelled that someone had not told him already. Rayna was, as George Carey in a drunken moment had observed not long previously, "a smashing little filly". In all the circumstances, it seemed she would be less productive of trouble than Ruth. She would have to be taught—Wilding wrinkled his nose—to use perfume with more discretion. There were other things she must learn, too, and the rôle of teacher did not seem an unpleasing one.

"Good evening, Mr Wilding," came a bell-like voice from behind him.

"Good evening," replied Wilding. "Who is that?" Taking a clean handkerchief from his pocket, he flicked imaginary dust off a chair. "Come and sit down, won't you?"

Rayna's careful poise deserted her in the flicker of an eyelid.

"Who were you expecting?" she asked, spitting out her words viciously.

Rayna was still in the shadows, invisible to Wilding, who sat in the direct light of a hanging lamp. Pausing for a moment to regain her carefully studied poise, Rayna made her entrance. She approached into the pool of lamplight, her face cast into shadow by the hat. Standing swaying slightly from the hips, wincing from the pain of the constricting shoes, Rayna twirled her parasol most convincingly.

It was not deliberate cruelty which sent Wilding into peals of uncontrollable laughter, for he would have been almost superhuman if he had not laughed. The ensemble—the gold *lamé* evening gown, designed to be worn by a woman three times Rayna's age, the pink parasol and the ridiculous hat, no less than the gigantic shoes which peeped out from beneath the frock—was grotesque in the extreme. A black rage swept over Rayna as she stood there watching while Wilding rolled in helpless laughter. She wanted to say a thousand bitter, ugly, cruel things, but her rage was too intense for mere words to act as a safety-valve. With all her strength and the speed of a cat, Rayna slapped Wilding's face, but even this did not check the bellows of his laughter. When Rayna began at length to laugh with him, her laughter was that of hysteria, which lasted only a few moments.

"What is wrong with me? Why do you laugh?" she stormed.

"There's nothing wrong with you, Rayna," replied Wilding in a kinder voice, realising a little of what the girl was suffering.

"Do you not like these clothes? To me," she said, with a defiant toss of the head, "they are very beautiful."

"Yes," Wilding agreed, "they are very beautiful. But you do not need clothes to make you beautiful."

Once again Wilding had to stifle the laughter that rose irresistibly to his lips. Rayna in that moment believed that she could endure anything on earth except laughter. Looking down into Wilding's mocking, up-turned face, she spat full at him as the measure of her rage. "If you do not like me in these clothes," she said, checking her sobs, "perhaps you like me better like this." With swift, savage movements she ripped the evening gown down the front and stood before him naked from the waist up, in all the glory of a pair of white linen drawers. In stepping out of the ruins of the gown, the gigantic shoes impeded her movements. Once again Wilding laughed, for to him the scene was irresistibly comic. Once again Rayna's reply was to spit at him, but this time his eyes grew dark with anger.

"That," said he angrily, "is not polite. I see that I shall have to teach you manners." Throwing her over his knee, he administered half a dozen really hard slaps, which stung furiously.

Rayna lay across his knees unresistingly. "More please!" she said coaxingly, turning a smiling face up to his. . . .

*   *   *   *   *

Rayna's unceremonious entrance into Wilding's solitary life seemed to both of them a most excellent arrangement. To Rayna the first weeks were, for the most part, blissful. Now, and for the first time in her life, her animal beauty was the object of the admiration which, in her eyes, it merited. It was not for any qualities of the mind that Wilding found her an amusing companion. "My beautiful little hell cat!" was how he described Rayna to her face. She did not mind what noun or nouns were qualified, always provided that one of the adjectives of pulchritude be used. So long as her beauty was never allowed to recede into the background, she was happy.

The first clash of wills occurred when Rayna, during the hours immediately before and after dinner, demanded the right to chatter inconsequentially, disappearing from time to time into the spare room to change into new finery. Her first experiment at wearing European clothes was her last. She could not even survey the tattered garments she had bought so hopefully without an angry scowl at the recollection of the laughter they had evoked. Wearing her new finery, she liked to pirouette round the veranda and, if Wilding did not utter extravagant expressions of admiration, she would fly into a rage.

The first time it was amusing. She pleased Wilding most when she was angry because, under stress of anger, she stripped off even the thin veneer of propriety which, at times, she wore quite convincingly. In the throes of anger or any other passion she lost all control, becoming, if anything, more beautiful. After a while, however, the enormous egoism which went with her beauty became a little wearisome.

By longstanding habit, Wilding devoted the hours immediately before and after dinner to reading and to his private correspondence. "Go away, Rayna!" he said one evening impatiently, when her importunities had become a nuisance. "I've some letters to write."

"Who are you writing to?" she asked suspiciously.

"That's none of your business. Go away and play."

"I am not a child any more," was the angry retort.

"All right. You are not a child. But for God's sake, shut up!"

"You do not love me, or you would want to talk to me and see my new clothes."

"No, I don't love you, and unless you want to be spanked hard, don't mention the word love here."

"Spank me, please," said Rayna disconcertingly.

"Go away!" reiterated Wilding. "I don't want to talk and I don't want to listen to you. You only talk nonsense, and I'm not in the mood for nonsense. I'm not interested in your clothes. In fact," he added, turning his back, "the only time I'm interested in you at all is when you're in bed."

"Lovely!" said Rayna, clapping her hands gleefully and trying to drag Wilding from his chair. "Then let's go to bed. I am not hungry. I do not want any dinner."

Wilding continued with his writing, trying to catch up with some weeks arrears of correspondence which had accumulated, largely owing to Rayna's insistent demands for the admiration, which she regarded as her right. To her, admiration was as necessary as food.

For ten minutes, or so, there was silence, broken only by the scratching of Wilding's pen and an occasional mutinous sigh from Rayna, who sat scowling and fuming with indignation at being thus neglected.

She chose to creep across the veranda to look over Wilding's shoulder at the moment when he was beginning to pen a polite note to Ruth Carey, returning a pile of magazines and thanking her for the loan of them. He had, in fact, only written the two words:

"Dear Ruth", when he was nearly scalped by two fists which dragged out handfuls of hair, while a set of sharp teeth bit the lobe of one ear, causing it to bleed profusely. Rayna hurled at Wilding every vile word she knew in English and in Sinhalese, and in the latter language her invective was highly picturesque. Wilding, by this time, was so angry that his first impulse was to give her a thorough beating. He refrained, however, because as he already knew, at the cost of his own dignity, Rayna preferred chastisement to being ignored.

"You were writing to that woman!" Rayna stormed, when a little coherence had returned to her. "What were you going to write to her?"

"I was only going to tell her," replied Wilding, "how beautiful she is. Do you not think she is beautiful?"

Rayna's reply defies the typographer's art.

"If you will stay just like that," said Wilding, looking with the eye of an artist at Rayna, who stood, eyes glinting, fists clenched, teeth bared and the skin drawn tight over high cheek-bones, the very picture of Fury, "I will paint you, and I shall be famous."

"You think," said Rayna, smiling sweetly, her mood changing in a second, "that I am beautiful?"

With a despairing laugh, Wilding returned to his writing. He completed the letter to Ruth, adding a paragraph more than he had originally intended, to the effect that, if she were free the following afternoon, he would like to play tennis and dine at the Big Bungalow. The only way, it seemed, of making clear to Rayna her position in his bungalow, was to ignore her for a little time. Otherwise, despite her beauty and the gaiety of her presence, she was in process of becoming an intolerable nuisance.

The following afternoon Wilding and Ruth played a few sets of violent tennis together, meeting on the cool, pleasant basis of tennis itself. They both enjoyed the game enormously. Of the three sets they played, Ruth won one.

The evening was not so easy or pleasant. George Carey, hating himself for it, could not forget the suspicions which Ruth had planted in his mind regarding Wilding. Every instinct in him called to him to force Ruth either to withdraw what she had said, or to amplify it. But there was a little inner voice which urged him not to do so.

If the suspicions, which now would not be stilled, were well-founded —and Carey told himself they might be—then he had the advantage of being forewarned. If, on the other hand, they were ill-founded, provided he did nothing, no harm would be done. But to a man of his nature, it made contact with Wilding difficult and uncomfortable. To hide his own ill-ease that evening he drank a great deal more than he had been drinking for many weeks. At dinner he fell asleep three times, awakening to Appuhamy's experienced touching of his right elbow. After dinner he applied himself to the whisky decanter with more than usual enthusiasm. He was soon too drunk to be amusing.

More to spare George the humiliation of being seen in his present condition, than for a desire to walk with Wilding in the moonlight, Ruth led the way to the garden. Here, strangely enough, they behaved like two light acquaintances. Ruth, despite her air of gaiety, felt horribly embarrassed, while Wilding, who was not embarrassed at all, kept the talk upon the plane which she seemingly preferred. Ruth, he still thought, was a delightful woman and a pleasant companion.

As they strolled they talked a little wistfully of London, the bombing raids and the current theatrical productions. Neither of them had seen *Chu Chin Chow, The Maid of the Mountains, The Lilac Domino,* or the other successes, whose melodies were on every lip. They indulged for a while in nostalgia, that vicarious pleasure of the exile.

Yes, Wilding decided, Ruth had that rare gift of intelligence, which was not at the expense of charm, as so often happened with intelligent women.

"You know, Ruth," said Wilding, spontaneously giving expression to some of his thoughts, "you're the nicest companion imaginable. I've only realised lately how much I owe to you. Whether you did it consciously or not, I don't know, but you helped me more than you will ever know to get out of myself when I came back. Thank you," he added, turning to implant a light kiss on her forehead. It was the friendly kiss of a brother for a sister, but to Rayna, lurking in the shadows, watching every movement, listening to every word, it was charged with hideous meaning.

Perhaps happily for them, neither Wilding nor Ruth glimpsed the searing hatred and jealousy which held Rayna in their grip, nor was able to see how the lovely young animal had reverted to primaeval savagery. This moment in the garden had implanted in Rayna's heart an implacable hatred for Ruth which, no matter what might happen, would never die.

For Wilding, the weekend at the Big Bungalow was the forerunner of several others. The reasons which prompted him to alter his habits were complex. Primarily, he went because he liked it as a change. He was aware, too, because his perceptions were very keen, of a difference in George Carey. The difference was too subtle to be pinned down and catalogued, but he was aware of a certain drawing-away, and he wondered at it. By seeing more of George Carey, he felt, he would understand what lay behind it. His absences from home served, too, to spare him some of the importunities of Rayna's vanity and, by giving her a sense of insecurity, to keep her in her place.

He knew, without any shadow of doubt, that this changed attitude of George Carey's had nothing to do with his relations with Ruth, for Carey was not the kind of man who could keep such suspicions to himself. The change, therefore, must be something to do with Elephant Walk. This puzzled him the more. Geoffrey Wilding, like the rest of his fellow-men, was a queer mixture. He was by way of being a perfectionist in the sense that he did things to the best of his ability, or he did not do them at all. He had given Elephant Walk of his best, and he knew with certainty that there was not one single detail of the work and responsibility which had been entrusted to him which had not been faithfully and conscientiously carried out. He knew, too, that George Carey was too good a planter himself to have any doubts upon the subject or, having doubts, to waste any time setting them at rest.

Why, then, had this subtle, barely perceptible drawing-away on George Carey's part, taken place? By a process of elimination it did not take Geoffrey Wilding very long to reach the conclusion that was, in fact, the right one: that Ruth lay behind this change.

When he troubled to do so, Geoffrey Wilding could make himself very charming to men and women and could exercise a domination over them which was not apparent. He had the knack of showing himself in a good light when it suited him to do so. If, as he believed, Ruth were the key to George Carey's attitude, it meant only that he had lost the power to charm and, in some degree, to dominate Ruth.

In reaching this conclusion, Wilding fell far short of doing justice to Ruth or of understanding the tortuous thinking of an unhappy woman. He could not realise—perhaps easy conquests in the past and vanity were responsible for this—that his power over Ruth had been an animal, physical power, but never a mental one. He did not realise that he was dealing with a divided personality, one which, furthermore, he himself had divided. He believed it lay in his power to lead Ruth once again a willing slave into the slough of bodily passion, but what he did not know was that, in so doing, because she would be disgusted at her own frailty, he would be driving her spiritually in the opposite direction from that which he desired. If he were to study his own inclinations now entirely, he had no more use for Ruth physically. With Rayna at his beck and call, there was no room for any other woman in his life, except intellectually. But since it seemed expedient to do so, he resolved to exercise his domination over Ruth in the only way he understood.

The paradox of it all was too deep and obscure for even the subtleties of Geoffrey Wilding's mind, for he had read Ruth Carey's character wrongly. The more she wronged George Carey, the more deeply she felt her loyalty to him and the more determined she became, cost her what it might in suffering, to give him a spiritual loyalty, even if she had failed to give him bodily fidelity.

*   *   *   *   *

June 24th, 1918 was Tommy's third birthday, in honour of which George Carey had planned one of the magnificent picnics for which Elephant Walk was famous. Everyone in the district—which meant John Gilliland and Robbie Norman—was coming and, in addition, several spare rooms in the Big Bungalow were being opened for old friends from other districts, who were coming to spend a few days, and who had never, because of the incidence of war, seen Tommy.

The site chosen for the picnic was a famous one in Elephant Walk annals: a grassy knoll half-way down to the factory where a dam, which provided the factory with water power, also made an excellent swimming-pool.

Tommy, in whose honour the party was given, had arrived in a palanquin carried by two coolies, specially chosen for their sure-footedness. Beside him, easily able to maintain the cracking pace set by the coolies, was Rayna.

Ruth, who rode just behind Tommy, found herself wondering about Rayna's strange behaviour during recent months, and was glad to see the girl again after an absence of some weeks. Since Rayna's position at Elephant Walk was strictly that of Appuhamy's grand-niece and she was in no sense of the word an employee, Ruth had no right to question her comings and goings. She was happy to note, however, that Rayna had brought back with her something of her old warmth, gaiety and friendliness. She seemed to adore Tommy, and Tommy in his turn loved to have her near him. Rayna, Ruth reflected, was in many ways as much of a child as Tommy and most certainly derived almost as much pleasure as he did from the childish games she played with him.

Towards Ruth, Rayna's manner seemed the same as it had been in happier days, but with a subtle difference upon which Ruth found herself unable to put her finger. If anything, the last months had heightened Rayna's beauty. She was more ripe, mature and better poised. The loveliness was still there, but some of the spontaneous gaiety seemed not so much less gay as less spontaneous.

The party arrived at the picnic ground to find, in the shade of a giant mango tree, two enormous trestle tables already erected, one for the guests and the other for serving. Here, in a profusion which gladdened Appuhamy's heart, recalling the splendid old days, were delicacies such as imported pheasant—canned but excellent; the ham of a young boar cured with sugar, in the Virginia fashion; fresh-water crayfish, served with golden mounds of mayonnaise; a magnificent cold hump of beef, without which no Carey picnic was ever complete. There was, in addition, a delicious Madras curry, served with mounds of white and flaky rice. For those with a sweet tooth, there was a bowl of fruit salad and a rich concoction compounded of the whipped cream of young coconuts, crushed almonds, honey and white of egg. To set off these delicacies were the finest linen, cut glass and silver, giving the feast a final touch of splendour.

"Now, darling," said George Carey to Ruth, when the meal was ended, "you're going to taste something you've never tasted before: real 'Monkey Coffee'." Monkeys, he went on to explain, found the few coffee bushes which had survived the blight decades previously. They, better than men, knew the exact moment to gather the perfectly ripe berries, judging them by colour. Their stomach acids were not strong enough to penetrate the tough outer skin of the berries, which passed unharmed through them, to be eliminated in small piles on the rocks where they could be gathered easily.

"It's perfectly clean, darling," George assured Ruth, seeing the look of disgust on her face. "Before being used, the berries are pulped and the skins removed. Mark my words, you've never tasted coffee as good."

Ruth did not believe the story until taken to see two coolies eagerly collecting a small sack of "Monkey Coffee".

During the afternoon a few of the more daring spirits, Ruth among them, swam in the dam, making quickly for the shadow of the mango tree afterwards to avoid the dire possibilities of sunburn.

Tommy, realising that all the excitement was for him, chortled with delight. Like most children, he loved to be the centre of attraction. He and Rayna had evolved a game of their own, played with a multi-coloured rubber ball, which spent most of its time lost in the undergrowth a few yards down the slope from where the picnic tables had been laid.

Watching Rayna and Tommy thus, and secretly a little ashamed of her feelings, Ruth became aware of a tinge of jealousy, that her son could be so utterly happy, to the exclusion of everyone else, in the company of this lovely but strange-natured girl, who hovered on the fringe of life at the Big Bungalow. Thus impelled, Ruth went to join the game. After some twenty minutes of play, during which she became over-heated, Ruth and Tommy, sprawling towards the ball, lay for a few moments laughing and exhausted, while the ball itself trickled into the undergrowth, disturbing in its passage a drab green reptile horror, coiled in sleep. Ruth's first thought was for Tommy, who lay between her and the disturbed snake. With a quick, violent motion, which caused the child to cry with pain, Ruth seized him and threw him over her own body, calling to Rayna, who stood watching: "Quick, Rayna! Pick Tommy up and take him away. There's a snake here!"

Eagerly Rayna gathered Tommy into her arms, retreating a few paces to safety. As she did so, the snake struck, retreating at once into the undergrowth. On her ankle Ruth felt a sharp pain, not particularly severe, as though she had been stung by a wasp. Pulling down her stocking, she saw two tiny punctures in the skin, so faint that, had she not seen the snake herself, she would not have been troubled.

"George," she called, trying to keep the alarm out of her voice so as not to spoil the party, "will you come down here a minute, please?"

"What is it, darling?" asked George, going to where Ruth was sitting on the grass.

"I think," she replied, "that I've been bitten by a snake."

"Quick! Show me," said George. "What kind of a snake was it?"

"I don't know, George," said Ruth helplessly. "It was a sort of dirty browny drab green and mottled."

"You've got to be more precise than that, Ruth," said George anxiously. "Did you notice, for example, a hood?" Ruth shook her head.

In silence George opened a small flat tin box which he always wore at his waist-belt when out on the estate. It contained first-aid necessities for snake-bite. With quick, deft hands he put a tourniquet above Ruth's right knee and, withdrawing from the box a lancet, said: "Sorry, darling. This is going to hurt, but it's got to be done—now."

With the lancet he made two swift criss-cross cuts over the marks left by the reptile's fangs. The cuts bled profusely.

"Listen, darling," Carey said slowly. "Listen to me very carefully. You may have been bitten by a rat-snake, which is more or less harmless. More probably you've been bitten by a cobra or by a *tic-polonga*. Either of them is very dangerous. I'm not going to prompt you, but if I'd seen the snake, I could have told the difference. The danger is, don't you see, darling, that the treatment for the two bites is entirely opposite. Try to recall and describe exactly what you saw. And, Ruth darling, there isn't much time to lose."

By this time the rest of the party, realising that something untoward had happened, came down the slope to where George kneeled beside Ruth.

"It's no good, George," said Ruth. "I was too badly frightened to notice the details. All I can tell you is that it was a snake—I daresay about five or six feet long."

"Had it a thick, blunt head, do you think?" persisted George.

"It's no good, George. I just don't know. But," she added, "Rayna saw. She could tell you."

Rayna, with Tommy clasped in her arms, had not moved a step. She was standing very stiffly, her face almost expressionless, except for a faint smile playing elusively about her lips.

"You saw the snake, Rayna," said Carey roughly. "What was it? Mrs Carey's life depends on what you say," he added in an undertone.

"I saw the snake, yes," said Rayna calmly. "But my eyes were all for Tommy. I did not notice what kind of a snake it was."

George Carey knew that Rayna was lying, because he knew that no girl born and brought up in a Sinhalese village could ever be in the slightest doubt as to the identity of the snake she had seen. It must have been one of the three species he had named.

"If you saw the snake, Rayna," said Carey savagely, seizing her by the shoulders, "you must know what kind it was. Tell me, or by God I'll shake the life out of you!"

Rayna, with eyes which had turned to pin-points, returned George Carey's gaze unflinchingly. "You may do what you please," she replied slowly. "I do not know what kind of snake it was."

Realising that time was passing and that there was nothing more to be gained from Rayna, George Carey kneeled down beside Ruth again. "Listen, darling," he said. "Rayna either can't or won't tell us. I've got to gamble. In the hundreds of times I've been here I've seen snakes before. They were almost always cobras. *Tics* are very rare here."

"How do you mean, gamble, George?"

"Listen to me carefully. You may be able to tell me exactly how

244   *ELEPHANT WALK*

you feel and from that I'll be able to tell what bit you. The cobra bite slows down the action of the heart. If it was a cobra, you'll feel terribly tired and want to sleep. On the other hand, if it was a *tic,* the action of the heart would be accelerated. Whisky is the best thing for a cobra bite but, I've got to speak plainly, Ruth darling, it would be fatal for a *tic* bite. Do you understand now what I mean when I say I'm going to gamble? I'm going to assume that it was a cobra, because the probability is that it was. Do you understand me?"

"Yes, I understand perfectly, George," said Ruth calmly. "You do as you think best."

"Do you feel anything?"

"In myself, no. But there's a dull throbbing pain in my ankle. It hurts—quite a lot."

"Well, whatever the brute was," said George, "I've bled most of the venom out of you. Now," he laughed, "it's going to be my turn to see you drunk because, Ruth, you're going to be very drunk for a great many hours."

John Gilliland was already standing by with a whisky decanter and glass. George Carey poured from it close on half a pint of raw spirit. "Get that down your throat, Ruth darling," he said. "It doesn't matter how ill you are. Get it down your throat!"

Ruth gagged on the raw spirit, but somehow forced it down. The world began to swim. After that she did not care.

Roughly bandaging Ruth's ankle, George helped her to her feet. He and Gilliland then walked her up and down, forcing her to keep awake.

Some twenty minutes later Ruth, as through a mist, heard George's voice.

"Thank God, Gilly!" he said. "If it'd been a *tic,* she wouldn't be alive now. It must have been a cobra."

For Ruth during the next hours there were odd patches of agonising consciousness. Her head reeled with the fumes of whisky, while her limbs were held in the grip of a terrible lethargy. All she wanted was to go to sleep, but always at her side were two men. Sometimes it was George Carey and John Gilliland, Robbie Norman and Wilding, while at other times two other male guests, whose names she could not remember, walked her up and down, denying her the sleep for which her soul craved. Every time she was slipping off into blissful, delightful unconsciousness, they brought her back to consciousness. With every hour that passed, although she did not know it, she was slowly, barely perceptibly, creeping back towards life and strength.

In the few precious moments which had been wasted in talk, the deadly cobra venom—for such it was—had entered her blood-stream. The whisky, pills which contained strychnine, and the enforced exercise had kept her awake, kept her heart pumping, little by little overcoming the lethargy whose end is death.

In the late afternoon Ruth, between relays of men, was forced to stagger back on foot up the long hill to the Big Bungalow, where for many hours they kept her walking, walking, walking, when every fibre in her cried for the solace of sleep.

At length, only Rayna, Appuhamy and a few servants were left at the picnic ground. When they were alone and beyond the reach of any possible eavesdropper, Appuhamy turned to Rayna. "You knew," he said, "that it was a good snake?" *

"I knew," replied Rayna.

"Why did you not speak?"

"I am not God," said Rayna, the skin drawn tightly over her cheek-bones and lips. "It was God who sent the snake, and only God knew whether He wished the woman to live or to die."

"Had it not been a cobra, you would have allowed her to die?"

"Of course. It would have been God's will."

"Then," said Appuhamy, who knew unhappily that he was responsible for the fierce hatred which consumed Rayna, "if you were willing thus to see her die, you are more wicked than I believed possible."

"You talk like a fool!" retorted Rayna. "I allowed her to live, did I not? I had only to say that it was a *tic*. I did not say that because, as I told you, I am not God. It was for God to say whether she was to live or to die, not Rayna. But I hoped and prayed that she would die. . . ."

"You should have told the truth, child," said Appuhamy, appalled but not at all astonished by what he heard. "It is as wrong to gamble

* A colloquialism for the cobra, because the cobra is credited with having saved Buddha's life.

with the life of another—even the life of one whom you hate—as it is to kill."

"I did not gamble, I tell you," said Rayna. "I did not send the snake. I did not tell the snake to leave one and to bite another. It is nothing to do with me. Do you hear me? Nothing, nothing! Let her die or let her live! It is for God to decide."

"It seems," said Appuhamy in a heavy voice, "that God wished the woman to live. There must, therefore, be a purpose, for there is always a purpose."

Appuhamy was a Buddhist by birth and upbringing, even if not orthodox in all his beliefs. He understood, therefore, better than he seemed to understand, Rayna's attitude.

As a Buddhist, Corea, the Big Bungalow cook, would not kill even a chicken, but many a time he had caught a chicken, held it while a low-caste Tamil cut off its head, and had then cooked and eaten it. Between this and actually striking the blow which killed the chicken, Corea was able, by the tortuous ways of Buddhist hair-splitting, to see a difference.

Rayna had not conjured up the cobra which had bitten Ruth. She had not conspired even to allow Ruth to cross its path. She had remained coldly, implacably neutral, leaving Ruth's fate to a higher tribunal.

Appuhamy had progressed far beyond mere literal obedience to Buddhist teachings. He believed—and in this he was one of a very small minority—that the spirit of the teachings was of more account than the letter. Rayna's hatred for Ruth, strong as it was, would not permit her to kill, but, seeing no further than the letter of the law, she did not feel impelled by its spirit to save a life which she believed stood between her and the man she wanted.

When it was sure that Ruth would recover, Rayna accepted the decision with the same indifference that she would have shown if the cobra bite had proved fatal. Either way, she had played no part whatever.

✳

✳

✳

✳

✳ **CHAPTER EIGHTEEN** ✳ ✳ ✳ ✳ ✳ ✳

Heat brooded heavily over the low country. An oppressive silence lay like a blanket over the jungle. Monkeys sat crouched in shady tree-forks, their almost ceaseless chattering silent. Even the raucous voices of myriads of the parrot family were stilled. The sultry, oppressive heat accounted only in part for the deathly silence which had come over the jungle and over the wide clearing where, a few weeks previously, had been a waterhole and mud wallow, whose surface was now a crust of dried mud whose cracks would grow wider that day as the sun rose above the surrounding trees. Every living thing in the jungle was aware of great events afoot; the greatest, perhaps, they were ever privileged to witness.

Beside what had once been the waterhole, motionless as a graven statue, stood an Old Bull elephant, his flank deeply scarred by old wounds. One of his ears hung at a queer lopsided angle. On his flank were two very recent bullet wounds. They were not serious, as bullet wounds go, but there were times when they were very painful.

The Old Bull was not happy. At the base of one tusk, deeply buried in a mass of gristle and bone, decay had begun, and any leverage exerted upon the tip of the tusk, however slight, caused a suction which exposed the nerve at the base, subjecting him to blinding, searing waves of pain as a reward for any carelessness.

Occasionally, as he stood there, the Old Bull flapped his great ears, listening intently and, hearing nothing, allowed himself to be lulled for a few minutes into the belief that he was not going to hear what he feared to hear and what, in his innermost heart, he knew he would hear before long. It came before the sun had lifted over the tree-tops, as it had come for the last many mornings at the same time: the brazen trumpeting of another bull, who hovered a few hundred yards distant in the shelter of the jungle. There were challenge and mockery in the sound. On the previous mornings it had been so far distant that it had been possible to ignore it, to pretend to those who looked to him for leadership that he had not heard it. But this morning these others, the cows who stood huddled in the shade some eighty yards distant, had not only heard the sound but knew now beyond any shadow of doubt that he had heard it, too. Pretence, therefore, was no longer possible.

There is an ancient piece of wisdom among the Elephant People, handed down to them from the time when the world was very young. It has taught them all down through the ages the simple truth that, if the Elephant People are to survive as unchallenged monarchs of the jungle, he who would be the sire of future generations, must prove his fitness. For a very long while the Old Bull had been lord and master of the herd. The calves who played and fretted at their mothers' sides were his sons and daughters. That they were sleek, bounding rubber balls of health and baby strength was proof, if proof were needed, of his fitness to sire them.

They had been splendid years which were gone: roaming the mountains and the plains; enduring the fierce heat and drought; wallowing in the cool, healing mud when the rain fell; feeding off sweet grasses when they grew and reaching up into the trees for tender foliage when the earth began to parch. But the Old Bull was haunted by the consciousness that these splendid days were nearly over.

Once again the still morning air was rent with the trumpeted challenge of this other bull. Nearer this time. So near that the cows, huddling under the trees, shuffled their feet uneasily as they caught the hot, lusty smell of him. They were looking now in the direction of their lord and master who, thus far, had remained silent but who, if pride and tradition meant anything to him, must ere long reply.

The Old Bull was not a coward. He had proved that in a dozen battles. But he was tired. He wanted only to be left alone, to be able, in a few more years, to die in peace.

A third time there came the insolent trumpeted challenge of the newcomer, who now revealed himself in the open as a fine, strong young bull, sleek as the Old Bull himself had once been, and eager to take the prize which he sensed now lay within his grasp. The Old Bull threw up his trunk, blasting a trumpeted acceptance of the challenge offered. His voice was deeper than that of the challenger, more resonant. It was laden with all the anger, bitterness, heartache and futility of old age. The cows, huddled under the trees, shuffled their feet approvingly. They had known that in this great crisis their lord and master would not fail, would not prove himself devoid of the pride and courage which had enabled him to survive the embattled years.

The battle could not now be long delayed. Before the sun set the Old Bull would have established his right and fitness to sire another generation of the Elephant People, or he would have gone down to defeat and its inevitable consequence, oblivion.

The Old Bull was in no hurry. Let his younger opponent wear himself out with impatience if he would. As the challenged, it was for the Old Bull to seek, not only the place, but the time of the duel, and already his keen eyes were scanning the terrain with a view to using every conceivable advantage—and there were pitifully few—given him by age and superior cunning.

The Old Bull lumbered slowly towards a young tree, testing the tip of his left tusk upon it. The blinding pain which resulted told him what he already knew: that if he were to emerge victorious, he must do so without the aid of the sick tusk.

The challenger approached closer, now standing at a distance of no more than fifty yards. He was hot and impatient for the fray; hot and impatient, too, because of the smell of the cows, between whom and himself stood the Old Bull, their lord.

The Old Bull took up a stance where his left flank and the sick tusk were protected by a dense clump of trees which stood in the centre of the clearing. If the young bull wished to attack, he must do so from an angle which gave him no time to gather much speed for the kind of headlong, reckless, charging onslaught favoured by impatient young bulls. If the challenger could only be trapped into over-confidence, the day was not yet lost, for the art of jungle fighting is not learned in theory, but in the hard school of combat itself.

When the challenger's rush came, it came obliquely at the Old Bull's right flank. The latter, seeming to flinch from contact, caused the challenger to check in his stride and swerve inwards, in so doing losing most of the advantage of the attack. As he passed, the Old Bull's sound right tusk ripped a deep furrow down the other's left flank, while above the thunder of feet the sound of tearing hide and flesh came plainly to the watchers under the trees, whose ears were cocked to catch every sound.

Pain, however, does not deter a young bull, and this one came back again. A lunge on the part of the Old Bull, followed by the tremendous impact of his massive head against the other's flank, knocked the challenger off his feet, sending him rolling across the dusty arena, with the breath driven out of him. It cooled some of his ardour. Perhaps, in those seconds, the challenger recognised the superior cunning of the Old Bull and began to realise that tactics such as these were not going to help. He, too, was learning cunning which, if he learned his lesson well, would stand him in good stead over the years to come.

The sun was approaching its zenith when the young bull came in to attack a third time. Swinging clear of the other's formidable right tusk, he drove his body as a wedge between the Old Bull and the trees which sheltered his left flank and, although he did not know it, in that second he won the battle. His left tusk interlocked with the Old Bull's sick left tusk. A hideous, enormous leverage was applied to the decayed root, where a quivering, agonising nerve lay exposed to the least pressure. The young bull felt his opponent go limp. Of the two, the Old Bull was still the stronger, if the less active. Braced for a tremendous struggle with locked tusks, the young bull felt the other slipping away from him. The Old Bull had reached the white-hot limit beyond which nature has decreed that no creature can endure pain. Gusts of pain, sheets of searing agony enveloped his huge body, leaving in its wake the recklessness of despair. He no longer sought to protect the sick tusk. The pain had reached the point where it could never be greater, where it sapped reason, set prudence to flight and, instead of being just a part of life, became life itself. There was nothing but pain.

In his blind maniacal fury, his vast bulk quivering with the waves of agony which racked it, the Old Bull turned upon the challenger, seeking to rend, trample and destroy, and if, in the process, he himself were destroyed, it seemed in those hideous moments so very unimportant.

After some five minutes of savage fighting at close quarters, at a cost to the Old Bull which he himself did not stop to reckon, the young bull retreated in awe at the savage torrent of fury he had unleashed and, as he retreated, blood poured from a deep gash, more than a foot in depth, on one shoulder, while another long furrow in the flank paralleled the first. He was earning the scars which would identify him over the years ahead, and he did not relish them. Some of the fire went out of him, only to be rekindled as a gentle breeze came up the clearing, bringing with it the hot, urgent smells from the cows who stood, aloof and neutral, watching the battle.

The fourth and last attack brought the Old Bull to his knees and, try as he would, he could not rise. There was no pain now, only a dull insensibility which made everything seem unreal. The Old Bull did not hear his younger opponent's triumphant trumpeting. He was spared the sight of the cows who, for so many years, had roamed the jungle and plains with him, coyly, submissively, almost eagerly, turning to their new lord and master.

The young bull went off alone into the shade of the jungle. The cows ambled over towards where the Old Bull lay prostrate. What memories were evoked as they surveyed him thus, lie buried among the eternal secrets, but when a few moments later, from the direction in which the young bull had disappeared, there came a short, sharp trumpeted command, they flapped their ears and, without another glance at their fallen lord, obeyed the summons.

It was sundown when the Old Bull staggered numbly to his feet. Destiny had turned the full circle. They had been good years, but they were over. Now, before in a few days, a few weeks or a few months, he died, the urge came to him to breathe once more the cool air of the hills, to soothe his tired and aching body in the rich mud of a mountain wallow, and to savour once more the tender sweetness of the herbage which grew up there in the myriad dells and valleys where he had frolicked as a calf.

Some three painful miles had to be covered to the nearest water-hole which had not dried up in the heat. The water was foul and almost opaque, but as the Old Bull lay down and rolled in the rich mud at the margin, his thirst quenched, he felt better. An impatience possessed his soul to be on his way.

Summer lightning, flickering up there in the hills, beckoned him onwards. He rose to his feet, threw up his trunk and trumpeted a low, mournful, wistful note in which were subtly blent the agony of defeat and the hope for peace at the end. Up there, where the summer lightning played, there was peace.

*   *   *   *   *

Esmeralda was, as George Carey had pointed out, hog-fat and needing exercise. Ruth, in the saddle for the first time for over six weeks, knew a feeling of profound thankfulness that health and strength and an unclouded outlook had returned to her.

George Carey's prompt action had saved her life. But only just. During the awful time of doubt as to what had bitten her, while the precious seconds ticked away, some of the cobra venom had entered her blood-stream, and she had fought what had at one time looked like a losing battle with death.

The weeks of convalescence had been slow, for during them Ruth had been haunted by the memory of the ice-cold, implacable face of a Sinhalese girl, who had stood aside saying "I do not know". Rayna had known, for Ruth remembered that for whole seconds, which had seemed as long as minutes, the girl's eyes had been fixed upon the crawling horror. She had known and had kept her mouth closed. Only a deep and bitter hatred could have allowed her thus to remain silent and, to a hot-blooded young woman, such hatred, Ruth realised, could only stem from jealousy. Jealousy of what? There could only be one answer: jealousy of Geoffrey Wilding. No one could know, and Ruth herself did not want to know, what fancies might have been in Rayna's mind to prompt her to such awful callousness.

During the time she lay sick, it had been difficult for Ruth to dismiss these things from her mind. Now, with Esmeralda cantering beneath her, it seemed as though they had never existed.

During her convalescence, Geoffrey Wilding had been a constant and, Ruth was bound to admit it, cheerful, charming and attentive visitor, who had helped her in her climb back to health. He had brought books, marked with paragraphs he thought she would like. He had spent hours at the piano, playing gay, lilting music. One day he had brought a spray of the most glorious orchids Ruth had ever seen. "Oh, how lovely, Geoff! Where did you get them?" she had asked, her face flushed with pleasure.

"They come from a little plateau at the top of Ratnagalla Peak. They grow in festoons from the mossy wall of an old Buddhist shrine."

"Do you mean at Gem Cottage?"

Wilding had nodded. "In a little while," he had said, "I'll take you up there. You'll be able to gather orchids—more kinds than you ever dreamed of—until you're tired of them, and then"—his eyes had held hers meaningly—"there'll be the rest of a long day we can spend together."

"No, Geoff," Ruth had said coldly. "You've been very sweet since I've been ill and I appreciate it. But all that's over. It's not only over, it never happened. Do you understand me? I've got you out of my system and I don't intend to allow you to creep back into it—ever. During these last weeks I've had a lot of time to think, Geoff. Sick people have very clear minds sometimes. I think I had. I saw many things clearly: you, me, George, Tommy. But more than all, I saw myself, and I didn't like what I saw. Twice I thought I was going to die, and I knew that I didn't want to die, feeling as I did, unclean and horrible. I won't forget ever how I felt then, and I don't intend to allow myself ever to feel like that again."

Although Ruth had not known it, Geoffrey Wilding, surveying her thoughtfully as she spoke, had realised with something of a shock that she was speaking the sober truth and not, as he had suspected at first, play-acting for effect.

Much of the pleasure he had derived from association with Ruth had sprung from the knowledge of her helpless inability to fight against him. It had pleased him to know that she needed him, while he needed her not at all. Now, to learn from her lips that she was free of him and to realise that this was a fact, had come as a blow to his self-esteem. The suggestion of going together again to Gem Cottage had been made at most only half seriously. He had made it because it fed his self-esteem to see the look of misty longing which he had expected to see in Ruth's eyes.

"You are lucky, Ruth," Wilding had said in a low, tense voice. "Damnably lucky."

"I don't understand, Geoff. What do you mean? Why am I so lucky?"

"You are lucky," he had continued sadly, "to be able to discard me like an old coat, put me out of your life so easily and lightly. Isn't that lucky? I wish," he had said, his voice broken with emotion, "I could do the same. Anyway, Ruth," he had continued, rising to his feet, "it's good to see you looking well again. I'd take it easy for a bit, if I were you. You've been pretty sick. If you want anything more to read, let me know, because, you see, I don't think I shall be coming over here to see you any more. Probably it's best that way."

A few seconds later he had gone, and Ruth had been free to put whatever interpretation she pleased upon the manner of his going.

As she had heard him ride away, Ruth had been thankful because, in her innermost heart, she knew that he had not become quite so unimportant to her as her words had suggested. Realising this after he had gone, although she had not realised it before, she had been thankful that he intended to stay away from her and thus make things easier.

If, as he had ridden away that day, it had been given to Ruth to see a little of what was in Geoffrey Wilding's mind, some of her perplexities would have disappeared and so many things might have been different.

Ruth turned Esmeralda's head towards the high hills and across the broad shoulders of Ratnagalla Peak. Up here, it always seemed, the clear, sparkling air made clear thinking possible, and she wanted to think.

Some forty minutes later, tingling with exhilaration after a sharp gallop, Ruth lay on a green bank watching while Esmeralda nibbled daintily in a patch of tender grass. At last, she felt with thankfulness, life was becoming simpler, more normal. Within limits she believed herself able to control a situation which not long since had seemed out of all control.

During these last weeks George Carey and Tommy, perhaps because of the bond of anxiety, were closer than they had ever been. Tommy no longer cried piteously for Rayna, and George's first thought on returning home was always for Tommy. Some of the haunted look had gone from George Carey's eyes. He seemed to be at peace with himself and with his surroundings. He no longer drank with his erstwhile hunger for drink. He was more alert in mind and body. Subtly, because it is of its very essence subtle, a quiet happiness seemed to have descended upon the Big Bungalow, or at least upon those who dwelled in it.

Appuhamy's eyes had lost their bitter antagonism, and there had been times lately when it seemed to Ruth that something almost like affection, certainly approval, beamed from them. Ruth did not deceive herself. She knew that Appuhamy never would, never could, like her for herself. She was beginning to understand a little better the mind-processes of this loyal, single-minded man. There was only one way to Appuhamy's heart, and Ruth, without knowing it, had stumbled upon it: to make George Carey happy. Appuhamy, because of his changed attitude, had ceased to be a problem. In any case, the old man was sick and ailing these days.

There were, as Ruth saw things, lying on the greensward looking up into a peerless blue sky flecked with gay white clouds, only two great obstacles which stood between her and the course she had mapped out for herself. One, the biggest of all, perhaps, was the Big Bungalow itself. She could never achieve real happiness there. Its brooding, sombre immensity seemed to kill gaiety at birth. There still brooded over it—however fanciful, Ruth could not escape the thought—the dour, self-willed, egotistical personality of old Tom Carey. It was as much in evidence as the sombre sheen of the teak itself. It did not obtrude itself unless some change, however small, was planned. Then it seemed to rise in wrath to accept the challenge offered, and at these times Ruth felt the struggle was hopeless. It was not worth while. Home was a refuge, not a scene of constant battles. By the time she had won her little victories, the taste of them had been ruined.

This obstacle, Ruth believed, would soon be removed. George Carey, in his blundering way, was beginning to understand and sympathise. They had only spoken the once about leaving the Big Bungalow and building another more in keeping with the times and their needs, but Ruth, because George was very transparent, knew that he was turning this over in his mind, and she believed that, before long, he would see things as she saw them.

The other great obstacle was Geoffrey Wilding. Except for a casual passing greeting when he had come to see George Carey on business, she had not seen him since, with shoulders which seemed hunched sadly, he had ridden away from the Big Bungalow.

It came to her as she lay there, and for the first time, that the word love had never been used by either of them in the other's presence. There had been a time when she herself had believed she loved Geoffrey Wilding. That time was gone. What she had thought to be love had been no more than animal passion, whose fires were almost dead. Nevertheless, as she knew from experience, his presence could re-kindle them. Deeply buried beneath cold, grey ashes, there was still one small glowing ember, waiting for the winds of chance and opportunity to fan it into a white hot blaze. It might never happen, but the threat was there. It hung always in the background of consciousness. There were times when, however stout her resolution, the mention of Geoffrey Wilding's name made her breathe differently, made a pulse pound loudly in her throat.

Ruth knew, as she lay there alone in peace and solitude, drenched with the golden sunlight of late afternoon, that there was not room at Elephant Walk for Geoffrey Wilding and herself. One of them would have to go. That one must be Geoffrey Wilding. If, as he had implied by his manner at their last meeting, his affection for her was something more than a mere physical attraction, then the opportunity to prove this was at hand.

Suddenly, it all became very clear. Leaping into the saddle, Ruth cantered briskly homewards. She did not draw rein until she reached the fork at the top of the estate. The right fork led to the Big Bungalow, the left to Geoffrey Wilding's bungalow. So often in life a fork in the way was a symbol, having a far deeper meaning than the mere turning to the left or to the right, Ruth mused, as she paused there in a mood of indecision. A strange feeling swept across her that the decision she must make in the next few seconds would have far-reaching consequences. With a quick movement she turned Esmeralda's head to the left and, with a touch of the whip upon the tired mare's flank, set off at a brisk trot in the direction of Geoffrey Wilding's bungalow.

❋

❋

❋

❋

❋ **CHAPTER NINETEEN**   ❋ ❋ ❋ ❋ ❋ ❋

After a long and tiring day in the fields Geoffrey Wilding, as he approached his bungalow, was filled with a pleasant sense of anticipation. It wanted a little more than half an hour to sunset. Before darkness fell he would be able to enjoy the luxury of a clean shave, denied to him in the early morning because of the hazards of using an open razor by the flickering light of an oil lamp. There would follow the exquisite sensation as ice-cold spring water cleansed his body of stale sweat, the delight of a clean shirt, fresh, crisp white duck trousers, a pair of light-weight woollen socks and comfortable slippers.

In imagination Wilding already saw himself stretched out in a long chair, sipping one, or at the most two, long, cool whiskies-and-soda. From the valley beneath there would filter upwards the evening sounds of contentment, the crude scents of aromatic wood-smoke as the rice pots simmered, while closer at hand there would be the sensuous fragrance of frangi-pani blossom, always more penetrating in the evening.

Geoffrey Wilding—and he himself would have been the first to admit it—was a sensualist. His finely-tapered, sensitive fingers enabled him to derive pleasure from the touch of fine linen, the handling of a well-bound volume, the smooth perfection of ivory piano keys, no less than the soft resilience of tender young flesh. He thought of his body as a keenly-tuned musical instrument from which, in the hands of an expert, every kind of melody to fit every kind of mood could be drawn at will. Someone, he thought, as he forced his tired horse into a canter—probably Oscar Wilde—had said that the height of sensuality was restraint. Yet so few of those who sought to exploit the senses understood this eternal truth.

Instinctively, his thoughts turned to George Carey, who sought what he would never find at the bottom of a whisky glass, dulling appreciation by over-indulgence; of Ruth who, as he saw her, sought spiritual peace by the mortification of the flesh, not realising that total abstention from anything was as much a form of excess as over-indulgence. There were so few people, he reflected, who understood the meaning of the word restraint, who understood true moderation in anything. Cats understood it. Almost alone among the predatory animals they were able to titillate the senses, playing with a mouse, prolonging the exquisite pleasure of killing, until not even feline self-restraint could endure more.

Shaved, bathed, clad in clean clothes and sipping his first whisky-and-soda, Geoffrey Wilding allowed his fancy to wander untrammelled. For him this was always the perfect hour of the day. Indeed, knowing how important it was to him, he had for a long while planned his days so that he should arrive home pleasantly tired, but not so tired that aching muscles pre-occupied the mind to the exclusion of other thoughts. To achieve this, a nice balance and sense of judgment were needed. As to everything else he attempted, he gave to this important problem much thought and care. Relaxed, but not slumped, in a long chair, his senses were keenly alive, ready to play all the wonderful melodies there were in the world for those with the wit to see them, hear them, smell them, taste them and touch them.

For several minutes Wilding watched while a gecko on the wall behind his desk manœuvred himself into a patch of shadow as he stalked an unsuspecting fly. The final, unerring pounce did not come until the pleasures of anticipation had been well savoured. Beside these the swallowing of the fly was secondary.

Wilding as he watched felt a kinship with the gecko. Each of them, he mused, understood at least one of the ways to extract the most from mere transitory pleasures.

For dinner there was to be a clear soup; a jungle cock cooked *en casserole* with red wine; a cheese *soufflé* and a cup of black monkey coffee. It was enough to satisfy a healthy appetite, tickle a clean palate and yet leave room for meditation.

To Geoffrey Wilding the most delightful prospect of all for the evening which lay ahead was that of solitude. Appuhamy, it seemed, was sick, and Rayna, with a sense of duty which was quite surprising, had undertaken to spend the night in his house, to look after him. She was a superb young animal but, as Wilding thought of an evening free of her senseless chatter, overweening vanity and insatiable lechery, he sighed with relief.

He picked up a newspaper three days old, from which it seemed, as he skimmed the headlines, that the war was approaching its closing phase. The giant machine of German power, which had once seemed irresistible, was proving brittle under the strain. His own part in it seemed so far off and remote as to be unreal, and he was able to read the news with a detachment he might show regarding events on another planet.

Wilding hoped, as he contemplated the imminent end of the war, that George and Ruth Carey would, as they planned, spend much of their time abroad, travelling and amusing themselves. It would give him the opportunity he wanted to become indispensable to Carey. With the latter absent for one year, he knew he could achieve this. Carey's fifty years, in addition to the handicap of whisky, would ensure that he could never resume more than a nominal control of Elephant Walk.

The picture conjured up was very pleasing. Wilding smiled as he surveyed it, but a moment later his smile turned to annoyance as, in the near distance, he heard the sounds of an approaching horse.

*   *   *   *   *

Appuhamy's bed had been pulled out on to the balcony of his little house. He lay there propped up by pillows, surveying all the old familiar scenes which were so deeply ingrained into his life that they had become a part of him. He knew the exact moment in the afternoon when the shadow of Ratnagalla Peak would touch the ridge on the far side of the valley. He could tell, without looking, in which field the pluckers were working, by the snatches of laughter which came from time to time through the still afternoon air. At four o'clock, the hot, aromatic smell of cinnamon, coming from the kitchens, told him that for his tea that afternoon George Carey was eating cinnamon toast.

Appuhamy was tired rather than ill. There had been times lately —and he was acutely ashamed of them—when he had neglected his tour of the Big Bungalow in the daily search for signs of dirt or neglect. His heart was playing him funny tricks. It fluttered strangely, leaving him short of breath and a little bewildered. He was not frightened of death. Indeed, during these last years, he had come to look forward to it as to a homecoming. His only fear now was that bodily weakness was going to make death a long, drawn out, empty futility.

When Rayna climbed up on to the balcony, it looked like the premises of a silversmith in a large way of business. On a table beside the bed were piled, in incalculable hundreds, massive silver spoons and forks of all shapes and sizes; thirty-six silver tankards and a vast agglomeration of silver rose-bowls, cigarette boxes, trays and other objects, each piece heavily embossed with the elephant head which had seemed to Tom Carey, in his strength and pride, a designation more fitting than the family crest to which his claim had been dubious.

Appuhamy had passed the day happily cleaning the silver. It was a task which he loved and which he had never during the long years delegated to an underling.

"Why do you do that when you are ill?" asked Rayna irritably.

"I do it, child, because I love it. Tell me, what news do you bring to an old man?"

"You have not noticed my new clothes," Rayna replied, ignoring the question, standing where the sunlight fell upon a silk blouse of canary yellow and a skirt of the same colour, slashed with royal blue. "Do you not think they are beautiful?"

"They are beautiful, child," said Appuhamy, sparing the merest glance. "But to look beautiful in this world is not enough."

"For me it is enough," replied Rayna.

"While you are still beautiful, maybe, but when you are old and ugly—and that comes to all of us—to remember that you were once beautiful will not be enough."

"When I am old and ugly," said Rayna, who did not like the trend of the conversation, "I shall kill myself."

"Others who have said that, child, have lived to a ripe old age. Tell me, what news is there of the young man Wilding?"

"He thinks I am very beautiful, but sometimes he becomes very angry with me. One day I think he loves me very much. The next day I am not so sure."

"You are happy with him?"

"Yes, I am happy," replied Rayna in a thoughtful voice, which suggested that her happiness was qualified. "But when I told him that I was coming here to spend the night with you, he was not at all angry. Indeed"—the words came out grudgingly—"I think he was pleased."

"Perhaps you talk too much, child. Remember, he is a studious young man. He reads many books."

While Rayna was busying herself preparing tea, Appuhamy found time to be glad that, over four years previously, he had undertaken the long journey to Rayna's village to fetch her. At one time it had seemed that all his plans were in vain. But now, with Rayna installed in Wilding's bungalow, the threat of public shame and dishonour which had hung like a black cloud over the Big Bungalow was, it seemed, lifted. The woman—in Appuhamy's thoughts Ruth would always be "the woman"—had mended her ways. She was behaving as a wife should behave. It had not escaped Appuhamy's keen eyes that these many weeks the door which divided the woman's room from the master's had been unlocked. The child Tommy was now learning to bask in the smiles of his father. (Appuhamy had schooled himself lately to think of George Carey as Tommy's father. It made so many things easier.) The happiness, which seemed in the past to have eluded this magnificent home, had slowly, imperceptibly, crept into it. Silently, almost unseen, like a wraith of mist, it was there. It could be felt as one stepped from the servants' quarters on to the broad veranda. It could not be defined nor pinned down, but it was there. And the knowledge made Appuhamy's tired old heart lighter.

Rayna chattered unceasingly. Sipping his tea, Appuhamy nodded sagely from time to time, as though he heard and appreciated every word. He had long learned the art of sifting the pitifully few grains of wheat from the chaff of Rayna's chatter, allowing the latter to blow away, unnoticed and unheard.

Rayna was too preoccupied to see, about half an hour before sundown, the shadow of anger which passed across Appuhamy's face. For a few moments his eyes became dull and heavy, his brow deeply knit. Rayna's back had been turned to the high slopes of tea land which rose in the direction of Ratnagalla Peak. She had not therefore seen, as Appuhamy had seen, a chestnut mare and her rider pause at the spot where two ways forked. Several minutes had passed while horse and rider remained motionless. Appuhamy, during that time, believed he could sense some of the turmoil in the mind of that solitary horsewoman up there among the flushing tea. He felt her indecision almost as poignantly as though it had been his own. He longed and prayed in his own fashion that, when the mood of indecision should pass, she would turn her horse's head to the right, in the direction of the Big Bungalow, which was her home. It was because he saw her turn Esmeralda's head to the left, in the direction of Geoffrey Wilding's bungalow, that his face darkened with anger.

Appuhamy knew, from many overheard snatches of conversation between George and Ruth Carey, that the latter knew nothing at all of Rayna's whereabouts. She could not be aware, therefore, that Rayna had, for some many weeks, been installed as Geoffrey Wilding's mistress. This, he decided, after due deliberation, was a pity. It was time the woman's eyes were opened.

"Rayna child," said Appuhamy, "I am feeling much better. It was kind of you to visit an old man. It has cheered me. Nevertheless, the thought has come to me that you should not leave the young man Wilding alone tonight. Beauty, even such rare beauty as yours, is apt to be forgotten when it is out of sight. That, do you not agree, would be a pity? The young man is now facing a lonely evening and a lonelier night. Think of his joy when he sees you return!"

"You think," said Rayna horror-struck at the very idea, "that in one night he could forget that I am beautiful?"

"Young men are very strange, child. In such a matter, if you will be guided by an old man, you will leave nothing to chance. There is a lantern downstairs. Take it, for darkness will have fallen before you reach home."

"If," said Rayna, unable to conceal her haste, "you have no need of me, it is as well perhaps that I should return to him. He might— who knows?—be lonely."

"Yes," echoed Appuhamy, "he might be lonely. The clothes are pretty," he called to Rayna who was, by this time, half-way down the steps. "Be careful lest, in your haste, you tear them upon thorns by the way."

*   *   *   *   *

Wilding, who had recognised Ruth, was standing outside his bungalow to help her dismount when she arrived.

"Let me mix you a drink," he said as he led her on to the veranda. "I'm afraid I shall have to ring for a glass. How darned inhospitable one glass looks on a tray!"

A few moments later, clutching her glass tightly, Ruth was fumbling for words. "I expect, Geoff," she said, still a little out of breath, "you're wondering what has brought me here at this hour."

"Who am I to question anything when a lovely vision drops from the sky?" replied Wilding in a way which failed to conceal his curiosity.

"I've come, Geoff," Ruth said soberly, "to ask something very big of you. Very, very big!"

As he sat there, Geoffrey Wilding experienced a feeling akin to that he had known when approached by someone wanting to borrow money. His face became a mask. He appeared to be listening intently, but his mind was working fast.

"I've come," Ruth continued, "to ask you to leave Elephant Walk. There's not room for us both here, Geoff, and I—well, I have to stay. I'm trying to rebuild my life, but with you here as—as a constant reminder of things I'd like to forget, it just isn't possible. I don't say this unkindly, Geoff. Understand that. But I want to forget you. Forget you as completely as though you'd never lived; and while you're here, while I never know when we're going to meet, I can't. That's all."

"Surely, Ruth," said Wilding, with a faint note of reproach in his voice, "you can't complain that, since we last met, I've obtruded myself or made things difficult for you?"

"You're a man, Geoff, and perhaps—I don't know—men see things differently. I've suffered a great deal because of you, Geoff—more than you'll ever know. But the suffering hasn't been any the less real because you didn't realise it. With your help, I've made a mess of my life. More than that: I've been unfair to two people who have a right to look to me for love and loyalty. I've failed them. But I'm not going to fail them any more and—well, I want your help."

"You speak of your own suffering, Ruth," said Wilding in a quiet, restrained voice, finding time as he spoke to wonder whether his old power over her still existed. "Do you think I haven't suffered? Do you think I haven't been through hell here sometimes, alone with my thoughts, knowing that a few miles over the hill you were there, living with another man? Do you think I've no imagination? No feelings? I've tried to be strong, Ruth; tried to shut you out. Then a picture comes between me and my peace of mind. I see you in the arms of the great clumsy baboon of a man you married. I see him slobbering over you, mauling you. It never ceases to torture me . . . and then you come here and talk to me of your sufferings, tell me I should go away. . . ."

"I've come to you, Geoff—thrown myself on your mercy—to ask you to give me a chance to make something of my life," said Ruth simply.

"You feel nothing for me? Is that it, Ruth?"

"Nothing, nothing at all, Geoff," said Ruth in a cold, dead voice. "Even if I did," she went on, "I'd stifle it and not allow it to make any difference to the life I intend to make for myself and for others."

Geoffrey Wilding was a close student of human nature, a keen observer of human character and motive. With those whom he knew well, he seldom made mistakes. He had enjoyed the knowledge that he was necessary to Ruth and was loath, although he had no clear intention of exploiting the knowledge, to surrender one iota of the satisfaction it gave him. Since she had raised the question, it would be interesting, he reflected, to know just how valid was her claim to have put him out of her life. She felt nothing for him. Nothing at all. Those were her words. Well, he would see.

"Ruth," Wilding said in a low voice charged with emotion, "I just don't know how to reply to you. Are you so blind that you can't see that, almost from the very moment we first met, I've loved you to distraction? Your fingers, the perfume of you, your laughter, your hair—you yourself, are twined around my heart. Even if I wanted to, I couldn't escape from you. I haven't said much about these things, Ruth darling, because, foolishly I suppose, I was brought up to believe that declarations of undying love to a married woman didn't amount to very much and were sometimes rather cowardly. As I saw things, if you were going to break up your life with George, the first move had to come from you. So I bottled up all the things I wanted to say to you. Now, you come along and ask me to go. Don't you think I've wanted to go a hundred times? If I'd studied my own peace of mind, I'd have gone a long while ago. I don't expect you've ever even troubled to think why I stayed. I had a funny notion, Ruth, that you might need me here, even if only as a friend. That's why I've stayed."

Ruth, listening to this declaration, began to feel old, worn and shattered. It shed a new and almost unbelievable light on Geoffrey Wilding. Never, in the moments of her greatest infatuation for him, had even vanity persuaded her to believe that she meant so much to him. She had come here to break bonds, but her coming had created a new one: the knowledge that he, too, had suffered. Was it part of the punishment for the law she had transgressed, she wondered, that now, when she was trying so desperately to make amends for the past, new difficulties were being put in her way? Even from the depths of her own misery Ruth was able to feel a surge of warm sympathy for the man whose grave face and unhappily hunched shoulders told their story so eloquently.

The fates, during the years which had passed since Ruth first met George Carey, had not been kind to her. That she had aided and abetted them in their unkindness did not ease the ache in her heart.

It is a human urge in times of great stress to turn towards elemental things for comfort. Ruth, without realising why, looked out towards the mountains, where the summer lightning flickered softly, mysteriously, so impersonal and aloof that her own problems became dwarfed. There was a wordless yearning in her eyes as she looked up into the hills for comfort.

Perhaps the gods who rule the thunder and the lightning heard the instinctive prayer which went up to them, for it seemed that suddenly, in the twinkling of an eye, they realised that they had been too unkind to her and that, because it is the prerogative of the gods to redress balances, the time had come to smile upon her.

As Ruth turned her head away from the summer lightning playing upon the mountains, and back to the realities of her own life, the gods, seeking to make amends, sent a breeze to stir a curtain. In the precious little moment while the curtain was parted, Ruth saw into a lighted room, on the far wall of which was a full-length portrait in oils of a lithe, lovely Sinhalese girl, naked from the waist up, her firm young rounded breasts held with a queenly arrogance. The portrait was the portrait of Rayna. In the right-hand bottom corner were the initials of the painter, J.G.W.

Just as the little breeze died and the curtain was falling back into place, Ruth caught a brief glimpse of something which, in a few seconds, brought to an end all her perplexities and indecision: behind the curtain, in an attitude of listening, stood Rayna herself. The face contorted with fury told its own story. It was so unlike the smiling child-woman who had beguiled the weary hours with her during the time of waiting for Tommy; it reminded Ruth more of the cold, impassive mask Rayna had worn when she had denied knowledge of the identity of the snake on Tommy's birthday picnic—a mask in which there had been no mercy.

It did not take Ruth more than a moment to digest the fact and its implications. Looking across at Wilding, with dawning comprehension in her eyes, she felt now only bitter contempt for this man who, a moment before, with words which she now realised had been no more than cold-blooded, deliberate lies, had stirred her to a mood of melting sympathy. As this realisation dawned on her, Ruth was conscious of a feeling of deep and profound relief. All her indecision was over. A great weight was lifted off her. Nothing mattered. In a few moments she would mount Esmeralda, ride back to the Big Bungalow, safe in the knowledge that nothing which had ever happened and nothing which could ever happen in the future could make her think with remorse or regret of Geoffrey Wilding. Contempt and disgust would be her only feelings for this man. In these last few fleeting seconds all his power to charm and hurt her had evaporated as though it had never existed. She was free. If he wanted to stay at Elephant Walk for the rest of both their lives, he could stay. His presence would mean to her no more than his absence.

Geoffrey Wilding looked up wonderingly at Ruth who, only a few moments before, had appeared upon the verge of tears. Now a little smile hovered upon her lips—a smile, moreover, which, because he feared he could read contempt in it, jolted him out of his inwardly amused, cocksure complacency. His poise began to desert him. His jaw dropped. There was blank horror and astonishment on his face, which turned quickly to black anger. He had demeaned himself to make his declaration of undying love, expecting to break down all Ruth's defences, and yet she sat there smiling to herself, as though she had not heard him. Making one last effort to stifle his pride and to bring Ruth to heel, Wilding turned appealingly to her, saying brokenly: "Ruth! I love you—and I expect I always will."

The curtain behind Geoffrey Wilding's chair moved. Rayna, tense as a coiled steel spring, moved slowly, softly across the few yards which divided her from Wilding. The skin was drawn tightly across her lips and cheek-bones, so distorting her loveliness as to make it almost unrecognisable.

Still smiling, Ruth sat and waited for what would happen next. She felt utterly detached now, a mere onlooker.

"So!" said Rayna's shrill voice, cutting like a knife into an atmosphere already too tense. "You love her! You think you will always love her!"

Like a tigress leaping on her prey, Rayna leaped at Geoffrey Wilding. At one moment he was looking at Ruth with anxious, uncertain eyes, at the next there were vivid scarlet slashes down his cheeks, from which the blood was dripping on to a clean white shirt.

Seemingly unmoved by this drama, Ruth rose to her feet, a smile of contemptuous amusement on her face. She looked so cool and poised that she shocked Rayna back from savagery to a sense of the proprieties.

As though a mask had been whipped off, Rayna began to smile.

"Good evening, Mrs Carey," she said politely. "It is so good of you to call upon—us. I am sorry I was out when you came. You will stay to dinner? Yes?"

"Thank you, no, Rayna. Dinner is waiting for me at home," said Ruth, walking to the top of the veranda steps. Before going out into the night, she turned.

Geoffrey Wilding had not moved, but a great change had taken place in him. His suavity and poise were gone. The scratches down his face had become rivulets of blood whose banks were strips of frayed skin, which looked dead and white. Ruth looked down at him for several seconds. She wanted to fix for ever in her mind the picture as he sat there, so that in the years to come, if he ever flitted across her memory, she would remember the cheapness of him. There surged over her a great thankfulness that she had never shared with this craven, deflated man the secret knowledge, which she would now carry to the grave inviolate, that her son Tommy was also his son. No, that was not true, Ruth told herself. This man who sat with blood pouring down his cheeks was not Tommy's father. Tommy's father had been a gay, reckless, devil-may-care, who had gone off to the wars and had never returned. This—this other man—was an impostor, the bare husk of a man winnowed by war. Thus he would remain in memory.

Rayna, in the manner of a polite hostess, accompanied her guest down the steps. A look of bewilderment and utter amazement appeared upon her face when, having mounted Esmeralda and before riding off into the night, Ruth leaned towards her and said, with genuine gratitude in her voice: "Thank you, Rayna—thank you very much."

* * * * *

"Thank God you're back, darling," said George Carey, as Ruth came up the veranda steps, looking serene and happy. "I was beginning to get badly worried. What happened?"

"I rode up into the hills after tiffin and, coming back, not realising how late it was, rode over to Geoff's bungalow and had a drink with him. Sorry if you were worried, dear."

"That doesn't matter, now that you're back," said George uneasily.

"You look upset about something," said Ruth. "What is it?"

"I'll tell you when you've changed. Shall I have a drink ready mixed for you?"

"Please, George—and a stronger one than usual."

Although curious to know what was troubling George, Ruth did not hurry. Nothing, it seemed, could be as important as the sense of freedom she hugged to herself.

Tommy, hearing her voice, was sitting bolt upright in his cot when she entered the night nursery. Folding him very tenderly in her arms, she held him until, with a deep sigh of contentment, he fell asleep. When she tucked him up for the night there was a smile across his chubby face, as though he, too, knew of the shadow which had been lifted from his own and his mother's life.

Looking at him thus, Ruth marvelled, for Tommy was amazingly like George Carey. There was a curiously similar expression about the full lips and the strong, pugnacious jaw. As she left the night nursery, Ruth had a sense of exaltation. For the first time in many months she felt able to face life with untroubled eyes.

In her own room Ruth scanned the impressive array of costly gowns which filled her wardrobe. The woman in her cried out to wear something sensational, something which would symbolise her new-found freedom. The urge was strong to wear all her jewellery until she dripped with gems to match her mood. Her hand paused several times, but none of the gowns, lovely as they were, had any special meaning. At length, with a gay laugh at the memories it evoked, she took from its hanger a simple thing of shot taffeta which had been made for her by a dressmaker at Shillingworth. It recalled to Ruth vividly the evening on which it had last been worn, and she believed—hoped—that it would recall something to George.

Her toilet completed, Ruth hurried out excitedly to the veranda. She warmed with pleasure when George said, as though he meant it: "You look simply smashing, darling. I've seen that frock before, haven't I? No, don't tell me . . . was it . . . wait . . . does this sound right?" He went over to the gramophone, and a few seconds later the Big Bungalow echoed to music of the *can-can.*

"You're right, George," said Ruth, her eyes misty with foolish tears of happiness. "I've never worn it since that evening. You laughed so much that you spilled a liqueur into my lap. If you look carefully, you can still see the stain."

"So you can! Keep the frock always, darling. Keep the stain, too . . . what a wonderful evening that was! I shall never forget it."

"Where's that drink you promised me, George?" Ruth asked, trying to control the mixture of laughter and tears which welled up in her. This great, simple-hearted, overgrown boy, with all his faults, had the power to pluck at her heartstrings in a way which would not be denied.

"No, George, not another, please!" said Erasmus aptly as George helped himself. There was mockery in the bird's mimicry but, Ruth realised with wonderment, it no longer had the power to hurt.

"By the way, dear," Ruth said, when their laughter had subsided. "What was it you were so serious about before I went to change?"

"Oh that!" said George, taking refuge behind a nervous laugh. "I've been meaning to speak to you about it for some time, darling, but 'pon my soul! I didn't like to . . ."

Ruth knew that George required time to come to the point in his own way, so she relaxed hopefully.

". . . I suppose I ought to have said this before, but now I must, darling," George blurted out. "For the future, you just mustn't go calling on Wilding or, for that matter, any other bachelor, unannounced. It—well, it just isn't done, if you know what I mean."

"Are you jealous, George? Is that what you mean?" asked Ruth wonderingly.

"Don't talk such absolute nonsense!" snapped George indignantly.

"Then, what do you mean?"

"I don't want you to think I'm telling tales out of school, darling," George rambled on, "but you've got to understand that life isn't— well, too easy for a chap like Wilding. It's pretty lonely up here, one way and another, you know. I've never talked about these things to you, darling, because I suppose I hoped it wouldn't be necessary.

Now, Wilding's a very good chap, if you know what I mean, but . . ."

"George!" Ruth implored. "Stop maundering and yammering and come to the point!"

"All right, darling, I will. The fact is that one has to be broad-minded about these things."

"What things, George?"

"Please, darling, don't make this more difficult than it is already. After all, you must admit that, for a chap like Wilding, life up here is not too gay—remembering that he's a bachelor, and all that. So you see, darling, it isn't very tactful, if you know what I mean, to go calling on a chap like that unannounced. After all, his private life is nothing to do with us. The fact is"—George's words tumbled over themselves in his eagerness to get them out—"I learned a few weeks ago that Rayna—she seemed to disappear a bit suddenly, if you re-member—is—well, in a sort of way keeping house for him. You must see that to have you popping down there unannounced, could be very embarrassing for the poor chap, if you know what I mean. He must be pretty lonely and—well, you can understand that he likes to have someone to chat with in the evening, and so on. So you see, dar-ling, the most tactful thing we can do is to pretend we know nothing. . . . I'm surprised that Appuhamy didn't tell me about it, because he must have known . . . probably the poor old chap thought I'd rather not know. . . . I only learned it, you know, through over-hearing coolie gossip. . . . Of course, I didn't let on that I'd heard. So, darling, if ever you want to pop over to Wilding's bungalow to borrow a book or anything like that, just remember the position and send over a chit to say you're coming. Then, when you arrive, every-thing'll be nice and tidy, if you know what I mean. . . ."

There was a great lump in Ruth's throat which made her croak.

"George dear, although you dither and waffle like an old woman, I think, all things considered, you're the nicest man I've ever met. Don't worry, dear. If I ever go to see Geoffrey Wilding again, I'll send heralds—mounted heralds with trumpets—on ahead to an-nounce my arrival."

A few moments later with her head pillowed on George Carey's shoulder, Ruth indulged in the rare luxury of tears.

"Hold me, George," she said in the small voice of a child. "I feel very safe—now. It's as though I've been lost in a dark forest filled with horrible things and have found my way home."

Appuhamy's temporary successor, wishing to announce that dinner was ready—the last dinner ever destined to be cooked for a Carey of Elephant Walk in the Big Bungalow—saw them thus and withdrew silently.

How long the dinner might have been kept waiting can only be a matter for conjecture for, at that moment, there came from the darkness outside an ear-shattering trumpeting and the sound of smashing timber.

*   *   *   *   *

Despite a body racked with pain and a mind saturated with vain longings, the Old Bull loped at a steady pace along the elephant trail which led across the plains to the foothills.

The events of the day were growing a little misty and vague when, as old familiar smells hit his nostrils, they returned poignant and clear. Somewhere in the vicinity, he knew, were his cows and his children, docile under the overlordship of another bull, the victor of the day's battle.

The thought of following the hot, fresh smells did not cross his mind, for there was no turning back now. The law, the ancient law, which governs the lives of the Elephant People, had taken its grim course. At dawn he had been undisputed lord, subject to no law except the age-old edict which demanded that he prove himself in battle. He had bowed to the law, and now he was nothing—less than nothing: a thing suspended in a void of pain and anguish, whose past was quickly dying, whose present was a torment and whose future— there was no future. He had come to the end of the road.

The cunning, the strength, the courage and the sagacity which, over the splendid years, had enabled him to keep the herd free from harm, these were guttering out like a spent candle.

The night was pitch black, illumined only for a few seconds at a time by the summer lightning, playing up there in the hills, beckoning to him, whispering of peace and oblivion.

The darkness did not matter, for the Old Bull knew every yard of the way he had travelled so many times before. Every rock, every big tree, every bend in the trail were graven into his mind until they had become part of him.

He turned aside for a few minutes to wallow in a rice field and, as he rose to his feet, he smelled, for the first time for many weeks, the hateful smell of Man. A village lay on the far side of the rice field. The golden glimmer of lamps shone through the trees. There was savage joy as he charged into the little cluster of tightly-packed, flimsily-built mud-and-wattle huts, scattering them like a whirlwind, without even pausing to see whether he had inflicted any hurt upon his ancient enemy, Man.

Man! The approach to the foothills was heavy with the scent of him. Villages dotted the plains. The Old Bull quickened his pace and did not check until he found himself breasting the lower slopes.

The trail for a while led up the dried bed of a torrent. In a careless moment his sick left tusk caught in the exposed root of a tree. The agonising wrench flooded his huge body with sheets of white hot, searing pain, which left no room for reason. For a few moments the Old Bull paused from sheer inability to continue. Until the pain subsided, the huge rippling muscles which had served him so well and so long, would not obey. He shivered, waited and, in a little while, was able to continue. Now, he trod the trail warily, keeping to the right-hand side so that the sick tusk should be spared any more contact.

The trail emerged from the torrent-bed, swinging along the razor-back of a spur which led down from the mountains. The going was easier. But here the smell of Man was everywhere.

Imagination was beginning to play queer tricks with the Old Bull. The immediate past receded from his mind and, as is the way sometimes with the very old, the remote past came up into the foreground of consciousness.

He was no longer a weary, beaten old bull, cast out from his kind, sick at heart and approaching very near to the end of his journey. He was once again a baby; a sleek, fat, round calf, resilient as a rubber ball, bounding along, tired but happy, at his mother's side, bent upon delightful adventures up there in the cool hills.

It was very good to be young again. No cares, no worries. Just a blind obedience to his mother who, in turn, obeyed her lord and master. To live was to feed joyously off tender green leaves and sweet-smelling herbage; to gambol in deep, cool mud wallows and to squirt water over himself and his playmates.

The illusion lasted untouched for several miles until, once again the hated smell of Man clouded everything, and in the distance there was a gleam of many lights from a huge structure which lay right across the trail.

He was still a baby bull. He paused to survey this monstrous thing, reared in his path. But the joy of youth was killed in him by the memories evoked.

Half a mile ahead, he remembered, was a deep pit, cunningly covered by light sticks and leaves. Into this his mother had plunged, to end her days in slavery. He had fallen on her back and had just managed to elude the men who came running with nets. There had been a loud explosion and a searing pain in his ear, which had never, since that day, been so acute as the other, because the torn muscle made it difficult to flap so as to catch the least sound.

As he stood thus, the Old Bull could feel the pain of the long furrow torn in his flank when, panic-stricken, he had crashed into a pile of timber, and a beam, sharply pointed at one end, had ripped through his tender young skin and flesh.

What hideous memories were evoked by the smell of Man! Man and pain and sorrow! Sorrow and pain and Man! They were the same. Wherever there was the smell of Man, there were pain and sorrow; and wherever there were pain and sorrow, there, somewhere lurking in the background, was Man.

The Old Bull knew now that he hated Man. In the elephant language, to hate was to destroy. Why else were the Elephant People given their great strength, their huge, round, massive feet and the power to destroy?

Softly, because although he hated Man, he also feared Man, the Old Bull approached closer to the long row of bright lights, until at length, at breast height, he came to a strongly-built wooden fence.

The smell of Man was so strong in the air that it blotted out all other smells. Up there, behind the lights, were plainly heard the voices of Man. And only the wooden fence between.

It was not in the nature of the Elephant People to come stealthily and furtively, like some slinking cat. The Elephant People were the lords of the jungle, who announced their coming in fitting style. As he set to work to batter down the wooden fence, the Old Bull, surveying with his beady little eyes the huge structure he had hated ever since he could remember, uttered a deep-throated trumpet of rage and defiance, which echoed among the hills.

It was the work of a few seconds to demolish the fence and, just ahead, was a flight of stone steps which led up to the lights. At the top of these steps his progress was impeded as his shoulders struck the overhanging eaves of the roof.

At long last his giant muscles had a task worthy of them. Summoning to his aid every ounce of strength, he heaved. A beam above his head loosened. He lifted his hind legs one step higher and again pressed upwards with all his might. There was a rending crash and, bewildered by the bright light, he stood upon the great veranda of the Big Bungalow.

Beside him, if he could have recognised them, were the feet of both his father and his mother, which had served these many years as umbrella-stands.

The light from a hanging lamp dazzled the Old Bull. Reaching up with his trunk, he tore the lamp and its chain from the roof beam to which it was fastened, hurling it into the brightness of a lighted room beyond. Down the long veranda there was another lamp, and another and another. There seemed no end to them.

Three or four shots rang out. To the Old Bull, in his rage and frenzy, the bullet wounds were of no more account than insect bites —if insects could have penetrated his thick hide.

* * * * *

From a knoll fifty yards behind the Big Bungalow, Ruth Carey, the limp form of the sleeping Tommy lying in her arms, stood watching while an inferno of flames shot up into the sky from what had been her home. Beside her, shattered and horror-struck by what he saw, stood George Carey, his left arm in use as a perch, from which a blasphemous parrot screamed obscenities at the flames.

The Big Bungalow had become a funeral pyre. Already the air

was hideous with the reek of scorching flesh, where an Old Bull elephant, narrowly missing death in that same spot more than fifty years previously, had completed the circle.

There was given to Ruth Carey in these tense, dramatic moments, a few seconds of time in which the human heart can become so very understanding. Tears were running down her cheeks: not for the home which was a roaring mass of flames, but for the brute beast whose vain longings had so often distorted her dreams, shattering the peaceful calm of the night—a brute beast who had dealt out justice at the end, as he understood justice.

The main roof beam, a massive, monstrous thing of teak, crashed down into the holocaust below, sending showers of golden sparks high into the sky. There was no fear in Ruth Carey's eyes as she saw the awe-inspiring sight, only a quiet peace and serenity.

"My God!" said George Carey, covering his face with his hands. "I can't stand any more. That's the end."

"No, darling," said Ruth softly, "it's the beginning."